Georges Feydeau was bor
Feydeau, was a stockbrok
who gained notoriety in 18
is probably the most brilliant farce writer of all time. His output was
vast, stretching from the *belle époque* to the 1920s. Among his best
known works are *Le Dindon* (1898), *La Puce à l'Oreille* (1907) and
Occupe-toi d'Amélie (1908). He died in Rueil in 1921.

John Mortimer is a playwright, a novelist and a lawyer. During the
war he worked with the Crown Film Unit and published a number
of novels before turning to the theatre. He has written many film
scripts, television and radio plays, including six plays on the life of
Shakespeare, the Rumpole plays which won him the British
Academy Writer of the Year Award, and the adaptation of Evelyn
Waugh's *Brideshead Revisited*. Three of his translations of Feydeau
plays have been performed at the National Theatre. Penguin also
publish his Rumpole stories: *Rumpole of the Bailey*, *The Trials of
Rumpole*, *Rumpole for the Defence* and *Rumpole and the Golden Thread*
in single volumes; *The First Rumpole Omnibus* containing *Rumpole
of the Bailey*, *The Trials of Rumpole* and *Rumpole's Return*; a volume
of his plays containing *A Voyage Round My Father*, *The Dock Brief*,
and *What Shall We Tell Caroline?*; *Edwin and Other Plays*: his ac-
claimed autobiography, *Clinging to the Wreckage*, which won the
Yorkshire Post Book of the Year Award for 1982; and *In Character*,
a series of interviews with some of the most prominent men and
women of our time. He has also edited and introduced *Famous Trials*,
a selection from the classic Penguin series.

John Mortimer lives with his wife and two daughters in what was
once his father's house in the Chilterns.

GEORGES FEYDEAU

THREE BOULEVARD FARCES

TRANSLATED AND INTRODUCED BY
JOHN MORTIMER

PENGUIN BOOKS

Penguin Books Ltd, Harmondsworth, Middlesex, England
Viking Penguin Inc., 40 West 23rd Street, New York, New York 10010, U.S.A.
Penguin Books Australia Ltd, Ringwood, Victoria, Australia
Penguin Books Canada Ltd, 2801 John Street, Markham, Ontario, Canada L3R 1B4
Penguin Books (N.Z.) Ltd, 182–190 Wairau Road, Auckland 10, New Zealand

First published in this translation by Penguin Books 1985
A Little Hotel on the Side (first produced as *L'Hôtel du Libre Echange* in 1894)
translation copyright © Advanpress Ltd, 1984
A Flea in Her Ear (first produced as *La Puce a l'Oreille* in 1910), translation
© John Mortimer (Productions) Ltd, 1968
The Lady From Maxim's (first produced as *La Dame du chez Maxim* in 1899)
translation © Advanpress Ltd, 1977

Made and printed in Great Britain by
Richard Clay (The Chaucer Press) Ltd,
Bungay, Suffolk

Filmset in Monophoto Photina by
Northumberland Press Ltd, Gateshead,
Tyne and Wear

To the memory of
JACQUES CHARON (1920–75)
who told me about Feydeau

CONTENTS

INTRODUCTION

Farce is tragedy played at about a hundred and twenty revolutions a minute. The story of *Othello* and the plot of Feydeau's *Puce a l'Oreille* have a striking similarity. Desdemona's lost handkerchief and Victor Emmanuel Chandebise's missing braces both give rise to similar misunderstandings, undeserved jealousies and accumulating catastrophe. Othello's mistake is the stuff of tragedy, Madame Chandebise's leads to events which move so quickly that we are left helpless with laughter and nobody dies.

What is at stake for the characters in Feydeau's farces is not their lives but their reputations. Feydeau's men are solid, bourgeois and middle-aged. His women, as he said, 'breathe virtue and are forthwith out of breath'. Social conventions are essential to farce. No one could write a successful farce about the misadventures of a set of Swedish teenagers in and out of the jacuzzi. The put-upon hero in a Feydeau play finds that the path of true love leads to immediate panic, as when four schoolgirls invade the bedroom where he has contrived a single chance of adultery, or his braces get borrowed and lost. It is the terror of losing their precious reputations which makes Feydeau's characters hide, lie and pretend to be each other. The advent of the permissive society, were it ever to come about, would make the continuance of farce writing impossible.

The great modern master of farce was born into a suitably middle-class family in 1865, in the street in Paris which now bears his name. His father, Ernest Feydeau, was a successful novelist and a stockbroker. It is clear that his son inherited his father's artistic and not his financial talents because the younger Feydeau eventually lost nearly all his considerable earnings from the theatre on the Stock Exchange. Georges Feydeau seems to have been a most likeable eccentric and, as is the case with many writers who produce a considerable body of work, basically indolent. Indeed, it is said that he was so lazy that when a friend told him that a beautiful girl had just entered a café by the door behind them, Feydeau said, 'describe her for me', to save himself the trouble of turning his head. When his wife decided to move to a larger apartment he went to stay for a weekend at an hotel opposite the Gare Saint-Lazare to be away from the disturbance, but once there he couldn't face the effort of moving out and the Hotel Terminus remained his home until he died, ten years later, in 1921, of a cerebral haemorrhage.

Feydeau's habits were entirely nocturnal. He spent the day writing or sleeping and only went out after sunset. He would sit in Maxim's where a token bottle of champagne stood on the table to protect the reputation of the establishment, for like at least two of his central characters, Pinglet and Dr Petypon, Feydeau drank only Perrier water. He was a sad, elegant man who sat with his hat tilted and a cigar between his fingers and never talked about his work. Late at night he would leave Maxim's and go to the kiosk on the corner of the street where he was often seen chatting to the newspaper seller until dawn. He was a man of great taste, whose walls were covered with paintings by Corot, Daumier, Delacroix and Renoir. He bought pictures by Cezanne and Van Gogh when those artists were still mocked and despised. In 1903 he had to sell all his pictures to meet his creditors. 'I don't in the least resemble my plays,' Feydeau once wrote. 'I never laugh in the theatre. I seldom laugh in private life. I am taciturn, somewhat unsociable.' And the greatest constructor of ingenious plots and outrageously logical situations added the information which will no doubt shock all movie producers who believe in 'outline treatments' and endless 'story conferences' and delight all true writers: 'My plays are entirely improvised,' he said; 'the whole and the parts, the design and the shape all fall into place while I am writing. And I have never made a first draft.'

I knew nothing about Feydeau and his plays until 1966 when I was asked to translate *Puce a l'Oreille* by Kenneth Tynan, who was then working at the National Theatre. I met the director, Jacques Charon, and he taught me, and the English actors, how these plays should be done. M. Charon was a plump, smiling associate of the Comédie Française, with the neatly brushed black hair and beady eyes of a mischievous schoolboy or an irreverent Abbé. Like many fat men he was light as a feather on his feet, and he could dance and water-ski with miraculous aplomb. He was a comic actor of genius and, knowing very little English, he acted all the parts for the benefit of the cast, being particularly hilarious as the ladies. The actors, who usually resent such demonstrations, loved him for it. I was privileged to remain Jacques Charon's friend until his ridiculously early death at the age of fifty-five, a tragedy to which his delighted habit of directing all day and acting at night no doubt contributed.

Jacques Charon said that the main qualification for an actor in a Feydeau farce was to be able to run a mile in the course of an evening:

and indeed the performers in these plays need to be middle-aged, out of condition, Olympic athletes. There is no time for moments of introspection or the niceties of light comedy. No time need be wasted at rehearsals in finding 'inner motivations' or discussing the psychological cause of Victor Emmanuel Chandebise's momentary impotence. Feydeau characters are driven by dedicated self interest and thrown wildly off course by unprovoked accidents and sudden panic. To alter a precept of Noel Coward's, they must remember the lines *and* bump into the furniture.

In his 1966 production at the National Theatre, then at the Old Vic, Jacques Charon taught English players how to act and English audiences how to enjoy Feydeau. Although the company has moved to larger quarters and Jacques Charon is no longer with us, his lessons, and the memory of his superb direction, remain a tradition in the company and each of these three translations has had its first production at the National Theatre. In the case of *L'Hôtel du Libre Echange*, the play was brought to the open stage of the Olivier Theatre, and Feydeau has been able to fill an auditorium of a size and shape he never dreamt of with his own extraordinary brand of laughter.

My aim in these versions has been to make the audience forget that they are listening to a translation and believe that they have a perfect understanding of idiomatic French. I have also tried to find an English equivalent of the slang of the 'Belle Epoque'. I confess that I have dared to add a collection of verbal jokes, lines which perhaps Feydeau or his characters couldn't find time for. Such jokes are mainly useful early in the evening. By the second act the players are usually running too fast and the audiences laughing too loudly to listen.

Feydeau has been called the greatest French dramatist since Molière. A contemporary, the poet and playwright Catulle Mendès, wrote, 'I continue to deplore the fact that M. Georges Feydeau uses his truly remarkable talent on plays that will be performed four or five hundred times but that will never be read.' I hope that this volume may do something to remedy that situation, as well as providing a salutary warning on the extreme, and often hilarious, perils of coveting your neighbour's wife.

JOHN MORTIMER
10 August 1984

A
LITTLE HOTEL
ON
THE SIDE

CAST OF FIRST LONDON PRODUCTION

A Little Hotel on the Side was first presented by the National Theatre Company at the Olivier Theatre, London, August, 1984

BENOIT PINGLET, *a building contractor*	Graham Garden
ANGELIQUE PINGLET, *his wife*	Deborah Norton
MARCELLE PAILLARDIN, *their next-door neighbour*	Dinah Stabb
HENRI PAILLARDIN, *her husband, an architect*	John Savident
MAXIME, *Paillardin's nephew*	Mathew Sim
VICTOIRE, *the Pinglets' maid*	Judith Paris
MATHIEU, *the Pinglets' friend*	Benjamin Whitrow
HEAD PORTER	Bill Moody
PORTERS	Charles Baillie, Melvyn Bedford, Robin Lloyd, Paul Tomany
VIOLETTE	Amanda Bellamy
MARGUERITE } *Mathieu's*	Deborah Berlin
PAQUERETTE } *daughters*	Katrina Heath
PERVENCHE	Kelly Marcel
BASTIEN, *the hotel manager*	Michael Bryant
BOULOT, *the hotel porter*	Robert Bathurst
ERNEST, *an actor*	William Sleigh
LADY	Janet Whiteside
CHERVET, *a schoolmaster*	Glenn Williams
INSPECTOR BOUCARD *of the Department of Public Morality*	Jeffry Wickham
FIRST CONSTABLE	Paul Stewart
SECOND CONSTABLE	Peter Changer

CONSTABLES AND HOTEL GUESTS Charles Baillie, Melvyn Bedford,
Judith Coke, Kate Dyson,
Robin Lloyd, Bill Moody,
Shan Stevens, Paul Tomany

The play was directed by
JONATHAN LYNN

Designed by
SAUL RADOMSKY

CHARACTERS

BENOIT PINGLET	A building contractor
HENRI PAILLARDIN	An architect. Pinglet's next-door neighbour
MATHIEU	The Pinglets' friend
MAXIME	Paillardin's nephew
BOULOT	Hotel porter
BASTIEN	Hotel manager
BOUCARD	A police inspector (of the Department of Public Morality)
ERNEST	An actor
CHERVET	A schoolmaster
ANGELIQUE	Pinglet's wife
MARCELLE	Paillardin's wife
VICTOIRE	The Pinglets' maid
VIOLETTE	
MARGUERITE	Mathieu's daughters
PAQUERETTE	
PERVENCHE	
A LADY	Ernest's lady friend
FOUR PORTERS, POLICEMEN	

The action takes place in Paris at the turn of the century.

ACT I

The office in the top-floor apartment of M. PINGLET, *a building contractor in Passy. From the windows we can see the tops of buildings, roofs, the Eiffel Tower, some tops of tall trees. At the far end of the room French windows lead out to a narrow balcony with a railing. The door, downstage right, leads to* MME PINGLET's *bedroom. At an angle upstage right is the door to an ante-room. Upstage left, also at an angle, another door leads to* PINGLET's *bedroom. A large white trestle table is upstage in front of the windows, on it papers, plans, a ruler, a T-square, various pens and pencils and a directory.*

There should be enough room to pass between the table and the windows. A very high stool stands in front of the table. There is a kind of chest of drawers covered with samples of tiles and stone between the windows and the angled door upstage left, and a large work table covered with books and rolled-up plans against the wall on the left between the angled door and the forestage. On the work table are a blotter, a pen and an inkstand and a pot of flowers. A mirror hangs above it and above that there is a shelf on which there are more rolled-up plans. There is a sofa at an angle downstage left. A small writing desk upstage right between the windows and the angled door on the right. A portfolio stands against the wall between this door and MME PINGLET's *bedroom door. Above the portfolio there is a clock attached to the wall and to its right a bell-pull. Framed plans, tinted drawings and plaster models of cornices and ornamental mouldings decorate the walls. There is an armchair and three chairs. The armchair is against the wall on the left, a chair is between the writing desk and the angled door on the right, there are other chairs on each side of the windows. The locks on the doors are practical. The angled door on the right can be bolted from the outside. The windows are open.*

As the Curtain rises PINGLET *is working on a plan at the table centre stage, his back to the audience.*

PINGLET [*sings as he works*]: 'Comes my love, with little fairy footsteps
Comes my love, tiptoeing o'er the grass ...'

[MADAME PINGLET *appears carrying two samples of material. She is a formidable and domineering lady.*]

[*singing*]: 'Comes my love, to fill my soul with gladness!'

MME PINGLET [*in a harsh voice*]: Pinglet!

PINGLET [*without turning round*]: There you are, Angelique, my dear heart!

MME PINGLET: My dressmaker's arrived.

PINGLET [*still not turning round*]: Wonderful news! Your dressmaker's arrived. What am I expected to do? Stand to attention and sing the 'Marseillaise'?

MME PINGLET: Stop working when I'm talking to you.

PINGLET [*aside*]: And when she talks it cuts you like a knife! [*To his wife*] Angelique, my dear heart. You see, I have to get these plans done today. They're for a charming little villa I'm building.

MME PINGLET: The charming little villa will have to wait its turn.

PINGLET: Of course, dear heart.

MME PINGLET: I've got these two fabrics. Which do you like best?

PINGLET [*looking at them*]: Is it for the old sofa?

MME PINGLET: No! It is for my new tea gown.

PINGLET [*pointing to one of the patterns*]: I rather like ... that one!

MME PINGLET: That settles it! I'll have the other.

PINGLET: It wasn't much use asking me, was it dear heart?

MME PINGLET: It was a great deal of use. I know you have the most appallingly vulgar taste. You pointed out the one I wouldn't be seen dead in.

PINGLET [*aside*]: Isn't she a little angel?

MME PINGLET: Get back to work then, Pinglet. Don't slack!

PINGLET: Of course, Angelique. My darling heart! [*He puts his tongue out at her as she goes out.*] Ugh! That's not a woman I've got in my house ... It's the Emperor of Japan! [*He returns to his work table.*] And to think I married her without my parents' consent. Of course, it was twenty years ago. If only we could've seen what they'd be like in twenty years' time we'd never have married them twenty years ago. I tell you, no son of mine would ever marry without my consent. If I'd ever had a son. Which I haven't. [*He shudders.*] Well, with Madame Pinglet the thing's unthinkable. Oh my God, no! Not that!

[*There's a knock at the door.*]

Come in! [MARCELLE *enters.* PINGLET *is delighted to see her, he cheers up enormously.*] Welcome! Welcome, dear Madame Paillardin.

MARCELLE: Good morning, M'sieur Pinglet. Receiving in your dressing gown?

PINGLET: We're next-door neighbours. We needn't stand on ceremony.

MARCELLE: I know. It's such a comfort. Your wife's not here.

PINGLET: She is conducting high level negotiations with her dressmaker. How's your husband?

MARCELLE: I haven't the faintest idea. [PINGLET *takes her hands and looks into her eyes.*]

PINGLET: What's the matter?

MARCELLE: Nothing.

PINGLET: Red eyes. You've been crying?

MARCELLE: Nothing much. Oh well. The same old story. A little difference of opinion.

PINGLET: Is he a brute?

MARCELLE: Of course he's not a brute. If only he were a brute there might be some faint hope for our marriage. He seems to find me considerably less attractive than a good drainage system. Please. Don't speak of it! It upsets me terribly. I must find your wife!

PINGLET: Through there. I think it's about time I had a few words with your husband. I might teach him to be a little civilized.

MARCELLE: Teach Paillardin to be civilized? You might as well teach a one-armed man to play the Beethoven Violin Concerto. [PINGLET *watches her go. He's very excited.*]

PINGLET: What spirit! What a beauty! What a woman! My wife's always saying that I'm finished. If she means finished with her, for once we're in complete agreement. But am I finished with Madame Paillardin? I tell you. I haven't even started with Madame Paillardin! Look here. That wonderful girl is married to a kind of ... a kind of fish-face! I mean, I can say it. He's my best friend. And your best friend's the one person in the world you can call a fish-face. If he weren't my best friend I might be rather rude about him. Of course, it simply wouldn't do to try and seduce your best friend's wife. Well, not unless you were absolutely certain of success. But let's be brutally honest about this. I'm not certain of success. I mean, I wouldn't want to play a dirty trick on my best friend if all I got out of it was a nasty slap in the face. Fine sort of friendship that would be! [*He unrolls the plan.*] Now, what's this deep sea moron of a next-door neighbour given me? Can you believe it? Limestone to support the weight of that beam. These architects! No practical sense whatever. And then we contractors have to get them out of their difficulties. Paillardin couldn't build a rabbit hutch that wouldn't blow over in a high wind. All the same, he's got a beautiful wife. [PINGLET *looks furiously at the plan as* PAILLARDIN *comes in.*]

PAILLARDIN: Morning, Pinglet, my dear fellow. Looks a little like rain, I think. [*Sees him glowering at the plan.*] What's the matter. You're not angry at all?

PINGLET: No. Delighted to see you. I'm not in the least angry. What the hell do you think you're playing at here? [*Shows him the plan.*]

PAILLARDIN: Playing at? Where?

PINGLET: Limestone to support that beam! God help us if a mouse sneezed anywhere near it.

PAILLARDIN: What do you expect me to use?

PINGLET: Use rock. Use your head! Anyway, limestone's far too expensive. I suppose you think an entire villa can be supported by architectural theory ...

PAILLARDIN [*sitting on the sofa*]: Oh, use what you like. Is my wife here?

PINGLET: Through there. With mine. And what *have* you been doing to her, Paillardin? Speaking as your best friend ...

PAILLARDIN: Has she been complaining?

PINGLET: She never complains! But you've only got to look at her, poor little thing. Eyes the colour of steak tartare.

PAILLARDIN [*bored with the subject*]: What's eating her? I'm a model husband. I haven't even got a mistress.

PINGLET: You haven't got a mistress! Are you neglecting *all* your matrimonial duties?

PAILLARDIN: She thinks I'm not 'loving' enough.

PINGLET: Why? Aren't you?

PAILLARDIN: What're things coming to? We live in a decadent age, Pinglet, old fellow. You're supposed to be 'loving' to your wife nowadays. Are you 'loving' to yours?

PINGLET: Well, hardly. Look at her. I mean, my wife's been twenty years in the bottle. That's all right for wine. It doesn't do much to improve the quality of a wife. Mine's corked!

PAILLARDIN: You're perfectly right. Marcelle's a newer vintage. But she can have a distinctly acid flavour. You know what I think, my dear Pinglet?

PINGLET [*aside*]: He thinks! An architect who thinks!

PAILLARDIN: I think that if you only get married for someone to go to bed with, well, you might as well take a mistress! [*He lights a cigarette.*]

PINGLET: What a delicate moral sense!

PAILLARDIN: No, but listen. I work hard. At night I climb into bed for the peculiar purpose of going to sleep. My wife doesn't accept that! She says it shows a lack of respect for her finer feelings.

PINGLET: Perhaps she has a point.

PAILLARDIN [*sitting back, his legs crossed*]: I don't care for hanky panky,

Pinglet. I'm not a ladies' man. Never have been. Haven't got the taste for it. I find all that side of life distinctly off-putting, somehow. That's why I got married!

PINGLET: All right! Very well. If you say so. You'd make a beautiful glacier.

PAILLARDIN: Me, a glacier! Are you such a little volcano?

PINGLET: You don't know me, do you? Beneath this calm, elegant exterior I am a cauldron! Boiling and bubbling with lava. Just at the moment I've got nowhere to erupt.

PAILLARDIN [laughs]: You a volcano!

PINGLET: Well, you've got absolutely no lava!

PAILLARDIN: I haven't?

PINGLET: And without lava a volcano's no more than a mountain with a boring little hole in the top.

PAILLARDIN [takes PINGLET's arm]: Now I remember what I came for ... I suppose you couldn't lend me your maid?

PINGLET: Victoire? What on earth do you want her for?

PAILLARDIN: She's for my young nephew, Maxime.

PINGLET: Ah. That makes it perfectly respectable?

PAILLARDIN: Why can't you take anything seriously? Maxime's a swot who thinks of nothing but his philosophy.

PINGLET: Philosophy, when he's a schoolboy? What's he got left for his old age?

PAILLARDIN: The point is ... he's starting his first term at the Lycée Stanislas to do his philosophy and I just haven't got a servant to take him there. You remember I gave mine the sack. She made blots with the furniture polish, all over my architectural drawings.

PINGLET [aside]: They should've built the blots. They'd probably have stood up better. Fool!

PAILLARDIN: What did you say?

PINGLET: I said, 'I'm glad he's going to a better school.' Why don't you take him? After all, he's your nephew.

PAILLARDIN: No time. I'm busy all day ... and tonight I'm sleeping away from home.

PINGLET: Ah ... Ha ... The glacier melts?

PAILLARDIN: Alone!

PINGLET: You astonish me!

PAILLARDIN: Oh, my dear friend! I've got to spend the night in this horrible hotel. They allege it's haunted. [Confidential.] One hears strange sounds of knocking at night.

PINGLET: Not the sort of thing you're used to at home.

PAILLARDIN: Certainly not! Knocking ghosts! Poltergeists. I'll wait till

I see them, and then I won't believe in them! No. My mind's quite made up, it comes from the drains.

PINGLET: Obviously.

PAILLARDIN: But the hotelier is asking to get out of his lease. The landlord's fighting the case and the Court's appointed me as the architectural expert! So I have to sleep there to decide the matter.

PINGLET: That the knocking ghosts are only a touch of collywobbles in the central heating?

PAILLARDIN: Exactly. [*He starts to go.*]

PINGLET [*calling him back*]: But you haven't made up things with your wife.

PAILLARDIN: How can I? She's been blubbing away all day. She does nothing but complain that I take every opportunity to stay away from her. She doesn't understand that the architect comes before the husband.

PINGLET: Oh my dear friend. Take care! Someone else may come before the architect.

PAILLARDIN: What can you mean?

PINGLET: You're playing a dangerous game. Wives, particularly your wife, are creatures of sentiment. And if ever your wife deceives you ... well, it'll be your own fault!

PAILLARDIN: My wife deceive me! She's not going to find a lover, just like that. That sort of thing only goes on in the theatre!

PINGLET: Of course. Quite right! Only in the theatre. God speed you, Paillardin.

PAILLARDIN: All right.

PINGLET: No. If your wife deceives you, I'll fall over backwards! [*Aside*] So will she with any luck! [*There is a knock at the door.*] Come in! [MAXIME *comes in with a book under his arm. He's a serious boy, wearing spectacles.*]

PAILLARDIN: Oh, it's you, Maxime.

MAXIME: My dear uncle. M'sieur Pinglet. Sorry to disturb you. I think I've lost the book I was reading. I may have left it here. [*He finds the book.*] Yes. Here it is ...

PAILLARDIN: What is it?

MAXIME: It's an extraordinarily interesting refutation of Descartes by Paine! 'The Treatise on the Passions'.

PINGLET: And how to put them to practical use?

MAXIME: It's philosophy! It has no practical use, m'sieur.

[VICTOIRE *comes in.*]

VICTOIRE: M'sieur.

PINGLET: Yes, what is it?

VICTOIRE: Madame's asking for you.

PINGLET: As usual.

VICTOIRE: She's with her dressmaker. She wants to consult your infallible bad taste.

PINGLET: All right. All right. Look here, Victoire. You're going to escort this young man to the Lycée Stanislas this evening.

VICTOIRE [*looking at* MAXIME]: Delighted, I'm sure.

PINGLET: No one cares whether you're delighted. The point is ... You will escort! [*To* MAXIME] What time do you need escorting?

MAXIME: I have to be there at nine, Monsieur Pinglet.

PINGLET: He has to be there at nine. Got that?

VICTOIRE: Delighted, m'sieur.

[*She goes to the table, arranges the papers, plans, etc.*]

PAILLARDIN [*to* PINGLET]: I say, Pinglet. Thanks awfully.

PINGLET: No trouble!

[MAXIME *starts to read, sitting on the sofa.*]

MME PINGLET [*shouts O.S*]: Pinglet!

PINGLET: Not a moment's peace! Off she goes again, like a fire alarm. [*Answering her.*] Here I am, Angelique. Just coming, dear heart. [*To* PAILLARDIN] My God, what a hornet that woman is! Buzzes round you the whole time and a terrible sting in the tail. Ever seen Madame Pinglet at a fitting, Paillardin? You'd be astonished at the rear elevation. It'll have you in stitches.

[*They go out.* MAXIME *is reading.*]

VICTOIRE: What's the book, M'sieur Maxime?

MAXIME: This? Oh. 'Treatise on the Passions'.

VICTOIRE: So what're you doing exactly?

MAXIME: Studying, the entire subject of love.

VICTOIRE: In that position? Can I help? [*She sits beside him on the sofa.*]

MAXIME: How can I study love with a woman sitting beside me?

VICTOIRE: I might be able to make the odd suggestion.

MAXIME: Do you read Descartes, Mam'selle Victoire? You can learn a lot from Descartes.

VICTOIRE: No. I only read tea leaves. You can learn a lot from them too. [*Aside.*] He's a nice boy. But on the timid side to look at him. I bet you're a daring young man, aren't you, M'sieur Maxime?

MAXIME [*reading*]: 'We can distinguish between the passion of a lover for his mistress and that of a father for his children as we can distinguish between love and lust ...' What did you say?

VICTOIRE [*moving very close to him*]: I bet you're ever such a daring young gentleman!

MAXIME: I certainly am not. I'm not daring at all. Not on any occasion.

[*Reading.*] 'Nevertheless they are similar as they are both forms of love.'

VICTOIRE [*moves even closer to him*]: If you're not daring what are you doing with your hand then ...?

MAXIME [*reading*]: 'A father desires nothing from his children that is not decorous and proper ...'

VICTOIRE: Decorous and proper. You're a fine one to talk!

MAXIME: It's not me talking. It's Descartes.

VICTOIRE: You young gentlemen are all as bad as each other! Taking advantage of a girl in my position. To put your warm little hand where it never ought to go!

MAXIME [*puzzled*]: Where have I put my hand?

VICTOIRE: On my knee. You dirty little devil, m'sieur!

MAXIME: Really, Victoire! Where've I put my hand?

VICTOIRE: Here!

  [*She takes hold of his hand and puts it firmly on her knee, holds it there tightly.*]

I bet that's all you think about at your age, isn't it? Putting your hands on girls' knees.

MAXIME: All I'm thinking about at the moment is philosophy.

VICTOIRE: Philosophy! [*She laughs.*] Is that what they call it nowadays?

MAXIME [*reading*]: 'Treating his children as extensions of his own being the father will strive for their good as he will for his own.'

VICTOIRE: No, M'sieur Maxime. I've had quite enough of this. Now you're going too far, my lad. Now you're taking liberties!

MAXIME: I haven't the faintest idea what you mean!

VICTOIRE: Really? A young gentleman like you. Is that what they teach you at the Lycée Stanislas?

MAXIME [*reading*]: 'Or even more so because he and his children make a greater entity!' [*To* VICTOIRE] What are you complaining about?

VICTOIRE: Your hand. It was bold enough when you put it on my knee. But now you've moved it up there! It's an outrage!

MAXIME [*a little impatient*]: Look, Victoire. How on earth am I going to learn about the nature of human love if you keep on interrupting me?

VICTOIRE: Just a touch. I could understand that. But keeping it there!

  [*She moves his hand and holds it firmly on her breast.*]

Your hot little hand. Such a long time. I'll have to complain to your uncle. Really I will!

MAXIME [*puzzled*]: What about?

VICTOIRE: What about? Don't act the innocent, M'sieur Maxime. Take it away this minute. Or I shall scream. I promise you!

  [*She holds his hand tightly on her breast.*]

MAXIME [*worried*]: Please don't scream!

VICTOIRE: Try and stop me.

MAXIME: I can't read about Descartes with people screaming.

VICTOIRE: Stop me then!

MAXIME: How?

VICTOIRE: Block up my mouth.

MAXIME: It's impossible. You've got my hand.

VICTOIRE: Simply place your mouth firmly on mine, m'sieur. Before I raise the roof and bring the whole family in here running . . . Stop! You brute! You masterful brute!

[*She puts her arms round his neck, pulls down his head and kisses him long and hard.*]

MAXIME [*regaining his breath, aside*]: What a curious sensation! Not altogether unpleasant.

VICTOIRE [*stands up and smoothes down her dress*]: Don't you ever do that again, young man. Or you'll be in serious trouble. Now I've got work to do. I shall see about escorting you later.

[VICTOIRE *leaves, stage right.*]

MAXIME: She seems angry. I hope I haven't upset her.

[*Noises, shouting and quarrelling O.S.* MAXIME *blocks his ears and goes on reading.*]

'The affection honourable people have for their friends is of the same nature'.

[MARCELLE, PAILLARDIN, PINGLET, *and* MADAME PINGLET *come in arguing.*]

PAILLARDIN: For God's sake, Marcelle. What's eating you?

MARCELLE: What's eating me? I'm leading the emotional life of a stuffed aubergine! All because of you!

MME PINGLET: Oh my dear. What will you say when you've had twenty years of so-called 'married life'!

PINGLET: Are you complaining? I've tried to make you happy?

PAILLARDIN [*to* MARCELLE]: So have I.

MME PINGLET:
MARCELLE: } You've tried to make me happy?

PAILLARDIN:
PINGLET: } Yes I have.

MARCELLE:
MME PINGLET: } No you haven't.

PAILLARDIN:
PINGLET: } Oh yes I have.

MARCELLE:
MME PINGLET: } Oh no you haven't.

[*They squabble amongst themselves.*]

MAXIME [*getting up*]: It's like trying to read Descartes in a parrot house! [*He goes.*]

MARCELLE: What I ask myself is ... Why on earth I'm married to this gentleman? He doesn't pretend to be a husband. He won't even go through the motions.

PAILLARDIN [*stung by his wife's rebuke*]: I say. That's a bit thick!

MARCELLE: He imagines that I got married for the pleasure of counting his dirty socks! He treats me like a laundry.

MME PINGLET: It's abominable.

PAILLARDIN: There's an element of exaggeration ...

MME PINGLET [*to* PAILLARDIN]: You know, we've been married for twenty years, but if my husband treated me like that I'd ... I'd obliterate him!

PAILLARDIN [*to* PINGLET]: Would she?

PINGLET: There's an element of boasting.

PAILLARDIN [*to his wife*]: What do you want then? Do you want me to stay at home this evening? Do you want me to give up my professional life for the sake of half an hour's ... hanky panky?

MARCELLE: Go on! Go and play with your drains. Whether you're here or there I find you equally distant.

PAILLARDIN: Oh, it's the same old story!

MARCELLE: I tell you, I'm going to start looking around. No one could stay an honest woman married to you.

PINGLET: In my opinion, Paillardin, old fellow. She's got a point!

PAILLARDIN: Don't you put your oar in!

MARCELLE: Just you watch out, that's all. One day someone else may give me all the treats I never get at home!

PAILLARDIN: You wouldn't!

MARCELLE: Why not? There's a lot of women much uglier than me who've found a little consolation.

PAILLARDIN [*laughing*]: You think I'd mind?

MARCELLE: Do you dare me? I won't be hard up for candidates.

PAILLARDIN: Go and find them then. Go on. Tell them to put up for election. [*He moves upstage.*]

MME PINGLET: Paillardin. Don't provoke her.

PAILLARDIN [*moving down again*]: She's provoking me! Oh, the happy, peaceful, glorious day when she finds her consolation! I only ask one thing of him, that he hangs on to her.

MARCELLE [*furious*]: Oh, M'sieur Pinglet!

PINGLET: This is mad! You're mad! He's mad!

MARCELLE: Oh, that's what's the matter with him, is it? [*to* PAILLARDIN] Remember. You wanted me to be unfaithful.

PAILLARDIN: I want it *passionately*! Good afternoon!

MME PINGLET: Look here, Paillardin. Give her a kiss. Make a fuss of her, why don't you?

PAILLARDIN: No, thank you very much. I'd rather step outside and kiss the Eiffel Tower. At least it wouldn't answer back. [*He goes.*]

MME PINGLET [*following him*]: Paillardin! Listen to me, Paillardin.

PINGLET [*at the door*]: Henri! You're making a terrible mistake. You'll regret it, my best friend. I sincerely hope you'll regret it.

[MARCELLE *sits down on the sofa, she's furious.*]

MARCELLE: All right! Quite all right! You heard what he said? You heard it, didn't you? A fine way for a husband to talk!

PINGLET: Yes. It was fine. It was marvellous! Marcelle, I love you. I have fallen for you, Marcelle, hook line and probably sinker.

MARCELLE [*gets up quickly*]: Pardon me?

PINGLET: That husband of yours is an absolute raving lunatic! Didn't I say to him all I was in honour bound to say? Didn't I behave exactly like his best friend?

MARCELLE: So far as I can remember.

PINGLET: I told him that he was making a terrible mistake. He was determined to go on. All right. He's made his bed. Someone else is going to lie on it! I hope. I mean, you remember what he said when you threatened to find a little consolation? 'All right', he said. 'Go on', he said. 'Find it', he said. Well. In my opinion it's your duty as a wife to do as he told you! If you don't find a lover, well, you won't be true to your marriage vows. Didn't you promise to love, honour and obey?

MARCELLE: There may be something in that.

PINGLET: And don't let him tell you that there are no candidates around. I am prepared to stand!

MARCELLE: You!

PINGLET: Me! Myself! Benoit Pinglet. I will stand. And let me say just one thing! You were insulted in my presence. You were challenged to find yourself a lover. The age of chivalry is not dead! At whatever personal cost and however hard the task, the honour of the Pinglets requires me to take up the challenge. I shall not sleep until my mission is accomplished. I shall be your lover.

MARCELLE: You, Pinglet?

PINGLET: Of course me Pinglet! Oh my God I love you! [*He tries to take her in his arms.*]

MARCELLE [*disengaging herself*]: But my duty to my husband ...

PINGLET: Oh, Marcelle – There are moments in life when we cannot think entirely of ourselves. We must make the supreme sacrifice and forget our duty to our husbands.

MARCELLE: But . . .

PINGLET: What about me? Don't you think it's painful for me to ignore my duty to Madame Pinglet? But I don't hesitate if the cause is just.

MARCELLE: Well, yes . . .

PINGLET: You have been insulted! And when one is insulted it's women and children last . . . and all hands to the guns.

MARCELLE: What guns?

PINGLET: The big ones. The guns of vengeance! They will go off . . . tonight. Bang! [*Aside*] With any luck.

MARCELLE: Vengeance!

PINGLET: Yes. Quick march. [*He takes her hand.*]

MARCELLE: What?

PINGLET: Shoulder to shoulder! [*He starts to pull her off towards his bedroom.*]

MARCELLE: Pinglet. Thank you. I appreciate your sacrifice. But I do find you terribly unattractive.

PINGLET: Don't hang about! Marcelle. Good grief? Have you forgotten what he did to you? In front of everyone!

MARCELLE [*furious*]: I'll never forget.

PINGLET: *Your* duty! Is he doing *his* duty?

MARCELLE: He certainly isn't.

PINGLET: All right. Then you don't have to do yours.

MARCELLE: I suppose you're right.

PINGLET [*taking her hands*]: When I think that he took the most beautiful little woman a fellow could ever dream of . . . and betrayed her for a slide rule . . . and a T-square.

[MARCELLE *cries, he wipes her eyes with her handkerchief.*]

MARCELLE [*crying*]: Yes . . . [*Taking back her handkerchief*] That's mine.

PINGLET: And he doesn't love you. He's not a ladies' man. Hasn't got the taste for it.

MARCELLE: You're right! Thank you. Thank you. You point out the hard path of duty. Your looks just make it a little harder, that's all.

PINGLET [*very tender, taking her in his arms*]: You shall see soon what sort of a gentle, tender, loving Pinglet I can be. A Pinglet who'll be worthy of you!

MARCELLE [*looking at him, moved*]: Oh, Pinglet! You *are* terribly unattractive but you know how to speak to a woman's heart!

PINGLET: Thank you, Marcelle. Thank you very much!

MARCELLE: God knows, if you'd asked me half an hour ago I'd've sent you packing. The idea would simply have given me the willies!

PINGLET: But I struck . . . when the iron was hot. The psychological moment!

MARCELLE: And now I say to you, 'Speak, Pinglet. Your word is my command!'

PINGLET [*taking her in his arms*]: Ah, Marcelle! Marcelle! I am transported to dreamland ...

[MADAME PINGLET *calls from O.S.*]

MME PINGLET [*O.S.*]: Pinglet! Pinglet!

PINGLET: And now I've woken up. [*To* MARCELLE, *who is disengaging herself from his arms.*] Marcelle. We haven't a moment to lose. Your husband's away tonight. You'll be free! And as for me, Pinglet! I'll be free as well.

MARCELLE: Yes?

PINGLET: I'll call for you and we shall go ...

MARCELLE: Go where?

PINGLET: Where? To paradise.

MARCELLE: Yes, but what's the address?

PINGLET: The address. I don't know yet. But I shall find out the address. I shall tell you and we shall take ... our terrible revenge! Heads down!

[*He separates from* MARCELLE *and steps in front of the table.* MADAME PINGLET *enters R.*]

MME PINGLET: Delightful friends you cultivate, Monsieur Pinglet! [*To* MARCELLE.] Your husband really is a bit of a peasant, you know.

PINGLET: What's he done now?

MME PINGLET: When I tried to use my most gentle persuasion, as a peacemaker, to save your marriage from the rocks, my dear Marcelle, can you imagine what he said?

MARCELLE: No.

MME PINGLET: 'Take your long nose out of my business, you old hornet'.

PINGLET [*delighted*]: He called you a hornet? [*Without conviction.*] I can't believe it.

MME PINGLET: Neither could I.

PINGLET: He said that to you? And you're so much older than he is.

MME PINGLET: I can't see what age has got to do with it. [*To* MARCELLE.] Oh, my dear. If my Pinglet ever behaved like that!

MARCELLE: What would you do?

MME PINGLET: No doubt about it. I'd find myself a lover.

PINGLET [*stifling his laughter*]: Oh, Angelique. Dear heart. You wouldn't!

MME PINGLET: I certainly would.

PINGLET: A masochist!

[VICTOIRE *comes in with the post.*]

VICTOIRE: Madame. A dress has arrived next door for Madame Paillardin

MARCELLE: Just a little frock I had run up for myself.

MME PINGLET: Take it, my dear. And may your little frock make up for your disastrous marriage. Goodbye, Madame Paillardin.

MARCELLE: Goodbye. [*To* PINGLET.] Goodbye to you too.

PINGLET: Goodbye. [*Under his breath.*] So it's all settled.

MARCELLE: Goodbye. [*Under her breath.*] My husband has been asking for it.

PINGLET [*cheerfully*]: And I'm going to get it!

    [MARCELLE *goes.*]

VICTOIRE: Oh Madame. Your post.

MME PINGLET: Very well. Leave it there. [*She sits on the sofa, opens letters.*]

PINGLET: Now ... to discover a secret and mysterious rendezvous. Oh, what a fool I am. Of course! [*He hits the table as he thinks of it.*] The Paris directory.

MME PINGLET: Less noise, Pinglet. Victoire, I shall be dining out.

PINGLET [*aside*]: Dining out! It's all going like clockwork. [*To* MME PINGLET] Where will you be dining out, exactly, dear heart?

MME PINGLET: At my sister's. At Ville d'Avray. She's not getting any better.

PINGLET [*aside*]: Nor is she.

MME PINGLET: She's not well. Read that, if you can read. [*She hands him a letter.*] And if I don't come back tonight, don't be disappointed.

PINGLET: I'll try and bear it. As bravely as I can.

MME PINGLET: Have you got that in your head, Victoire? M'sieur will dine here alone.

VICTOIRE: Very well, madame.

    [VICTOIRE *goes out R.* PINGLET *leafs through the directory, with his back to his wife.*]

PINGLET: H ... H ... O ... Hotels ...

MME PINGLET [*opening a letter*]: Ah. My dressmaker's sent in his bill.

PINGLET [*aloud*]: Ah ... Ha! Found it!

MME PINGLET: Found what?

PINGLET: Found out that your dressmaker's sent in his bill.

MME PINGLET: I know. I told you that!

PINGLET: Of course.

MME PINGLET: You do say the most useless things from time to time.

PINGLET [*between his teeth*]: Yes. Dear heart. Of course I do. Yes, of course. [*Aside, reading*] Hotel Summertime. No. Hotel Bristol. No. Hotel of the Penguin and the Fair Lady. What a ridiculous combination! The Grand Hotel of the Bicycle. The Hotel of the Heroic Fireman.

MME PINGLET [*opening a second letter*]: Good heavens!

PINGLET: What?

MME PINGLET: Whoever sent these to *me*?

PINGLET: What are they?

MME PINGLET: One ... Two ... Three ... circulars. From a hotel.

PINGLET: A hotel?

MME PINGLET: Listen to this. It's perfectly shocking. 'The Free Trade Hotel, 220 rue de Provence. Specially caters for married couples. With or without each other!'

PINGLET: With or without each other. It says that? In black and white!

MME PINGLET: See for yourself. [*She shows him the brochure.*]

PINGLET [*delighted*]: With or without each other. In black and white!

MME PINGLET: In my opinion it's a hotel for monkey business.

PINGLET: I'm afraid you may be right. [*Aside*] Monkey business. Exactly what I need! [*Aloud*] Rooms at all prices.

MME PINGLET [*reading*]: Special reductions for season ticket holders! It's disgusting!

PINGLET [*delighted*]: Disgusting! [*Aside*] I shall get a season ticket. [*He puts the prospectus in his pocket.*]

MME PINGLET: I can't imagine who would bombard me with salacious brochures.

PINGLET: *I* certainly can't.

> [*She tears up the other brochures and throws them on the floor.* VICTOIRE *comes in.*]

VICTOIRE: Madame. There's a gentleman to see you.

MME PINGLET: A gentleman?

VICTOIRE: His card. [*She hands a card to* MME PINGLET.]

MME PINGLET: Oh, it's Mathieu! Bless my soul. It's our old friend Mathieu.

PINGLET: Mathieu from Dieppe? He must be here on holiday. Run along, Victoire. Show him up!

VICTOIRE: Yes, m'sieur.

MME PINGLET: Victoire. Clear up this mess.

> [VICTOIRE *gathers up the torn up brochures, looks at them as she goes out.*]

MME PINGLET: Mathieu's here. Our dear friend.

PINGLET: Mathieu! Who was so kind to us when we took our holiday in Dieppe.

MME PINGLET: Put us up for two weeks. Lobster thermidor till it came out of our ears. And he's such a brilliant conversationalist!

PINGLET: Of course. He's a barrister.

> [VICTOIRE *shows in* MATHIEU.]

VICTOIRE: In you go, m'sieur.

> [VICTOIRE *goes.*]

PINGLET: There he is! Come in then, dear old Mathieu.

MME PINGLET: What a wonderful surprise!

PINGLET: How good of you to visit us!

MME PINGLET [*waving to the sofa*]: Do make yourself thoroughly at home!

PINGLET: And let me have your umbrella. Poor old Mathieu. He's soaked to the skin!

MME PINGLET: Of course he is. It's raining outside.

PINGLET: Now, to what do we owe this totally unexpected pleasure? [*He puts the umbrella by the window.*]

MATHIEU: Oh my – my friends. I'm so – so ... I'm so – so.

PINGLET: Only so-so?

MATHIEU: I'm so – so glad to see you. I'm mad ... Mad ... Mad!

PINGLET: Surely he's exaggerating?

MATHIEU: I'm mad ... [*He kicks up his leg and cries out.*] Madame Pinglet's greatest admirer! [*To* MME PINGLET] You're such a stupe ... stupe ... stupe ...

MME PINGLET [*aside*]: Is he working himself up to calling me stupid?

PINGLET: Try and keep calm, Mathieu. Please try and keep very calm.

MATHIEU: Such a stupe ... [*Kicks*] ... endously generous woman!

PINGLET [*sitting on the sofa*]: What on earth's the matter with him? [*To* MATHIEU] Has something happened to you, old fellow?

MATHIEU: Wha ... Wha ... Wha ...

MME PINGLET: He wants a glass of water.

MATHIEU: Wha ... [*Kicks*] Whatever do you mean?

PINGLET: It just occurred to me ... It's hardly noticeable, of course, but listening to you very carefully, can one just detect ... a slight impediment in your speech?

MME PINGLET: And when we stayed with you in Dieppe, you hardly drew breath. No trouble then.

MATHIEU: It was s ... summer then. During that fort ... fort ... fort ...

PINGLET: Fortnight?

MATHIEU: Two weeks. Every d ... day was Ho ... Ho ... Ho ... Ho ...

MME PINGLET: ⎱ Ho! Ho! Ho! [*They join in, laughing appreciatively.*]
PINGLET: ⎰

MATHIEU: Not finished. Every day was ho [*He kicks up his leg and cries out.*] Hot! In fine weather I can talk as well as anyone. But when it's raining. Pi ... Pi ... Pi ... Pi ...

PINGLET: We get the idea ...

MATHIEU: Pitilessly. Ma-ma, Ma-ma, Ma-ma-ma.

PINGLET: Mother?

MATHIEU: Ma – my stutter comes back.

PINGLET: The man's a walking barometer!

MAIHIEU: When it's stormy I can't fu ... fu ... fu ...

34

PINGLET: Steady on, old fellow! Ladies present.

MATHIEU: Fu ... [*He kicks.*] Function!

PINGLET: Not a word?

MATHIEU: Not a w ... w ... word!

MME PINGLET: But as a barrister it must be terribly difficult for you. What do you do if it comes on to rain when you're in court?

MATHIEU: I have to ask the judge if I can have a wee ... a wee ... a wee ...

PINGLET: Does that make you feel better?

MATHIEU: A wee ... [*He kicks.*] Week's adjournment!

MME PINGLET: Dear old Mathieu. You haven't forgotten us! Just arrived in Paris and your first call is on the Pinglets.

MATHIEU: I remember so well your arse ... your arse ... your arse ...

MME PINGLET: I can't believe my ears!

MATHIEU: Your asking me to stay.

MME PINGLET: Oh, I see.

MATHIEU: You said if I came to Paris I must stay under your roo ... roof. You m ... meant it?

PINGLET: Of course we did.

MME PINGLET: The idea of you staying anywhere else! This *is* a treat for us.

PINGLET: Stay as long as you like. Two days. Or three. Promise us you'll stay three days!

MATHIEU: N ... n ... n ... No!

MME PINGLET: We insist!

PINGLET: Just to please us.

MATHIEU: No!

MME PINGLET: We really shall be quite cross if you go anywhere else.

MATHIEU: I shan't go anywhere else. I'm staying here for a m ... m ... m ... month.

MME PINGLET: It seems a little on the long side.

MATHIEU: Not at all.

MME PINGLET: We wouldn't want to impose on you to stay with us for a *month*.

MATHIEU: You're not.

PINGLET: We're really delighted! [*Less enthusiastic*] Quite delighted.
   [MATHIEU *takes off his overcoat.*]

MME PINGLET [*aside to* PINGLET]: A month's a bit steep. We only stayed with him for two weeks.

PINGLET: But there were two of us. Two weeks each. It adds up, you know.

MATHIEU: I won't be a na-na ... na-na ... nuisance!

PINGLET: A nuisance! How could you be a nuisance? We've heaps of space. And you're travelling light. Just a bachelor with an overnight bag!

MATHIEU: Well, not exactly. I've brought a little surprise for you.

PINGLET: Really! Angelique, my heart. This dear old fellow has got a little surprise for us!

MME PINGLET: A surprise! That's charming. He thinks of everything.

[VICTOIRE comes in.]

VICTOIRE: I ought to warn you, madame. Someone's bringing up a trunk.

MATHIEU: Oh yes. It's mine.

[A PORTER comes staggering in with a trunk on his back. He's panting, exhausted.]

PORTER: It's like climbing the Himalayas.

[VICTOIRE goes out.]

MATHIEU: Oh lay ... Lay ... Oh, lay ...

PORTER: Ole to you, m'sieur. A Spanish gentleman is he?

MATHIEU: Oh ... [Kicks] Lay it down.

PINGLET: Monsieur told you to lay it down over there.

PORTER: If you say so, m'sieur.

[PINGLET helps the PORTER.]

MATHIEU: How much do I owe you?

PORTER: Forty sous.

[MATHIEU pays him.]

MME PINGLET [looking at it]: What an absolutely gigantic piece of luggage.

PINGLET: It has a distinct look of Napoleon's tomb. We'll have it taken to your room.

[VICTOIRE comes in.]

VICTOIRE: Madame, there are more porters with more trunks.

PINGLET: ⎱
          ⎰ More?
MME PINGLET:

[FOUR PORTERS come in with four trunks, all gasping.]

MATHIEU: Oh yes. They're all m ... mine!

MME PINGLET: One ... Two ... Three ... Four! We're being taken over.

MATHIEU: It's my little surprise.

MME PINGLET [delighted]: Surprise. Words fail me.

PINGLET: I thought you were travelling light.

MATHIEU: Pinglet. I've got no change. Be a good fellow and see to these por ... por ... por ...

2nd PORTER: Of course we're poor, climbing half way to heaven for forty sous.

3rd PORTER: I've done myself a permanent injury.

MATHIEU: Por ... [*Kicks*] Porters.

PINGLET: Here. And that's all you're getting. Why don't you go down to the kitchen. Get yourselves a milk ... glass of water.

[*He gives the* PORTERS *money; they go grumbling.*]

What sort of little surprise is it that needs *four* trunks?

MME PINGLET: So generous! Well, we might as well open them ...

MATHIEU: Why?

[MATHIEU *stops her.*]

MME PINGLET: Why? For our surprise ...

MATHIEU: No!

MME PINGLET: He wants to keep us in suspense!

MATHIEU: The surprise is cu ... cu ... cu ...

PINGLET: Custard glasses?

MATHIEU: Cu ... [*Kicks*] Coming!

PINGLET [*dodging his kick*]: Missed me again.

MME PINGLET: The suspense is killing us. Really you're too kind.

PINGLET: I've known generous men in my time. But our dear old friend Mathieu's generosity is un-pa ... un-pa ... un-pa ... Christ, he's got me doing it!

MATHIEU: Unparalleled?

PINGLET
MME PINGLET } [*take his hand*]: Congratulations!

MATHIEU: I don't stutter for other people.

[VICTOIRE *comes in.*]

VICTOIRE: Madame. There are some little girls just arrived by train. They've come up the stairs and they seem quite excited.

MATHIEU: Little girls. Are there four of them?

VICTOIRE: Probably. I wasn't counting.

MATHIEU: Then they're mine!

VICTOIRE [*going*]: That's it then.

MATHIEU [*to the* PINGLETS]: Hey p ... p ... presto. My surprise.

MME PINGLET: *Four* little girls?

PINGLET: For us? I mean, I quite like little girls, in moderation, but ...

MATHIEU: They're my daughters!

PINGLET: No!

MATHIEU: When we met in the summer I was a bachelor. My wife had been dead for eight years.

PINGLET: And presumably still is?

MATHIEU: Yes. My girls were in a convent. But they had to come out of the convent. A lot of the girls there had mum ... mum ... mum ...

PINGLET: Mummys? And theirs had passed away?

MATHIEU: Mum ... [*Kicks*] Mumps! So I went to collect them and I said

37

to myself ... the poor Pinglets. They've never seen my g ... g ... girls.
So I thought I'd give you a little surprise.

MME PINGLET: Is *that* his surprise?

PINGLET: I'd call it more of a shock.

MATHIEU: So I came on ahead to announce them.

MME PINGLET: But the trunks?

MATHIEU: My little girls' bits and pieces.

PINGLET: They're travelling heavy.

[GIRLS' *voices O.S.*]

Probably moving in with their furniture.

MATHIEU: Come along in girls.

[*The* FOUR GIRLS *enter.*]

PINGLET: He seems to have made the most of Madame Mathieu while she
was with us!

MATHIEU: I want my chilled ... chilled ... chilled ...

PINGLET: What's he want now, champagne?

MATHIEU: Chilled ...

GIRLS: Dren!

MATHIEU: Children. You've often heard me speak of Monsieur and
Madame Pin ... Pin ...

GIRLS: Glet!

MATHIEU: There they are! Large as life. Surprise them! Give them a great
big ha-ha, ha-ha, ha-ha. Hug!

[*The* GIRLS *chorus 'M'sieur Pinglet Madame Pinglet!' and embrace the*
PINGLETS.]

PINGLET
MME PINGLET } [*trying to escape from the girls*]: Yes. Yes. They're totally charming but ...

MME PINGLET: But it's an invasion!

[*The rain stops.*]

PINGLET: The biggest since the Franco-Prussian war!

MME PINGLET: We had no idea you'd gone in for daughters, in quite such
a big way.

MATHIEU [*pleased with himself*]: I am extraordinarily fertile!

PINGLET: I suppose you'll be taking them straight to another convent.

MATHIEU: No, no. I'm waiting for the mumps to disappear from theirs.

PINGLET: But where are they all going to stay?

MATHIEU: Here, of course.

MME PINGLET: Say that again?

MATHIEU: We're all going to stay here.

PINGLET: I'm afraid that's unthinkable! Out of the question!

MATHIEU: But you both said ...

PINGLET [*advancing on* MATHIEU]: We naturally say all sorts of idiotic things on holiday, when we're trying to be polite.

MATHIEU: Oh?

PINGLET: You took me at my word. If you'd come alone, well, we'd've put up with you. Now you've gone too far. What do you think this is? A marine barracks!

MATHIEU: If I'd thought it was a marine barracks I certainly wouldn't have brought my children here! They are young girls, m'sieur!

PINGLET [*taps him on the chest*]: I'm astonished! Absolutely astonished. [*To* MME PINGLET.] What's he think we're doing, opening a house for stray orphans? This is Paris! Not the provinces. We don't all pile in together in mud huts.

MME PINGLET: It's all your fault, Pinglet! If you didn't scatter invitations around like confetti ...

PINGLET: It's not my fault. You said it was the least we could do. You said, 'We've been here a fortnight. We've got to invite him.'

MME PINGLET [*touches* MATHIEU *lightly*]: Of course I invited you. I never thought for a moment you'd accept.

PINGLET: And was it my fault that he turned up?

MME PINGLET: Of course it's your fault. If you'd just mentioned it in passing it might have all been forgotten. We'd've made the gesture. That was all that was intended. But no! You had to keep inviting him all the time, like a parrot with a one track mind. You insisted! Of course the poor fellow felt obliged to take you up on it. And bring the whole tribe with him.

PINGLET: Don't find excuses for him. [*To* MATHIEU] *Naturally* it's all my fault.

[MATHIEU *stands up, surprised but resigned.*]

MATHIEU: If I understand your drift Pinglet, you don't want us to stay with you!

PINGLET: Got it in one! There's no room!

MATHIEU: Very well. Come along, children. Thank Monsieur and Madame Pinglet for their wonderful welcome.

THE GIRLS [*shaking the* PINGLETS' *hands*]: Thank you, m'sieur. Thank you for having us, madame.

PINGLET: Don't mention it! [*To* MME PINGLET] Angelique. My dear heart. You couldn't see if the porters are still getting their breath back in the kitchen. They could take away the impedimenta.

MME PINGLET: As soon as possible.

[*She goes.* MARCELLE *enters from the right.*]

MARCELLE: All these trunks! It looks like a railway station.

PINGLET: We're getting rid of them. Do come in, my dear.

MATHIEU [*sees* MARCELLE]: Madame!

PINGLET [*introducing them, delighted*]: My dear lady. Allow me to present Monsieur Mathieu. The old friend you've heard us talk about so often. And his descendants! Madame Paillardin. [*Under his breath to* MARCELLE] I've found exactly what we were looking for. You're still on?

MARCELLE: Absolutely!

PINGLET: Eight o'clock tonight at the corner of the Avenue du Bois and the Rue de la Pompe. Be in a cab with the blinds pulled down. I'll be wearing a white carnation and carrying 'the Building Contractor's Gazette'.

MARCELLE: Why?

PINGLET: So you can recognize me.

MARCELLE: But I know you already.

MATHIEU [*to* PINGLET]: After all that ... where can I take my family?

PINGLET: I'll see to you in a minute.

MARCELLE [*under her breath, to* PINGLET]: Where are we going?

MATHIEU [*aside*]: If only I knew of a small, family hotel.

PINGLET: The Free Trade Hotel. 220 rue de Provence.

MATHIEU: Thanks. The Free Trade Hotel. [*He thinks the address is meant for him and is writing it on his cuff.*] 220 rue de Provence. Well then. Good afternoon.

[MME PINGLET *comes back with the Porters who remove the trunks.*]

THE GIRLS: Goodbye m'sieur. Goodbye madame.

MATHIEU [*on his way to the door*]: Goodbye, Madame Paillardin. [*To* PINGLET] You know where we'll be.

PINGLET: Where?

MATHIEU: At the hotel.

PINGLET: Oh yes. That's where you'll be. Off you go!

MME PINGLET: Goodbye! I'm off to my sister's.

[*The* MATHIEU FAMILY *and* MADAME PINGLET *go.*]

PINGLET: Oh, Marcelle. My little spring flower! If only you knew how happy I am. [*Laughs happily.*]

MARCELLE: It's no laughing matter!

PINGLET: Your husband's gone?

MARCELLE: Oh yes. And he hardly bothered to say goodbye. He'll be sorry!

PINGLET: Listen. My wife's out to dinner. Your husband's gone. Before we make the supreme sacrifice, shall we have supper together?

MARCELLE [*nobly*]: Whatever hardships are in store, I shall be brave!

PINGLET: Eight o'clock at the corner of the Avenue du Bois ...

MARCELLE: And the rue de la Pompe.

[*She is prevented from going out by* MADAME PINGLET *entering, followed by* VICTOIRE *with a tray.*]

MME PINGLET: Are you leaving us, my dear?

MARCELLE [*feeling her forehead*]: I think I'm coming up for a cold.

MME PINGLET: Then you ought to be tucked up in bed.

PINGLET: I quite agree.

[MARCELLE *goes,* PINGLET *sits on his stool, looks at the tray.*]
What on earth's that?

MME PINGLET: Your dinner, of course. Victoire has to take young Maxime to the Lycée.

PINGLET: My dinner?

MME PINGLET: What's the matter with you, Pinglet? Haven't you ever seen a dinner before? Go along, Victoire.

[VICTOIRE *goes.* PINGLET *stands up casually.*]

PINGLET: My dinner? I don't think I care for it. On second thoughts, I think I'll go to a restaurant. You're going to see your sister. I'm a bachelor and tonight I'll stand myself a rattling good meal!

MME PINGLET: In a restaurant? I forbid you to go to a restaurant!

PINGLET: What's the harm in a restaurant?

MME PINGLET: You're a married man! Married men don't go to restaurants on their own. What would people at the other tables say?

PINGLET: I suppose they'd say, 'Oh, look. There's a married man having dinner on his own.' What do you want them to say?

MME PINGLET: The day you go trotting off to a restaurant on your own, I shall be beside you. Placing the order!

PINGLET [*faintly*]: Everyone'll envy me, I'm sure.

MME PINGLET: Don't try to butter me up. Tonight you have your dinner here! On a tray.

PINGLET: When're you going to stop treating me like a child?

MME PINGLET: When you grow up!

PINGLET: I don't care what you say. I shall go to a restaurant.

MME PINGLET: No, you shan't!

PINGLET: I shall!

MME PINGLET: Shan't!

PINGLET: Shall!

MME PINGLET: Very well, my fine little fellow. I'll have to teach you a lesson.

[*She takes the key out of the door stage right.*]

PINGLET [*trying to grab it*]: Give it to me!

MME PINGLET [*pushing him back*]: Make way for me, Pinglet.

PINGLET: Will you give me that key? I insist on having my key! A husband has every right to his own key!

41

MME PINGLET: No!

PINGLET: Yes!

MME PINGLET: Don't argue!

> [MME PINGLET *slaps his face.* PINGLET *sits, his hand to his face. She goes out and bolts the door after her. He shakes the door, trying to get out.*]

PINGLET: You haven't! You wouldn't! You *would*!

MME PINGLET [*from outside*]: Good night, M'sieur Pinglet. See you tomorrow.

> [PINGLET *goes into* MME PINGLET'S *room and comes back.*]

PINGLET: They're all locked! She's a methodical woman. [*Mimes it.*] She's shot all the bolts. But with one leap . . . Pinglet was free!

> [*He opens a drawer in the chest of drawers, finds an extremely long rope ladder, fixes it to the balcony and climbs quickly and joyfully out of the window.*]

END OF ACT I

ACT II

The hotel. It is obviously a seedy and down-at-heel place with dirty, tasteless wallpaper of a blue floral pattern and cheap furniture. The stage is divided into three parts.

On the left-hand side, a hotel room. Against the wall, downstage left, a little round table with a faded cover. Upstage to this, a door leading to a bathroom. At an angle, further upstage still, a chimney-piece. Facing the audience, at the end, a bed, covered with an eiderdown, with flowery chintz curtains hanging from a mahogany ring screwed into the ceiling. Downstage right, the door on the landing. The door opens inwards and away from the audience. A straw-seated chair in the middle near the front of the stage. A zinc clock with a globe on the chimney-piece. On each side of it two candlesticks with candles and two painted porcelain vases with artificial flowers and plumes. A crocheted bedcover on the eiderdown. On the bedside table, a jug, a glass and a sugar bowl.

The central part of the stage is the landing. The door of the above bedroom downstage left. Above it, the number '10' painted on the wall. Behind, upstage and at the far end facing the audience, the staircase which leads up from below, going from left to right. Facing the audience, another door with the number '9' above it. This room is on the level of the third step. From here on the stairs turn right and disappear up into the ceiling. The audience should be able to see the staircase going up as far as possible. Downstage right, a board, on which keys hang from numbered hooks, is attached to the wall which separates the landing from the right-hand room. Below the board, a small table with drawers. On it, flat copper candlesticks. One of them has been lit. A straw-seated chair in front of the table. Beyond the table, further away from the audience, a door which leads to the room on the right. This is number '11'. The door opens inwards and away from the audience.

The third part of the stage is a large room, a kind of dormitory. On the left between the door and the front of the stage, along the wall, is an iron bedstead with a small mirror above it. Opposite, downstage right, are two more iron bedsteads facing the wall. A chair in front of the first one. Upstage a door behind the second bed which leads to a bathroom. There is a window at an angle further

43

upstage still. Below it a fourth bed along the wall. At the far end, facing the audience on the right, a door leading to another bathroom (the door opens inwards). A chair between the bed and the door. At the far end on the left, a wooden bed with white curtains (just like the one in the room on the left). Behind the bedhead which is on the right, a chair. A curtain-hook on the wall near the bedhead. A bedside table in front of it. A small round table with a cover in the centre of the room between the bed on the left and those on the right. Grey wallpaper on the walls and ceiling.

The doors on the left and right of the landing should have practical locks with keys. It should also be possible to bolt the left-hand door from the inside. It is eight-thirty in the evening. As the curtain goes up the rooms on the left and right are in darkness. Only the landing is lit by two gas burners placed between the doors on the left and right and the stairs.

BASTIEN, *the manager, is sitting at a table on the right of the landing. He holds up two candles.*

BASTIEN: Two candles [*cuts them in half*] one and one makes four candles ... makes four candles. It may not sound much but in the thirty years I've been manager of this select establishment, man and boy, cutting the candles in half has made me six thousand francs. I'm not cheating them. Most of our clients prefer the dark.

[BOULOT, *the under porter, comes rushing down the stairs.*]

BOULOT: Oh, my sainted aunt, M'sieur Bastien! If you'd seen what I've seen!

BASTIEN: I probably have. What was it?

BOULOT: I knocked, just like you told me, on the door of number 32. I promise you, I took every precaution. And then a voice said, 'Come in'.

BASTIEN: What did you do?

BOULOT: I went in.

BASTIEN: This story is full of surprises.

BOULOT: Surprises! I was shocked, M'sieur Bastien. I was horrified! There was a naked woman in there!

BASTIEN: Amazing!

BOULOT: Nakeder than naked! Like a shelled egg, M'sieur Bastien. And she said 'Porter!' she said. 'Fetch me a pack of cards.' Well, M'sieur Bastien. What could I do?

BASTIEN: You could've fetched her a pack of cards!

BOULOT: A naked woman, playing patience? It's against nature!

BASTIEN: Seems natural enough to me.

BOULOT: Life's totally different in the Provinces!

BASTIEN: We've got to educate you, my little Boulot. We've got to make a Parisian out of you! When you've been here a couple of weeks you won't give a toss for a naked woman playing patience. 'Madame,' you'll say, 'just pop your Black King on your Red Queen,' and leave it at that. Now be a good lad and go and knock on number 9.

BOULOT: Number 9? What's she wearing in there?

BASTIEN: Number 9's not a woman, Boulot. Number 9's a bone-headed schoolmaster who thinks he can enjoy our facilities and not settle our account. We'll keep his trunk and kick M'sieur Chervet out!

BOULOT: Is he the gentleman who's always threatening to blow people's brains out?

BASTIEN: That's just his little joke.

BOULOT: But what if he blows *mine* out?

BASTIEN: Then you come straight back here and tell me all about it. Jump to it, Boulot!

BOULOT: If you say so, M'sieur Bastien. [*He is in front of number 9.*] Not a very attractive assignment! [*He knocks timidly on the door.*]

CHERVET [*a furious shout from within*]: Come in, then, damn you!

BOULOT [*leaps back, terrified, from the door*]: I'd even rather play patience with the lady upstairs. [*He goes into number 9.*]

BASTIEN [*standing up*]: When *he's* been here thirty years he'll've got used to it.

    [*The bell rings.*]

BASTIEN: What've we got here? Not regulars!

    [ERNEST, *a down-at-heel actor, comes in with a large, blowsy* LADY *on his arm.*]

ERNEST: Varlet! There you are. Have you, by any conceivable chance . . .

BASTIEN: I don't answer to 'varlet'.

ERNEST: Sirrah . . .

BASTIEN: I suppose I answer to 'sirrah'. Yes, m'sieur. We certainly have, m'sieur. [*In honeyed tones.*] Just what m'sieur is looking for. A charming little love nest where you and Madame can snuggle down and no questions asked. And what a delicious morsel Madame is, if I may say so, m'sieur. A morsel for a monarch! M'sieur is clearly a man of taste and discernment.

ERNEST: I didn't ask for your opinion, peasant!

BASTIEN [*still smiling*]: Understood, m'sieur. I'm the soul of tact and discretion. M'sieur's in luck's way tonight. Number 22's available.

ERNEST: Is number 22 where the two fat tarts from Pigalle always go?

BASTIEN: Yes, m'sieur. But we'll put m'sieur in there with one.

ERNEST: Insolent dog! This lady is a lady of breeding. She is a person of

refined taste and genteel education, closely connected with the aristoc-
racy. She is a woman of the world.

BASTIEN: All right. We'll let you up there with one woman of the world.

ERNEST: You know who I am of course.

BASTIEN: Of course I do. Who are you?

ERNEST: I am Ernest 'Casanova' Couet. The great leading actor of the
Théâtre des Batignolles.

BASTIEN: Casanova? The name's familiar . . .

ERNEST [to his companion]: You see, my dear. My fame goes before me.
[Under his breath to BASTIEN] To be absolutely frank with you, and not
putting on side or anything . . . she's a Duchess!

BASTIEN: Is she now? Congratulations! All the more reason for taking
her up to number 22. It was in that room that the Crown Princess of
Poland spent her wedding night with her major-domo. [To the lady]
You'll be thoroughly at home there, madame.

ERNEST [under his breath to BASTIEN]: But doesn't a fellow pay through
the nose for a Princess's room?

BASTIEN: What's that to you, m'sieur?

ERNEST: What do you mean, 'What's that to me'? It's my money, isn't
it?

[A terrific noise from number 9. BOULOT comes shooting out of the
door.]

BOULOT: Oh, m'sieur Bastien! He keeps saying he'll blow my brains out,
and he won't leave without his luggage!

ERNEST: What are those noises off?

BASTIEN: A customer leaving. Chervet! Come here a minute!

[CHERVET, looking very fierce, appears at the door of number 9.]

CHERVET: What do you want?

BASTIEN: You see the stairs? You see the front door? Be so very kind as
to deprive us of your company.

CHERVET: When do I get my luggage?

BASTIEN: When you pay your bill.

CHERVET: Very well! I've got a friend or two in the Department of Public
Morality. Perhaps you'll stop larking about with my luggage when the
police descend on you!

ERNEST: ⎱
HIS LADY: ⎰ Not the police here?

CHERVET: Certainly the police! [To ERNEST] And I can tell them a thing
or two about this hotel.

ERNEST: ⎱
HIS LADY: ⎰ What?

BASTIEN: When you've quite finished, Chervet.

CHERVET: I'm talking to this gentleman. Call this a hotel! What a dump! Deserves a skull and crossbones in the Michelin. And the fleas . . .

BASTIEN: That's not true. We spend a fortune on flea powder!

CHERVET: Flea powder! It chokes the guests and the fleas adore it. Added to which the place is haunted. . .

ERNEST: ⎤
⎬ Haunted?
HIS LADY: ⎦

BASTIEN: Chervet! Put a sock in it!

CHERVET: Evil spirits! Knocking ghosts! Poltergeists. That room's the worst. [He points to the room on the right.] Jam packed with ghosts every night of the week. It's so bad they turned it into a dormitory for the staff, and now the staff are scared stiff to go in there.

LADY: Oh, horrors!

BASTIEN: Grossly exaggerated!

CHERVET: It's got so serious they're calling in an expert. True or not?

ERNEST: This is no place for 'Casanova' Couet. [He moves away.] You can dispose of number 22!

BASTIEN: M'sieur's not going?

ERNEST: M'sieur certainly is. Come, Duchess.
    [He goes. His LADY follows.]

BASTIEN [to CHERVET]: Now look what you've done!

CHERVET: Not enough. [To BASTIEN] You haven't heard the last of me! [To BOULOT] There are brains round here that need blowing out. If anyone can find them. [He goes.]

BASTIEN [calling after him]: You'll get thrown out of worse places than this.

BOULOT: He's lost us two clients!

BASTIEN [sits down]: Clients! Don't talk to me about clients. I'm sick of them. All the same, I wouldn't've minded seeing how 'Casanova' Couet of the Théâtre des Batignolles made love to a real live Duchess.

BOULOT: You'd never have seen that?

BASTIEN: Why not?

BOULOT: They might not have asked you to join them.

BASTIEN: Silly noodle! [He gives him a small slap on the cheek.] I'd've seen them all the same.

BOULOT: How?

BASTIEN: How? [Shrugs his shoulders.] What a simple soul! [He shows BOULOT a drill.] You know what that is, noodle?

BOULOT: It's a drill! For making holes.

BASTIEN: Exactly! When I fancy a person . . . [He turns the drill.] I get myself an eye-full! Through a small but convenient hole in the wall.

BOULOT: No!

BASTIEN: Oh yes! I've seen some of the most beautiful women in Paris ... with the naked eye! And all free, gratis, and for nothing!

[PAILLARDIN *appears on the staircase.*]

PAILLARDIN: Manager! Where's the manager?

BASTIEN [*very firmly*]: At your service, m'sieur. M'sieur is expecting someone? I know *exactly* what m'sieur's looking for. A charming little love nest where you and your madame can snuggle down and no questions asked.

PAILLARDIN: No! Thank you, no! I'm not expecting anyone. I am Paillardin, Monsieur Henri Paillardin. The learned architectural expert appointed by the commercial court.

BASTIEN: Oh, m'sieur, I understand! The haunted chamber! It's a little nest of enchantment.

[*A bell rings.*]

Jump to it, Boulot. A customer's ringing. Look alive now, my lad. One two, one two! [*To* PAILLARDIN] Oh yes, m'sieur. The ghosts honour us with their presence. Every night. Lively spirits they are too. They kick up the most terrible shindig. They crack the walls! They chuck the furniture about! Like removal men!

PAILLARDIN: That's quite enough! I can investigate perfectly well on my own. Now where is this eventful room?

BASTIEN: The one on the left, m'sieur. If you'll allow me to light a candle.

[*He lights a very small candle.*]

PAILLARDIN: Lead on, to the haunted chamber!

[*They both go into the room on the right.*]

BASTIEN: Rather you than me!

PAILLARDIN: Seems perfectly peaceful.

BASTIEN: The spirits are always quiet at this time of night.

PAILLARDIN [*plugging his pun*]: In low spirits, perhaps?

BASTIEN [*on whom this joke has no effect*]: But just you wait.

PAILLARDIN: Wait until when?

BASTIEN: Until midnight, of course. When the lights are all off. The spirits get up to their tricks then.

PAILLARDIN [*plugging his joke painfully*]: Probably just *high* spirits.

BASTIEN: High spirits, eh? [*Gets the joke at last, laughs dutifully.*] M'sieur the learned expert is a wit! But m'sieur the learned expert shall see what he shall see.

[*Sound of singing from above.*]

PAILLARDIN: What's that? The spirits tuning up?

BASTIEN: No, m'sieur the learned expert. Just some of the young men from the Galeries Lafayette getting a bit above themselves with the girls from the lingerie department. I'll go up and read the riot act. [*He goes out.*]

PAILLARDIN [*opens his bag*]: My cigars! My hair brushes:

BASTIEN [*shouting up the stairs*]: This is a respectable establishment!

VOICE FROM ABOVE: Tell us another!

BASTIEN: Some people come here to sleep.

1st VOICE FROM ABOVE: That's not what we've paid for.

2nd VOICE FROM ABOVE: Why don't you put a sock in it, then?

BASTIEN: Put a sock in it? I'll teach you to put a sock in it!

PAILLARDIN [*appearing*]: I say. Garçon.

BASTIEN: Half a jiff, m'sieur the learned expert. I'll be back in half a jiff.

[PAILLARDIN *goes back into his room leaving his door open.* BASTIEN *disappears up the stairs as* PINGLET *comes into the hotel smoking an enormous cigar and carrying* MARCELLE's *bag.*]

PINGLET: He'll be back in half a jiff. [*Looks round.*] It seems a nice, quiet little hotel.

MARCELLE [*looking round*]: It's horrible! Where on earth did you find it.?

PINGLET: It may be a little lacking in style. But it's just exactly what we want! In an AI De Luxe establishment we'd certainly be recognized. I don't suppose we'll meet any of our friends here.

MARCELLE [*looking about*]: Not if they like clean wallpaper ...

PAILLARDIN [*sneezing in his room*]: Tishoo!

PINGLET [*hearing him*]: Bless you!

PAILLARDIN [*hearing him and taking off his hat*]: Thank you very much!

PINGLET: Don't mention it. [*Tenderly to* MARCELLE] And who cares about the hotel? We're together, darling Madame Paillardin, and that's all that matters. [*He stops and sniffs.*] Christ! What an extraordinary smell of ... The drains could do with a little attention. Oh good. Here's the lackey!

[PAILLARDIN *goes into the bathroom at the end of his room. There's darkness in his room.*]

BASTIEN: At your service, m'sieur. [*Very servile*] I know exactly what m'sieur's looking for. A charming little love nest where you and madame can snuggle down and no questions asked ... And what a delicious morsel madame is, if I may say so, m'sieur. A morsel fit for a monarch! M'sieur is clearly a man of taste and discernment.

PINGLET: How dare you speak to me like that! This lady's my wife.

BASTIEN: No!

PINGLET: Yes!

BASTIEN: No!

PINGLET: Yes!

BASTIEN: No. M'sieur's carrying the suitcase.

PINGLET [*aside*]: The fellow's a psychologist. [*To* BASTIEN] Have you a little something available on this floor?

BASTIEN: More than a little something, m'sieur. A luxuriously appointed salon which we delight in calling ... [*He points to the left.*] Number 10. That's where the Crown Princess of Poland spent her wedding night with her major-domo.

PINGLET: Perfect! [*To* MARCELLE] I told you it was a respectable hotel.

BASTIEN [*picking up a lighted candle as they go into the room on the left*]: There you are, m'sieur. Your bathroom. You're in luck's way tonight. Hot and cold running water and our guests are cordially invited to partake of it. [*He lights the candles on the mantelpiece.*]

PINGLET: Madame Paillardin. May I call you Marcelle, darling?

MARCELLE [*embarrassed*]: Ssh! He's still here.

PINGLET: Oh yes. So he is. [*General embarrassment.*] Very well. I shall take this room.

BASTIEN: Good night m'sieur, madame! [*He goes.*]

PINGLET: At last! [*He takes* MARCELLE *in his arms.*]

[BASTIEN *comes popping back in.* PAILLARDIN *comes out of his bathroom and crosses his bedroom on his way out to the hall.*]

BASTIEN: Your key. Best of luck, m'sieur!

[BASTIEN *goes out onto the landing.* PAILLARDIN's *there.*]

M'sieur's not leaving us already?

PAILLARDIN: Just for a breath of fresh air. I'll have a beer in the café opposite. Back in half an hour.

BASTIEN: Very good, m'sieur. M'sieur will find his candle waiting for him.

[PAILLARDIN *goes out.* BASTIEN *goes up to the floor above.*]

PINGLET [*still smoking his cigar*]: Marcelle! [*He takes her in his arms again.*]

MARCELLE: Pinglet!

PINGLET: Oh ... I'm no longer Pinglet to you. Call me Benoit!

MARCELLE [*shrugs*]: If you like. Why? [*She disengages herself and moves away.*]

PINGLET: It's my name of course. Benoit Pinglet! Marcelle! Marcelle! The terrible hour of vengeance on your appalling husband has arrived! You'll get your own back – on your own back!

[PINGLET *tries to grab* MARCELLE.]

MARCELLE: Look out! You're going to set me on fire!

PINGLET: On fire with love! [*The cigar's still in his mouth and he's puffing out smoke as he embraces her again.*] I love you, Marcelle! More than anything in the world.

MARCELLE [*coughing*]: It's like being cuddled by a chimney! [*She pushes him away.*]

PINGLET: Oh! [*Takes out his cigar, looks at it.*] Pardon me.

MARCELLE: Can't you throw it away?

PINGLET [*doubtfully*]: It cost me forty sous. I was planning to smoke it right down to the end.

MARCELLE [*hurt*]: So I take second place, to a forty sous cigar?

PINGLET [*going to the fireplace*]: You're right! When it's an affair of the heart, what does money matter? [*He throws the cigar away and returns to* MARCELLE.] And you're staggeringly beautiful!

MARCELLE: How do you like my dress? Do you like me in puce?

PINGLET: It's perfectly all right. In fact, yes. I like you in or out of puce!

MARCELLE: It came from the dressmaker this evening! You're the first person to see it on.

PINGLET: The dress! What's the dress matter? The dress is nothing but the dish which contains the delicious little cutlet! [*With passion*] So far as I'm concerned, it might as well not be there. It's unnecessary. It doesn't add anything to your beauty. We can get on perfectly well without your dress! I want you desperately, Madame Paillardin. [*He hurls himself on her.*] Marcelle!

MARCELLE [*struggling*]: Oh, good heavens! What's got into you, Pinglet? M'sieur Benoit! Do please be careful!

PINGLET [*holding her in his arms*]: I want you! I've wanted you ever since you moved in next door. And came in to borrow a stick of sealing wax. I didn't want to give you the sealing wax, I wanted to give you ...

MARCELLE [*getting away from him*]: The champagne's gone to your head!

PINGLET: Nonsense. Everything's done me good! The miraculous Marcelle, the beautiful Beaujolais, the charming Chartreuse, the soothing cigar. My wife says smoking and drinking make me ill. Look at me! I'm in the pink! I've never felt better in my life!

[*He takes* MARCELLE *in his arms and sits on the chair. The chair breaks. He falls to the ground. He shouts at the chair.*]

Stupid chair!

MARCELLE [*bursting out laughing*]: You look so funny!

PINGLET [*aside*]: Now she finds me ridiculous.

MARCELLE [*laughs*]: You haven't done yourself an injury?

PINGLET: An injury? Of course not. I did it on purpose. I do a little tumbling at times. Just to amuse the ladies. [*He gets up.*] Idiotic chair! [*He picks up the chair.*] And it's the only one! [*He throws the chair out onto the landing.*] Clear out! And don't come back. [*Aside*] Now then. Let's get on with it. [*He tries to take her in his arms again.*] Marcelle!

MARCELLE [*pushing him away and laughing*]: If only you could have seen yourself!

PINGLET [*put out*]: Well, I couldn't. I had to leave that to you.

MARCELLE [*still laughing*]: I looked down. And you suddenly seemed to have shrunk!

PINGLET: It isn't really very funny!

MARCELLE: No, of course it isn't! [*She stuffs her handkerchief in her mouth to stop herself laughing.*] You're absolutely right ... It's not ... funny ... at all!

[*On the landing* BOULOT *sees the broken chair.*]

BOULOT: It's the chair from number 10. Who put it there?

[PINGLET *embraces* MARCELLE.]

PINGLET: My dear Marcelle!

[BOULOT *goes into* PINGLET's *room with the chair and starts back in surprise.*]

BOULOT: Pardon me!

MARCELLE: ⎱ Oh!
PINGLET: ⎰

BOULOT: M'sieur. I didn't know this room was taken ... I'm just putting your chair back for you.

PINGLET [*furious*]: No! Take it away! I never want to see it again!

BOULOT: But m'sieur. It belongs in here.

PINGLET: Not any longer. I've thrown it out. I've had quite enough of it! You and that chair. Get out, both of you! [*He pushes* BOULOT *out onto the landing.*]

BOULOT: She's a bit of a morsel, that young lady. I wouldn't mind seeing more of her. [*He gets an inspiration.*] The drill ... Why not? [*He gets out the drill.*]

BASTIEN [*from above*]: Boulot! Boulot!

BOULOT: I'm coming. I'm coming. [*He puts the drill away and starts upstairs.*]

PINGLET [*anxious*]: My God! What a peculiar sensation.

MARCELLE: What's the matter?

PINGLET: I'm not sure. It's a cold sweat! Now it's a hot sweat! Rising steadily. It must be excitement. Nothing to worry about. [*He takes her in his arms again passionately.*] Marcelle! We're alone at last. I wish you could see what's going on inside me. I can feel my heart ... My heart. Oh my God! My heart's going pit-a-pat! In an alarming manner!

MARCELLE [*concerned*]: You've gone terribly pale, Pinglet! Benoit! Are you all right?

PINGLET: Just feeling a little dickie. The ticker ... and all that.

MARCELLE [*frightened*]: Sit down, for heaven's sake!

PINGLET [*looking round desperately*]: Where? The chair's gone.

52

MARCELLE: Sit on the table then.

[PINGLET *sits on the little round table.*]

PINGLET: Oh, Marcelle! I'm terribly sorry. The happiest moment of my life. And I'm not up to snuff? Better in a minute. [*Grips his stomach and moans*] Oh ... my God!

MARCELLE: Hang on. I'll get you something to drink. [*She starts to prepare water and sugar.*]

PINGLET [*in rueful despair*]: It was the cigar. I told you it was the cigar. It doesn't matter. Better soon. The cigar and the champagne. Me! And all I usually drink is water ... Oh, my God! [*He stands up.*]

MARCELLE [*stirring the sugar in the water*]: You poor thing!

PINGLET: I feel terrible. And my wife's not even here!

MARCELLE [*bringing him the glass*]: Do sit down!

PINGLET: I can't! I've got to keep on the move. I need fresh air.

MARCELLE: Then I'll come with you.

PINGLET: No! No, I've got to go it alone. Help, I'm suffocating!

MARCELLE: Take your jacket off.

PINGLET: What a brilliant idea. [*He takes it off.*] Oh, I'm sinking!

MARCELLE: Come along now. Brace up!

PINGLET [*with despair*]: I feel very near the end.

MARCELLE: Don't say that! No one could be seen dead in this hotel!

[*She wipes his forehead with her handkerchief which she wets with water from the glass.* BOULOT *appears with the drill.*]

BOULOT: Now then. After all, Bastien does this all the time. [*Tapping the wall*] Where are we going to start drilling? There! That seems nice and yielding. [*He starts to drill.*]

PINGLET [*leaning back against the wall*]: Oh, that feels so refreshing ... and beautiful, Marcelle.

BOULOT: Just a little spy hole ... down there ... and they'll be none the wiser!

MARCELLE: Better?

PINGLET: Oh yes! Your touch ... is so exciting!

[*The drill is now through the wall. As it first touches him* PINGLET *wriggles with a sort of ecstasy.*]

BOULOT: That's going in nice and easy. No hard core there.

PINGLET [*startled as the drill goes further*]: Oh, my God!

MARCELLE: What is it?

PINGLET: A kind of pricking sensation in the lower ... the lower back.

MARCELLE: That's a good sign. It means the blood is draining out of your brains.

PINGLET [*a sharp cry*]: Ouch!

MARCELLE: What did you say?

53

PINGLET [*hurling himself away from the wall*]: Oh! Ouch! Oh! It's agony ... sudden agony!

BOULOT: What's the matter with it? [*He pulls the drill out.*]

PINGLET: Ooh! Help! Ouch! Appalling sensation!

MARCELLE: What's the matter now?

PINGLET: An indescribable pain. Just as though someone were trying to penetrate my ...

MARCELLE: Thoughts?

PINGLET: No ... ow!

MARCELLE: It's a sort of seizure.

BOULOT [*looking at the end of his drill*]: Rising damp! [*He touches it.*] And red in colour.

MARCELLE: You look terrible! Shouldn't we send for a doctor?

PINGLET: Just give me air. All I need is air. [*He fans himself with* MARCELLE's *hat.*] And a cup of camomile tea.

[BOULOT *is on all fours, looking through the hole.*]

BOULOT: Now let's have a little look-see.

PINGLET [*opening the door*]: Lackey! [*He falls over* BOULOT's *back.*] What on earth are you doing down there?

BOULOT: Keeping my ear to the ground. I thought I heard m'sieur calling.

PINGLET [*in a strained voice*]: I need air. Show me to a garden, a terrace, even a little balcony!

BOULOT: Straight upstairs, m'sieur. Turn right. End of the corridor ...

PINGLET: Thank God!

MARCELLE [*appears at the door and speaks to* BOULOT]: And please bring m'sieur a hot water bottle.

PINGLET: Yes! That's what I want. A hotty! [*He goes up the stairs, calls to* MARCELLE] You will wait for me!

MARCELLE: Don't worry!

PINGLET [*disappearing*]: The happiest day of my life. And I'm feeling dreadfully sick!

MARCELLE [*to herself*]: Poor Pinglet! [*To* BOULOT] Quick. Camomile tea. Any sort of tea. So long as it's camomile.

BOULOT [*shrugs*]: Everything's shut. Just a minute. That brute we just chucked out next door! He was always making tea. He'll have the necessary. [*He goes into* CHERVET's *room.*]

MARCELLE [*goes into her room*]: What a chapter of accidents!

BOULOT [*who has collected* CHERVET's *tea things*]: Here we are, madame! All the tackle. [*He goes back into* MARCELLE's *room.*]

MARCELLE: Put it down there ...

BOULOT [*putting it down*]: Very well, madame.

MARCELLE: Are you sure the gentleman won't catch cold, up there on the balcony? He's in a most delicate state of health.

BOULOT [*lighting the spirit lamp under the kettle*]: Don't worry, madame! The air is exceedingly balmy. Not a bit like this morning when it was raining cats and dogs. Now it's a beautiful moonlit night. [*He winks at her.*] A night for lovers!

[MATHIEU *enters with his* DAUGHTERS.]

MATHIEU: Come along now, children. Come along ...

THE GIRLS: We're coming, Papa. Here we are, Papa.

MATHIEU [*talking quickly and volubly as they come in*]: Well, here we are and where's the porter? I mean, I've never seen a hotel like this before. Anyone could just walk in off the street. I mean, we might have been burglars so far as anyone knows. We might have been cut-throats, footpads, murderers or confidence tricksters! Pickpockets even! The front door bell is absolutely useless! It's clearly only there for swank!

VIOLETTE: Oh, Papa! Anyone can tell it's stopped raining!

MATHIEU: Obviously. But I can't imagine why Pinglet recommended this place. Perhaps it's gone downhill rapidly. All the same, it's late. We'll stay one night. Not worth getting your trunks up, girls. Tomorrow we'll find somewhere else.

MARGUERITE: I like AI De Luxe hotels ... with soft carpets and perfumed soap in the bathrooms ...

THE GIRLS [*one after the other*]: So do I ... So do I ... So do I ... So do I!

MARCELLE [*to* BOULOT *as the kettle boils*]: Very well. You can go now. Don't forget the hot water bottle.

BOULOT: Certainly, madame. [*He goes out onto the landing.*] That poor invalid's lady friend is an absolutely charming morsel!

THE GIRLS: There's the porter!

BOULOT: My God. What do they think this is? A boarding school?

MATHIEU: Look here, porter. This place was recommended to me by M'sieur Pinglet.

BOULOT: M'sieur Pinglet. But of course! [*Aside*] Never heard of him.

MATHIEU: Now then. What accommodation can you offer for me and my daughters?

BOULOT [*aside*]: His daughters? [*To* MATHIEU] These are *all* your daughters, m'sieur? [*Aside*] The fellow must breed like a rabbit.

MATHIEU: Look sharp about it. What can you show us?

BOULOT [*looking at the keys on the board*]: Let me see now. I'm never going to find enough rooms for ... all of you. [*Aside*] I've got an inspiration! The haunted room! Can't let that for love or money. [*To* MATHIEU.] If you're not too finicky, m'sieur, I think I might have something available.

MATHIEU: Lead us to it.

BOULOT [*takes the candle and goes up to number 11*]: This way, m'sieur. [*He shows them into the room.*] Here we are – the State Apartment.

MATHIEU: It's a barracks!

BOULOT: It's all we can offer, m'sieur. And with four girls and your good self it's very suitable. Look, five beds exactly.

MATHIEU: But a Papa can't sleep in the same room as his daughters. It's out of the question!

BOULOT: M'sieur can hop into bed first and pull the curtains round him when the young ladies undress. And we can offer segregated toilet accommodation. [*He shows them the bathrooms.*]

MATHIEU: I suppose we've got no choice. [*He takes* BOULOT's *candle.*]

BOULOT: None whatsoever, m'sieur. [*He quickly takes one of the short candles from the landing and swops them over.*]

MATHIEU: And how am I expected to pay for your State Apartment?

BOULOT: To *you*, m'sieur. And seeing you come recommended by Monsieur Whatshisname ... What would you say to ... seven francs a night? All in.

MATHIEU: Sounds reasonable.

MARCELLE [*coming out of her bathroom*]: What on earth's Pinglet up to? He's been gone for hours.

MATHIEU [*to* BOULOT]: Very well, my man. We'll take the room. [*He puts his candle down on* PAILLARDIN's *cigar box.*]

BOULOT: Excellent, m'sieur! Good night, m'sieur. Sleep well, young ladies.

THE GIRLS: Sleep well, porter!

[BOULOT *goes out onto the landing.*]

MARCELLE: Perhaps he's been taken poorly again! I'm beginning to worry about him. [*She goes towards the door onto the landing.*]

MATHIEU: But I must have a candle for my girls. [*He goes towards the door onto the landing.*]

MARCELLE [*coming out onto the landing, to* BOULOT]: I say, porter!

MATHIEU [*doing the same thing*]: I say, porter!

MARCELLE [*turning to him*]: M'sieur Mathieu!

MATHIEU [*turning to her*]: Madame Paillardin. Unless I'm very much mistaken.

MARCELLE [*turns her back on* MATHIEU]: No ... Well ... Yes. As a matter of fact it is.

MATHIEU: I had the pleasure of meeting you at the home of our mutual friends, the Pinglets.

[*On the right the* GIRLS *are making themselves at home.*]

MARCELLE [*worried*]: No. No. The pleasure was mine. Entirely.

BOULOT [*surprised*]: Amazing! They know each other.

MATHIEU: Well, what a lovely surprise. [*Calls*] Children!

MARCELLE: No, please, m'sieur ... Don't trouble your children.

MATHIEU: But of course. It's no trouble, madame! Come along, children. Who do you think I've found? Madame Paillardin. Madame *Paillardin*!

MARCELLE: My God! He's shouting my name!

BOULOT: She's called Madame Paillardin!

[*He goes into the room on the left to see if the kettle's boiling. The* GIRLS *come out to greet* MARCELLE *with enthusiasm.*]

GIRLS: Madame Paillardin! What a lovely surprise! How are you, Madame Paillardin? It's Madame Paillardin! [*etc.*]

MARCELLE [*aside*]: Children! That's all I need. [*She greets them with embarrassment.*]

BOULOT [*comes to the door*]: Madame Paillardin. Tea is served.

MARCELLE: Madame Paillardin! He said 'Madame Paillardin'. He knows my name! [*Very worried*] My tea. Oh, thank you. Thank you very much!

MATHIEU: Your tea? Are you a resident here?

MARCELLE: No. Not at all! That is to say ... Yes! Well, it was my husband's idea, as a matter of fact. We're just moving house and so ...

MATHIEU: We're in luck's way. We've got the room next door. We shall be neighbours!

BOULOT: Madame Paillardin. Your tea is served!

MARCELLE [*aside*]: He's driving me insane! Is he going to announce my name to the nation?

BOULOT: Madame Paillardin. Your tea ...

MARCELLE: Thank you very much. M'sieur, I'd love to stand here chatting to you. But my tea calls! [*Going to her door*] I'm sure you don't want to join me. [*She goes into her room.*]

[MATHIEU *follows her.*]

MATHIEU: But I'd be delighted! What could be more welcome than a cup of good, hot tea!

GIRLS: Oh yes. Good, hot tea! How lovely! What a treat!

MATHIEU [*to* BOULOT]: Hurry up, my man! Fetch the cups. And look sharp about it.

BOULOT: As you say, m'sieur.

MATHIEU: Come along, children. We're all going to pay a call on Madame Paillardin!

MARCELLE: Help! His jacket.

[*She hides* PINGLET's *jacket behind her as* MATHIEU *comes into the room.*]

MATHIEU [*looking round*]: It's really very pleasant here!

MARCELLE [*sliding towards the bathroom*]: I quite agree. Delightful, isn't it?

[*Aside.*] My God! How on earth will I get rid of them?

MATHIEU: Come along in, children.

[*They come in as* MARCELLE *disappears into the bathroom with* PINGLET'S *hat and jacket.*]

MARCELLE [*comes back smiling*]: Very well then. Do sit down.

MATHIEU: We don't want to seem difficult. But isn't there a slight short-age of chairs?

MARCELLE [*forcing a laugh*]: Shortage of chairs? Oh yes. Very witty! Most amusing ...

BOULOT [*coming into the room*]: The tea cups, m'sieur. [*He puts down a tray with five cups and the sugar bowl.*]

EVERYONE: Tea! At last ...

MATHIEU: Fetch us some chairs, porter. And look lively now!

BOULOT: Very well, m'sieur.

[BOULOT *goes to* CHERVET'S *room.*]

MATHIEU: Run along, children. Help the porter. The furniture here seems notable by its absence.

MARCELLE [*aside*]: Oh my God! Will they never go? And Pinglet's bound to come back in a minute.

MATHIEU: If I may, I'll put a little more water in the pot.

MARCELLE [*hopeless, aside*]: He's going to start cooking now! [*Aloud*] Oh do as you like ...

[BOULOT *comes back carrying a chair and the* GIRLS *have a chair each.*]

BOULOT: Your chair, m'sieur.

MARCELLE [*aside*]: Pinglet! Look what you've landed me in!

[*Everyone sits down.*]

BOULOT: I'm going for the bottle.

MARCELLE: What bottle?

BOULOT: The poor invalid's hot water bottle.

MARCELLE: Of course. Yes. Now! Do it!

[BOULOT *goes.*]

[*Aside*] This charming family's going to kill me! [*Not thinking what she's saying.*] Please. Do all sit down ...

MATHIEU [*sitting judicially on his chair*]: We are sitting down. Apart from that, Madame Paillardin. Is there something troubling you?

MARCELLE [*nervous*]: Troubling me? Of course not. I feel totally relaxed.

MATHIEU: Come along, children. Make yourselves useful! Pour out the tea.

[*The* GIRLS *do so.*]

What about our old friend Pinglet, madame? Do you ever see anything of him, these days?

MARCELLE: Oh, hardly ever! You know how it is in Paris. We've quite lost touch. Of course, I'm a great friend of dear Madame Pinglet. That's why I was there today ...

[PINGLET *appears on the landing, extremely cheerful.*]

PINGLET: Oh, I'm feeling so much better. I've had a breath of fresh air and I've said 'goodbye' to my dinner. I'm fit as a fiddle! And ready for anything! [*Singing*]

'Take me where the ladies dance all night,

Take me where the bubbly makes you tight!

Take me where the kisses feel just right ...

In Monte Carlo!'

MATHIEU: So you've lost touch with Pinglet?

MARCELLE [*wincing as she hears him singing*]: Oh, completely. Absolutely lost touch.

[PINGLET *comes into the room. All the* MATHIEU FAMILY *stand up, astonished.*]

THE MATHIEUS: Pinglet!

PINGLET [*astonished*]: The Mathieus!

MARCELLE [*who has risen, aside to* PINGLET]: It's all up with me!

PINGLET [*aside*]: Where did they spring from?

MATHIEU [*grasping* PINGLET's *hand*]: Pinglet! My dear old friend! Your ears must be burning. We were talking about you!

THE GIRLS: Yes. Yes. We were talking about you. Your ears must be burning.

PINGLET: How very kind of you.

MATHIEU: But do tell me, Pinglet. Do you usually go out in your shirt sleeves?

PINGLET: Oh. No. Not at all. Er. Well, you see. My jacket was torn. So I took it to the tailor. Just in the next street, as a matter of fact. And he said he'd do it in a quarter of an hour, so I said to myself, 'Hello', I said, 'I've just time to pop in and say hello to Madame Paillardin.'

MARCELLE: So kind of you. So very kind.

GIRLS: So kind.

[*Awkward pause.*]

PINGLET: So ... hello!

MARCELLE: Hello!

MATHIEU: Hello!

VIOLETTE: A lovely cup of hot tea, M'sieur Pinglet. [*She hands him one.*]

PINGLET: Tea. How thoughtful of you!

MARGUERITE [*with the sugar bowl*]: Sugar, M'sieur Pinglet?

[*He starts putting in lumps.*]

PINGLET: How very kind. [*Aside*] My God ... I didn't exactly come here to have tea with the Mathieu family!

   [*He is still putting sugar in his tea.*]

MARGUERITE: You've got a sweet tooth, M'sieur Pinglet.

PINGLET: Not at all. Can't stand sugar.

MATHIEU [*drinking his tea*]: Tell me, my dear old friend. What's the news in Paris?

PINGLET: The news? Well, we got rid of Marie Antoinette. We had a revolution! Some time ago, of course.

MATHIEU: And your wife? She's still keeping well? Since this afternoon?

PINGLET: Quite well. Thank you. How about yours?

MATHIEU [*hurt*]: You know perfectly well! She died eight years ago.

PINGLET: So she did! I shan't bother to ask after her then. [*Aside*] Why won't they go?

BOULOT [*coming in from the left with a large stone hot water bottle*]: Ah, there you are, m'sieur. Here's m'sieur's hot water bottle.

MARCELLE [*aside*]: That's all we need!

PINGLET [*aside, taking the hot water bottle*]: The tactless idiot! [*Burns his hand on the bottle.*] Ouch!

MATHIEU: What've you got there, Pinglet? Ginger beer?

PINGLET: Yes. No! Hot hands. Every time I pass this hotel I order a hot water bottle.

MATHIEU: Really?

PINGLET: Oh, yes. They're famous here for their good, old fashioned hot water bottles. Hot water bottles are the spécialité de la maison! My wife, my dear heart Angelique, always says, 'If you're passing the Free Trade Hotel, do bring me back one of their glorious old hot water bottles.' Isn't that right, Madame Paillardin?

MARCELLE: Yes, of course. Quite right. Splendid hot water bottles! [*Embarrassed.*] They're quite the thing here. In Paris.

BOULOT: But, m'sieur ...

PINGLET: That's quite enough! We don't want to hear any more from you, lackey, go along now. Leave the room!

BOULOT [*going to the door on the right*]: Very well, m'sieur. [*He goes out, up the stairs and disappears.*]

PINGLET [*to* MARCELLE]: Madame, I'm sure you must be tired. [*Shouts in* MATHIEU's *ear*] She must be *tired*! [*To* MARCELLE] I'm not going to keep you up a moment longer. Allow me to take leave of you. I'm going now. Don't try and stop me. Goodbye!

MARCELLE [*yawning*]: Well, as a matter of fact ...

MATHIEU [*rising*]: You're tired? But you should have told us. Come along, children. Back to our room. Show a little tact and discretion.

[*He takes his chair and starts out, followed by his* DAUGHTERS.]

PINGLET [*to* MARCELLE, *pretending to follow* MATHIEU]: I knew how to flush him out!

MATHIEU [*to* MARCELLE]: Good night, dear Madame Paillardin. You must go straight to bed now.

PINGLET: Of course she must!

[*He pushes* MATHIEU *and, in the general confusion, they all, including* PINGLET, *pick up a chair.*]

[*Aside to* MARCELLE] I'll go down to put him off the scent. Back in a minute! Stay exactly where you are!

[PINGLET *goes out onto the landing.*]

MARCELLE [*shutting the door*]: This is a pretty kettle of fish!

MATHIEU [*holding out his hand to* PINGLET]: Good night, my dear old friend. My respects to dear Madame Pinglet!

PINGLET [*putting his chair into* MATHIEU'*s hand*]: So kind! So very kind!
[*He goes off downstairs.* MATHIEU *gets rid of the chair.*]

MATHIEU [*going into his room*]: Come along in, children.

MARCELLE: That's enough! That's quite enough! No more adventures! I've learned my lesson ...

GIRLS [*kissing their father*]: Sleep well, Papa!

VIOLETTE: We're going to get undressed.

MATHIEU: Oh, very well. There are your ... facilities. [*He points their bathroom out.*] But quietly now! Madame Paillardin wants to sleep.

MARCELLE: I'm not staying a minute longer in this horrible hotel! As soon as Pinglet gets back ... [*She puts on her coat.*]

MATHIEU [*yawns*]: I'm longing for my bed.

MARCELLE [*searching her room*]: My hat! What an evening! Now my hat's done the vanishing trick!

MATHIEU: It's been a long day.

MARCELLE: Did I put it with Pinglet's bits and pieces? [*She takes the candle into the bathroom. The room's in darkness.*]

MATHIEU [*looking round his room*]: I think we'll do pretty well here. This room has a sort of rustic simplicity which I find rather appealing. [*He sees* PAILLARDIN'*s things.*] Good gracious! We've got the luxury of a full toilet set. Tortoise-shell combs! Ebony backed brushes, with the initials of the hotel proprietor! [*He brushes his hair.*] All the comforts of home! Paris hotels are miles ahead of anything we've got in Dieppe. Now, a cigar before turning in! [*He gets out a very small cigar.*] There's not much of it, but it's quite enjoyable, such as it is. [*He sees* PAILLARDIN'*s box of cigars.*] A cigar box! 'Regalias' hand rolled on the thighs of Cuban beauties, at least eighty centimes a piece. Save that for a rainy day. [*He puts away his cigar.*] An AI hotel de luxe! Seven francs a day and a box of cigars thrown in! [*He takes all the cigars and lights one*] No wonder Pinglet recommended it.

MARCELLE [*coming out of her bathroom*]: Incredible! My hat's disappeared.

MATHIEU [*smoking, his candle in his hand*]: An excellent smoke. I can't think how they make a profit!

MARCELLE [*still searching*]: And Pinglet's vanished again. Where on earth's he got to? [*She opens the door.*]

MATHIEU [*seeing* PAILLARDIN'*s night shirt on the bed*]: And a night shirt. Silk from Sulkas. And bedroom slippers. They really think of everything ... [*He picks up the slippers.*] What service! Never known anything like it.

[PINGLET *appears carrying his hot water bottle.*]

MARCELLE [*on the threshold*]: There you are at last!

PINGLET [*very quiet, looking round him fearfully*]: Here I am at last!

MATHIEU: There's only one thing missing. A nice, comforting hot water bottle! I'll get the porter to bring one.

MARCELLE [*to* PINGLET]: Come in. Don't hang about!

[MATHIEU *goes out onto the landing with his candle in his hand. It's dark on his right.*]

[*Seeing him*] Drat that man! [*She bangs the door shut.*]

PINGLET [*aside*]: Mathieu! [*He is rooted to the spot.*]

MATHIEU: Good heavens! It's you, Pinglet! [*He puts his candle on* BOULOT'*s table.*]

PINGLET [*very embarrassed*]: Oh, yes. It's me. Pinglet. I had to come back up because there's something I simply had to tell you.

MATHIEU: What?

PINGLET [*babbling*]: Not that it's all that important. But I might as well tell you. As I'm here ...

MATHIEU: Which you obviously are.

PINGLET: Well, I think you ought to know this. I was downstairs and I heard people talking. Apparently things were hotting up in Parliament this afternoon.

MATHIEU [*uninterested*]: Oh, really?

PINGLET: Oh yes! There were questions asked about the Budget! I mean, this may astonish you. The Budget came up for discussion! And the Minister of Finance has really been caught with his trousers down. Figuratively, of course!

MATHIEU [*bored*]: Of course.

PINGLET: Well. Where's it going to end? That's what I ask myself. My God, where will it end? And I said there's only one person who knows the answer to that sort of question. Good old Mathieu! So I came straight up here to ask your advice.

MATHIEU: On the Budget! What on earth do you expect me to do about it?

PINGLET [*cheerfully*]: All right then! The Budget bores you. Understood! We'll say no more about the Budget. Good night to you. I'm on my way ... [*He starts to leave.*]

MATHIEU: Good night. But thanks for thinking of me ...

PINGLET: Don't mention it. Back to your room now. High time you were in bed, old fellow.

MATHIEU: I'm waiting for the porter to bring me a hot water bottle. You told me they were particularly good here.

PINGLET: A hot water bottle! Oh, for God's sake have mine. [*Giving it to him.*]

MATHIEU: I wouldn't dream of it. Robbing you ...

PINGLET: You're not robbing me. [*Aside*] It's stone cold anyway. [*Aloud*] I'll pick another up on my way out.

MATHIEU: It's terribly kind of you.

PINGLET: Not at all. Think nothing of it. Now then, for God's sake. Get into bed! You must be exhausted.

MATHIEU [*standing calmly in his doorway smoking his cigar*]: I certainly am. Good night to you, Pinglet my dear old fellow.

PINGLET [*waiting for him to go into his room*]: Good night to you! Good night!

MATHIEU [*waving him goodbye*]: Good night!

PINGLET [*moving towards the stairs*]: Good night! What are you waiting for? [*Smiling mirthlessly at* MATHIEU.] Good night to you! [*He goes off down the stairs.*]

MATHIEU [*going into his room*]: Charming chap! Forgot my candle.

[*He goes back to the landing and finds himself face to face with* PINGLET, *who has come back. He smiles at him.*]

MATHIEU: Still there, old fellow?

PINGLET [*embarrassed*]: I forgot to shake hands.

[*He grasps* MATHIEU's *hand and runs back downstairs.* MATHIEU *goes back into his room.* PINGLET *takes advantage of this and shoots into* MARCELLE's *room.*]

MATHIEU [*going into his bathroom*]: Time to get undressed.

[*Darkness on the right.*]

PINGLET [*in* MARCELLE's *room*]: I managed it!

MARCELLE: At last! I thought you'd never get back.

PINGLET: But my dearest one. I had to shake off that abominable Mathieu. What a limpet that fellow is!

MARCELLE: Limpet? The man's a leech!

PINGLET: There must be at least a thousand hotels in Paris and he has to pick on this one! Just my luck!

MARCELLE: Exactly! Well, put on your hat and jacket and let's go home. Please!

PINGLET: My hat! My jacket? Where are they?

MARCELLE: In the bathroom.

PINGLET: Oh, thanks. [*He goes into the bathroom.*]

MARCELLE: Oh and whatever have you done with *my* hat?

PINGLET [*putting on his jacket*]: Your hat? What about your hat? It must be somewhere.

MARCELLE: Somewhere? *Where?* Will you kindly tell me that!

PINGLET [*agitated*]: Where? Well, I really don't know. When you took it off I put it on the bed ... Oh, now I remember. When I was suffocating I used it to fan myself a little. And then I must have just popped up to the balcony with it in my hand. I suppose I left it upstairs! [*He laughs foolishly.*] What a silly billy I am!

MARCELLE [*very angry*]: I suppose you think that's very funny! Really, Pinglet. You're a genius. Why on earth did you take it in the first place? Oh, go and get it then. I'll wait for you.

PINGLET: Yes. Wait for me! Only wait for me, Marcelle.

MARCELLE: Well hurry up. I'm at the end of my tether!

[PINGLET *rushes out and bumps into* BASTIEN.]

PINGLET: Oh!

BASTIEN: Can I help you, m'sieur?

PINGLET [*running upstairs*]: I don't need your help! No, thank you. I know where I'm going. I know exactly where I'm going. [*He vanishes.*]

BASTIEN: Just as well.

MARCELLE [*very nervous*]: It's the last straw! I'm worn out. From now on ... Total fidelity!

[*She goes into the bathroom.* BASTIEN *is on the landing and hears the bell.*]

BASTIEN: Good. Good. More guests! [*He sees* PAILLARDIN.] Ah. It's the monsieur the learned expert back.

PAILLARDIN [*coming up the stairs*]: In person!

BASTIEN: M'sieur the learned expert is going to bed?

PAILLARDIN: If that is quite convenient to you. You have my candle?

BASTIEN: Here it is, m'sieur the learned expert.

PAILLARDIN [*smiles*]: And have your worthy ghosts made their appearance yet?

BASTIEN: Not so far as I am aware, m'sieur the learned expert.

[BASTIEN *gives* PAILLARDIN *his candle.*]

PAILLARDIN: Perhaps they were caught in the traffic. [*He goes into the room on the right.*]

BASTIEN: Laugh while you can, m'sieur the learned expert. Laugh while you can! [*He follows* PAILLARDIN *into the room.*]

PAILLARDIN [*laughing and looking round the room*]: The haunted chamber doesn't look particularly haunted to me. I just hope your ghosts have the good manners to let a fellow get a decent bit of shut-eye.

BASTIEN: They probably heard you say that, m'sieur the learned expert.

PAILLARDIN [*seeing his open cigar box*]: Some joker's been at my cigars!

BASTIEN: M'sieur the learned expert?

PAILLARDIN: I told you. My cigars. The box was full when I went out. Who's been at my cigars, eh?

BASTIEN: I have absolutely no idea, m'sieur.

PAILLARDIN: You have absolutely no idea? Well, my cigars didn't suddenly decide to go out for a breath of fresh air.

BASTIEN [*gloomily*]: It's obvious, isn't it.

PAILLARDIN: What's obvious?

BASTIEN: It's the supernatural. Up to their usual tricks, m'sieur!

PAILLARDIN: Don't make me laugh. Whoever saw a ghost smoking a Havana cigar?

BASTIEN: I don't see why not. You do it.

PAILLARDIN: Look at this! My brushes. My comb! All at sixes and sevens. The ghosts have been brushing their hair ...

BASTIEN: Seems the most likely explanation.

PAILLARDIN: I think I'm beginning to get to the bottom of this little mystery. There's some thieving rascal who pays calls here pretending to be a ghost.

BASTIEN: Oh ye of little faith!

PAILLARDIN: All right. Run along now, my man. I'll have it out tomorrow – with your superior.

BASTIEN: As you say, m'sieur. I hope you sleep as well as possible. [*Very gloomily.*] Under the circumstances. [*Going out onto the landing, aside.*] And I hope some bloody great ghost comes and gives you a slosh around the chops, m'sieur the learned expert.

PAILLARDIN: Oh yes! There's a thief at work here. That's perfectly obvious. [*He looks at his brush.*] He's even left his filthy thieving hairs in my brushes!

[*He puts his brushes and combs back in his bag.* PINGLET *is coming down the stairs.*]

PINGLET: Nothing! Not a sign of her wretched hat. And I've searched high and low.

65

PAILLARDIN [*looking at the bed*]: My night shirt and bedroom slippers! The fellow's a nightwear robber and he's made a killing! [*He hangs up his hat.*]

PINGLET [*on the landing*]: Marcelle's going to cut up pretty rough about her hat! Never mind. I'll just have to tell her the truth. Courage, Pinglet! [*He goes back into the room on the left.*]

PAILLARDIN: I'll just have to sleep in my clothes. At least if anything supernatural crops up I'll be ready for action.

[*He lies on the bed and starts to read a book.* MARCELLE, *coming out of her bathroom, meets* PINGLET.]

MARCELLE: Back at last! Give me my hat and let's go.

PINGLET: Marcelle. I want you to be very brave about this.

MARCELLE: Why've I got to be brave? Tell me, Pinglet. Why?

PINGLET: I have not recovered your hat. Some swine's pinched it!

MARCELLE: Who?

PINGLET: He didn't leave his card.

MARCELLE: Charming! Never mind. Luckily I brought my little mantilla. [*She puts on a lace mantilla.*] Well. What are we waiting for?

PINGLET [*going out onto the landing, followed by* MARCELLE]: Very well! The order for retreat.

MARCELLE: What an evening! It's taught me a lesson ... What a lesson! [*They go down the stairs.*]

PAILLARDIN [*yawning*]: I'm absolutely whacked. Can't think what's the matter with me. Can't keep my eyes open.

[*He puts out his candle.* MARCELLE *comes shooting back up the stairs, followed by* PINGLET.]

MARCELLE: Oh, my God! It's Maxime!

PINGLET: Your husband's nephew here with Victoire, my maid! The younger generation's got absolutely no sense of morality! In there!

[*They go back into the room on the left.*]

MARCELLE: Shut the door!

PINGLET [*in a panic*]: But the key! Where on earth's the key? What happened to the key?

MARCELLE: Lock the door! Never mind the key!

PINGLET: I can't lock it! Not without the key. [*He points to the bathroom.*] In there!

MARCELLE: Is there a key?

PINGLET: There's a bolt on the door. Quick!

MARCELLE [*rushes in after him*]: What a night! My God! What a nightmare! [VICTOIRE *and* MAXIME *appear.* VICTOIRE *is carrying* MAXIME'S *books.* MAXIME *has a satchel.*]

BASTIEN: This way, m'sieur. Welcome to the Free Trade Hotel.

MAXIME [*to* VICTOIRE]: This is a serious step we're taking, mademoiselle ...

VICTOIRE: Oh, don't keep on about how serious it is.

BASTIEN [*in honeyed tones*]: Now, may I say that I know exactly what m'sieur and madame are looking for! A charming little love nest where you and madame can snuggle down and no questions asked! M'sieur is clearly a man of taste and discernment.

MAXIME [*very worried*]: Oh ... yes. Do you really think so?

BASTIEN: By a happy chance I am able to offer m'sieur and madame room number 9. It was in that very room that the Crown Princess of Poland spent her wedding night, with her major-domo. You'll be thoroughly at home there, madame!

VICTOIRE: In a princess's room!

BASTIEN: In this hotel, madame, you bed down with the élite!

VICTOIRE: Oh, I know. We've read your brochure. That's it then. We'll take number 9.

BASTIEN: That's wonderful. [*Starts to laugh.*] You'll have the time of your young lives in number 9. [*He is laughing, looking at them.*]

MAXIME [*to* VICTOIRE]: He's laughing at me! Even the porter's laughing at me!

VICTOIRE: Don't worry. Let him laugh!

BASTIEN [*lighting a candle*]: If madame and m'sieur would condescend to enter ...

[VICTOIRE *tries to drag* MAXIME *into the room.*]

MAXIME: Mademoiselle. Careful. Please. I really don't know where all this is going to end ...

VICTOIRE: Why not come in and find out?

MAXIME [*goes into number* 9]: I'm all prepared, anyway. Thank God I've revised my Descartes.

[BASTIEN *follows them. It is dark on the landing.* PAILLARDIN *is asleep on the bed. The* MISSES MATHIEU, *wearing their nightdresses, come out of their bathroom.*]

VIOLETTE [*putting down her candle*]: Early to bed! [*She sits down on the right.*]

MARGUERITE: That's going to be my bed!

PERVENCHE: I want that one. It looks lovely and big.

PAQUERETTE: No. I bag that one!

PERVENCHE: I bagged it before you bagged it!

PAQUERETTE: You're a liar. I saw it hours ago.

PERVENCHE: You saw it but you never bagged it, did you?

PAQUERETTE: Anyway, you smell!

[*An argument starts.*]

VIOLETTE [*whispers*]: Don't make such an unholy row, girls! Papa told us not to.

> [*They all sit on their beds and take off their stockings.*]

How lovely it's going to be ... To slip between the sheets. [*She gets into bed.*] Crikey! It's freezing!

BASTIEN [*coming out of number 9*]: Sweet dreams, m'sieur! Sleep well, madame! [*He goes down the staircase.*]

THE GIRLS: Let's have your candle. No, it's mine! Mine! You thief! That's my candle! etc. etc.

> [*They quarrel over the candle, which drops onto the floor and goes out. There is darkness on the right and on the landing.*]

VIOLETTE: That's our candle gone!

PERVENCHE: Butter fingers!

> [*They light their night lights, which are small spirit lamps.*]

VIOLETTE: What lovely night lights! Do we look like little elves ...?

PERVENCHE [*standing up on her bed*]: Or terrible ghosts!

VIOLETTE [*standing up on her bed*]: That's what we are! I'm the headless hunter of Honfleur!

PAQUERETTE [*standing up on her bed*]: I'm the strangled Sister of Soissons!

MARGUERITE [*standing up on her bed*]: I'm the noseless Nun of Nantes!

> [*They are all standing up on their beds.* PERVENCHE *starts to sing.*]

PERVENCHE [*singing*]:

> 'Knock! Knock! Knock!
> Wake up ghosts, come out of your graves!'

THE GIRLS [*singing*]:

> 'Wake up ghosts, we're going to dance
> Up and down the roads of France
> Rattling bones till break of day
> The Headless Hunter leads the way!'

PAILLARDIN [*waking up, terrified*]: The ghosts are here! Oh my God!

> [*The* GIRLS *get off their beds and dance round the room.*]

THE GIRLS [*singing*]:

> 'Knock! Knock! Knock!
> Wake up ghosts, come out of your graves,
> Wake up ghosts, we're going to dance
> Up and down the roads of France!'

PAILLARDIN [*astride the end of his bed, his arms in the air in a wild gesture of exorcism*]: Evil spirits, avaunt!

THE GIRLS: Aha! It's a man! Ooh! Help! etc. etc.

> [*The* GIRLS *see him and with terrified shrieks they take refuge in* MATHIEU'*s bathroom.*]

PAILLARDIN: The ghosts! The knocking ghosts! Help! Help!

[*He rushes out onto the landing.* VICTOIRE *comes out onto the landing, followed by* MAXIME.]

VICTOIRE: What's going on?

PAILLARDIN [*shouting*]: Help me! Help me!

VICTOIRE [*face to face with* PAILLARDIN]: Monsieur Paillardin!

MAXIME: My uncle!

[MAXIME *rushes back into number* 9. VICTOIRE *hides behind the curtains on* MATHIEU's *bed*.]

PAILLARDIN [*rushing up the stairs and shouting*]: The ghosts have arrived! The knocking ghosts! Get thee behind me Satan! Beelzebub! Let a good man rest!

[MATHIEU *comes out of his bathroom, carrying his candle.*]

MATHIEU: What's all the fuss about? A man in here? Where on earth's the man? In the bed? I don't see any man.

[*He pulls aside the bed curtains and sees* VICTOIRE.]

VICTOIRE: Oh!

MATHIEU: Excuse me, madame! [*He starts to laugh.*] They told me you were a man. You're quite clearly not a man at all! [*He goes back into the bathroom.*] What on earth was all that fuss about? It's not a man at all. It's a woman!

[*Darkness in the room.*]

THE GIRLS [*O.S. in the bathroom*]: No . . . No, Papa. It really *is* a man.

MAXIME [*coming out onto the landing*]: My uncle's cleared off. I'd better rescue Victoire. [*He goes into* MATHIEU's *room.*] No one about! [*He calls in a whisper.*] Victoire!

VICTOIRE [*peeping out of the bed curtains*]: Here I am!

[MATHIEU *comes out of the bathroom, followed by his* GIRLS.]

MATHIEU: Here you are, my children. See for yourselves!

[MAXIME *and* VICTOIRE *give small cries and hide.*]

VIOLETTE: My dear Papa. I can assure you. It's a man. We saw him. Large as life!

MATHIEU: And I've got eyes as well. What're you suggesting? That I've reached my time of life and I still can't tell a man from a woman? Let me tell you, I have memories! [*He sees* VICTOIRE *creeping out onto the landing.*] There you are, you see. I know what I'm talking about. It's a perfectly obvious woman!

[MAXIME *creeps out onto the landing.*]

THE GIRLS [*seeing him*]: No, no, Papa! Look. Look closely! Can't you see? It's a man!

MATHIEU [*disturbed*]: Could it be both?

MAXIME: Let's go.

VICTOIRE: Yes let's!

[MAXIME *and* VICTOIRE *disappear down the stairs.*]

MATHIEU: We've got to get to the bottom of this! [*He goes to the door and calls.*] Porter! Porter!

[BOULOT *appears.*]

BOULOT: What's all the noise about?

MATHIEU: Oh, porter. What on earth's going on? There are men and women, of both sorts, in our room!

BOULOT: Really, m'sieur? Then undoubtedly m'sieur has seen them.

MATHIEU: Seen what? Who are they ...?

BOULOT: Who are they? Indeed! Those whose names we dare not speak, m'sieur. But you were in the haunted room.

EVERYONE: The haunted room!

[PAILLARDIN *appears at the top of the staircase, coming down with great care.*]

BOULOT: Oh yes, m'sieur! Those men and women you were talking about. They're not men and women of this world, m'sieur. They are the departed! But they do not rest in peace, m'sieur. They come back here to haunt our visitors. We call them 'the knocking ghosts'!

THE GIRLS [*with little cries of terror*]: The knocking ghosts! Poor, troubled spirits!

[*The* GIRLS *go up the stairs still uttering little screams. They terrify* PAILLARDIN, *who runs up the stairs in front of them.*]

MATHIEU [*following his children*]: Children! I don't know what's got into you. Running round the hotel in your nightgowns! What would they say at the convent? Children! Children!

[*He disappears up the stairs.* BOULOT *follows him.*]

BOULOT: A curse is on our house! A terrible curse!

[PINGLET *comes out of his bathroom, followed by* MARCELLE.]

PINGLET: What's all the hullabaloo? Are we on fire?

MARCELLE: Whatever it is, it's nothing ordinary. Let's get out of this place before I die of terror.

PINGLET Yes, but careful! Don't take any risks. [*He opens the door a crack.*]

MARCELLE: Oh, the joy of not being in this ghastly hotel!

PINGLET [*looking round the landing*]: The coast's clear!

MARCELLE [*comes out onto the landing with a sigh of relief*]: Safe at last!

[PAILLARDIN *comes rushing madly down the stairs.*]

PAILLARDIN: The ghosts are back! The knocking ghosts!

MARCELLE [*terrified*]: Oh, my God! Get back in!

PINGLET [*following her in*]: Is there someone there?

MARCELLE: Oh no. Only my husband!

PINGLET [*terrified*]: Help! [*He bangs the door shut.*]

PAILLARDIN [*who has seen them without recognizing them*]: Thank God. Living beings! [*He tries to pull open the door.*] Open up there! Let me in! For mercy's sake!

PINGLET [*holding the door on the other side*]: This is private property. No entry! Absolutely no entry!

PAILLARDIN [*pulling*]: Please! I beg of you. I'm in terrible danger from ghosts! For God's sake let me in!

PINGLET [*on the other side*]: No entry!

MARCELLE: Don't let him in!

PINGLET: No entry! I may not have much choice. He's stronger than I am.

PAILLARDIN: Open up there.

> [*The door gives way and* PAILLARDIN *comes in from the left.* PINGLET *is sent flying back into the fireplace.* MARCELLE *grabs* PAILLARDIN'S *hat and pulls it right down over her head, hiding her face.*]

PAILLARDIN: My hat's gone! Excuse me, madame, that's my hat you're wearing!

MARCELLE [*hanging onto the hat*]: Help me! Help me!

> [PINGLET *extricates himself from the fireplace. His face is covered with soot.*]

PAILLARDIN: Aaah! The chimney sweep?

> [PINGLET, *driven beyond endurance, punches* PAILLARDIN, *kicks him out onto the landing.*]

It's another ghost! A knocking ghost! They're in a terrible mood tonight! [*He rushes off down the stairs.*]

> [PINGLET *returns to* MARCELLE.]

PINGLET: Well. I think that's seen him off the premises.

MARCELLE [*taking off her hat*]: At last! What a narrow squeak! [*She has the hat off and looks at* PINGLET.] My God! A blackamoor!

PINGLET: No! No, it's me. Pinglet.

MARCELLE [*weakly*]: This night'll be the death of me. You Pinglet? You've undergone some sort of colour change ...

PINGLET: Oh, that. That's not important ...

MARCELLE: When I think back. On what we've lived through! It makes me feel completely dizzy!

PINGLET: It's all over now. We can breathe again.

MARCELLE: What a blessed relief!

PINGLET: Isn't it marvellous! Our troubles are over, Marcelle. We're safe at last.

> [*Sound of raised voices and police whistles.*]

What the devil's that?

MARCELLE: Not something new?

BASTIEN [*rushes madly up the stairs*]: Oh, my God! It's the police! The police! Make yourselves scarce, messieurs and mesdames! It's the Department of Public Morality. 'The Morals' are after us! [*Going up the stairs*] 'The Morals' are after us!

MARCELLE [*to* PINGLET]: What's he talking about?

PINGLET: 'The Morals'. The Department of Public Morality. That is to say, the police. We're absolutely and completely – in the soup!

MARCELLE: The police! No! That's the last straw! I'm leaving now.

[*They both go out onto the landing where* MARCELLE *sees* INSPECTOR BOUCARD *coming up the stairs with his* CONSTABLES.]

My God! An inspector!

[*She rushes into the room on the left and bangs the door.* BOUCARD *sees her.*]

BOUCARD: There goes one of them. [*To his men, pointing to* PINGLET] Arrest him, lads!

PINGLET [*struggling with the* CONSTABLES]: I can assure you, m'sieur. There's a perfectly innocent explanation!

CONSTABLE: Tell us down at the Station.

BOUCARD: There's a woman in there!

[*The* CONSTABLE *tries to open the door.* MARCELLE *holds it on the other side.*]

MARCELLE: No entry! Absolutely no entry!

BOUCARD [*to the* CONSTABLE]: Force it!

[*The door gives way. The* CONSTABLE *goes in.*]

MARCELLE: I'm lost!

CONSTABLE: Come along with me, madame.

PINGLET [*who is being held by a* CONSTABLE]: The poor woman!

MARCELLE: I can't believe it!

BOUCARD: Bring her out here.

[MARCELLE *is being brought out onto the landing.*]

MARCELLE: It's all a terrible mistake, m'sieur. I'm a completely honest woman!

PINGLET: She's perfectly right. She's a completely honest woman.

BOUCARD: So much the better. [*To* PINGLET] No one asked your opinion! Constable. Take the gentleman through there! [*He points to the room on the right.*]

PINGLET [*resisting*]: Now look here, my man!

CONSTABLE: Come along now. We've heard quite enough from you.

[*They take him into the room on the right.*]

BOUCARD [*to* MARCELLE]: And as for you, madame. Don't give me any fairy stories. Name and identity, if you please.

MARCELLE: But, m'sieur. What on earth's this all about? I'm here with my husband.

BOUCARD [*shrugs*]: I did say, no fairy stories.

MARCELLE: But it's perfectly true! I'm the wife of the gentleman ... The gentleman your men have just taken in there.

BOUCARD [*smiling at her*]: Oh, yes, of course. The lawful wedded wife! Proud possessor of a marriage certificate! I'm quite sure you are. And would it be taking too much of a liberty to inquire madame's name?

MARCELLE: But, m'sieur ... [*Aside.*] My God. It's the only way out! [*To* BOUCARD] Certainly. My name's Madame Pinglet.

BOUCARD: Very well, madame. [*To the* CONSTABLE] Bring back that individual, constable. [*He points to the right.*]

    [*The* CONSTABLE *goes to the door.*]

CONSTABLE: All right, you. The Inspector wants you.

PINGLET [*crossing the landing, aside*]: That poor little helpless woman! She won't have had the presence of mind to give a false name.

BOUCARD [*to* PINGLET]: All right, m'sieur. Full name please. No fairy tales!

PINGLET [*aside*]: Got it! It's the only way to save her. Thank God I'm brilliant! [*To* BOUCARD, *with great self confidence.*] I really can't understand what this is all about. It's perfectly above board. This lady is my wife!

MARCELLE [*seeing a ray of hope*]: Of course I am.

BOUCARD [*aside*]: Could they be fooling me by telling the truth? [*To* PINGLET] Just your name, m'sieur. If you please.

PINGLET: Madame's already told you it, I'm sure. [*Very loud and clear.*] I am Monsieur Henri Paillardin!

MARCELLE: Oh, my God!

BOUCARD [*very polite*]: Thank you so very much, m'sieur. It's just exactly as I thought!

MARCELLE [*aside*]: He's sunk me!

PINGLET [*aside, very pleased with himself*]: I've saved her!

    [BOULOT, BASTIEN, MATHIEU *and the* GIRLS *appear, followed by the* CONSTABLE.]

BOUCARD: Take the whole boiling down to the Station!

ALL: To the Station!

[*Tears, shouts, protestations, etc.*]

CURTAIN

ACT III

The same set as Act I.

When the curtain goes up the room is deserted and the window at the far end is open as it was at the conclusion of the first act. The clock strikes seven. PINGLET, *still covered in soot, appears at the window climbing up his rope ladder. He jumps over the hand-rail, pulls up the ladder, puts it under his arm and sits, tired and dejected, on the window sill. He stands up, almost immediately, tip-toes over to the angled door on the right and makes sure that it is still shut. Then he goes to the chest of drawers and puts away the rope ladder hurriedly. He takes off his jacket, his waistcoat and his hat and takes them into his bedroom, through the door at an angle stage left. He comes back as fast as he can to hang up another jacket near the fire. He takes a handkerchief out of his pocket and knots it around his head. A second handkerchief goes around his neck. He then comes downstage and faces the audience.*

He is now quite pleased with himself.

PINGLET: My God! What a night! What a ghastly night ...! But it's all over. At least Madame Pinglet wasn't there ... She must have been the only one. And when she gets back ... She'll find me looking like a man who's just got out of bed.

[*Knock at the door.*]

Is that you dear heart? It can't be her. Anyway, she's got a key. She never knocks.

VICTOIRE [*calls, O.S.*]: It's me, m'sieur. Victoire.

PINGLET: The little baggage! She was at the Free Trade Hotel ... with the rest of the world! But I can't tick her off about it without giving myself away. [*Calls.*] What do you want?

VICTOIRE: Your hot chocolate, m'sieur.

PINGLET: Oh, very good. Wheel it in ...

VICTOIRE [*O.S.*]: How can I? The door's locked.

PINGLET [*aside, taking a key out of his pocket*]: Of course it is! Well, go and ask madame for it.

VICTOIRE [*O.S.*]: But madame's not back yet, m'sieur.

PINGLET: Not back! Good heavens. Her sister must have taken a turn for the worse. It must add greatly to the terrors of being ill, having Madame Pinglet looming up at your bedside!

VICTOIRE [*O.S.*]: So what does m'sieur want me to do?

PINGLET: Do what you like. I haven't got the key. You'll have to wait till madame comes back.

VICTOIRE [*O.S.*]: Very well, m'sieur.

PINGLET: Of course I could open it. But if I do ... bang goes my alibi! All the same. What a night! What a terrible night! Dragged off to the police station like a couple of pick-pockets, and I hardly got time to steal a kiss!

[*He sits on the sofa.*]

The Free Trade Hotel! I'd've had a more passionate evening at the Building Contractors Annual Dinner! Anyway, why should the Department of Morality complain about me and Marcelle? Her husband wasn't complaining.

[*There's a knock at the door, he gets up.*]

Who's there? Who's there ... ?

MARCELLE [*calling in a hushed voice from the other side of the door*]: Pinglet! It's me.

PINGLET: Who's me?

MARCELLE [*O.S.*]: Me. Marcelle!

PINGLET: At last! Are you alone?

MARCELLE [*O.S.*]: Of course I am. Open up!

PINGLET: Half a minute. [*He unlocks the door.*] Now. Pull the bolt on your side.

MARCELLE [*O.S.*]: There! It's pulled.

PINGLET [*letting MARCELLE in*]: Come on in. Look slippy! [*He closes the door and locks it with a double lock.*] Oh, Marcelle! What a night! My God what a night! ... We've gone through a baptism of fire.

MARCELLE [*moving upstage, very agitated*]: Oh, Pinglet! Pinglet! You've ruined my reputation!

PINGLET [*following her*]: Don't be ridiculous. I haven't ruined anything. I mean, just because we happen to have been in a hotel together ... What's that got to do with it? Anyway, we're not undesirable characters. Police raids are only meant for undesirable characters.

MARCELLE: Looking at you, Pinglet, I suppose you might be described as extremely undesirable. I always thought so.

PINGLET: Marcelle!

MARCELLE: Better call me Madame Paillardin. In the circumstances.

PINGLET: Darling Madame Paillardin. Your husband need never know!

MARCELLE: He'll find out somehow. The police'll never leave us alone now ... And the newspapers ... We're doomed, Pinglet! We're both doomed!

[*She collapses onto the sofa.* PINGLET *kneels in front of her.*]

PINGLET: Chin up, Madame Paillardin. We've got absolutely nothing to feel guilty about. Worse luck. [*He kisses her.*] Try to be very brave.

[*He looks at her critically, having covered her face with soot.*]

I say, old thing. You've got a smut on your nose.

MARCELLE: A smut? Me? Well, you must have put it there.

[*She leads him to the looking glass.*]

Just look at your face!

PINGLET: Mine? [*He looks at himself.*] Oh, my God! Soot! From the fireplace. The chimney can't have been swept for years. I'd've had a fine chance of convincing Madame Pinglet that I've just got out of my lonely bed. Troubles! Nothing but troubles and tribulations!

[*He starts to wash his face with water from a carafe.*]

MARCELLE: Oh yes! What tremendous troubles! What terrible tribulations! [*Matter of fact*] After you with the water.

PINGLET: But it might have been worse. We might have spent the night in the cells, like the others. But thank God the Inspector trusted us! He gave us bail.

MARCELLE: Well, of course! That was because he could see the sort of people he was dealing with.

PINGLET: And because I stumped up five thousand francs! [*Showing her his face*] All gone now, has it?

MARCELLE: Just a little speck. On the end of your nose. [*Clutching his arm*] Five thousand francs!

PINGLET: I offered him the choice. My word as a gentleman or five thousand francs. He took the money. Oh, and I have to prove our identity to his satisfaction by this afternoon.

MARCELLE: That's torn it! You can't possibly prove that you're Monsieur Paillardin! I know exactly what's going to happen! We're going to have the Moral Squad round here. In full force!

PINGLET [*scrubbing his face*]: Don't worry your pretty little head. Just as soon as I'm looking presentable I'm going straight to the Prefect of Police.

MARCELLE: The Prefect of Police?

PINGLET: Who else? When you were safely tucked up in bed ...

MARCELLE [*mirthless laugh*]: Safely!

PINGLET: Well ... dangerously then. I, Benoit Pinglet, called on the Prefect.

MARCELLE: What happened?

PINGLET: He was out. At a Police Ball. Very thoughtless of him. I waited until seven o'clock this morning.

MARCELLE: And then?

PINGLET: He went straight to bed. No matter. I shall go back. He is a close personal friend.

MARCELLE: Of yours?

PINGLET: Oh yes. I am very close to Monsieur le Prefect.

MARCELLE [*very nervous*]: What on earth are you going to tell him?

PINGLET: I shall speak to him, as though he were my priest.

MARCELLE: But he isn't.

PINGLET: I shall make a clean breast of it.

MARCELLE: I'll never be able to speak to him at parties ...

PINGLET: I'll say, 'A woman's honour is involved.' He will respect the secrets of the confessional.

MARCELLE: You're certain?

PINGLET: I'm damn sure. I'll get away with a few dozen Ave Marias and a subscription to the Disabled Constables Seaside Holiday Fund ...

MARCELLE: It would have been so easy not to have landed us in all these complications. Why on earth did you have to call yourself Monsieur Paillardin when you're obviously Monsieur Pinglet?

PINGLET: Well really. Wasn't it just a tiny bit your fault? If only you hadn't said you were Madame Pinglet when everyone knows you're Madame Paillardin!

MARCELLE: Excuse me! I only called myself Madame Pinglet so they'd think I was your wife!

PINGLET: Excuse me! I only called myself Monsieur Paillardin so they'd think I was your husband!

MARCELLE: But use your common sense, my dear Pinglet. If you've got any left! How on earth are you going to convince the Inspector that your wife's called Madame Pinglet when you've made it perfectly clear to him that your name's Paillardin?

PINGLET: Let's be perfectly honest about this, old girl. When I said I was Paillardin, how on earth was I to know that you'd gone to the extra-ordinary lengths of introducing yourself as Madame Pinglet?

MARCELLE [*irritated*]: Well, if you didn't know that you should have kept your mouth shut!

PINGLET [*aside*]: Women! They've got an answer for everything.

[*There's a knock at the door.*]

Who's there?

PAILLARDIN [*O.S.*]: It's me! Paillardin!

MARCELLE [*whisper*]: Oh God! My husband ...

PINGLET: Ssh! [*To* PAILLARDIN, *through the door*] What do you want, old chap?

PAILLARDIN [*O.S.*]: I want to speak to you. Open the door!

PINGLET: I can't. My wife's locked me in and gone off with the key.

PAILLARDIN [*O.S.*]: What a woman!

PINGLET: Tell you what. Go outside. Get the gardener's long ladder. The one with the extension ... And come in by the window!

PAILLARDIN [*O.S.*]: I'll go and get the ladder.

PINGLET: There's a brave fellow!

MARCELLE: Now! Let me out.

PINGLET [*listening*]: Wait! His footsteps are dying away. [*He opens the door.*] Out you go!

[*He goes to the window to see if he can see* PAILLARDIN *and comes back.*]

Bolt the door after you.

MARCELLE: Oh, all right. What a night!

[*She goes.* PINGLET *shuts the door after her.*]

PINGLET [*going to the window*]: Yes. Indeed yes. My God! What a night!

[*He shouts down to* PAILLARDIN.]

Are you there, old chap?

PAILLARDIN [*O.S.*]: Coming up! My dear fellow. Aren't you ashamed to be treated like that – by a woman!

PINGLET: Just part of the wear and tear of married life!

PAILLARDIN [*O.S.*]: My God. If my wife ever treated me like that! Of course, she wouldn't dare. The poor little thing loves me far too much.

PINGLET: Steady on. Mind how you go.

[PAILLARDIN *appears and climbs in at the window. He has a huge black eye.*]

PAILLARDIN: Oh, my friend. What a night I've had, what a night!

PINGLET: Is there something the matter with your eye, old chap?

PAILLARDIN: There are more things in heaven and earth, Pinglet, than are dreamt of in your philosophies ...

PINGLET: What sort of things?

PAILLARDIN: Supernatural manifestations! Oh, I was like you once. I used to scoff. No longer! I have seen, Pinglet, what I have seen. And I tell you, quite frankly, I never want to see it again.

PINGLET: Oh, really? What's that?

PAILLARDIN: Ghosts! Troubled spirits of the departed.

PINGLET [*laughing*]: Ghosts! Poor old Paillardin. He's seen ghosts!

PAILLARDIN: Oh yes. I thought I was very clever when I agreed to sleep in that accursed hotel! I put it all down to the central heating. What a fool I was! I tell you. I'd hardly put my head on my pillow in the haunted room when I was wide awake. And I saw them! Devilish apparitions. With unearthly voices. They were dancing, a wild, terrible, frenzied dance. Singing. Singing in a way that was hardly human!

[PINGLET *is laughing.*]

Mock on, Pinglet! Mock on. I shall never forget that blood chilling song.

[*He sings.*]

> 'Wake up you ghosts, we're going to dance
> Up and down the roads of France,
> Rattling bones till break of day
> The Headless Hunter's on his way!'

It would have frozen your blood!

PINGLET [*aside*]: It would have done. If they'd sung like that!

PAILLARDIN: I didn't stand on ceremony! I gathered up my bits and pieces and I was off, like a bat out of hell! Oh, that room ... That damnable hotel bedroom! It was horrible. I fled and saw two normal human beings in another room ...

PINGLET [*not thinking*]: Number 10.

PAILLARDIN: Number 10? Why should it have been number 10?

PINGLET: Oh, I don't know. Why shouldn't it have been number 10?

PAILLARDIN: All right. Let's say it was number 10. I moved over to it and saw ...

PINGLET: Yes?

PAILLARDIN: A woman!

PINGLET: Ah ...

PAILLARDIN: Or at least, something that looked like a woman ... something in a dress and with ... [*He gestures, showing breasts, etc.*] I couldn't tell if it had a head, because of my hat.

PINGLET: It was over your eyes?

PAILLARDIN: No.

PINGLET: No?

PAILLARDIN: It was over *its* eyes.

PINGLET: Remarkable!

PAILLARDIN: The accursed apparition was wearing my hat. But the dress. Oh yes. I'd know that dress anywhere.

PINGLET: My God!

PAILLARDIN: It was a sickening sort of puce colour. The colour of old blood, Pinglet!

PINGLET [*aside*]: Damn!

PAILLARDIN: But at that very moment! Now this was witchcraft! Devilish

witchcraft! A ghostly chimney sweep materialized from the fireplace'
An evil spirit, of course.

PINGLET: Naturally.

PAILLARDIN: Supernaturally! A ghostly chimney sweep, about your size.

PINGLET [*positive*]: Couldn't have been. Must've been bigger.

PAILLARDIN: What do you mean? 'Must've been bigger'?

PINGLET [*confused*]: Chimney sweeps are always bigger. Even after death.

PAILLARDIN: You could be right. I hardly had time to measure. Before
I knew where I was it fell on me savagely and gave me a punch in the
face, and then I got a kick up the . . .

PINGLET: It was the kick that gave you the black eye?

PAILLARDIN: No. It was the punch. Never again. I tell you. I'll never set
foot in that hotel again! Oh, my dear old friend. God preserve you from
the knocking ghosts! [*He sits on the sofa.*]

PINGLET [*aside*]: He really believes in ghosts. [*To* PAILLARDIN] And does
your lady wife believe these tales of the supernatural?

PAILLARDIN: My wife? I haven't seen her yet. When I got home I knocked
and knocked at her bedroom door. No answer!

PINGLET [*aside*]: We're lost!

PAILLARDIN: She was sleeping like a log. [*He rises.*] I had to spend the
rest of the night in my dressing room.

MAXIME [*O.S. from the garden*]: Uncle! Are you there, uncle?

PAILLARDIN: That sounds like young Maxime! [*He goes to the window.*]

PINGLET [*following him*]: So it does.

PAILLARDIN [*calling down to* MAXIME]: Why aren't you at school, young
man?

MAXIME [*O.S.*]: I can explain everything, uncle.

PAILLARDIN: I hope you can. Come up the ladder.

MAXIME [*O.S.*]: Right you are.

> [PINGLET *sits.* MAXIME *appears at the window with a cigarette in his
> mouth. He stays there.*]

Good morning, M'sieur Pinglet. Morning, uncle. I say, uncle, wherever
did you get that shiner?

PAILLARDIN: That's not the point. The point is, why aren't you at school?

MAXIME: Ah. That. I was just going to tell you. Last night. I must have
forgotten to wind up . . .

PINGLET: Wind up what?

MAXIME: My watch, m'sieur. So I got the time wrong last night and
when I got to the Lycée yesterday evening, I was too late. The gates
were locked!

PAILLARDIN: What on earth are you talking about? Is this some sort of
joke?

MAXIME: I promise you. I've never been more serious in my life.

PINGLET [*aside*]: Not a bad little actor. He was tucked up with Victoire in the Free Trade Hotel!

PAILLARDIN: So why didn't you come straight back home?

MAXIME: Oh, uncle. It was much too late, and you were out, weren't you? And I didn't want to upset auntie.

PAILLARDIN: Don't beat about the bush, boy! Where did you spend the night?

MAXIME: They gave me a room, at the 'Continental'.

PAILLARDIN: Are you sure?

MAXIME: Do you doubt my word?

PINGLET [*aside*]: Nothing like a little philosophy to teach you how to lie through your teeth!

MAXIME: And when I got to the Lycée Stanislas this morning the head-master wouldn't let me in without a letter from you, uncle.

PAILLARDIN: We'll see about that.

MAXIME [*aside*]: Thank God he never recognized me at the hotel!

MARCELLE [*O.S. behind the door*]: Henri! Henri!

PAILLARDIN: That sounds very much like my wife. [*To* MARCELLE *through the door*] Here I am, my dear.

MARCELLE [*O.S. behind the door*]: All right. Open up.

PAILLARDIN: Can't be done. Madame Pinglet's got the key. I had to come up through the window. I'm here with good old Pinglet.

MARCELLE [*O.S.*]: Oh, are you ...?

PINGLET: Good morning to you, Madame Paillardin.

MARCELLE [*O.S.*]: Oh. Good morning to you, M'sieur Pinglet.

PINGLET [*greeting* MARCELLE *as though he could see her*]: And how are we feeling this morning? I do hope you slept well.

MARCELLE [*O.S.*]: Only so-so, I'm afraid. I had rather a restless night.

PINGLET: Oh, poor old you. I'm so sorry.

PAILLARDIN: Talk about restless nights! What about me? You know what happened to me?

MARCELLE [*O.S.*]: Not really. What?

PAILLARDIN: You won't believe this. You know the Free Trade Hotel?

MARCELLE [*O.S., very positive*]: Of course I don't! Never heard of it!

PINGLET: No! Never heard of it! Never in our lives. What on earth's the Free Trade Hotel? I've no idea where it is even.

MARCELLE [*O.S.*]: Neither have I. No idea at all!

PAILLARDIN: Of course you don't know it. It's an extremely dubious hotel. Why on earth *should* you know it?

PINGLET: Exactly. Dubious place! [*Laughs*] How on earth would we know it?

MARCELLE [*O.S., almost at the same time*]: How on earth would we know it?

PAILLARDIN: Well. Let me tell you about this nightmarish hotel. Half a minute. It's not very convenient talking to you through a door. I'll just hop out of the window and come round by the garden. With you in a jiffy.

MARCELLE [*O.S.*]: Oh, all right.

PAILLARDIN [*to* PINGLET]: Do you mind? We had a few cross words yesterday. East wind blowing, you know. I'd like to make peace with my wife. [*He goes to the window.*]

PINGLET: Well, of course. Make it up at once.

PAILLARDIN [*to* MAXIME]: Out of the way, boy. I want to get down.

[MAXIME *disappears.* PAILLARDIN *is sitting astride the window. He speaks to* PINGLET.]

Want to join me?

PINGLET: What? Me? Oh no. I'll stay here. I'll stay. [*Aside*] Thanks very much. You want to ruin my alibi?

[*He goes to open the door but then goes back to the window.*]

Put the ladder away. Don't forget!

PAILLARDIN [*O.S.*]: Oh, very well.

MARCELLE [*O.S.*]: Has my husband gone down?

PINGLET: The coast's clear.

[MARCELLE *unbolts the door.*]

MARCELLE: What did he say?

PINGLET: He doesn't know a thing! He's not at all suspicious.

MARCELLE: Oh, thank God!

PINGLET [*agitated*]: He didn't see anything. Except your dress. Your puce dress. That's all he saw of you last night. Burn it! Bury it! But, by all that's holy, don't ever let him get a glimpse of it.

MARCELLE: I'm glad you told me. I'll see to it at once.

PINGLET: He's coming up the stairs. Make yourself scarce!

[*He shuts the door in her face.*]

The bolt! Shoot the bolt!

[*We hear the sound of the bolt.*]

Safe at last! [*He sits.*] But I'm beginning to get bored in here. [*He gets up.*] I hope to God my wife comes back soon and sets me free. I know her sister's ill, but I can't stay in here for ever!

VICTOIRE [*O.S.*]: M'sieur! Are you there, m'sieur?

PINGLET: What is it, Victoire?

VICTOIRE [*O.S.*]: Telegram for you, m'sieur.

PINGLET: Push it under the door.

VICTOIRE [*O.S.*]: Here it comes!

[*The telegram slides under the door.* PINGLET *picks it up.*]

PINGLET: Probably from the hornet! [*Opens it.*] From the hornet's sister!
[*Reads it.*] 'We're extremely worried.' She's worried! 'Angelique didn't
arrive for dinner. We waited for her in vain.' She waited in vain for
Madame Pinglet! Lucky old her! 'Is she ill? Telegraph at once!' What's
it all mean? My wife isn't with her sister? Let me see, let me see. Last
night she set out for . . .

[*His face lights up.*]

Could she have been kidnapped? [*Disappointed*] Afraid not. These days
acts of heroism are far too rare. Could it be . . . Could it possibly be . . .
[*He starts to laugh.*] That Madame Pinglet . . . She too! She set out on
a little adventure?

[*He stops laughing.*]

It's not possible. Unless she had a blind date! Literally!

MME PINGLET [*in a tremulous voice from behind the door*]: Pinglet . . . Are
you there, Pinglet?

PINGLET [*depressed*]: I knew it was too good to last. She sounds a bit shaky.
Now's the time to get out of bed!

[*He goes into his room.*]

MME PINGLET [*O.S.*]: Oh, Pinglet. My dear, dear Pinglet! My little Benoit!
[*She comes in with a huge black eye.*]

What a night! My God what a night I've had! [*Taking off her cape.*]
Benoit. My dearest husband. Where are you?

PINGLET [*O.S.*]: What? Who's there? Who's waking me up?

MME PINGLET: It's me. And I'm still alive. Thanks be to God!

PINGLET [*O.S.*]: For small mercies!

MME PINGLET: When you know what I've suffered . . . Oh, Benoit! When
you hear of the terrible dangers I've been through . . . While you were
safely tucked up in bed. Where are you?

PINGLET: Here!

[*He appears at the door of his room.* MME PINGLET *falls into his arms.*]

MME PINGLET: I'm so happy to see you again, my darling!

PINGLET: Any particular reason?

MME PINGLET: What a night! What a night I've had . . . What troubles
and tribulations!

PINGLET [*aside*]: That same old song!

[*Taking his wife's head in his hands.*]

Good grief. What a shiner!

MME PINGLET: Oh, Pinglet! Pinglet! You nearly lost me!

PINGLET [*calm*]: *Nearly?*

MME PINGLET: I swear it. Doesn't that distress you?

PINGLET: Of course. [*Aside*] So near and yet so far.

MME PINGLET: Oh, my dear. A terrible accident ... *nearly* snatched me from you!

PINGLET: Don't tell me that again. It's breaking my heart ...

MME PINGLET: You're such a good, kind man. I took a cab, as you know, to Ville d'Avray. Everything was going so well.

PINGLET [*bored*]: The travels of Madame Pinglet.

MME PINGLET: We were quite contented, all three of us.

PINGLET: All three?

MME PINGLET: The cabbie, the horse and your dear, devoted wife. And then a train whistled ... and the horse bolted, terrified, and ...

PINGLET: I nearly lost you!

MME PINGLET: The cabbie dragged on the reins. He tried to stop the horse. Impossible! Picture me, Pinglet! Flying across the countryside. Galloping at breakneck speed. Not a soul about. No one to help us. It's in such moments of terror, Benoit, that one thinks of one's husband.

PINGLET: I think of you in moments of terror, too.

MME PINGLET: I said to myself ... [*with emotion*] 'If only he were at my side!'

PINGLET: You're too kind!

MME PINGLET: Anyway. You weren't there. So I lost my head. I opened the cab door ... and leapt!

PINGLET: Leapt?

MME PINGLET: Leapt into the void! Nearly to my destruction!

PINGLET: *Nearly?*

MME PINGLET: After that ... I remember nothing! All I know is that I awoke about dawn, in a rude peasant hut. Among rude peasants who seemed pleased to see me alive.

PINGLET [*aside*]: Not rude. Just dense!

MME PINGLET: But they were good, kind people. I'm sorry I only had a hundred francs in my purse. I wanted to give them all that we possess.

PINGLET: That might have been over generous.

MME PINGLET: But they saved my life!

PINGLET [*between clenched teeth*]: Exactly!

MME PINGLET: And so this morning when I was feeling well enough to travel, they took me in a rustic cart ... as far as the Arc de Triomphe! I got a cab and here I am!

PINGLET [*calmly*]: How terrible.

MME PINGLET [*crying*]: Oh, Pinglet! When I think of it. When I remember that ghastly moment. Your poor little wife ... [*She sobs.*]

PINGLET: Brace up! There's nothing for you to cry about.

MME PINGLET: Poor Pinglet! What would you have done if you'd lost me?

PINGLET [*taking her in his arms*]: I tell you one thing. I'd never have married again!

    [VICTOIRE *comes in with the letters.*]

VICTOIRE: The post, madame.

MME PINGLET [*pointing to the sofa*]: Just put it down there, Victoire.

PINGLET: I'll get dressed.

MME PINGLET: Oh yes. Off you go! I feel quite dizzy. It must be the reaction. What I need is a nice hot bath!

    [*She sits on the sofa.*]

VICTOIRE: Madame. I don't know whether madame has noticed. But madame has an absolutely terrific black eye!

MME PINGLET: It's none of your business. It's my eye, isn't it? Go and run my bath, Victoire. And pour in a good dollop of lime flower oil.

VICTOIRE: In Madame's eye?

MME PINGLET: No. In Madame's bath. [*Picks up the letters*] Servants nowadays!

    [VICTOIRE *goes.* MADAME PINGLET *opens a letter.*]

PINGLET [*singing, O.S.*]:
    'Comes my love, with little fairy footsteps!
    Comes my love, tip-toeing o'er the grass!'

MME PINGLET [*reading the letter*]: What's all this? 'The Department of Public Morality'. What on earth can the Department of Public Morality want with me? [*Reading the letter*] 'You are hereby summoned to present yourself at this office in connection with the case you are concerned in and to bring proof of your identity'! What can it mean?

    [*Reading*]

'To Madame Pinglet who was discovered in a compromising position with a certain Monsieur Paillardin during police investigations last night at the Free Trade Hotel. [*Astonished*] Me! Police investigations! With Paillar ... In the ... Free ... Trade ... It's a madman! A maniac! I've had a letter from a maniac! [*Very agitated*] What's it say again? [*Tries to read it.*] The letter's a hallucination! Am I going mad?

    [PINGLET *comes in with one of his boots in his hand.*]

PINGLET: Disaster!

MME PINGLET: Yes!

PINGLET: A button's come off my boot!

MME PINGLET: Thank God you're here!

PINGLET: What's the matter?

MME PINGLET [*deeply disturbed*]: This letter! Am I going mad? It says ... It makes ... The most appalling suggestions. Take it, Pinglet. Read it. [*She gives him the letter.*]

PINGLET [*glancing at it*]: Oh, my God! From the police ... So soon?

MME PINGLET: Go on! Read the dreadful thing!

PINGLET [*aside*]: Now we're in the soup!

[*Reading*]

'You are hereby summoned . . . Proof of identity . . . To Madame Pinglet who was discovered in a compromising position with a certain Monsieur Paillardin last night at the Free Trade Hotel'!

MME PINGLET: That's me! Me? *I* was discovered in a compromising position with Monsieur Paillardin!

PINGLET [*aloud, to* MADAME PINGLET, *with a grand gesture*]: Miserable woman! Your sins have found you out!

MME PINGLET [*flabbergasted*]: What?

PINGLET: You admit it! Found in a compromising position with my best friend.

[*He hits the table with his boot.*]

Messalina!

MME PINGLET: No. No. I'm your little Angelique! You don't believe . . .

PINGLET: Get thee behind me. Sinner!

[*He takes her hand and pulls her aside.*]

MME PINGLET: But Pinglet!

PINGLET [*furiously, to* MADAME PINGLET]: So, Cleopatra of Old Nile! What did you get up to with Paillardin, eh? What tricks?

MME PINGLET: Nothing! Absolutely nothing. It's all a bad dream!

PINGLET: So that summons is a dream, is it? I didn't know the police were given to daydreaming. [*Dramatically*] The game's up, madame! You'd better make a clean breast of it.

[*He takes her by the wrists.*]

Admit it!

MME PINGLET: Pinglet! You misjudge me terribly!

PINGLET [*in a terrible voice*]: *Admit it!*

MME PINGLET: You don't want me to admit something that's not true?

PINGLET [*brandishing his boot*]: I don't care about that. *Admit it!*

MME PINGLET [*on her knees*]: Spare me, Pinglet!

VICTOIRE [*coming in briskly*]: Did someone call?

PINGLET [*calmly, to* VICTOIRE]: Oh, Victoire. Could you sew a button on my boot? [*Giving it to her.*] And make sure it stays on this time! The last one popped off.

VICTOIRE: Certainly, m'sieur. [*Exits.*]

PINGLET [*furious, to* MADAME PINGLET]: And you were the woman I trusted. I had faith in you. I used to boast to my friends. 'All right,' I'd say. 'My wife is a sour faced, stunningly boring old battle axe, but at least she's faithful!' I can't even pay you that compliment any more. At your age!

MME PINGLET: I tell you. It's lies. All lies!

PINGLET: I see it all now! I see why you locked me in here. So you could satisfy your filthy lust with the architect next door.

MME PINGLET: I never dreamed ...

PINGLET: I suppose your poor ill sister lives at the Free Trade Hotel. A place of ill repute in the rue de Provence!

MME PINGLET: I've never been there in my life. Why do you say it's in the rue de Provence? Who told you it was in the rue de Provence?

PINGLET [*taking the summons*]: It says so in the summons. [*Looks*] Oh no! It doesn't!

MME PINGLET: I've told you the truth! The whole truth! Nothing but the truth! The horse bolted. Those poor peasants cared for me!

PINGLET: And where are these poor peasants, eh? Tell me that.

MME PINGLET: In their village. I suppose.

PINGLET: And where is their village?

MME PINGLET: Oh, God. I should've asked them. But we'd travelled so far and I never dreamt ... Listen! I've just thought. Paillardin! Paillardin will tell you the truth. He's accused with me. Paillardin can explain everything!

PINGLET: We shall see.

[*He's looking out of the window.*]

Speak of the devil! Here comes your precious paramour. Walking across the garden in a particularly brazen manner. [*He calls down.*] Paillardin! Paillardin!

PAILLARDIN [*O.S.*]: What's the matter?

PINGLET [*severely*]: Come up here a moment! I want to talk to you!

PAILLARDIN [*O.S.*]: What do you want to say?

PINGLET: Come up and you'll find out! [*To* MADAME PINGLET] And as for you, madame. When your accomplice is here I don't want you to breathe a word. Not a gesture. No signals. You understand? Complete silence in the face of the Court!

MME PINGLET [*praying dramatically, her hands raised to heaven*]: How long? How long, oh Lord ... Shall thy innocent ones suffer? [*As* PAILLARDIN *comes in*] Lighten our darkness, I pray you. And bring forth the truth!

PAILLARDIN [*puzzled*]: What do you want?

PINGLET [*very serious*]: You may approach the Seat of Judgement.

PAILLARDIN [*laughing*]: The Seat of Judgement? What're you playing at?

MME PINGLET: Oh, Paillardin. Tell him ...

PINGLET: Be careful, madame! No hints! If you speak to him I'll have you for Contempt of Court ... [*To* PAILLARDIN] Now then, Paillardin. Perhaps you'll tell us where you spent last night. The truth now!

PAILLARDIN: Last night? I was at the Free Trade Hotel, of course.

MME PINGLET [*astonished*]: Where?

PAILLARDIN: 220, rue du Provence.

PINGLET [*triumphant*]: You have heard the evidence, madame!

MME PINGLET [*astonished*]: Am I going mad? Is it possible that I ...? With ...? Did ...? Oh no! Not that! Never that!

PAILLARDIN [*aside*]: What's eating them?

PINGLET [*to* PAILLARDIN]: And who were you with at the Free Trade Hotel? Come along, m'sieur! Don't fence with me! Just answer the question.

PAILLARDIN: I was alone.

PINGLET [*terrible voice*]: Don't lie, m'sieur. You were with my wife!

PAILLARDIN: What?

PINGLET: The game's up, Paillardin! You are my wife's lover!

PAILLARDIN [*astonished*]: Me?

MME PINGLET [*to her husband*]: You see!

PINGLET: Silence, madame!

PAILLARDIN: Very funny, Pinglet. Extremely humorous! Of course you're joking.

PINGLET: Am I? Am I joking? Read that!

[*He gives him the summons.*]

Is that a joke?

PAILLARDIN: What've you got there?

[*He reads it.*]

'To Madame Pinglet who was found in a compromising position with Monsieur Paillardin during police investigations last night at the Free Trade Hotel.'

[*He starts to laugh.*]

Oh, delicious! Very comic. Highly comical. You are a terrible old joker, Pinglet!

PINGLET: A joker? Do I look like a joker?

MME PINGLET: My husband has got the idea that I could ... That I did ... With *you*! Yes. I promise you!

PAILLARDIN: Me? Your lover! [*In fits of laughter*] What a joke. What a wonderful joke!

PINGLET: Don't try and laugh it off, m'sieur.

PAILLARDIN: But you can't be serious. You honestly think that *I*? You need your head examined!

PINGLET: Let me remind you. The Summons!

[MADAME PINGLET *throws herself onto the sofa, despairingly.*]

PAILLARDIN: Me ... The lover of ... Now listen to me, my dear fellow. Be reasonable. I mean, I've got absolutely nothing against your wife. For all I know she may cook a very tolerable Blanquette de Veau. She may do reasonable plain sewing. I'm sure she's a dab hand at potting meat. But me . . . hanky panky with Madame Pinglet! I mean, look at her! I mean look at her!

PINGLET: I think you'd better not insult my wife, just at the moment.

MME PINGLET: Is he insulting me?

PINGLET: Oh yes, madame! That's the sort of man he is. He put you on a pedestal and now he's knocking you off it. He squeezed the juice out of you and now he casts you aside like an old bit of dried up lemon.

PAILLARDIN: The whole thing's ridiculous!

PINGLET: Oh yes. [*Shows him the summons*] Then how do you explain that?

PAILLARDIN: I don't know. Someone's got a weird sense of humour. And the proof of that is – why haven't I got a summons too? If I was involved in your wife's so-called love affairs, wouldn't they have summoned me as well? And I've had nothing! Nothing, you hear? All right. Until I get a summons like that I shall deny all the charges. And I'll go on denying them while there's breath left in my body!

[VICTOIRE *enters with a letter and* PINGLET's *boot.*]

VICTOIRE: Excuse me, m'sieur. A policeman just arrived with this for Monsieur Paillardin.

PAILLARDIN [*opening the letter*]: What on earth is it?

PINGLET [*triumphant*]: You know perfectly well!

PAILLARDIN [*reading very quietly*]: 'To Monsieur Paillardin who was discovered in a compromising position with Madame Pinglet during the police investigations last night at the Free Trade Hotel.'

PINGLET: Hasn't that rather taken the wind out of your sails?

PAILLARDIN [*astonished*]: This is ridiculous!

MME PINGLET [*resigned*]: Destiny's got it in for us! What can we do about it?

PINGLET: Are you still going to deny the charges, with your last breath?

PAILLARDIN [*astonished*]: I simply can't understand it!

VICTOIRE: Your boot, m'sieur. [*She gives it to* PINGLET.]

PINGLET: Oh, thanks. [*To* PAILLARDIN] Miserable! Miserable sinner!

VICTOIRE: What've *I* done, m'sieur?

PINGLET: Oh, clear off. I wasn't talking to you.

VICTOIRE: Very well, m'sieur.

[*She goes.* MARCELLE *comes in.*]

PAILLARDIN: Marcelle!

PINGLET: Ah, madame! You came at a most convenient moment. You see that wretched man?

MARCELLE [*astonished*]: I see my husband.

PINGLET: That's him. He's my wife's lover!

MARCELLE: Him!

PAILLARDIN: ⎫
MME PINGLET: ⎭ Oh, my God!

PINGLET [*aside to Marcelle*]: There's not a word of truth in it. Just pass out in my arms.

MARCELLE: Right oh! [*She falls into his arms in an apparent faint.*]

PAILLARDIN: But it's a lie. All lies. Oh, my God! [*To* PINGLET] You must be mad to tell her that! Marcelle! Marcelle, my dear little wife! [*He slaps her hands.*] Quick. Smelling salts immediately!

MME PINGLET: I've got some.

   [*She goes into the room on the left.* PAILLARDIN *follows her.*]

MARCELLE [*opening her eyes, and in a very faint voice*]: Where am I?

PINGLET [*very quickly and quietly to her*]: They both got summonses. From the police. So to get us out of a hole, I accused *them*! You twig?

MARCELLE: I twig!

PINGLET: Faint again. Go on, faint!

   [MARCELLE *lets her head fall back onto* PINGLET'*s shoulder.* PAILLARDIN *comes back with the smelling salts.* MADAME PINGLET *is with him.*]

PAILLARDIN [*threatening* PINGLET *with the bottle as though it were a revolver*]: M'sieur, your conduct is unworthy of a gentleman!

PINGLET: You're a fine one to talk! [*Businesslike*] Don't hold the bottle up there. You'll corrode her poor little neglected nostrils. Give it to me. [*He snatches the bottle.*]

PAILLARDIN: She looks terrible! My God. What a tragedy! Water! We need water!

PINGLET [*under his breath*]: That's quite enough, Marcelle. Don't over do it!

MARCELLE: All right. [*Pretending to revive*] Aaah!

MME PINGLET: She's coming back to life!

PAILLARDIN [*to* MARCELLE]: Marcelle. I beg you. Don't believe a word he says.

MME PINGLET: It's lies! All lies ...

PINGLET: They were only caught together. In a compromising position. In a police raid – on a hotel of ill repute!

MARCELLE [*without conviction*]: How horrible. [*To* PINGLET] Do I have to faint again?

PINGLET [*under his breath*]: Don't bother. Try getting extremely angry.

MARCELLE [*under her breath*]: Oh, very well. [*Shouts at* PAILLARDIN] Aaah!

MME PINGLET [*afraid*]: She's absolutely livid!

PAILLARDIN: Marcelle. Please. You can't believe everything you read in summonses. [*He tries to take her arm.*]

MARCELLE: Let me go, Paillardin. I suppose she was one of your so-called spooks!

PINGLET: Oh yes. For your husband it was knocking ghosts. For my wife it was a run-away cab horse. And by a strange coincidence they both came home with black eyes! And they expect us to believe that they got their two shiners on separate occasions!

MARCELLE: *Two* shiners!

PAILLARDIN: All right. We've had quite enough of this! You're both sure that we were caught having hanky panky in a dubious hotel ...

PINGLET: Quite, quite sure!

PAILLARDIN: All right. We'll all four of us go off to the Police Station and see if the Inspector identifies us.

MARCELLE: ⎫
PINGLET: ⎭ No! Oh no! We couldn't possibly do that!

MME PINGLET: That's it! What a wonderful idea! We'll all go to the Police Station!

[*Two of them take the other two by the hands, trying to pull them out of the room.*]

PINGLET: ⎫
MARCELLE: ⎭ No! It's a terrible idea! Really quite stupid! Oh no!

PAILLARDIN: Oh yes! You brought the accusation! You'll go through with it! Only the Inspector can settle this once and for all. Down to the Police Station ...

[VICTOIRE *appears and announces*]

VICTOIRE: Monsieur Mathieu!

PINGLET: ⎫
MARCELLE: ⎭ Him!

[VICTOIRE *goes.* MATHIEU *appears.*]

MATHIEU: What a night, my friends! What a terrible night!

PINGLET ⎫
MARCELLE ⎭ [*aside*]: Oh, my God!

MATHIEU: Good morning to you, Pinglet.

PINGLET [*taking him by the shoulders and pushing him*]: Is it good? Is it a good morning for you? Go and wait for me in my room on this good morning. We're rather busy!

MATHIEU: Yes, of course. Good morning, Madame Paillardin. Good morning, Madame Pinglet. I say, has something happened to your eye?

MME PINGLET: Oh no! Nothing at all.

MATHIEU [*still being pushed by* PINGLET, *he stops*]: If only you knew what happened to me since I left here yesterday evening!

PINGLET [*pushing him*]: You can tell us all about that later.

MATHIEU: My daughters and I spent the night in the cell ...

PINGLET [*quickly*]: In the Select Hotel. [*He turns him round.*] Take no notice of this fellow. He stutters ... Can't make head or tail of a word he says.

MATHIEU: What do you mean ... I stutter? I don't stutter at all!

PINGLET [*despairingly, aside*]: Please God! Let it rain!

MATHIEU [*moving downstage again*]: Happily they realized who we were this morning and we were given our freedom!

PINGLET [*rushing to him*]: So much the worse! Come on. For God's sake. Get into my room. In there! In there! [*He takes him by the shoulders.*]

MATHIEU: I've had quite enough of Paris. We're taking the first train back to Dieppe.

[*They change direction.*]

PINGLET: Oh yes? Then it's that way. Over there! Over there! In there! In there!

MATHIEU: Not yet.

PINGLET: Oh! All right. Then it's that way. In there! [*He pushes him into his room.*]

PAILLARDIN: This is getting boring!

[MATHIEU *opens the door and comes out of* PINGLET's *room.*]

MATHIEU: What about the rest of you? How did you get on there last night?

PINGLET: I slept like a log. Thank you very much [*He seizes him.*]

MATHIEU: I say. Careful!

PINGLET: Come along now! [*He pushes him back into his room and shuts the door.*]

MME PINGLET [*to* PAILLARDIN]: What do you suppose he meant by, 'How did you get on there last night?'

PINGLET: Oh, didn't you know? It's typical! Dieppe dialect. When you want to ask someone how they slept ... In Dieppe you always say, 'How did you get on there last night?'

MME PINGLET: How very interesting. I never knew that!

PAILLARDIN: Right! We're off to see the Inspector.

[*He and* MADAME PINGLET *take the others by the hands.*]

PINGLET:
MARCELLE: } No! No! [*They resist.*]

VICTOIRE [*comes in and announces*]: Inspector Boucard of the Department of Public Morality.

EVERYONE: The Inspector!

PINGLET: Hold on tight!

PAILLARDIN: Excellent. Just in time!

PINGLET [*aside*]: Our goose is cooked!

[*He turns his back on* BOUCARD, *who is entering.*]

PAILLARDIN ⎱ [*to* BOUCARD]: Come along in, Inspector.
MME PINGLET ⎰ This way, Inspector!

BOUCARD: Monsieur Paillardin!

PAILLARDIN: I'm Paillardin.

[*He leads* BOUCARD *downstage.*]

BOUCARD: Forgive me, m'sieur. I didn't recognize you at first. After all, you were covered with soot!

PAILLARDIN: *I* was?

BOUCARD: But I remember you perfectly now.

PAILLARDIN ⎱ What's that?
MME PINGLET ⎰

PINGLET [*under his breath to* MARCELLE]: He remembers him! That's not bad.

PAILLARDIN: You remember me, m'sieur?

BOUCARD: Of course. You're the fellow I caught with Madame Pinglet at the Free Trade Hotel.

MME PINGLET: Me? You caught me?

PAILLARDIN: Me? With her?

BOUCARD [*turning to* MADAME PINGLET]: Madame Pinglet. Of course!

MME PINGLET: Of course I'm Madame Pinglet!

BOUCARD: You must forgive me. Last night I could hardly see you for lace.

MME PINGLET: Me?

BOUCARD: But now I can identify you perfectly. We get pretty skilled at identification you know, in the Department of Public Morality.

EVERYONE: What?

BOUCARD [*aside*]: She's a bit of an eye-sore!

MME PINGLET: You can identify me?

PINGLET [*delighted, to* MARCELLE]: He can identify her. He's a sleuth in a million!

PAILLARDIN: M'sieur. You can't possibly identify us. For the plain and simple reason that you never saw us in the Free Trade Hotel.

BOUCARD: And I suppose I never arrested you! Never questioned you! Never let you out on bail!

PAILLARDIN: It wasn't us. It was a couple of jokers impersonating us.

BOUCARD: Anyway. It's of absolutely no importance.

PAILLARDIN ⎱ Of no importance!
MME PINGLET ⎰

BOUCARD: I'm only sorry that my fool of a secretary sent out those summonses. Now I know who you are, m'sieur, we can consider the matter closed. M'sieur, are you not Monsieur Paillardin, Architect and Learned Expert appointed by the Court in Building and Allied Matters?

PAILLARDIN: I don't see what that's got to do with it. It's immaterial!

BOUCARD: For you, perhaps. But not for me! It's a bit of luck, running into you. Here's the problem. I've bought this little property in the country. And the beams, riddled with woodworm! And the dry rot ...!

PAILLARDIN [*impatient*]: M'sieur. It doesn't matter about your dry rot! What matters is last night!

BOUCARD: I told you. Don't worry about it. You've got a permanent address? Means of support? A bulging bank account? Then you're of no concern whatever to the Department of Public Morality.

PAILLARDIN: But we're of concern to that lady and gentleman! [*He points to* PINGLET *and* MARCELLE.]

BOUCARD [*greeting them*]: M'sieur! Madame!

[*They return his bows with their backs still to him.*]

PAILLARDIN: Our respective spouses took your summonses to mean that last night we actually ... Well! I demand my rights. You must make it clear that you can't possibly identify us!

BOUCARD: I keep on telling you that!

PAILLARDIN: No you don't. You say you can't remember our faces. At least tell them that you didn't arrest *us*!

BOUCARD: You're making things very difficult for me.

PAILLARDIN: Try and remember! Take a good look at us.

MME PINGLET: If you can't remember the woman's face, think of her size, her figure perhaps.

[PINGLET *masks* MARCELLE *from* BOUCARD.]

BOUCARD: Well ... I seem to remember that the lady was a little less substantial. It may have been an optical illusion. My office is on the largish side, so the lady may have appeared somewhat dwarfed by it. Architecture can be extremely deceptive.

PAILLARDIN: Well, really!

BOUCARD: But one thing I do remember!

[EVERYONE *listens.*]

The female person in question was sporting a somewhat vulgar and ostentatious dress, puce in colour.

MME PINGLET: And I haven't got such a thing!

MARCELLE [*positive*]: Nor have I!

PINGLET [*under his breath*]: Shut up!

PAILLARDIN [*to* MARCELLE]: No one's talking about you!

BOUCARD [*to* MADAME PINGLET]: I'm sorry, madame. That's the best I can do. My recollection's extremely vague ...

PAILLARDIN: Then set up an inquiry.

BOUCARD: An inquiry?

PAILLARDIN: You arrested a lot of people last night. Let's see if any of *them* can identify us.

BOUCARD: Brilliant! I've got a list.

PAILLARDIN [*taking the list from him*]: Let's have a look. Gaston, the Bull of Boulogne. Never met him. Adèle Dubois, known as the 'Flea'. Bastien Morillian, hairdresser. M'sieur le Juge de . . .

BOUCARD: Better not read that out!

PAILLARDIN: Oh, very well. Monsieur Mathieu and his alleged daughters.

MME PINGLET: Mathieu! Which Mathieu? We've got a Mathieu here this morning.

PINGLET [*aside*]: Damn!

BOUCARD: Here?

MME PINGLET: In this very apartment! And he has no less than four daughters!

PAILLARDIN: And he spent the night in the cell . . .

PINGLET: Select Hotel.

PAILLARDIN: No. No. You said that. He meant in chokey!

BOUCARD: Must be one and the same individual.

MME PINGLET: Well, for goodness sake. Let's ask him. [*Calling*] Mathieu! Mathieu!

MARCELLE [*under her breath to* PINGLET]: The ground's opening beneath our feet!

PINGLET: I wish it would!

MME PINGLET [*opening* PINGLET'S *door*]: Come out, Monsieur Mathieu.

PAILLARDIN [*also calling*]: Come out! Come out!

MATHIEU [*appearing*]: What is it now?

PAILLARDIN [*taking his hand*]: Come along. Don't be nervous.

MATHIEU: My God, the police again! What've I done now?

[*He tries to escape.* PAILLARDIN *holds him.*]

PAILLARDIN: ⎤ M'sieur Mathieu! You can solve the mystery!

BOUCARD: ⎬ M'sieur Mathieu! Only you can save us

MME PINGLET: ⎦ Yes, M'sieur Mathieu! You can jog my memory.

MATHIEU: Don't all speak at once!

PINGLET [*aside*]: And the awful thing is .., He's not stuttering.

PAILLARDIN: Last night you were in the Free Trade Hotel?

MATHIEU: Where I was arrested for no apparent reason. With my daughters. Thrown into the cells! Me, a barrister-at-law!

PAILLARDIN: No one cares about all that. The point is, did you see Madame Pinglet and me there at all?

MATHIEU: You and Madame Pinglet? Certainly not.

MME PINGLET [*to* BOUCARD]: There! You see?

MATHIEU: When I think of my poor children. Up till now they've had no sort of criminal record ...

PAILLARDIN: I told you. No one's interested in all that. The point is, did you see somebody else?

MATHIEU: Of course I saw somebody else!

BOUCARD:
MME PINGLET: } Who? Tell us who?
PAILLARDIN:

MARCELLE [*to* PINGLET]: I know what he's going to say!

PINGLET: The game's up!

MATHIEU [*to* PINGLET, *laughing*]: Listen to this, Pinglet. They're asking me who I saw at the hotel last night!

PINGLET [*with a terribly forced smile*]: Oh, really?

MATHIEU: And shall I tell them who I saw? Shall I?

[PINGLET *tugs at the tail of his coat.*]

Leave my coat tails alone, why don't you?

MATHIEU [*to* MADAME PINGLET]: Well. I'll tell you. I saw ... I saw quite clearly ...

[*There's a sudden thunder clap. The rain pours down outside.*]

I s ... s ... s ... s ...

MME PINGLET: What's the matter with the man?

MARCELLE [*aside*]: He's stuttering!

[PINGLET *leaps on a chair and holds his arms up to heaven.*]

PINGLET: Rain! Blessed rain! Thanks be to God! My prayers are answered!

BOUCARD [*to* MATHIEU]: Take a grip on yourself, m'sieur. You will kindly answer the question!

MATHIEU: Ugh! Yes ... I s ... s ... s ... at the Fre ... Fre Fre ... Tr ... Ho ... Ho ... Ho ...

PAILLARDIN: Come along now. It's not funny!

PINGLET [*aside*]: He's stuttering well today!

MATHIEU: At the Ho ... Ho ... Ho ... Ho ...! [*He kicks.*]

PAILLARDIN: We'll never get it out of him.

BOUCARD: I've had a little idea ...

EVERYONE: An idea!

BOUCARD: A solution to this difficult case! He can make a written statement.

PAILLARDIN:
MME PINGLET: } Yes, yes. So he can! A written statement!

BOUCARD: Now. Sit you down, m'sieur. [*Gets out paper and a pen.*] And just write out your evidence. Tell us exactly who you saw.

MATHIEU: I s ... s ... s ...

MARCELLE [*to* PINGLET]: We're finished, Pinglet!

PINGLET: We're cooked!

PAILLARDIN:

BOUCARD: } Go on! Go on! Write it down!

MME PINGLET:

> [*As they gesture to* MATHIEU *to write,* MAXIME *comes in with his hat in his hand.*]

MAXIME: What a lot of people! [*Aside*] Oh, my God! It's the fellow from last night. [*He puts his hat over his face.*] If he recognizes me it's all up!

> [*He sees* PINGLET'*s briefcase, he puts it on his head, puts his hat on top and starts to climb out of the window.* MATHIEU *points him out to* PAILLARDIN *and* MADAME PINGLET.]

MATHIEU [*seeing* MAXIME, *shouts out*]: Stop thief!

> [PAILLARDIN *runs to the window.* BOUCARD *follows him.*]

BOUCARD: Excuse me, m'sieur. That's my job!

> [PAILLARDIN *grabs one of* MAXIME'*s arms,* BOUCARD *the other.* BOUCARD *tries to pull off the briefcase.*]

Open up, m'sieur. We all know you're in there!

MAXIME [*struggling*]: Leave me in peace. I'm not doing any harm.

BOUCARD:

PAILLARDIN: } Take off that thing! Take it off?

MAXIME: No! No! Let me alone!

> [PAILLARDIN *pulls off the briefcase.*]

EVERYONE: Maxime!

BOUCARD: That's the individual!

EVERYONE: Who?

BOUCARD: The male person I saw covered in soot.

EVERYONE: Maxime! It was Maxime!

PAILLARDIN: You young scoundrel! Was it you?

MAXIME: I have no idea what you're all talking about.

BOUCARD: The charge is ... You were the fellow at the Free Trade Hotel. Found in a compromising position.

MAXIME: How did you know.

EVERYONE: It was Maxime!

PINGLET: Did you hear! Did you hear? He confessed!

MATHIEU: B ... b ... b ... but ... I s ... s ... s ...

PINGLET: Shut up!

MME PINGLET [*to* MAXIME]: Young man! I don't suppose you'll dare to suggest that you were up to monkey business with me?

MAXIME: With you? God forbid!

BOUCARD: So who was it? I have a strong suspicion that the individual in question may have been of the female variety.

EVERYONE: A woman! You were with a woman. Who was it?

MAXIME: Oh, well then. Who cares? It was Victoire!

PAILLARDIN: Victoire? Victoire? Where is this Victoire?

MME PINGLET: In her room. She just went up to change.

PAILLARDIN: Leave this to me! [*He calls.*] Victoire! Come down! You're wanted immediately!

> [*He goes out to get her.*]

It's a matter of vital importance to us all!

MATHIEU: But I s ... s ... s ...

PINGLET [*pushing him*]: Oh, do shut up! No one else can get a word in edgeways!

MATHIEU: Very w ... w ... well!

> [*He starts to write out his statement.*]

PAILLARDIN [*O.S.*]: Come along, my girl.

VICTOIRE [*O.S.*]: But I haven't finished dressing!

> [PAILLARDIN *comes in, followed by* VICTOIRE, *who is wearing* MARCELLE's *puce dress.* MATHIEU *goes on writing at the bureau.*]

EVERYONE: The puce dress!

MME PINGLET: Where on earth did you get that dress?

VICTOIRE: It's just a dress. I was trying it on. Someone gave it to me.

PINGLET [*to* VICTOIRE]: Quiet, girl! Don't bother us with long explanations!

PAILLARDIN: So *you* were at the Free Trade Hotel last night!

VICTOIRE: Oh, m'sieur! However did you guess?

MME PINGLET: And you had the cheek to borrow my name!

VICTOIRE: I did what?

PINGLET: No explanations! I told you. We're all bored with explanations! Off you go now! We've heard quite enough from you!

> [*He pushes her towards the door.*]

MME PINGLET: But, my dear ...

PINGLET: And we've heard quite enough from you too. Thank you! [*To* VICTOIRE] I thought I told you to go. Stop hanging about like yesterday's lunch.

VICTOIRE: But you wanted me!

PINGLET: And now we don't want you any more! [*He pushes her out.*]

VICTOIRE [*going*]: Make up your mind!

MATHIEU [*holding up his statement to* BOUCARD.] My sta ... sta ... sta ...

PINGLET: Your statement? Well, we shan't be needing that now! Now we know exactly what happened. We don't need your statement at all! Quite unnecessary! [*He takes it.*]

EVERYONE: Quite unnecessary!

> [PINGLET *tears up* MATHIEU's *statement.*]

MATHIEU [*disappointed*]: Oh!

PINGLET [*looking at his watch*]: Look at the time! Quick! You'll miss your train back to Dieppe!

[*Everyone starts to push* MATHIEU *to the door.*]

EVERYONE: The train to Dieppe!

MATHIEU: But I s ... s ... s ... Damn! It's raining!

PINGLET: The sun's shining in Dieppe. Off you go!

EVERYONE: Off you go!

[MATHIEU *is pushed out by everyone.*]

PINGLET: Thank God that's over!

BOUCARD [*to* MAXIME]: Well, young man. I don't think you'll be hearing any more about last night. Allow me to return your five thousand francs to you. Just count it, will you? [*He gives him the money.*]

MAXIME: To me?

PINGLET [*aside*]: Ouch! He's giving him my five thousand francs!

MAXIME [*counting the money*]: *My* five thousand francs?

BOUCARD: Of course.

MAXIME: Why did you give it to *me*?

BOUCARD: Because you were the man committing the Immoral Act at the Free Trade Hotel.

MAXIME: Do they give you prizes for it? What a hotel! I'll go back there again!

PINGLET: I won't. Not ever. Not for the rest of my natural life! I'd rather spend the night with Madame Pinglet!

CURTAIN

THE END

A
FLEA
IN
HER EAR

CAST OF FIRST LONDON PRODUCTION

A Flea in Her Ear was first presented by The National Theatre at The Old
Vic on 8 February 1966

CAMILLE CHANDEBISE	Edward Hardwicke
ANTOINETTE PLUCHEUX	Sheila Reid
ETIENNE PLUCHEUX	Robert Lang
DR FINACHE	Kenneth Mackintosh
LUCIENNE HOMENIDES DE HISTANGUA	Anne Godley
RAYMONDE CHANDEBISE	Geraldine McEwan
VICTOR EMMANUEL CHANDEBISE	Albert Finney
ROMAIN TOURNEL	John Stride
CARLOS HOMENIDES DE HISTANGUA	Frank Wylie
EUGÉNIE	Petronella Barker
AUGUSTIN FERAILLON	Michael Turner
OLYMPE	Margo Cunningham
BAPTISTIN	Keith Marsh
HERR SCHWARZ	Peter Cellier
POCHE	Albert Finney
GUESTS AT THE HOTEL COQ D'OR	Janie Booth, Maggie Riley, David Hargreaves, Christopher Timothy, Lewis Jones

The play was directed by
JACQUES CHARON
Designed by
ANDRE LEVASSEUR
Lighting by
JOHN B. READ
Stage Manager
DIANA BODDINGTON

CHARACTERS

CAMILLE CHANDEBISE	Victor Emmanuel Chandebise's nephew and clerk
ANTOINETTE PLUCHEUX	Chandebise's cook
ETIENNE PLUCHEUX	Chandebise's butler
DR FINACHE	
LUCIENNE HOMENIDES DE HISTANGUA	Raymond Chandebise's friend, married to a Spanish gentleman
RAYMONDE CHANDEBISE	Chandebise's wife
VICTOR EMMANUEL CHANDEBISE	Head of the Paris branch of an insurance company
ROMAIN TOURNEL	Chandebise's friend
CARLOS HOMENIDES DE HISTANGUA	A Spanish gentleman
EUGÉNIE	The maid at the Hotel Coq d'Or
AUGUSTIN FERAILLON	The Manager of the Hotel Coq d'Or
OLYMPE	Feraillon's wife
BAPTISTIN	Feraillon's uncle
HERR SCHWARZ	A guest at the hotel
POCHE	The hotel porter

The action takes place in Paris at the turn of the century

ACT I

Afternoon in the drawing-room of the home of Victor Emmanuel Chandebise,
Head of the Paris office of Boston Life Insurance Company. Although it is a
comfortable house in the Boulevard Malesherbes there are some signs of business
activity, such as a filing cabinet and a desk. There is a French window opening
onto a balcony. The main entrance to the room is a pair of large double doors
centre stage which lead to a hall and a corridor. There are three other doors,
one stage right and two stage left, which lead to inner rooms.

When the curtain rises, CAMILLE *is discovered standing by the filing cabinet.*
His cleft palate makes his speech almost impossible to understand. ANTOIN-
ETTE *moves to* CAMILLE, *taps his shoulder and kisses him.*

CAMILLE: Hare foo. Please, please be careful!

ANTOINETTE: Calm down. The family's out.

CAMILLE: Hoh, yes ...

ANTOINETTE: Come on. Give us a kiss. Well, wake up!

[*Voices are heard off.* CAMILLE *goes to another room on the left.*
ETIENNE, *the butler, comes in ushering* DR FINACHE.]

ETIENNE: Come along in, Doctor.

[FINACHE *enters and puts his hat and stick on a small table.*]

ETIENNE [*to* ANTOINETTE]: What're *you* up to?

ANTOINETTE: Me?

ETIENNE: You!

ANTOINETTE: I came ...

ETIENNE: Go on.

ANTOINETTE: To ask about dinner.

ETIENNE: When the family's out! Back to your hot stove and bend over
it! We don't have cooks in the drawing-room.

ANTOINETTE: But ...

ETIENNE: Out!

[ANTOINETTE *goes out by the main doors, closing them.*]

FINACHE: The Lord and Master!

ETIENNE: That's the way to treat them. If you're not in charge of them they're in charge of you. And I'm not having that!

FINACHE: Excellent!

ETIENNE: You know, Doctor. That little wife of mine's as faithful as a poodle, but as jealous as a tiger. She comes in here to spy on me! She's got some strange idea – about me and the housemaid ...

FINACHE: How very strange ...

ETIENNE: Me? A housemaid? Really!

FINACHE: Ridiculous! If your master's not at home ...

ETIENNE: Don't worry. I've got time to kill – I'll keep you company.

FINACHE: I don't want to impose ...

ETIENNE: On my good nature?

FINACHE: Certainly.

ETIENNE: Think nothing of it.

FINACHE [*bows ironically*]: When will he be back?

ETIENNE: Quarter of an hour – at least.

FINACHE [*picking up his hat and stick*]: Oh, in that case ... However delightful your conversation –

ETIENNE: Too kind ...

FINACHE: – pleasure isn't everything. I've got a patient to see. Must finish him off.

ETIENNE: Oh ...

FINACHE: What? Oh, no – thank you very much. I'm cutting my visit short, not my patient's life. Back in a quarter of an hour ... [*He moves towards the door.*]

ETIENNE [*following him*]: I must let you go.

FINACHE: It's so hard to tear myself away. [*Handing* ETIENNE *a certificate*] If your master comes back before I do, give him this. Tell him I examined the customer he sent me and he's in first rate condition.

ETIENNE: Oh, yes.

FINACHE: Not that you care.

ETIENNE: No. [*He moves to the table and puts the certificate on it.*]

FINACHE [*moving down* c]: Nor do I. But since your master's the managing director of the Boston Life Insurance Company for Paris and the provinces ...

ETIENNE: The governor ...

FINACHE: The governor, if you prefer the word, should know that his Spanish insurance risk is A1. What's he call himself – Don Carlos Homenides de Histangua?

ETIENNE: His wife's here now! She's waiting next door for madame.

FINACHE: Amazingly small world! I examine the husband this morning
– and now the wife's next door.

ETIENNE: And they both had dinner here yesterday!

FINACHE: Unbelievable!

ETIENNE [*sitting by the table*]: Doctor. Seeing you're here . . .

FINACHE: You don't stand on ceremony, do you?

ETIENNE: Me? Oh, no. I'm very easy-going. I want to talk to you because
I was having a word the other day with my good lady . . .

FINACHE: Madame Chandebise.

ETIENNE: Not the mistress, my good lady.

FINACHE: Your wife?

ETIENNE: Yes. Now when you've got this hammering inside you – do pull
up a chair . . .

FINACHE: Thanks. [*He sits by the other side of the table.*]

ETIENNE: Night and day! Both sides of the abdomen. Remorseless.

FINACHE [*putting his hat on the table*]: Now that's a condition we often
find . . .

ETIENNE: Yes?

FINACHE: With some gynaecological troubles.

ETIENNE: I see.

FINACHE: Probably the ovaries.

ETIENNE: That's what I've got?

FINACHE: We'll have to have them out!

ETIENNE: Careful now. [*Rising*] If I've got them I'm keeping them.

FINACHE [*also getting up*]: I won't insist – on having them. Not for the
moment.

  [LUCIENNE *comes in from the side door – stage right.*]

LUCIENNE: Look here, excuse me. You're sure Madame Chandebise'll be
back?

ETIENNE: She said to me, she said, 'If Madame –' well, anyway . . .
whatever your name is.

LUCIENNE: Homenides de Histangua.

ETIENNE: That's right. She told me, 'Don't let her go. I've got to see her.'

LUCIENNE: That's what she said in her letter. I can't understand it. I'll
wait a little longer.

ETIENNE: That's perfectly all right. I was just passing the time of day with
the doctor.

FINACHE: He's delightful company.

ETIENNE: That's true. You know Dr Finache?

FINACHE: Madame.

ETIENNE: Chief Medical Officer of the Boston Life.

LUCIENNE: Ah!

ETIENNE: Tells me he saw your husband this very morning.

LUCIENNE: What a coincidence!

FINACHE: I had the honour of examining Don Carlos de Histangua.

LUCIENNE: My husband had himself examined? What on earth for?

FINACHE: Insurance companies are ridiculously inquisitive. But I must congratulate you. What a husband you have, madame! What a constitution! What stamina!

LUCIENNE [aside]: Don't I know it!

FINACHE: It's very flattering.

LUCIENNE: But exhausting!

FINACHE: You get nothing without working for it in this world.

ETIENNE: It's what Madame Plucheux dreams about.

LUCIENNE: Who on earth's that?

ETIENNE: My wife. Too much for me, I can tell you, she needs a man like madame's husband.

FINACHE: Then with madame's permission and the Spanish gentleman's consent – the thing might be arranged!

ETIENNE: God forbid!

LUCIENNE: Really, Doctor! Anyway, I couldn't allow it either.

FINACHE: I'm sorry. [Picking up his hat from the table] It's this ghastly butler. He makes me say the most idiotic things. Back in a quarter of an hour. Charming to meet you.

ETIENNE: It's when I lean forward like this they get me.

FINACHE: What?

ETIENNE: Those ovaries!

FINACHE: Oh, take three cascara tablets. That'll give them something to think about.

[FINACHE and ETIENNE go out of the main doors together.]

LUCIENNE [moving to the window R]: Seven minutes past one! [She picks up a magazine from the table.] This is what Raymonde calls counting the seconds till she sees me. Really! [She sits.]

[CAMILLE enters with a file and moves to the cabinet.]

CAMILLE [putting the file in the cabinet]: Ho – Hi – Hohiy. [Oh, I'm sorry.]

LUCIENNE: What did you say?

CAMILLE: Haham's ha—ing hor he hea Hon Hon Hife Cumbee? [Madame's waiting for the Head of the Boston Life Company?]

LUCIENNE: I'm terribly sorry . . .

CAMILLE: Haham's ha—ing hor he hea Hon Hon Hife Cumhee?

LUCIENNE [rising and backing away from him]: I can't understand a word you're saying.

CAMILLE: He harsed if H – Ham here Hee Hee Hirerector? [I asked if madame's here to see the Director?]

LUCIENNE [*moving to* CAMILLE]: No. Me. Franzuski – Franchese. Me French.

CAMILLE: He Hoo! [*Me too!*]

LUCIENNE [*backing to the window*]: Are you looking for the butler? I mean I don't belong here. I'm just waiting for Madame Chandebise and . . .

CAMILLE [*backing to the door up on the left*]: Ho Horry. [*So sorry.*] If madame's waiting for the head of the Boston Life Company.

LUCIENNE: Yes.

CAMILLE: Ho horry. [*So sorry.*]

[CAMILLE *goes.*]

LUCIENNE: What a monster!

[ETIENNE *comes in through the main doors.*]

ETIENNE: You're not bored?

LUCIENNE: No, but would you kindly explain – there was a man here . . .

ETIENNE: A man!

LUCIENNE: Spoke the most extraordinary language. Ho Horry H'am . . .

ETIENNE: It's Camille!

LUCIENNE: A foreigner?

ETIENNE: Not at all. The master's nephew. Blood relative. I see your difficulty. He butchers the language. Kills off his consonants entirely.

LUCIENNE: Good heavens!

ETIENNE: It's embarrassing till you get used to it. I'm just starting to understand . . .

LUCIENNE: He's giving you lessons?

ETIENNE: In time – the ear grows accustomed.

LUCIENNE: I suppose it must.

ETIENNE: The master's taken him on as a secretary. Who else would employ him?

LUCIENNE: A man with nothing but vowels to offer!

ETIENNE: It's not enough! He gives you the consonants when he's writing; but we can't all communicate by letter! Such a serious, steady boy. Handicapped! So far as anyone knows, madame, he's never had a woman in his life!

LUCIENNE: Really!

ETIENNE [*simply*]: Not so far as we know.

RAYMONDE [*off*]: Antoinette, my husband's not back yet – and have you seen Madame De Histangua?

ETIENNE: Madame's here. [*He opens the main door.*]

LUCIENNE: At last!

[RAYMONDE *comes in in a hurry and kisses* LUCIENNE]

RAYMONDE: My poor darling – I'm sorry. You can go, Etienne.

ETIENNE: Yes, madame. Madame will excuse me . . .

[ETIENNE *goes.*]

LUCIENNE: What's the matter?

RAYMONDE [*taking off her hat*]: I've kept you waiting. [*She puts her hat on a stool.*]

LUCIENNE: Have you. Really!

RAYMONDE [*moving above the table and putting her bag on it*]: I had to go such a long way. I'll tell you all about it, Lucienne. I wrote and asked you to come because – a terrible thing's happened. My husband's unfaithful!

LUCIENNE: Victor Emmanuel?

RAYMONDE: Exactly! Victor Emmanuel!

LUCIENNE: You take my breath away!

RAYMONDE: I'll expose him!

LUCIENNE: You mean you can prove it?

RAYMONDE: What? Oh, no. I can't. Oh, but I will . . .

LUCIENNE: What?

RAYMONDE: Prove it.

LUCIENNE: How?

RAYMONDE: I don't know. But you're here . . .

LUCIENNE: Well?

RAYMONDE: You're going to prove it for me!

LUCIENNE: Me?

RAYMONDE [*taking* LUCIENNE's *hand*]: Don't say 'no', Lucienne. We were bosom friends at the convent. All right, we've drifted apart over the years, but some things last! I left you Lucienne Vicard. Now I find you Lucienne Homenides de Histangua. The name's longer, but the heart's still in the same place. I always think of you as my best friend.

LUCIENNE: Of course . . . [*She sits in a chair.*]

RAYMONDE [*sitting on the sofa*]: So I naturally come to you when I have an enormous favour to ask . . .

LUCIENNE: Thank you very much!

RAYMONDE: So tell me what to do!

LUCIENNE: How do you mean?

RAYMONDE: To expose my husband. Trap him . . .

LUCIENNE: Is that why you dragged me here?

RAYMONDE: Well, of course.

LUCIENNE: How do you know he's trappable? He might be a model of virtue.

RAYMONDE: Him!

LUCIENNE: You've got no proof.

RAYMONDE: Certain things don't deceive you . . .

LUCIENNE: Including Victor Emmanuel?

RAYMONDE: What would you say if *your* husband, suddenly, after having been a husband – and what a husband! – suddenly stopped – like that! Between one day and the next.

LUCIENNE: I'd say – phew!

RAYMONDE: Is that what you'd say? You'd say 'phew'? That's what you would say. I was just like you. This endless love! That perpetual spring. Boring! Tedious! Oh, for a little cloud! A few obstacles. I even thought about taking a lover just for the worry of it.

LUCIENNE: You – a lover!

RAYMONDE: Certainly! You know, you get these moments. Oh, I'd even chosen him. Romain Tournel, to mention no names. He was here with you at dinner the other night. Didn't you notice how he stared at me? You astonish me. Well – we were on the very brink . . .

LUCIENNE: Oh!

RAYMONDE [*rising*]: He said, 'As your husband's my best friend I feel it's incumbent upon me to . . .' Well, why shouldn't I take a lover! Now my Victor Emmanuel's deceiving me!

LUCIENNE [*getting up*]: Shall I tell you something?

RAYMONDE: What?

LUCIENNE: You're secretly mad about your Victor Emmanuel.

RAYMONDE: Mad?

LUCIENNE: If you're not – why all the fuss?

RAYMONDE: Well, I may want to deceive him, but for him to deceive me! No! It's going too far!

LUCIENNE: I like your sense of morality!

RAYMONDE: Aren't I totally justified?

LUCIENNE: Yes, yes. Only look. What you told me doesn't prove anything!

RAYMONDE: What? When a husband's been a raging torrent for years, and then suddenly – pfutt! Nothing. Not a trickle . . .

LUCIENNE [*sitting at the table*]: Spain's full of dried-up rivers. But they're still in the same old beds . . .

RAYMONDE: Oh! . . .

LUCIENNE: You know, it's like those men in casinos, who try to impress everyone by risking millions and then one day – pfutt! – they're reduced to ten francs.

RAYMONDE: Ten francs would be all right, but he doesn't even play. All he does is walk round the table and watch.

LUCIENNE: All the better! It doesn't mean he's spending his money on someone else. He's just bankrupt.

RAYMONDE: Oh, yes? What about *that*, then? [*She takes a pair of braces from her bag.*]

LUCIENNE: What about it?

RAYMONDE: A pair of braces.

LUCIENNE: I can see that.

RAYMONDE: And who do you think they belong to?

LUCIENNE: Your husband, I assume.

RAYMONDE: You admit it!

LUCIENNE: Not exactly. I just presume that if you have a pair of braces about you they belong to your husband, *and no one else!*

RAYMONDE [*taking her handbag to the stool and returning*]: Precisely! And now perhaps you can explain why he got them this morning, through the post.

LUCIENNE: Through the post?

RAYMONDE: In a parcel which I opened by mistake, when I went through his letters.

LUCIENNE: Why go through his letters?

RAYMONDE: To see what's in them.

LUCIENNE: Sound reason ...

RAYMONDE: Well!

LUCIENNE: That's what you call a parcel 'opened by mistake'?

RAYMONDE: Of course it was a mistake. It wasn't meant for me.

LUCIENNE: I see ...

RAYMONDE: You agree that if someone posts him his braces, it's because he left them behind in some – *somewhere?*

LUCIENNE [*rising and moving down stage*]: It seems to follow.

RAYMONDE: Yes – and do you know where it was? This *'somewhere'?*

LUCIENNE: You're making my flesh creep.

RAYMONDE: 'The Hotel Coq d'Or', my darling.

LUCIENNE: What on earth's that?

RAYMONDE: Well, it's not the Christian Science Reading Room.

LUCIENNE: 'The Hotel Coq d'Or.'

RAYMONDE [*moving to the tallboy and taking out a box*]: Look! The box they came in. Printed label, and then, my husband's address: 'Monsieur Chandebise, 95 Boulevard Malesherbes.' [*She gives* LUCIENNE *the box.*]

LUCIENNE: The Hotel Coq d'Or.

RAYMONDE: And in Montretout, my darling. [*She takes the box back.*] A name that speaks volumes! It's repulsive! But it adds up! Now I can understand it all. [*She returns the box to the drawer.*]

LUCIENNE: Oh? Absolutely.

RAYMONDE: Of course I had my doubts. Just because my husband seemed to be going through ... a slight period of ...

LUCIENNE: Drought?

RAYMONDE: Exactly. I said to myself, 'Oh, well,' I said. 'What of it?' But now – this! This has sent me away – with an enormous flea in my ear ...

LUCIENNE: Obviously.

RAYMONDE: If you could see this hotel, darling. It looks as if it'd been carved out of nougat.

LUCIENNE: You mean, you know it?

RAYMONDE: I've just been there.

LUCIENNE: What?

RAYMONDE: That's why I'm late. I wanted to be quite sure! So I told myself, 'You must question the management.' But how do you question that type of management? They refused to remember anything.

LUCIENNE: That's the first rule of their profession.

RAYMONDE: You know what the terrible man there said to me?

LUCIENNE: What?

RAYMONDE: He said, 'Madame,' he said, 'if I gave away the names of my guests you'd be the first never to come here any more.' He said that to me! Then he shut up. Like a clam.

LUCIENNE: Oh, clam's too good for that sort.

RAYMONDE: You see – men stick together. We must rely on us! Now – you know so much more about these things than I do, darling.

LUCIENNE: I wouldn't say that.

RAYMONDE: You know the facts. And with your touch of genius.

LUCIENNE [sitting at the table]: There is that! Of course.

RAYMONDE: What shall I do?

LUCIENNE: Well, now. Let's see. Go to Victor Emmanuel – have it out with him!

RAYMONDE: Lucienne! You know he'd only lie to me! There's no liar like a man – unless it's a woman.

LUCIENNE [rising]: You're right. [Moving to RAYMONDE] Men and women are the only two of God's creatures who lie at all. Listen. There's one trick I've seen in plays and ...

RAYMONDE: What? Tell me.

LUCIENNE: It's pretty loathsome. I mean I'd only do it to a man. But – you take a sheet of highly perfumed writing paper and on it you write a burning, passionate letter ...

RAYMONDE: Yes?

LUCIENNE: To your husband.

RAYMONDE: Oh ...

LUCIENNE: As if it came from another woman – and you end up – by arranging a meeting!

RAYMONDE: A meeting?

LUCIENNE: Which you go to, naturally. And if he comes to meet you – you've got him!

RAYMONDE: Of course. You're right. It's rather revolting, but the old-fashioned ways are best. We'll do it now.

LUCIENNE: Good.

RAYMONDE: He might recognize my handwriting.

LUCIENNE: If you've written to him before.

RAYMONDE: But he doesn't know yours. [*Moving to* LUCIENNE] You're going to write it! Are you my best friend or not? [*She takes Lucienne's hand.*]

LUCIENNE: You're leading me into mortal sin ...

RAYMONDE: That's where you'll find my husband.

LUCIENNE: That won't do me much good apparently. [*Moving to the sofa*] All right. Give me the writing paper. [*She sits behind the desk.*]

RAYMONDE: Here.

LUCIENNE: Not yours. He'll recognize it.

RAYMONDE [*moving to a cabinet*]: Of course. Silly of me. This'll do. [*She brings out some paper.*] I bought it to give my dear little nephews for their thank you letters.

LUCIENNE: That! He'll think it's an affair with a cook. He'll never go.

RAYMONDE: You're right ... [*She returns the paper to the cabinet.*]

LUCIENNE: Haven't you got any decadent writing paper? Something suggestive ...

RAYMONDE: There's this mauve. It's not all that suggestive.

LUCIENNE: But drenched in perfume ...

RAYMONDE [*moving to a bell-push* R *and rings*]: I've got the stuff! A bottle of 'Scarlet Woman'. I was going to send it back – it makes me sneeze. Wait a moment.

[CAMILLE *comes in from the door on the left.*]

CAMILLE: Ho Horry. [*So sorry. He goes on speaking strangely.*]

RAYMONDE: Can I help you, Camille?

CAMILLE: Don't worry. I wanted to see if Victor Emmanuel was back.

RAYMONDE: Not yet. Why?

LUCIENNE: There's the post to be signed, and a contract.

RAYMONDE: He can't be much longer.

CAMILLE: I'll wait.

RAYMONDE: All right. What're you staring at, darling?

LUCIENNE: No – nothing, really ...

CAMILLE: You see Raymonde came home in the end. You didn't have to wait too long.

LUCIENNE: Honestly. I remember you perfectly – we even had a little chat.

RAYMONDE: What he said was – you didn't have to wait too long.

CAMILLE: That's it! That's it!

LUCIENNE: Not too long, thank you.

RAYMONDE: Camille Chandebise, our nephew. Mme Carlos Homenides de Histangua.

LUCIENNE [*rising and offering* CAMILLE *her hand*]: Delighted to meet you. You must excuse me. [*Withdrawing her hand before* CAMILLE *can kiss it*] I didn't catch all you said just now. A little hard of ...

CAMILLE: Hearing? I have an impediment – in my speech. I don't say words clearly.

LUCIENNE: Charming! Charming! [*Moving to* RAYMONDE] What's he talking about?

RAYMONDE: He says he has an impediment in his speech.

LUCIENNE: Really? Well, perhaps a little tiny – hitch. Now you mention it ...

CAMILLE: You're too kind.

　　[ANTOINETTE *comes in at the main doors.*]

ANTOINETTE: You rang, madame.

RAYMONDE: Yes. Fetch me a big bottle of perfume – you'll find it on the right of the dressing-table.

ANTOINETTE: Yes, madame.

RAYMONDE: You'll see a 'Scarlet Woman' ... smouldering on the label.

ANTOINETTE: Certainly, madame.

　　[ANTOINETTE *goes out by the door on the right, pinching Camille as she passes.*]

CAMILLE: Ouch!

RAYMONDE
LUCIENNE ⎫ [*together*]: What?

CAMILLE: Touch of neuralgia ...

RAYMONDE: In the ...

CAMILLE: Hi' ...

RAYMONDE: The change in the weather.

CAMILLE: I must get on with my work. [*Going*] Madame.

LUCIENNE: Sir!

CAMILLE: My respects.

　　[CAMILLE *goes out by the door on the left*]

LUCIENNE: I think it's wonderful. How do you understand?

RAYMONDE: Is *that* why you were staring?

LUCIENNE: Of course. [*She sits at the desk.*]

RAYMONDE: You get used to it. How sweet of you to pretend not to notice ...

LUCIENNE: I wouldn't hurt his feelings ...

　　[ANTOINETTE *returns.*]

ANTOINETTE: Is this the one, madame?

RAYMONDE: Thank you. Right – now before Victor Emmanuel gets back ...

[ANTOINETTE *goes out by the main doors.*]

LUCIENNE: Well, now how are we going to hook the fish?

RAYMONDE: That's the question.

LUCIENNE: The question is – where?

RAYMONDE: What?

LUCIENNE: Where did this mysterious lady become besotted with Victor Emmanuel?

RAYMONDE: Where do you suggest?

LUCIENNE: Been to the theatre lately?

RAYMONDE: Last Wednesday. The Palais Royal. We went with Monsieur Tournel ...

LUCIENNE: Monsieur Tournel?

RAYMONDE: Who's almost my lover ...

LUCIENNE: Oh, him. [*Writing*] Now – listen to this – 'Dear Sir, Having noticed you the other evening at the Palais Royal Theatre ...'

RAYMONDE: Doesn't that sound a little formal – for love at first sight?

LUCIENNE: Formal?

RAYMONDE: As if you were serving a writ. I'd come right out with it. 'I was the girl who couldn't take her eyes off you that night at the Palais Royal ...'

LUCIENNE: You've obviously got a talent for this sort of thing.

RAYMONDE: I was only saying what *I'd* write.

LUCIENNE: All right, I agree. 'I'm the girl who couldn't take her eyes off you –'

RAYMONDE: '– that night at the Palais Royal.' Hot, yearning – and simple.

LUCIENNE: You're really living the part, aren't you? 'You were in a box with your wife and another man ...'

RAYMONDE: Monsieur Tournel ...

LUCIENNE: 'Since then – you are all I dream of.'

RAYMONDE: Isn't that going too far?

LUCIENNE: Other people always go too far.

RAYMONDE: If you're sure ...

LUCIENNE: 'I'm ready to commit a folly. Will you join me? I'll be waiting for you today. Five o'clock. In the Hotel Coq d'Or in Montretout.'

RAYMONDE: The same hotel? Won't he be suspicious?

LUCIENNE: He'll be stimulated – beyond endurance. 'The room will be booked in the name of Monsieur Chandebise.'

RAYMONDE: 'I rely on you ...'

LUCIENNE: 'I rely on you.' Marvellous! I tell you, you've got a talent for this sort of thing.

RAYMONDE: I'm starting to learn ...

LUCIENNE [*writing*]: 'From one who loves you ...' Now – drenched in perfume ...

RAYMONDE [*giving* LUCIENNE *the perfume*]: Here we are!
  [LUCIENNE *sprinkles the letter.*]

LUCIENNE: That'll do ... [*She puts the perfume on the table.*]

RAYMONDE: Oh, dear!

LUCIENNE [*rising*]: Blotched!

RAYMONDE: What a shame.

LUCIENNE: Yes.

RAYMONDE: You'll have to do it again.

LUCIENNE [*sitting as before*]: Not at all! That'll come in very useful. [*Writing*] 'P.S. Why can't I stop crying when I write to you? Let them be tears of joy and not despair.' Private. To Monsieur Victor Emmanuel Chandebise. Ninety-five Boulevard Malesherbes. Now we need a messenger. Who can we send?

RAYMONDE: You, of course.

LUCIENNE [*rising*]: You're – not serious!

RAYMONDE: We can't send a servant – he'd be recognized. And I can't do it myself. I mean if my husband asked for a description of the woman who brought the letter – and got a description of me – the cat would just leap out of the bag! You're the one to do it!

LUCIENNE: Whatever next!

RAYMONDE: Are you my best friend or not?

LUCIENNE: I suppose so. You certainly make the most of it.
  [*The doorbell rings.*]

RAYMONDE: That must be my husband. [*She opens the door on the right.*] Hurry up. Out this way. Take the door on the right and you are in the hall.
  [LUCIENNE *collects her gloves and goes quickly.* RAYMONDE *replaces the cap on the perfume bottle, puts it back on the table, and moves down stage.* CHANDEBISE *enters, followed by* ETIENNE, *through the main doors.*]

CHANDEBISE [*giving* ETIENNE *his cane*]: You say the doctor called?

ETIENNE: Yes, sir.

CHANDEBISE: Good! Excellent! Go in, my dear fellow.
  [TOURNEL *follows them in with a brief-case, which he puts on the table.*] Give me a moment. Must sign the post. [*He puts his hat and gloves on the table.*]

RAYMONDE: Camille's been waiting as if you were the Second Coming.

CHANDEBISE: Oh, it's you.

TOURNEL: Good morning dear lady.

RAYMONDE: Good morning, Mr Tournel. [*To* CHANDEBISE] Yes, it's me.

CHANDEBISE: I met Tournel on the stairs, so we came up together.

RAYMONDE: Oh, yes ...

TOURNEL: I've brought a list of new clients.

CHANDEBISE [*hitching up his trousers with his hands in his pockets*]: Splendid. You can give me that right away.

RAYMONDE: Are you having trouble with your braces by any chance?

CHANDEBISE: As a matter of fact I am.

RAYMONDE: Are they the ones I bought for you?

CHANDEBISE: What's that? Yes, of course.

RAYMONDE: They seemed to be – quite satisfactory.

CHANDEBISE: It's because I've pulled them up too tight.

RAYMONDE: Let me adjust them for you.

CHANDEBISE: Please don't bother. I can adjust them myself.

RAYMONDE: Have it your own way.

CHANDEBISE: Excuse me. Be with you in a moment.

[CHANDEBISE *goes by the door stage left.*]

TOURNEL: Carry on! Carry on!

CAMILLE [*off*]: A – Harst. [*At last.*]

CHANDEBISE [*off*]: All right! Some people don't have to rush round all day ... [*He closes the door.*]

TOURNEL: Oh, Raymonde! Raymonde! You're all I dream of!

RAYMONDE: Not now, thank you very much. Not when he's unfaithful.

TOURNEL: What?

RAYMONDE [*moving towards the door on the right*]: That sort of thing's perfectly all right when you've got nothing else on your mind.

TOURNEL [*following her*]: But, Raymonde – Raymonde, you said – you let me hope ...

RAYMONDE: Did I? I suppose I did. But he didn't have his braces then. Now that he's got his braces – goodbye!

[RAYMONDE *goes by the door on the right.*]

TOURNEL: She's going to be a hard nut to crack! Braces. What's she talking about? Braces!

[CAMILLE *comes in from the left.*]

CAMILLE: Monsieur Tournel, my uncle is asking for you.

TOURNEL [*smiling*]: What?

CAMILLE: My uncle is asking for you.

TOURNEL [*crossing to the table*]: Don't talk with your mouth full, old boy, it's rude. [*He picks up his brief-case.*]

CAMILLE: Wait. 'My uncle is ask-ing for you!'

TOURNEL: My uncle is asking for you! Why not say so!

[TOURNEL *goes out of the door on the left.*]

CAMILLE: What an uncouth fellow! Extraordinary thing! I go to all the trouble of fetching him and he gives me a mouthful of abuse!

[FINACHE *and* ETIENNE *come in through the main doors.*]

ETIENNE: The master's back.

FINACHE: Good.

ETIENNE: I'll tell him.

[ETIENNE *goes out stage left.*]

CAMILLE: It's a bit thick! I say to him, most politely, 'My uncle is asking for you.' He makes me repeat it. I write it down for him, and he has the ice-cold nerve to come back with, 'All right, why couldn't you say so?' It's the last time I do a favour for a pig like that!

FINACHE: You rehearsing a dramatic monologue?

CAMILLE: It's you, Doctor! I was just complaining about a certain person who ...

FINACHE: Oh, all right. Don't explain. Well, you young scallywag? Been on the tiles lately?

CAMILLE: Oh! Shhh!

FINACHE: Of course. You're supposed to be the virginal young Camille. You've got to keep up your reputation ...

[FINACHE *and* CAMILLE *circle each other.*]

CAMILLE: Please!

FINACHE: Doctors have a way of catching little plaster saints with their trousers down. I must say it's very funny. Everyone thinking that you're so innocent.

CAMILLE: I suppose it is really ...

FINACHE: Have you taken my advice?

CAMILLE: What?

FINACHE: The Hotel Coq d'Or.

CAMILLE: Please!

[FINACHE *and* CAMILLE *circle again.*]

FINACHE: Why? We're alone – between friends. You've been there?

CAMILLE: Yes.

FINACHE: What did I tell you?

CAMILLE: Oh!

FINACHE: Isn't it? When I want a little – relaxation I never go anywhere else. All right, come down to earth and go and fetch your uncle.

CAMILLE: Yes, of course.

FINACHE: While I think of it, I'll give you your infernal machine.

CAMILLE: What infernal machine?

FINACHE: What I promised you. At least you'll sound like a human being.

CAMILLE: You've got it!

FINACHE: Now your trouble is – the roof of your mouth hasn't formed properly. The sounds don't bounce off it. They float up – and they get lost somewhere behind your face.

CAMILLE: That's it.

FINACHE [*producing a box with a false palate in it*]: So – I've brought you a sounding board. Isn't it pretty?

CAMILLE: Let's see. [*He takes the box.*]

FINACHE: A silver roof to your mouth.

CAMILLE: Oh!

FINACHE: Not everyone can say that.

CAMILLE: I'll be able to speak!

FINACHE: What?

CAMILLE: I'll be able ... [*He starts to insert the palate.*]

FINACHE: Not yet! First soak it in boracic. Who knows where it's been!

CAMILLE: You're right! No, but I said. I shall be able to speak.

FINACHE: Of course you will be able to speak! With a little talent you'll be in the *Comédie Française*.

CAMILLE: Ah! I'll soak it in boracic.

CHANDEBISE [*off*]: Camille!

FINACHE: Just a minute. They're calling you.

CAMILLE: Tell them – I'll be back in a minute.

[*CAMILLE goes out by the main doors.*]

CHANDEBISE [*off*]: Camille!

[*CHANDEBISE comes in from the door on the left.*]

FINACHE: He'll be back in a minute.

CHANDEBISE: Finache!

FINACHE: He's got something to see to. Keeping well?

CHANDEBISE: Thank God it's you – just the man I wanted to see.

FINACHE: I was here earlier. Etienne told you?

CHANDEBISE: With Histangua's certificate.

FINACHE: It's on the table.

CHANDEBISE: It seems he's a good risk.

FINACHE: First rate.

CHANDEBISE: Thanks.

FINACHE [*sitting at the table*]: What did you want to see me about?

CHANDEBISE [*also sitting at the table*]: Yes. Well. Now – I wanted to consult you. It's rather a delicate matter. But, quite frankly, a most extraordinary thing's happened to me.

FINACHE: What sort of thing?

CHANDEBISE: It's not very easy to explain. Well. You know I have an extremely attractive wife ...

FINACHE: Hear, hear!

CHANDEBISE: Good! And no one's less interested in other women than your humble servant.

FINACHE: Ah.

CHANDEBISE: What do you mean 'Ah'? Why do you say 'Ah'?

FINACHE: I really don't know.

CHANDEBISE: I'm telling you! Raymonde's everything to me. Wife and mistress. And I don't wish to boast but between you and me, I'm a first-rate husband!

FINACHE: Ah?

CHANDEBISE: What do you mean 'Ah'? Why do you keep saying 'Ah'?

FINACHE: I really don't know.

CHANDEBISE: I'm telling you! To say I'm first-rate's an understatement ...

FINACHE: Delighted to hear it. I suppose all this is leading somewhere.

CHANDEBISE: Of course it is. You've seen a play called *Nothing to Declare* at the Palais Royal?

FINACHE: What?

CHANDEBISE: I asked you if you'd seen *Nothing to Declare*.

FINACHE: Yes and no ...

CHANDEBISE: What's the matter? You've either seen it or you haven't ...

FINACHE: Well, actually both. I had a close friend in my box.

CHANDEBISE: So there were gaps.

FINACHE: Quite a few.

CHANDEBISE: Never mind! You got the general idea. Nice young man on his honeymoon. He's about to give his wife lesson number one in the grammar of matrimony when a customs officer bursts in with a quite inopportune cry of 'Nothing to declare?' Brutally interrupts his train of thought.

FINACHE: I remember, vaguely.

CHANDEBISE: Vaguely! Obviously the customs officer didn't burst into your box!

FINACHE: That's perfectly true.

CHANDEBISE: Not to make a long story out of it – it became an obsession with the young fellow. Every time he felt an impulse to reopen negotiations with madame he saw the customs officer and heard that terrible 'Nothing to declare'. And then, hey presto! Nothing to declare!

FINACHE: What a bore for him.

CHANDEBISE [*rising*]: Decidedly! My dear chap. That's exactly what happens to me!

FINACHE: What?

CHANDEBISE [*pacing down the room*]: One fine day. No. One ghastly night about a month ago, I was extremely amorous, as is my wont. I expressed my desires to Madame Chandebise who appeared to welcome them. And then, hey presto!

FINACHE: The customs man arrived!

CHANDEBISE: Yes. What? No! But I was in a terrible trouble. I don't know what. I felt I'd become – a little child again.

FINACHE: That was a bit hard.

CHANDEBISE: You could put it more happily. At first – I didn't worry. I had a glorious past behind me. I said to myself, 'Chandebise. A reverse today, revenge tomorrow.'

FINACHE: That's life!

CHANDEBISE: But the next day unfortunately I said to myself, 'Steady now, old fellow. If you're going to do the same as yesterday ...' Damn silly to put ideas in a man's head just when he needs all his confidence. I was overcome with anxiety and once again. Nothing to declare!

FINACHE: Poor old Chandebise.

CHANDEBISE: I'm afraid it is 'poor old Chandebise'. It's an obsession. Now I don't even say to myself, 'Tonight – can I?' I say, 'Tonight – I can't!' It never fails. Steady on! Hardly the moment for laughing.

FINACHE [*rising and moving to* CHANDEBISE]: What? You don't expect me to treat your case as a tragedy! It happens every day. You're simply the victim of auto-suggestion. Now! It's up to you. All you need is a little strength of character. If you want it you can do it.

CHANDEBISE [*unconvinced*]: Oh, yes!

FINACHE: If instead of saying, 'Can I', you must simply say – [*very positive*] – 'I can'. That'll do it. Never doubt yourself in this life. You should have told your wife all you told me, quite clearly, and calmly ... I mean, she'd have had a good laugh, and you'd have enjoyed the joke together. You'd've both put your shoulders to the wheel. And rolled straight through the Customs.

CHANDEBISE: Perhaps you're right.

FINACHE: Apart from that I prescribe – plenty of outdoor exercise. I'll listen-in to your chest. You work too hard. Desk-bound. Round shoulders. That's why I prescribed special American braces. I bet you're not wearing them!

CHANDEBISE [*taking off his jacket*]: Oh, yes, I am. I gave Camille my other braces. But these are pretty unsightly.

FINACHE: You're the only one who sees them.

CHANDEBISE: It's not true! My wife almost poked her nose in there ...

FINACHE: That'll never do. Come on, let's listen to your chest ...

CHANDEBISE [*unbuttoning his waistcoat*]: One humiliation after another ...

LUCIENNE: Tell your mistress I'm here ...

CHANDEBISE: Oh! [*He buttons his waistcoat.*]

ETIENNE: Certainly, madame.

[LUCIENNE *comes in through the main doors.*]

CHANDEBISE: See you later. It's you, dear lady ...

LUCIENNE: Of course it's me. Are you quite well?

CHANDEBISE: Perfectly well, thank you. [*He puts on his jacket.*] You're calling on my wife?

LUCIENNE: Calling back. I had a few – little jobs – but I've seen her already – and this gentleman.

FINACHE: A delightful encounter.

CHANDEBISE: Then – no need for introductions. Did you notice any – signs of nervousness?

LUCIENNE: In him?

CHANDEBISE: No, no. In my wife. I don't know what was wrong with her this morning. Got out of bed the wrong side ...

LUCIENNE: I didn't notice anything.

CHANDEBISE: So much the better.

[RAYMONDE *comes in from the door on the right.*]

RAYMONDE: There you are.

LUCIENNE [*moving to* RAYMONDE]: Hullo again. [*They whisper together.*]

RAYMONDE: All right?

LUCIENNE: Fine. It's on its way.

RAYMONDE: Splendid.

[ETIENNE *comes in through the main doors with the letter.*]

ETIENNE: Sir.

CHANDEBISE: What?

LUCIENNE: Here it is!

ETIENNE: By special delivery. Personal to the master.

[ETIENNE *goes.* RAYMONDE *moves towards* CHANDEBISE.]

CHANDEBISE: For me? Excuse me ... [*He opens the letter.*] Good heavens!

RAYMONDE: What is it?

CHANDEBISE: Oh, nothing very much ...

RAYMONDE: Bad news?

CHANDEBISE: Just something about the business ...

RAYMONDE [*aside*]: Oh, yes. Liar! [*Moving to* LUCIENNE] Let's go. Now it's perfectly obvious.

[RAYMONDE *and* LUCIENNE *go out by the door on the right.*]

CHANDEBISE: My dear fellow, women are remarkable creatures! You'll never guess what's happened to me.

FINACHE: What?

[TOURNEL *comes in through the door on the left.*]

TOURNEL: You gave me the slip ... [*He puts his case on the table.*]

CHANDEBISE: Come in. Nothing private ...

TOURNEL: What is it then? Hullo, Doctor.

FINACHE: Oh, hullo, Tournel.

CHANDEBISE: You chaps must amuse yourselves. I've got to go somewhere. I've made a conquest.

TOURNEL ⎫
FINACHE ⎭ [*together*]: What?

TOURNEL: *You?*

FINACHE: *You*, Chandebise!

CHANDEBISE [*moving between them*]: That's taken the wind out of your sails. Listen. And I'm not making this up. 'I'm the girl who couldn't take her eyes off you, that night at the Palais Royal ...'

TOURNEL: *You!*

FINACHE: *You*, Chandebise!

CHANDEBISE: Me! Chandebise! She couldn't take her eyes off me ...

TOURNEL [*taking the letter*]: 'You were in a box with your wife and another man ...'

CHANDEBISE: 'Another man.' That's you, Tournel. [*Taking the letter*] 'Another man' 'X'. The first one she saw, a blurred anonymous individual. Moth-eaten.

TOURNEL: Thank you.

CHANDEBISE: 'Since then you're all I dream of.'

TOURNEL ⎫
FINACHE ⎭ [*together*]: No!

CHANDEBISE: I'm all she dreams of! What've you got to say to that?

TOURNEL: Is that there?

CHANDEBISE: Oh, yes, my dear fellow. It's there all right.

FINACHE: I'm afraid it is.

TOURNEL: Damned odd! Don't you find that damned odd?

FINACHE: People have morbid dreams occasionally.

TOURNEL: Depends on what they ate the night before.

CHANDEBISE: You may choose to mock ...

TOURNEL: I must say I do ...

CHANDEBISE [*going on reading*]: 'I'm ready to commit a folly. Will you join me?' Poor little creature. She's got it badly. Wouldn't you say so?

FINACHE: Oh, I don't know ...

CHANDEBISE: After what you've heard ...

FINACHE: Is *that* all?

CHANDEBISE: 'I'll be waiting for you today. Five o'clock. At the Hotel Coq d'Or.'

FINACHE [*startled*]: The Hotel Coq d'Or. [*He sits at the table.*]

CHANDEBISE: Yes. In Montretout.

FINACHE: If she knows that place, she must be well broken in.

CHANDEBISE: Why? Is it one of those hotels?

FINACHE: It's where I go, for my little adventures.

CHANDEBISE [*sitting at the table*]: These places are unknown – to the pure in heart!

FINACHE: But I'm sure Tournel ...

TOURNEL: I may have just heard the name ...

CHANDEBISE: Oh. My dear fellows ...

TOURNEL ⎫
FINACHE ⎭ [*together*]: What?

CHANDEBISE: She wept!

TOURNEL ⎫
FINACHE ⎭ [*together*]: No!

CHANDEBISE: I'm afraid so. Half a minute. 'P.S. Why can't I stop crying when I write to you? Let them be tears of joy and not despair ...' Poor little broken heart! No good saying she's not totally sincere! Look. Drenched. [*He gives* TOURNEL *the letter.*]

TOURNEL: Oh, my dear fellows ...

CHANDEBISE ⎫
FINACHE ⎭ [*together*]: What?

TOURNEL: What does she mix her tears with to make them smell so overpowering?

CHANDEBISE [*rising and moving to* TOURNEL]: Did you notice anyone ogling us?

TOURNEL: No! That is – I did notice something. But I thought it was meant for me.

CHANDEBISE [*snatching the letter from* TOURNEL]: Oh. For you? Really. What a fool I am! Of course, it's obvious.

[FINACHE *rises and moves down stage.*]

TOURNEL ⎫
FINACHE ⎭ [*together*]: What?

CHANDEBISE: It wasn't me she fancied. It was you!

TOURNEL: Me?

CHANDEBISE: Certainly! She mistook you for me. And when someone pointed to our box and said my name, naturally, as she only had eyes for you ...

TOURNEL: You really think so?

CHANDEBISE: Oh, yes, I'm certain of it.

TOURNEL: Ah. Perhaps so. Yes.

CHANDEBISE: Look at me! Do I sweep girls off their feet? Poor old Chandebise. But you ... It's perfectly natural. It's your function in life!

His function in life. You're used to making conquests. You've the looks.

TOURNEL: Well now. I wouldn't go as far as that ...

CHANDEBISE: Why not. It's no secret.

FINACHE: You don't know your own strength.

TOURNEL: I may have a certain boyish charm. That's about all ...

CHANDEBISE: Boyish charm! Women have committed suicide for you. True? Answer yes or no!

TOURNEL: Just – one, actually.

CHANDEBISE: Ah.

TOURNEL: And besides, she recovered.

CHANDEBISE: That's irrelevant!

TOURNEL: Anyway the whole thing's a bit mysterious. She poisoned herself eating mussels.

CHANDEBISE ⎱
FINACHE ⎰ [together]: *Mussels?*

TOURNEL: I'd just left her. She told everyone she did it in a fit of despair. But I must say I wouldn't choose a plate of *moules marinières* as a suicide weapon. Too risky.

CHANDEBISE: Come on! There's no mistake. The letter's meant for you.

TOURNEL: What do you think? Doctor?

FINACHE: Well ...

CHANDEBISE: But of course! And since the letter's meant for you, you're the one who must go ...

TOURNEL: Oh, I couldn't do that!

CHANDEBISE: Anyway! I'm not free this evening. We've got a dinner for our American director and ...

TOURNEL: It's impossible.

CHANDEBISE: You're dying to go.

TOURNEL: Am I?

CHANDEBISE [*moving to* TOURNEL]: Look at your nose. It's twitching.

TOURNEL: My God, it is! All right. I accept.

CHANDEBISE: Such a tease! Be off with you!

TOURNEL: It suits me. I was looking forward to another little – adventure. It was all arranged. But it'll have to be postponed.

CHANDEBISE: Who with?

TOURNEL [*turning to* CHANDEBISE]: With er – I couldn't possibly tell you.

CHANDEBISE: He couldn't possibly tell me! What a tease you are.

TOURNEL: Your unknown beauty'll do me for the moment.

CHANDEBISE: Take her, with my compliments!

TOURNEL: Too kind! So. Let's have the letter.

CHANDEBISE: You don't need it. You've only got to go to that hotel and ask for the room booked in my name. I mean, I don't get letters like that dropped through the post every day of the week. Some day I want my grandchildren – if I manage to produce grandchildren – I want them to come across this letter stuffed away in some attic and say, 'Grandpa must have been a damned good-looking fellow to excite such a desperate passion.' At least I can be good-looking for posterity. Come on, Finache, old man. Come and hear my chest. [*He picks up his hat and gloves.*]

TOURNEL: What about the signatures ...

CHANDEBISE: I'll be with you in two ticks. We'll go in there, Finache. No one'll disturb us.

[FINACHE *and* CHANDEBISE *go out by the door on the left.*]

TOURNEL: The Hotel Coq d'Or. Who's this poor girl who's so besotted with me?

[RAYMONDE *comes in from the right.*]

RAYMONDE: Isn't my husband here?

TOURNEL: In there with the doctor. Shall I call him?

RAYMONDE: Don't bother him now. Could you say I've gone out with Madame de Histangua and if I'm late he's not to worry. I may dine with a lady friend ...

TOURNEL: He'll probably be out too.

RAYMONDE: Why?

TOURNEL: He's got a dinner, for his American director.

RAYMONDE: He said *that*, did he? Not that I mind, in the least; but it just isn't true. The dinner's tomorrow! I saw the invitation ...

TOURNEL: He's made a mistake then. I'll tell him.

RAYMONDE: Don't get excited. He knows exactly what he's doing. An alibi! So he can come creeping home late and say he mixed up the date. He can't fool me ...

TOURNEL: Why should he tell me fairy stories?

RAYMONDE: You mean he saves them up for me?

TOURNEL: Of course not! You're putting words into my mouth.

RAYMONDE: Very clever! While my husband's unfaithful you know you won't get anywhere with me – so you want me to believe he's pure as the driven ...

TOURNEL: But he is. I'm speaking the truth!

RAYMONDE: Really! Well, it makes no difference, he still doesn't – oh, good-bye!

TOURNEL: Raymonde ...

RAYMONDE: Vanish!

[RAYMONDE *goes out through the door on the right.*]

TOURNEL: She told *me*, to vanish!

[CAMILLE *comes in with a glass and a bottle of boracic acid.*]

CAMILLE: Hullo. Monsieur Tournel. You in a better temper now?

TOURNEL: You! Vanish!

[TOURNEL *goes out left.*]

CAMILLE: What an uncouth fellow! [*Putting the boracic in the glass*] Boracic acid – so hard to come by. There! [*He puts the palate in the glass and places it on the mantelpiece.*] Soak yourself, my silver roof! Soak yourself clean!

[ETIENNE *comes in through the centre doors followed by* HOMENIDES.]

ETIENNE: Monsieur Don Homenides de Histangua.

[ETIENNE *goes.*]

HOMENIDES: Buenos días.

CAMILLE: Monsieur Histangua.

HOMENIDES: Where is Señor Chandebise?

CAMILLE: He'll be with you in a minute. He's with his doctor.

HOMENIDES: I want to see the Señor Chandebise!

[CHANDEBISE *and* FINACHE *come in from the left.*]

CAMILLE: Here they are.

FINACHE: Just take my advice. That's all.

CHANDEBISE: I understand.

HOMENIDES: My old friend. Buenos días.

CHANDEBISE: Very well, thank you . . . [*He shakes hands with* HOMENIDES.]

HOMENIDES: And the doctor. In fine health?

FINACHE: Naturally. You all right? I've got to rush away.

HOMENIDES: I excuthe . . . [*He puts his hat, gloves and stick on the sofa.*]

FINACHE: Goodbye. [*He opens the main doors.*]

ALL: Goodbye.

FINACHE: Whoever get's there, good luck at the Hotel Coq d'Or.

[FINACHE *goes.*]

CAMILLE: Silly old fool!

HOMENIDES: Tell me . . . My wife here?

CHANDEBISE: Certainly. With mine.

HOMENIDES: I thought tho.

CHANDEBISE: I'll tell her . . . [*He starts to move away.*]

HOMENIDES: Chandebise, I called on your company today. I thaw your doctor.

CHANDEBISE: He told me.

HOMENIDES: He told me – 'Por favor to make a little water'.

CHANDEBISE: What?

HOMENIDES: Pee – piddle – *pith!*

CHANDEBISE: Ah yes!

HOMENIDES: Why did he do that?

CHANDEBISE: What?

HOMENIDES: To make me – pith?

CHANDEBISE: Well obviously – to discover if you're a good risk.

HOMENIDES: But I came to insure my wife!

CHANDEBISE: You should've told me.

HOMENIDES: I thaid I want inthurance. You didn't ask me for who.

CHANDEBISE: Well, no harm done. Your wife can just pop into the company office and ...

HOMENIDES: Be subjected – to the same humiliation?

CHANDEBISE: Well, of course.

HOMENIDES: I'm not wanting that.

CHANDEBISE: But ...

HOMENIDES [*moving slowly towards* CHANDEBISE]: I'm not wanting *that!* I'm not wanting *that!* I am not wanting that!

CHANDEBISE: Now. Be reasonable. It's in our rules.

HOMENIDES: I break your rules. I have already pithed for her.

CHANDEBISE: That's not allowed.

HOMENIDES: Bueno. Then no inthurance. Terminado!

CHANDEBISE: Surely you're not so possessive ...

HOMENIDES: An affront – to the man of dignity.

CHANDEBISE: Or jealous.

HOMENIDES: Jealouth? Me? I am never jealouth.

CHANDEBISE: Of course you have no reason to be jealous of your wife. I'm sure of that.

HOMENIDES: Not only that! She knows that I would be terrible. She wouldn't dare detheive me ...

CHANDEBISE: Oh, yes?

HOMENIDES [*producing a revolver*]: You thee thith little toy?

CHANDEBISE: Put it away! Good heavens – don't play with things like that!

HOMENIDES: Not dangerous. Just a deterrent.

CHANDEBISE: All the same.

HOMENIDES: If I just catch her – with another man. He'll get a ball of shot in the back which will pass through and come *out of the back!*

CHANDEBISE: Out of – his back?

HOMENIDES: No! Hers!

CHANDEBISE: What? Oh, I see. You think they might possibly be like – well, like ...

HOMENIDES: I think? What do you mean I think?

CHANDEBISE: Nothing. Really, nothing at all.

HOMENIDES: She knows what'll happen. I told her. On the wedding night ...

CHANDEBISE: Charming for her!

[TOURNEL *comes in from the left.*]

TOURNEL: Oh, there you are, old chap.

CHANDEBISE: Half a moment.

TOURNEL: No, listen. You know I've got – an urgent appointment.

CHANDEBISE: Of course. Get the forms out. I'll be with you in a second.

TOURNEL: Oy ... !

[TOURNEL *goes back through the door on the left.*]

HOMENIDES: Who's that man?

CHANDEBISE: Monsieur Tournel.

HOMENIDES: Monsieur Tournel?

CHANDEBISE: One of our agents – and a personal friend.

HOMENIDES: Aha?

CHANDEBISE: Charming fellow. Tournel, do meet ... Oh. He's not there
Pity. He's only got one fault ...

HOMENIDES: Yes?

CHANDEBISE: Women! He never stops. It's quite fantastic.

HOMENIDES: Well ...

CHANDEBISE: He's in a hurry. He's got a girl waiting for him now. Or
perhaps she's not waiting for him either. You see, she sent her steaming
little love letter – to me!

HOMENIDES: Truly? Who is thith girl?

CHANDEBISE: A mystery. Not signed.

HOMENIDES: Perhaps – one of those anonymous perthons.

CHANDEBISE: But she must be a woman of the world. Sophisticated.
Married probably.

HOMENIDES: Why you thay this?

CHANDEBISE: What?

HOMENIDES: Why you thay this?

CHANDEBISE: Oh. Why I thay this? Well, the way it's written. Loose
women are much more straightforward, not so sentimental. Here, have
a look ... [*He holds out the letter.*]

HOMENIDES [*taking the letter*]: Good joke! A poor idiot of a husband! Being
cheated!

CHANDEBISE: That makes you laugh?

HOMENIDES: Such a good joke! [*He looks at the letter.*]

CHANDEBISE: He's got a lovely nature!

HOMENIDES: Ah!

CHANDEBISE: What?

HOMENIDES: Caramba! The moment of truth! Caramba!

CHANDEBISE: What's the matter?

HOMENIDES: Her handwriting! [*He produces his revolver.*]

CHANDEBISE: *What?*

HOMENIDES [*seizing* CHANDEBISE *and bending him over the table*]: Mongrel! Snake! Reptile!

CHANDEBISE: There – there, old fellow.

HOMENIDES: My faithful bulldog! Here, boy, here!

CHANDEBISE: He's got a dog with him?

HOMENIDES: There you are!

CHANDEBISE: Steady now ...

HOMENIDES: My wife thends you letters!

CHANDEBISE [*escaping and running round the table*]: Certainly not! Anyway how do you know it's her? These days all women write alike ...

HOMENIDES [*loading the revolver*]: I know it!

CHANDEBISE: Anyway I'm not going to see her. It's Tournel.

HOMENIDES: The man who wath here! Good! I shall kill him!

CHANDEBISE: I'll stop him going. It'll be all right ...

HOMENIDES [*stopping him*]: I wish it conthummated. Then I have my proof – and I will kill beautifully!

LUCIENNE [*off*]: Raymonde, dear, we really ought to hurry.

RAYMONDE [*off*]: Yes, dear, I'm ready.

HOMENIDES: My wife's voice! [*Forcing* CHANDEBISE *down to the door on the left.*] Get in there!

CHANDEBISE: Histangua, my dear friend ...

HOMENIDES: Si! I'm your friend! But I'll kill you like a mongrel dog. Go on. Or I fire.

CHANDEBISE: No – no ...

[CHANDEBISE *goes in through the door.* HOMENIDES *locks the door and pockets the letter and revolver.* LUCIENNE *and* RAYMONDE *come in through the door on the right.*]

LUCIENNE: Darling, here you are!

HOMENIDES: Si! Here I am.

RAYMONDE: Monsieur de Histangua.

HOMENIDES: Madame, I trust you are well. And your huthband ...

RAYMONDE: Well, yes, thank you very much.

HOMENIDES: And los niños – the little ones.

RAYMONDE: Well, I haven't any little ones.

HOMENIDES: Pity. Well – thooner or later ...

RAYMONDE: Thank you.

LUCIENNE: What's the matter?

HOMENIDES: Nothing the matter. Nothing! Nada ...

LUCIENNE: I'm going out with Raymonde. You don't mind?

HOMENIDES: Bueno. Go. I beg you. Go!

LUCIENNE: Goodbye, then.

RAYMONDE: Goodbye, dear M. De Histangua. [*She moves and opens the main doors.*]

HOMENIDES: Adiós, madame. Goodbye.

LUCIENNE: Qué tienes, querido mío? Qué te pasa por que me pones una cara así? [*What has happened to you, darling? Why do you make that face?*]

HOMENIDES: Te aseguro que no tengo nada! [*I can assure you nothing has happened to me!*]

LUCIENNE: What an impossible creature!

[RAYMONDE *and* LUCIENNE *go out through the main doors.*]

HOMENIDES: She rejects me! Without thame! Thore! Thrumpet!

[*Knocking is heard off from the room where* CHANDEBISE *is imprisoned.*]

HOMENIDES: Thut up – or I fire!

[TOURNEL *comes in through the other door on the left.*]

TOURNEL: Isn't Chandebise in here?

HOMENIDES: The other man! Tournel! No, Señor. He is not here.

TOURNEL: All right, if you see him be so good as to tell him I've left all the proposal forms in his office. He's only got to sign them.

HOMENIDES: Bueno! Bueno!

TOURNEL: I simply can't wait any longer.

HOMENIDES [*following him*]: Go! Go on! Go! Go – or I'll ...

TOURNEL: Or you'll what?

HOMENIDES: Nada, Señor. Absolutely nada! Go then. You'd better go.

TOURNEL: All right. Curious individual. Good day.

[TOURNEL *goes through the main doors.*]

HOMENIDES: Ah – I'm choking. I need a drink. [*He drinks from the glass on the mantelpiece.*] Filthy French drink! [*He puts the glass on the table, spluttering as* CAMILLE *comes in from the left.*]

CAMILLE: Monsieur Histangua. All alone? [*He offers his hand.*]

HOMENIDES [*grabbing him by the throat*]: You ... ! Oh, you. So happy you're here. I'm going now.

CAMILLE: Oh, yes!

HOMENIDES: When I go I authorize you – to unlock your mathter.

CAMILLE: My mathter?

HOMENIDES [*collecting his stick, gloves and hat from the sofa*]: Oh, thameless! Lustful! Lecher! Who would think my mujer would think to a lover!

[HOMENIDES *goes through the main doors.*]

CAMILLE: My mujer think to a lover! You can't understand a word he says. My mathter? What mathter? [*He unlocks the door.*] You ... ?

[CHANDEBISE *comes out cautiously.*]

CHANDEBISE: Has he gone?

CAMILLE: Who?

CHANDEBISE: Ho – Homenides.

CAMILLE: Yes.

CHANDEBISE: And – his wife?

CAMILLE: She went out with Raymonde.

CHANDEBISE: Good. And Tournel?

CAMILLE: He's just left.

CHANDEBISE: Him, too. How terrible. There's not a moment to lose. Who can we send down there to stop them? I know – Etienne.

CAMILLE: What's 'down there'?

CHANDEBISE: Down there's the – *Place*. The what-do-you-call-it? – 'down there'. Good God, we're sitting on a volcano. We're about to witness a ghastly tragedy. Perhaps – a double murder!

CAMILLE: What are you talking about?

CHANDEBISE: Look. I've got time to run round to Tournel's before the dinner. My hat! Where's my hat?

CAMILLE: What on earth's happening?

CHANDEBISE: No time to explain. If Tournel comes back – tell him not to go. He knows where. His life's at stake.

CAMILLE: His life's at stake?

CHANDEBISE: Understand? His life's at . . .

CAMILLE: Yes, yes. Stake.

CHANDEBISE: What dramas! Oh, my God! What dramas!

[CHANDEBISE *goes out stage left.*]

CAMILLE: I feel it in my bones – something's going on.

[TOURNEL *comes in through the main doors.*]

TOURNEL: I left my brief-case . . . [*He moves to the table.*]

CAMILLE: Monsieur Tournel!

TOURNEL: Here it is. [*He picks up his case.*]

CAMILLE: For God's sake. Don't go you know where. Your life's at stake!

TOURNEL: What did you say?

CAMILLE [*pushing* TOURNEL *round to the door*]: Don't go you know where. Your life's at stake.

TOURNEL: Let me alone! I can't understand a word you say. [*He moves to the main doors.*]

CAMILLE [*following him*]: Monsieur Tournel! Monsieur Tournel!

TOURNEL: To hell with you! Goodbye!

[TOURNEL *leaves, slamming the main doors.*]

CAMILLE [*moving to the mantelpiece*]: My roof. Oh, dear God! My silver roof . . . [*Seeing the glass on the table*] There you are! [*He puts the palate in his mouth and speaks normally.*] Monsieur Tournel! Monsieur Tournel!

[CHANDEBISE *comes in through the door on the left.*]

CHANDEBISE: Who are you yelling at?

CAMILLE [*speaking clearly*]: At Monsieur Tournel. I've never known such an uncouth fellow! I gave him your message perfectly clearly. He simply wouldn't listen.

CHANDEBISE: My God! He spoke!

CAMILLE [*running up* C]: Monsieur Tournel! Monsieur Tournel! Listen to me, Monsieur Tournel!

> CAMILLE *goes out of the main doors, as the lights Black-Out and –*

THE CURTAIN FALLS

ACT II

The Hotel Coq d'Or in Montretout. Evening.

A small, ornate but down-at-heel hotel. A staircase leads to a landing and the upper rooms. Below this is a central corridor leading to the hotel entrance and another passage leading left to other rooms in the hotel. Downstairs left is Schwarz's bedroom door. The right side of the stage is taken up by a small bedroom, with a bathroom door and a bed on a small raised platform. This bed is on a revolve which can turn to reveal a similar bed in the room behind it. The door to this back room is visible to the audience.

When the curtain rises, EUGÉNIE, a maid, is seen standing on a chair and cleaning the door to the small bedroom. FERAILLON, the Hotel Manager, comes in bristling and goes to the bedroom door. He speaks in a military manner.

FERAILLON: Eugénie! Eugénie!

EUGÉNIE: Yes, M'sieur?

FERAILLON: What are you doing?

EUGÉNIE: I'm finishing the room, M'sieur.

FERAILLON: You call this room done, do you?

EUGÉNIE [*getting off the chair*]: Looks all right to me.

FERAILLON: Do you call this a made bed? It looks as if it's been used once or twice since this morning.

EUGÉNIE: Fancy that!

FERAILLON: Are you implying that there's something dubious about this hotel?

EUGÉNIE: Oh, I'd never say that!
     [OLYMPE *enters with linen.*]

FERAILLON: I tell you this is a respectable establishment! Only married couples come here.

EUGÉNIE: But not at the same time.

[OLYMPE *puts the linen on a table and looks in the mirror*]

FERAILLON: Mind your own business. If they're both married, it is twice as respectable. Now let's get this bed straightened.

EUGÉNIE: Oh, for heaven's sake!

FERAILLON: It's a matter of urgency! [*He moves to the stairs.*]

EUGÉNIE: He gets on your nerves. [*She tidies the bed.*]

OLYMPE: What are you on about, Feraillon.

FERAILLON: That girl needs a sharp lesson. If I'd had her under me in the regiment, I'd have made her jump about a bit.

[EUGÉNIE *goes.*]

OLYMPE: Now then, Feraillon.

[BAPTISTIN *comes in from the corridor and tiptoes to a bedroom door.*]

FERAILLON: Oh, I'd have made her double up, about turn. I'm not making any innuendoes.

OLYMPE: I should hope not!

FERAILLON: I can't stand that type of conversation. [*He sees* BAPTISTIN.] Where've you sprung from? Some filthy bar, I suppose ...

BAPTISTIN: Me?

FERAILLON: It's five o'clock. On sentry go! Do you want to work or not?

BAPTISTIN: Yes.

FERAILLON: All right. Go to bed! [*Seizing* BAPTISTIN *by the collar*] Here's a perfectly useless individual, offered a golden opportunity to be bed-ridden with the rheumatics, and I pay him for it! Why? Because I've got too much family feeling to leave an old uncle of mine in the gutter. And how does he repay me? By creeping out in the afternoons. By hanging round the bars ...

BAPTISTIN: Listen.

FERAILLON: Filthy, depraved, drinking dens which should be closed in the name of public morality. And if we needed a ghastly old wreck in your absence, who'd have taken your place, you ghastly old wreck? Not me, I do assure you! What would we do in a sudden emergency? Who'd have saved us from a nasty case of *in flagrante*?

BAPTISTIN: But I knew ...

FERAILLON: Silence on parade! And go to your room. To bed!

[BAPTISTIN *goes to the door behind the room with the revolving bed.*]

My family's doing all right. All take and no give ...

[SCHWARZ *comes in and moves to* FERAILLON.]

SCHWARZ: Hat ein schönes, kleines Mädchen nach mir gefragt?

FERAILLON: What!

SCHWARZ [*to* OLYMPE]: Hat ein schönes, kleines Mädchen nach mir gefragt?

OLYMPE: Gefragt? No gefragt at all.

[SCHWARZ *goes into his room.*]

FERAILLON: What did he say?

OLYMPE: I have a feeling he's looking for someone.

FERAILLON: It's morbid. Chattering away in Prussian! I don't talk like that to him.

OLYMPE: He doesn't know our language.

FERAILLON: That's no excuse! I don't know his.

[EUGÉNIE *enters with a jug.*]

OLYMPE: Poor fellow. He's come here three times and every time he's been let down.

FERAILLON: If he behaves like that with women I can understand it.

OLYMPE: There you are, then! [*Picking up the linen*] I'll pop these up in the linen cupboard.

FERAILLON: Let the girl do that, Eugénie!

EUGÉNIE: Yes?

FERAILLON: Is the bedroom done?

EUGÉNIE: Oh, yes, M'sieur.

FERAILLON: It's always done when you want it done.

EUGÉNIE: And when it's done it's always ready to be done again.

FERAILLON: Quite enough of your philosophy. There's a pile of sheets! Take them up to the linen cupboard.

EUGÉNIE: Me?

FERAILLON: Who else?

[EUGÉNIE *takes the linen.*]

EUGÉNIE: Donkey work! [*She starts up the stairs.*]

OLYMPE: While I think of it. Don't let that room. It's reserved specially.

FERAILLON: Who for?

OLYMPE: Monsieur Chandebise. [*Taking a telegram from her garter*] You remember him?

EUGÉNIE: Oh, yes. The gentlemen that Halked Hike Hat?

OLYMPE: That's him.

[EUGÉNIE *moves and looks over* OLYMPE's *shoulder.*]

FERAILLON: He's coming today.

OLYMPE: Yes. Here's his telegram. All right, Eugénie.

EUGÉNIE: Oh, yes, madame. Thanks for asking.

OLYMPE: I mean. All right! That will be all ...

EUGÉNIE: Oh, yes. Sorry. [*Facing front*] How very embarrassing!

OLYMPE: Go up the back stairs. Then you won't bump into our clients with your pile of sheets.

EUGÉNIE: Yes, madame.

[EUGÉNIE *goes upstairs.*]

OLYMPE: Here's what the telegram says – 'Keep me same room as last time. Five o'clock. Signed Chandebise.' This is the one he had last time.

FERAILLON [*rising*]: That's all right. [*He goes into the small bedroom.*] I'll just inspect the quarters. That's better.

OLYMPE [*following him*]: What about the bathroom? The bathroom's vital! [OLYMPE *goes out through the bathroom door.*]

FERAILLON: And our camouflage system! Make sure my old idiot uncle's on duty. [*He presses a button beside the bed, which revolves and disappears as the bed from the room behind appears with* BAPTISTIN *on it.*]

BAPTISTIN: My rheumatism. I'm a martyr to it. Can't move hand or foot . . .

FERAILLON: Not now, you fool! It's only me!

BAPTISTIN: You! You're always on at me; but here I am. Manning my post.

FERAILLON [*pressing the button*]: That's what I pay you for. We'll file you away for future reference.

[*As the bed turns,* OLYMPE *re-enters.*]

All present and correct. Where's Poche?

OLYMPE: In the cellar, getting the wood up.

FERAILLON: In the cellar? Poche? Are you out of your mind, woman? You know his one weakness, and you send him down to the cellar.

OLYMPE: The wine's locked up. He's quite safe.

FERAILLON: If you knew the old beggar! It's no good him saying he's broken himself of the habit. I know him of old. Had him under me in the regiment. Good as gold Monday to Saturday – but straight after Church Parade, the Sunday morning piss up!

OLYMPE: It's fashionable – on Sundays.

FERAILLON: He started the fashion. Did I put him on a charge? Oh, no. I preferred to give him a beautiful hiding which kept him straight till the following Saturday. Then, on Sunday, he'd start all over again. Apart from that he was a credit to the Service, honest, hard-working . . . and, thank God, loyal! Oh, I could chase that one! It was a real pleasure to knock him about. Whenever I got my boot to him, he was a perfect gentleman.

OLYMPE [*putting her hand on his shoulder*]: You give such beautiful beatings . . .

FERAILLON: Well, yes. I had a certain talent, in that direction. I'm getting past it now. But he's the sort of servant I like. Not this modern type of domestic you have to go down on your knees and beg them to do you a favour. When I discovered Poche had drunk himself out of the army and was selling matches up the Champs Elysées, I gave him a job at once!

OLYMPE: You're a good boy.

[POCHE *comes shambling in from the corridor and salutes. Although shabbily dressed as a Hotel Porter, he has a strong physical resemblance to Victor Emmanuel Chandebise.*]

FERAILLON: Talk of the devil! What was it, Poche?

POCHE [*holding out a telegram*]: Dispatches from the front, chief.

FERAILLON [*taking the telegram*]: Dispatches from the front! Right! Thanks. My God, you're an ugly-looking brute these days, Poche. You finished staring at me, half-wit? Chandebise again. [*Reading.*] 'Keep me a good room ...'

[EUGÉNIE *comes downstairs.*]

OLYMPE: He's got one!

FERAILLON: 'And show anyone in who asks for it in my name.' Got it, you pair of ... ? If anyone asks for the room reserved for Chandebise, show them in there!

EUGÉNIE: All right.

POCHE: Orders received and understood, chief!

FERAILLON: To your posts!

[EUGÉNIE *goes.* POCHE *stands still.* FERAILLON *grabs him and twists him round to face the stairs.*]

Are you deaf, you stinking Cossack? Pa-rade dis—miss! Happy as a babe unborn. He loves me! Wake up – get moving! [*He kicks* POCHE.]

[POCHE *moves up two stairs.*]

By the right! Hipe – hipe!

[POCHE *marches on upstairs.*]

OLYMPE: He's harmless, anyway.

[SCHWARZ *comes in from his room.*]

SCHWARZ: Entschuldigen Sie mich, bitte, ein Fräulein, ist ein hübsches, junges Fräulein für mich gekommen?

FERAILLON: What!

SCHWARZ: Ein hübsches, junges Fräulein – für mich?

FERAILLON: No, I don't think so.

SCHWARZ: Donnerwetter nocheinmal – danke schön.

[SCHWARZ *goes back to his room.*]

OLYMPE: The demon lover!

FERAILLON: Damn jack in the box.

OLYMPE: Makes you jump out of your skin.

[FINACHE *comes in down the central corridor.*]

FINACHE: Good afternoon, Colonel.

FERAILLON ⎱ [*together*]: ⎰ Hullo, Doctor.
OLYMPE ⎰ ⎱ Afternoon, Doctor.

FINACHE [*moving to* OLYMPE *and kissing her hand*]: My dear Madame Feraillon. Have you got a room for me?

OLYMPE: Always one for *you*, Doctor.

FINACHE: No one's – asked for me?

FERAILLON: Not yet, Doctor.

FINACHE: Just as well ...

OLYMPE: We haven't seen you for more than a month.

FINACHE: I've been flitting from flower to flower.

FERAILLON: That's no good. You must be faithful.

FINACHE: But not always to the same girl.

FERAILLON: I mean faithful to us ...

FINACHE: That's better.

FERAILLON: If you were faithful in love – we'd be out of business.

FINACHE: How true. Coming in here – it's like going into an enchanted forest! I didn't see your man at the desk.

OLYMPE: Poche?

FINACHE: What, Poche? No, Gabriel.

FERAILLON: You didn't know? It's been so long! He was dismissed the service!

FINACHE: Oh, why? He was so decorative ...

FERAILLON: Too damned decorative.

OLYMPE: He started having affairs with the clients.

FINACHE: You don't say ...

FERAILLON: We can't have that. A man's got to feel safe to bring his mistress here without having her snaffled by the uniformed staff. We've got our reputation ...

FINACHE: Of course you have.

FERAILLON: You must have discipline! Speaking as an old soldier ...

FINACHE: So he's a genuine colonel. [*He sits.*]

OLYMPE: Perfectly genuine!

FERAILLON: Ex-Regimental Sergeant-Major Feraillon of the Twenty-ninth Foot. That's why they call me colonel.

FINACHE: In civil life ...

FERAILLON: Oh, in civil life what's a rank or two, here or there? What do you think, my dear? Number Ten for the doctor?

OLYMPE: Yes ... [*She moves to the stairs.*]

FINACHE [*rising*]: Isn't Number Five free?

FERAILLON: Afraid not.

    [OLYMPE *goes up the stairs.*]

FINACHE: Oh, dear ...

FERAILLON: Number Ten has all the same – facilities.

FINACHE: Number Ten'll have to do.

OLYMPE: I'll get it ready for you.

FERAILLON [*turning and blowing kisses to* OLYMPE]: You do that, my little angel.

[OLYMPE *returns the kisses, and goes.*]

FINACHE: What a perfect gem she is!

FERAILLON: A very genuine type of woman.

FINACHE: I often feel – I've seen her before.

FERAILLON: Oh, yes. Didn't you ever hear of the beautiful Castana? Her they used to call 'The Copper-Bottomed Contessa'?

FINACHE: The name's familiar ...

FERAILLON: She was the Duc de Choisel's mistress – for many years.

FINACHE: Wasn't there a Freemason's dinner, where she was served up stark naked with the pêche melba? On a silver plate – with sponge fingers!

FERAILLON: You've hit it! That's her. That's my wife! I married her.

FINACHE: Congratulations!

FERAILLON: She fell for me when I was a sergeant of the Twenty-ninth. I was a handsome young fellow. Anyway, she always relished something in uniform.

FINACHE: The Copper Bottomed – of course!

FERAILLON: That's it! She – she wanted me to live off her ...

FINACHE: Really?

FERAILLON: I didn't fancy it. Well, she had a bit in the bank, and her powerful attractions, and her reputation of course. I tell you. She was a catch! So, I proposed marriage, and we worked it out that way.

FINACHE: Good for you!

FERAILLON: I made my position quite clear. From now on, I said, orgies are out! And no more gentlemen. I don't know about you, but when I take a wife, gentlemen are definitely out of the question.

FINACHE: I think you're perfectly right.

FERAILLON: Respectability! I told her, from now on. So we opened up this little business.

FINACHE: You're a wise man!

FERAILLON: We live pretty modestly. Putting by for our old age. I was thinking about what you mentioned the other day, life insurance!

FINACHE: You're coming round to it?

FERAILLON: I'm forty-four now, and Madame Feraillon's fifty-two, give or take a little.

FINACHE: Good! They say there should be seven or eight years between a husband and wife ...

FERAILLON: It might be better if the wife was younger ...

FINACHE: If there's no alternative, it's got to be the husband.

FERAILLON: Obviously! Now if I can insure my poor darling, so that when she passes away ...

FINACHE: Insure her! At fifty-two. You'd be much cheaper.

FERAILLON: I don't care which. Just so long as when *she* dies ...

FINACHE: No! It'd be when *you* die ...

FERAILLON: When I die? Oh, I'm not thinking of myself, it's *her* I'm worried about ...

FINACHE: We'll work something out. Come and see us.

FERAILLON: When?

[OLYMPE *comes downstairs.*]

FINACHE: Any morning. I'm there from ten to eleven. The French branch of the Boston Life Assurance Company. Ninety-five Boulevard Malesherbes ...

FERAILLON: Boulevard Malesherbes. Who do I ask for?

FINACHE: Our managing director. I'll warn him.

FERAILLON: Very kind of you.

OLYMPE: Would you like to see the room, Doctor?

FINACHE [*going upstairs*]: Of course I'd like to see it. I'm longing to see it! Let me know as soon as anyone asks for me.

[FINACHE *goes upstairs.* OLYMPE *follows.*]

FERAILLON: Love! It's a beautiful thing!

[SCHWARZ *comes in from his room.*]

SCHWARZ: Haben Sie ein schönes Fräulein für mich?

FERAILLON: Stop doing that!

SCHWARZ: Ein hübsches, kleines Mädchen?

FERAILLON: Shut your hole!

SCHWARZ: Bitte?

FERAILLON: Shut your hole!

SCHWARZ: Schart – ja – hohl?

FERAILLON [*moving to* SCHWARZ]: That's right – I have the honour to request you to shut your hole.

[RAYMONDE *comes into the hotel. She is veiled.*]

SCHWARZ [*shaking* FERAILLON'S *hand*]: Ach so! Jawohl! Schart ja hohl!

FERAILLON: It's a pleasure.

SCHWARZ [*seeing* RAYMONDE]: Ach! Freude!

FERAILLON: At your service, madame.

RAYMONDE: You have a room booked for Monsieur Chandebise?

FERAILLON: This way, madame. [*He goes to the small bedroom.*]

[RAYMONDE *starts to follow, but is stopped by* SCHWARZ, *who dances round her, singing.*]

SCHWARZ: Eins, zwei, drei, vier, fünf, sechs, sieben, acht,
      Neun, zehn, elf, zwölf,
      Ich werde auf dich warten!

[SCHWARZ *dances off to his room.*]

RAYMONDE [*shaken*]: Insane?

FERAILLON: No, madame. Merely Prussian. Here for the Exhibition.

RAYMONDE: Exhibition, cheeky fellow! [*Taking off her veil*] No one's asked for the room yet?

FERAILLON: No. No one. Bless my soul. Aren't you the lady who called this morning. If I'm not very much mistaken.

RAYMONDE: What?

FERAILLON: I knew my tact and discretion would impress you, madame. Testing us out, were you? I thought you planned to bring a customer, but not so soon.

RAYMONDE: Please! Don't imagine that . . .

FERAILLON [*moving to the bedroom door and opening it*]: Say no more. If madame would be so good.

[RAYMONDE *goes into the bedroom.* FERAILLON *follows.*]

RAYMONDE: Huh!

FERAILLON: It's our most comfortable room, madame. [*Moving to the bed*] The bed . . .

RAYMONDE: I don't want anything to do with the bed!

FERAILLON: Oh, well! Pervert! [*He opens the bathroom door.*] Here's the bathroom, complete with hot and cold, bath, bidet, shower . . .

RAYMONDE: Thank you. I have no intention of moving in.

FERAILLON: Well! Now there's this little convenience I'd like to show madame. Comes in very useful in a sudden case of *in flagrante*. On each side of the bed madame will find a button . . .

RAYMONDE: I can see it for myself. Please leave me alone.

FERAILLON: But, madame . . .

RAYMONDE: I don't need you any more . . .

FERAILLON [*moving to the bedroom door*]: Well – all right then. Always at your service. [*He bows and leaves the bedroom.*]

RAYMONDE: Goodbye! Tactless fellow!

[RAYMONDE *goes into the bathroom.*]

FERAILLON: Stuck-up bitch! Poche!

[POCHE *comes staggering downstairs with a log basket. He is Chandebise's double, and played by the same actor.*]

POCHE: Yes, Chief!

FERAILLON: Finished lugging the logs?

POCHE: Report for orders, Chief!

FERAILLON: Get your uniform on. This isn't the place for it. It's time for the customers to arrive. On parade!

[*Number 4 rings on the buzzer board.*]

POCHE: Yes, chief.

FERAILLON [*moving to the board*]: Someone's ringing. It's that Prussian. Go and see what he wants.

POCHE: Yes, chief. [*He puts the basket down and opens* SCHWARZ'S *door.*]

SCHWARZ [*off*]: Herein!

[POCHE *goes.* TOURNEL *comes into the room.*]

TOURNEL: Good evening. Which is Monsieur Chandebise's room?

FERAILLON: This way, sir. Pardon me for mentioning it, but you're not Monsieur Chandebise.

TOURNEL: I'm here to – represent his interests ...

FERAILLON: Oh, yes – the telegram said we were to let in whoever asked for the room in his name. Madame's already there.

TOURNEL: Ah – and how does she look?

FERAILLON: Do you really need my opinion?

TOURNEL: As a matter of fact – I don't actually know her.

FERAILLON: Ah?

TOURNEL: So, before I get involved – what's she like? Long in the tooth?

FERAILLON: Oh, no. Cheer up, sir. She may not have the sweetest character in the world, but she's certainly pretty.

TOURNEL: I didn't come here for her character ...

FERAILLON: Of course you didn't. [*Knocking and going into the small bedroom*] Well, now, here's the room ...

[TOURNEL *comes into the bedroom.*]

SCHWARZ [*off*]: Schnell!

[POCHE *comes in from* SCHWARZ'S *room.*]

POCHE: Coming right away, sir. He asked for a 'shut ya hole'. God knows what this is. I'll give him a vermouth!

[POCHE *picks up the log basket and goes up the central corridor.*]

FERAILLON: No one here! I'll find her for you. [*He knocks on the bathroom door.*]

RAYMONDE [*off*]: Who's that?

FERAILLON: Your gentleman's arrived.

RAYMONDE [*off*]: Good!

FERAILLON [*to* TOURNEL]: Madame's in there.

TOURNEL: Excellent.

FERAILLON [*going upstairs*]: Good luck, sir!

[FERAILLON *goes.*]

TOURNEL: Thanks. Well. This is all very pleasant. Nicely done up. Oh, the bells. If you're bored there's always target practice. Now. I know what's expected of me, but I don't know how to make it *new*. What about ... ? Yes. I'll play a boyish prank. [*He lies on the bed and covers himself up.*]

[RAYMONDE *comes in from the bathroom.*]

RAYMONDE: So! There you ... Well, where is he?

TOURNEL: Cuckoo!

RAYMONDE: Cuckoo. [*Moving to the bed*] You wait!

TOURNEL: Cuckoo!

RAYMONDE [*pulling the coverlet off*]: Take that! [*She slaps Tournel.*]

TOURNEL: Oh!

RAYMONDE: It's not him!

TOURNEL: Raymonde, it's you!

RAYMONDE: Monsieur Tournel!

TOURNEL [*rising and moving towards* RAYMONDE]: If I'd only known. Such a wonderful surprise.

RAYMONDE: What on earth are you doing here?

TOURNEL: What's it matter what I'm doing here? It's a great love story. A girl – is besotted with me. She saw me at a theatre and of course – the lightning struck! She wrote to me, and, out of the goodness of my heart . . .

RAYMONDE: How wrong you are!

TOURNEL: What's the matter, anyway? I don't know her! I don't even love her. But as for you – oh, my dream! My dream come true! There you are! In the flesh! All mine. The Gods are on my side. [*He puts his arm round her waist.*]

RAYMONDE [*moving away from him*]: Take your hands off me!

TOURNEL: No! No!

RAYMONDE: The letter wasn't for you! It was for my husband!

TOURNEL: Oh, come now. That's hardly very likely. I mean, he really is rather unattractive, not to say hideous. It's just that we were sitting together and this girl got us – muddled up and . . .

RAYMONDE: You're wrong again! *I* wrote the letter to my husband!

TOURNEL: *You* did?

RAYMONDE: Absolutely!

TOURNEL: You write love letters – to your husband?

RAYMONDE: I wanted to know if he'd been unfaithful – if he'd turn up here.

TOURNEL: You see! You wouldn't have me because he was unfaithful! He sent me so he's obviously faithful.

RAYMONDE: I suppose that's true.

TOURNEL: You know what he said, when he got the letter, *your* letter – he said, 'What does this woman want with me? Doesn't she know I'd never be unfaithful to my wife?'

RAYMONDE: He said *that?*

TOURNEL: Yes!

RAYMONDE: Oh, I'm so happy! [*She kisses* TOURNEL.] So happy!

TOURNEL [*returning the kiss*]: Oh, Raymonde, my darling. Now – aren't you sorry you ever doubted him? You were wrong to suspect him. And you've no right not to deceive him! Poor dear fellow!

RAYMONDE: Of course – you're right! It was horrible of me to suspect him. My dear Chandebise. It was too bad of me. Please, try and forgive me.

TOURNEL [*encircling her waist*]: Don't apologize. Just be mine!

RAYMONDE [*flopping in his arms*]: That'll be my punishment!

TOURNEL [*kissing her all over*]: Oh, Raymonde. I love you! I love you! Raymonde, my Raymonde!

RAYMONDE [*breaking free*]: Please, Tournel! Let me think for a moment!

TOURNEL [*following and grabbing her*]: Don't think at all! Strike while the iron's hot!

RAYMONDE: Monsieur Tournel! Half a minute ...

TOURNEL: Seize the moment – now, when our senses are inflamed – almost unbearably. We're off! [*Pulling her to the bed*] Come on! Come on ...

RAYMONDE: What? Where are you taking me?

TOURNEL: There – where happiness is waiting for us.

RAYMONDE: What? There! Are you mad? [*Breaking away*] What do you take me for?

[TOURNEL *falls on the bed.* RAYMONDE *moves away.*]

TOURNEL: But I clearly understood that you agreed ...

RAYMONDE: To be your mistress, yes! But not to go to bed with you! Do you think I'm a prostitute?

TOURNEL: Well, what are we going to do?

RAYMONDE: We will have a flirtation. Exchange looks, hold hands. I'll give you the best part of myself!

TOURNEL: Which part?

RAYMONDE: My head – and my heart.

TOURNEL: Oh! Pfhtt!

RAYMONDE: What else had you in mind?

TOURNEL [*rising*]: The thoughts of every true lover. What? When all the forces of nature are drawing us together. When even your husband throws me at you! After all it was your husband who sent me ...

RAYMONDE: My husband!

TOURNEL:. Yes. Your husband. You're the only one who's complaining. Look here, Madame Chandebise, you're in a minority.

RAYMONDE: Monsieur Tournel. Please, calm down!

TOURNEL: Do you think that'll satisfy *me?* Flirting? Exchanging looks? Half of you! And the wrong half ...

RAYMONDE: Monsieur Tournel ... !

TOURNEL: What can I do with your head and your heart?

RAYMONDE: Oh!

TOURNEL [*pacing up and down*]: No! It's a fine look-out for me! Withering in a vacuum! Continually frustrated! My reward? Little walks with madame. Taking the dog out when he feels the urge – to be taken out! Never! No! No! No!

RAYMONDE: Monsieur Tournel . . . !

TOURNEL: No! No! No! Since you don't seem to know the first rules of this game I'll have to instruct you!

RAYMONDE: My dear friend . . .

TOURNEL: Do you think I'll be made a fool of, in front of myself! Do you think I'll creep out of here the same poor idiot I came in . . .

RAYMONDE: Monsieur Tournel . . . please . . .

TOURNEL [*grabbing her*]: Never! You belong to me. [*He pulls her below him and up to the bed.*] And I want you!

RAYMONDE: Now then, Monsieur Tournel!

TOURNEL: No! No!

RAYMONDE [*pushing* TOURNEL *away and kneeling on the bed*]: One step and I ring . . . [*She pushes the button.*]
  [*The bed revolves, bringing on* BAPTISTIN.]

TOURNEL: Oh, ring! Please do! Wear out your finger! No one'll come in here.

RAYMONDE [*as she disappears*]: Help!

TOURNEL [*facing front, taking off his coat*]: You can shout for help all you want! [*Leaping on top of* BAPTISTIN] You're mine! I want you! I'll take you! Oh, Raymonde . . . My pretty one . . . ! Ah! [*He leaps up and grabs his coat.*]

BAPTISTIN: Oh, my rheumatics!

TOURNEL: Whatever's that?

BAPTISTIN: My poor rheumatics . . .

TOURNEL: Who let you in?

BAPTISTIN: What?

TOURNEL [*looking out of the bedroom door*]: And Raymonde. Where's she? Raymonde! [*Returning*] Raymonde! Raymonde! Raymonde! Where are you? She's gone! Vanished into thin air. Come back! Come back to me, my darling! Raymonde! Don't disappear!
  [TOURNEL *goes into the bathroom.* RAYMONDE *enters from the back bedroom.*]

RAYMONDE: Oh, my God! What's happened? Where am I? Monsieur Tournel! Monsieur Tournel! No! I've had enough of this hotel. I'm getting out!
  [RAYMONDE *goes up the central corridor.* SCHWARZ *enters from his room.*]

SCHWARZ: Hallo! Kellner! Hier ist niemand! Kellner! Kellner!

[RAYMONDE *comes back running.*]

RAYMONDE: My husband! My husband on the staircase!

[RAYMONDE *runs off.*]

SCHWARZ: Ach, mein Schatz, Herrlich!

[SCHWARZ *follows* RAYMONDE. POCHE *comes in down the central corridor.*]

POCHE: I can't find the vermouth. I gave it to Baptistin yesterday. [*Going to the small bedroom*] Baptistin. You there?

BAPTISTIN: Here I am!

POCHE: Tell me, old man, what have you done with the vermouth?

BAPTISTIN: In the next room. You know. On the cupboard.

POCHE: Oh, good.

[POCHE *exits into the back bedroom.* TOURNEL *comes in from the bathroom.*]

TOURNEL: No one there! Where is she? Vanished into thin air! [*He moves to the central corridor.*]

RAYMONDE [*off*]: Stop it at once! I don't even know you!

[RAYMONDE *comes in, followed by* SCHWARZ.]

TOURNEL: Ah! [*He comes down stage between them.*]

RAYMONDE: Please stop doing that! Leave me alone!

SCHWARZ: Mein Liebling, geh' nicht!

RAYMONDE: Sex maniac! [*She turns, slaps* TOURNEL, *then goes into the bedroom.*]

TOURNEL: Not again!

SCHWARZ: Danke schön!

[SCHWARZ *clicks heels and goes back to his room.*]

TOURNEL: Bitte, schön. Raymonde! Raymonde! [*He goes into the small bedroom.*]

RAYMONDE: It's all too much. My husband . . .

TOURNEL: Yes.

RAYMONDE: My husband's here!

TOURNEL: Oh, yes. What? Chandebise?

RAYMONDE: Victor Emmanuel. Disguised as a servant. What for? God knows! To spy on us I'm sure of that . . .

TOURNEL: It's not true!

BAPTISTIN: My rheumatics! My poor . . .

RAYMONDE: Ah!

TOURNEL: What?

RAYMONDE: In God's name! What's that?

TOURNEL: What? Oh, him. God knows. Some sort of invalid. He suddenly appeared! What the hell are you doing here?

BAPTISTIN: But you brought me in.

TOURNEL: Did I?

RAYMONDE: Get rid of him! Get rid of him at once ...

TOURNEL: I quite agree. Go on! Get out of here!

BAPTISTIN: If I'm in the way press that button. Then I'll go back where I came from.

TOURNEL [*pressing the button*]: Certainly. Right away.

[*The bed revolves removing* BAPTISTIN *and bringing on* POCHE, *with a bottle*]

RAYMONDE: That's the limit! Bringing on spectators!

TOURNEL: I promise you. I had nothing to do with it.

POCHE: Oi! Oi! What's happening now?

RAYMONDE: Oh, my God!

TOURNEL: Chandebise!

RAYMONDE: My husband. I'm lost ...

TOURNEL: My dear old friend! You mustn't believe all you see!

RAYMONDE: Don't pass judgement before you've heard us out!

POCHE: What's that?

TOURNEL: Appearances are perhaps against us. But we're completely innocent!

RAYMONDE: He's telling the truth! We never expected to meet one another ...

TOURNEL: It was all the fault of the letter ...

RAYMONDE: I started it all. I wrote it because ...

TOURNEL [*kneeling*]: You see? It's perfectly true.

RAYMONDE [*kneeling and putting her hand on* POCHE'S *knee*]: Forgive me! I thought you were deceiving me!

POCHE: Me?

RAYMONDE: Tell me you believe me! That you don't doubt my word!

POCHE: Of course. Of course. [*Laughing*] Have they gone mad?

RAYMONDE: I beg you, Victor Emmanuel! Don't laugh in that horrible cruel way. You hurt me so ...

POCHE: You don't like my laugh?

RAYMONDE: I can see – you don't believe me.

TOURNEL: The circumstantial evidence may be slightly against us ...

RAYMONDE: My God? How can we convince you?

POCHE [*rising and moving towards the door*]: Listen. I'm sorry but I've got to take the vermouth to Number Four.

RAYMONDE [*takes his arm*]: Victor Emmanuel! What's wrong with you?

POCHE: Me?

TOURNEL: I beg of you, my old friend. At a time like this, don't let's speak of vermouth!

POCHE: But Number Four's waiting for it! Look, here's the bottle!

RAYMONDE: Enough of this play-acting. [*She kneels.*] Please. Hurt me! Punish me! Beat me! Anything better than this icy calm.

TOURNEL [*also kneeling*]: Yes! Beat me, too!

POCHE: If you insist. But I assure you, madame ...

RAYMONDE: Madame! Madame! No longer your little Raymonde ...

POCHE: What?

RAYMONDE: Call me Raymonde ...

TOURNEL: Please ...

POCHE: What? All right. [*He kneels between them.*] I'd like to. But I assure you, madame ...

TOURNEL: Not madame. Not like a – business letter.

POCHE: Right! I assure you, Raymonde ...

RAYMONDE: Oh, God! Tell me you believe me!

POCHE: Oh, yes. I believe you.

TOURNEL: At last.

RAYMONDE: Kiss me then, darling. Aren't you going to kiss me?

POCHE: What, me?

RAYMONDE: Kiss me! Then I'll believe you still want me.

POCHE [*moving on his knees to* RAYMONDE]: Oh, I want you all right. [*He kisses her.*]

RAYMONDE: Ah ...

TOURNEL: That's the way!

RAYMONDE: Thank you! Thank you! [*She kisses* POCHE's *hand.*]

POCHE: Lovely silky skin!

TOURNEL [*rising and facing* POCHE]: Me, too! Kiss me, too!

POCHE [*rising*]: You, too?

TOURNEL: Then I'll know you believe me!

POCHE: All right. [*Facing front*] My God, he's a bit keen! [*He kisses* TOURNEL.]

TOURNEL: Now I feel better.

POCHE: Me, too. But I liked it best with the lady.

RAYMONDE: 'The lady.'

POCHE: Now I'm really going to take the vermouth to Number Four.

RAYMONDE [*rising*]: Oh, not again!

TOURNEL: Look, what's this private joke?

RAYMONDE [*stopping* POCHE]: Are you my husband or not?

POCHE: Me? Of course not. I'm the hall porter.

TOURNEL: What?

RAYMONDE: Victor Emmanuel – with a brain-storm!

POCHE: Not at all. Dear lady, it's all perfectly simple. You see, my name's Poche! [*He presses the button.*] If you don't believe me you can ask Baptistin!

[*The bed revolves bringing on* BAPTISTIN.]

RAYMONDE: Baptistin?

TOURNEL: Who's this ... Baptistin?

POCHE: The poor, sick gentleman.

BAPTISTIN: Oh, my rheumatics. My poor ...

POCHE [*sitting on the bed*]: No need to go into all that! Just say who I am ...

BAPTISTIN: Why? Don't you know?

POCHE: It is for the lady's benefit.

RAYMONDE: Yes. Who is this gentleman?

BAPTISTIN: He's Poche, of course.

RAYMONDE
TOURNEL } [*together*]: Poche!

BAPTISTIN: The hall porter.

POCHE: What did I tell you?

[FERAILLON *comes downstairs.*]

RAYMONDE: For heaven's sake. Could it be true?

FERAILLON: Poche! Poche!

[RAYMONDE *moves to the bedroom door.*]

TOURNEL: They can't be twins. It's not possible. It's a trick ...

FERAILLON: Poche! Where are you, Poche?

POCHE [*rising and trying to pass* RAYMONDE]: Here, chief! I'm sorry. Call to arms! My superior officer!

RAYMONDE: Your superior! Now we'll see ...

TOURNEL [*pushing* POCHE *and following* RAYMONDE]: Get out of my way!

[POCHE *sits on the bed steps.*]

RAYMONDE: Please ...

[POCHE *rises and moves to the bedroom door.*]

FERAILLON: Yes?

RAYMONDE [*pointing at* POCHE]: Tell us! Who is this gentleman?

TOURNEL [*pointing at* POCHE]: Yes.

FERAILLON: That's Poche!

POCHE: You see!

RAYMONDE
TOURNEL } [*together*]: Poche!

FERAILLON [*crossing to* POCHE *and kicking him round in a full circle*]: Poche! Here, with a bottle in his hand! You dog's dinner! You animal! You soak!

POCHE: See what I told you?

FERAILLON: You starting up again?

RAYMONDE
TOURNEL } [*together*]: What?

POCHE: But it's for Number Four.

FERAILLON [*taking the bottle from* POCHE *and kicking him round again*]: I'll give you Number Four.

POCHE: Yes, chief.

FERAILLON: Take that!

POCHE: You see –

FERAILLON: And that!

POCHE: – just as I told you –

FERAILLON: And that!

POCHE: – I could only be Poche!

FERAILLON: And get the hell out of here at the double!

[POCHE *goes up the central corridor.*]

So sorry about that. My porter's a sort of alcoholic mess.

[FERAILLON *goes.*]

RAYMONDE: The porter?

TOURNEL: Raymonde!

RAYMONDE: What?

TOURNEL: We have kissed the hall porter.

RAYMONDE: Just what I was thinking.

TOURNEL: I'm shattered! As like as two peas. Is it possible?

RAYMONDE: But – look at what happened. Those kicks! Victor Emmanuel might want to fool me, but he'd surely never stand being kicked up the ...

TOURNEL: Back.

RAYMONDE: Yes.

TOURNEL: Obviously.

RAYMONDE: All this emotion! I'm dry as a bone. For pity's sake – water!

TOURNEL [*searching his pockets*]: Where did I put it?

RAYMONDE: In the bedroom!

TOURNEL [*moving into the bedroom*]: Water! Yes, for God's sake, water. Where's water?

BAPTISTIN: In the bathroom.

TOURNEL: Thanks.

[TOURNEL *goes into the bathroom.* RAYMONDE *enters the bedroom.*]

RAYMONDE: Can you imagine? My husband a hall porter! [*She sits down.* POCHE *enters with a full log basket and moves to the stairs.* EUGÉNIE *comes downstairs.* POCHE *drops a log on the stairs.*]

BAPTISTIN: That's just like life – isn't it?

POCHE: Eugénie, put that back for me.

EUGÉNIE [*doing so*]: There you are, love.

RAYMONDE: I must have water.

[RAYMONDE *goes into the bathroom.* CAMILLE *and* ANTOINETTE *come into the hotel. He is now wearing the palate and his speech is normal. He is holding* ANTOINETTE's *hand.*]

CAMILLE: This way, my little chick. This is the scene of the crime, and your great big Camille's going to love every delicious minute of it. They must have kept us a room!

POCHE: Can I help you, sir?

CAMILLE: Yes, I want to know – Victor Emmanuel!

[CAMILLE *runs into the back bedroom.*]

ANTOINETTE: Sir!

[ANTOINETTE *runs into* SCHWARZ's *room.*]

POCHE [*going upstairs*]: What's wrong with everyone today? They keep calling me Victor Emmanuel.

[POCHE *goes upstairs.* EUGÉNIE *leaves.* TOURNEL *and* RAYMONDE *come in from the bathroom.*]

TOURNEL: Feeling better now?

RAYMONDE: Yes! No! I don't know. All this emotion! I think I'm going to faint.

TOURNEL: Please! Don't!

RAYMONDE: I'm not doing it for pleasure!

TOURNEL: Of course not. [*Taking* RAYMONDE *to the bed*] You ought to lie down a moment. Come on, stretch out on the bed.

RAYMONDE: I won't say no. [*She lies on* BAPTISTIN.]

RAYMONDE ⎫
⎬ [*together*]: Ah!
BAPTISTIN ⎭

[RAYMONDE *jumps up.*]

TOURNEL: Whatever is it? What? You again! You're always here!

BAPTISTIN: But you brought me in!

RAYMONDE: It's too much. Don't argue about it. Get rid of him! [*She moves on to the bed steps.*]

TOURNEL [*pressing the button*]: All right. Now! Back to where you belong!

[*The bed revolves bringing on* CAMILLE *under the coverlet.*]

RAYMONDE: It's very rude to keep whirling into people's bedrooms. [*She falls on to* CAMILLE, *then leaps up.*] Ah ... !

TOURNEL [*catching her*]: Look out! Here!

CAMILLE: What's happening? Help! It's an earthquake! Oh, dear ...

TOURNEL ⎫
⎬ [*together*]: Camille!
RAYMONDE ⎭

[TOURNEL *and* RAYMONDE *run from the bedroom.*]

CAMILLE: I'm terribly sorry. My bed ran away with me.

RAYMONDE: It can't be him. It speaks ...

TOURNEL: It speaks. It's not him! It's not!

CAMILLE [*rising*]: The bed ran away with me!

RAYMONDE: Let's go.

[RAYMONDE *goes up the central corridor with* TOURNEL *following her.*]

TOURNEL: Yes. Let's go!

CAMILLE [*looking through the door*]: Tournel and Raymonde! What're they up to? Suppose they recognized me! What's happened to Antoinette?

[CAMILLE *goes into the bedroom on the left.* RAYMONDE *comes back down the central corridor followed by* TOURNEL.]

RAYMONDE: Etienne! Etienne's here!

TOURNEL: The butler! My God, what a circus!

[RAYMONDE *and* TOURNEL *run off.* SCHWARZ *comes in from the left bedroom pushing* CAMILLE.]

SCHWARZ: Geh' weg! Geh' weg!

CAMILLE: But excuse me, sir ...

SCHWARZ: Ach, verflucht! [*He slaps* CAMILLE's *face so hard that* CAMILLE's *palate falls to the floor.*] Geh' doch weg, sage ich!

CAMILLE [*bending to pick it up*]: My palate! My palate!

SCHWARZ [*grabbing* CAMILLE *by the collar*]: Na, also! [*Kicking* CAMILLE *towards the upstage bedroom*] So eine Unverschämtheit!

[CAMILLE, *kicked by* SCHWARZ, *goes into the back bedroom.*]

SCHWARZ: Ach! Ich bin's, mein Liebling!

[SCHWARZ *goes back to his room.* ETIENNE *comes into the room.*]

ETIENNE: No one about? [*He picks up the palate.*] Quite a nice bit of work. It's damp ...

[EUGÉNIE *comes in and moves to* ETIENNE.]

EUGÉNIE: Did you want something, sir?

ETIENNE: Yes, miss, in the first place I've just found this valuable little object on the floor. For the moment I find its exact nature something of a mystery ...

[CAMILLE *comes out of the back bedroom.*]

CAMILLE: Oh, dear, what has happened to my silver roof?

EUGÉNIE: What a funny looking thing! Sort of ancient Egyptian brooch.

CAMILLE [*facing front*]: My God! Etienne!

[CAMILLE *retreats into the back bedroom.*]

EUGÉNIE: A lady must have dropped it. I'll hand it in downstairs.

ETIENNE: Very right and proper. And now tell me, has there been a lady asking for Monsieur Chandebise's room?

EUGÉNIE: Yes. ...

ETIENNE: And where is – this certain lady?

EUGÉNIE: Oh, I'm not allowed to tell ...

ETIENNE: I've got to see her! Her husband might intrude on her at any moment. He's a fiend and he'll certainly do her in.

EUGÉNIE: Good God!

ETIENNE: I've got to warn her!

EUGÉNIE: If it's like that – I saw her go in there. [*She points down on the left.*]

ETIENNE [*putting on his hat and moving left*]: Good enough! [*He knocks at* SCHWARZ's *door.*]

SCHWARZ [*off*]: Geh' doch weg!

ETIENNE [*opening the door*]: Begging your pardon – my wife!

[ETIENNE *goes into the room. A commotion is heard.*]

EUGÉNIE: What's going on?

[ANTOINETTE *comes in from the left and runs to the central corridor.*]

ANTOINETTE: Etienne. Etienne's here! Help me! Help!

[ANTOINETTE *goes.* ETIENNE *enters.*]

ETIENNE: Stop that woman!

[SCHWARZ *comes in from the left in his underpants.*]

SCHWARZ [*grabbing* ETIENNE *and swinging him round*]: Ach, du dummer Trottel!

ETIENNE: Ow!

SCHWARZ [*shaking* ETIENNE]: Ich werde dich umbringen.

ETIENNE: She's my wife! You've got no business to . . .

SCHWARZ: Na!

ETIENNE: Please. Leave me alone!

SCHWARZ [*throwing* ETIENNE *on the floor*]: Also und jetzt, geh' weg!

[SCHWARZ *goes out stage left.*]

ETIENNE: It's not right. I'm the wronged husband. I'm not the one who ought to be hit. [*He gets up.*]

EUGÉNIE: If you'd told me you were the husband . . .

[POCHE *comes downstairs with the log basket.*]

ETIENNE: You think I knew? It's too bloody much. Me! A gentleman's gentleman! And deceived! You little slut! Just you wait, that's all! Just you wait! [*He turns and sees* POCHE.]

POCHE: What is it?

ETIENNE: Sir – you're – carrying a log basket!

POCHE: Yes. I am carrying a log basket. Why not?

ETIENNE: Oh, sir! My dear sir. I've been deceived. My wife's unfaithful, sir!

POCHE: Bad luck!

ETIENNE: She did it in there, sir. With a Prussian . . .

POCHE: Herr Shutyourhole.

ETIENNE: He didn't tell me his name. But, as you're here, sir. As you don't need my services, may I give chase, sir? May I catch the little devil, and then – and then – I have your permission, sir?

POCHE: Go ahead.

ETIENNE: Thank you, sir. I'm so grateful. [*Moving to the hotel entrance*] Look out, you slut – I'm coming ...

    [ETIENNE *goes.*]

POCHE: I don't know if it's something they've eaten, but it's my opinion they're all barmy.

    [*The buzzer sounds, Room 7.*]

LUCIENNE [*off stage*]: Mind where you're going.

EUGÉNIE: Someone's ringing! [*Moving to the board.*] It's for you!

POCHE: For me – good, somebody wants me! Coming! Coming!

    [POCHE *goes.* LUCIENNE *comes in from the hotel entrance.*]

LUCIENNE: Extraordinary. I could have sworn that was Chandebise's butler.

EUGÉNIE: Can I help you, madame?

LUCIENNE: Oh, yes. Yes. A man nearly knocked me flying on the stairs. Wasn't he Monsieur Chandebise's butler?

EUGÉNIE: That's possible! He asked for a room booked in that name, madame. He said he came to warn a woman to make herself scarce as her husband was after her. And when he met the lady it turned out he was her husband, and he was after her, madame, and – it's a bit of a muddle, quite frankly!

LUCIENNE: I don't understand a word of it.

EUGÉNIE: I'm only telling you what I saw.

LUCIENNE: Anyway – which is the room booked in Monsieur Chandebise's name?

EUGÉNIE: The room boo ... Oh, it's that one. [*She points to the small bedroom.*]

LUCIENNE: Good. I'm going in there ...

EUGÉNIE: That's quite all right. I've been told to let anyone in who asks for it.

    [EUGÉNIE *goes upstairs.*]

LUCIENNE: Thanks. [*She knocks on the bedroom door.*]

    [CAMILLE *enters from the back bedroom.*]

CAMILLE: I do wish I could find my silver roof.

LUCIENNE: Nobody there! [*She knocks again.*]

CAMILLE: Madame Histangua! Oh God! Whatever next?

    [CAMILLE *goes quickly up the central corridor.*]

LUCIENNE [*entering the bedroom*]: No one here? It's not possible. Raymonde said: 'I'll expose my husband between five o'clock and ten past. Come at half past and it'll all be over.' Didn't she wait for me? Let's look in here.

    [LUCIENNE *goes into the bathroom.* CAMILLE *returns.*]

CAMILLE: Victor Emmanuel! It's Victor Emmanuel!

[CAMILLE *goes into the back bedroom.* LUCIENNE *comes back into the small bedroom on the right.*]

LUCIENNE: It's very odd! Never mind, I'm going. [*She crosses the bedroom.* CHANDEBISE *comes in from the hotel entrance.*]

CHANDEBISE: Who should I ask for? Ah ... You!

LUCIENNE: Monsieur Chandebise!

CHANDEBISE: At last, I've found you ...

LUCIENNE: What's the matter with you?

CHANDEBISE: Did you see Etienne by any chance?

LUCIENNE: Why?

CHANDEBISE: Because I sent him to tell you – you see I had a dinner. But then I discovered – my dinner's not till tomorrow! So I – I – rushed here to tell you ...

LUCIENNE: Tell me what?

CHANDEBISE: Oh, my poor child. What utter madness – to fall in love with me. *Me?*

LUCIENNE: *What?*

CHANDEBISE: I do understand. [*Taking her hand*] Of course I understand. Were you afraid to sign your adorable letter?

LUCIENNE: What letter?

CHANDEBISE: The one you wrote to arrange our little – rendezvous?

LUCIENNE: Oh! But what makes you think that was me?

CHANDEBISE: I didn't know who it was at first. But I showed it to your husband and ...

LUCIENNE [*removing her hand*]: You did *what?*

CHANDEBISE: He knew your handwriting at once ...

LUCIENNE: What are you trying to tell me?

CHANDEBISE: Of course, now he's perfectly capable of killing you!

LUCIENNE: Madre de Dios! Where is he?

CHANDEBISE: Probably just about to – breathe down our necks!

LUCIENNE: Our necks! Oh, my God! Don't just stand there! Run away! Help ... !

[LUCIENNE *runs away down the central corridor.*]

CHANDEBISE: Oh, the madness of love!

[CHANDEBISE *goes up the central corridor.* OLYMPE *comes in.*]

OLYMPE: Eugénie! Eugénie! Where's that girl got to?

[CHANDEBISE *returns breathless and appalled.*]

CHANDEBISE: It's him! Histangua. Abandon ship!

[LUCIENNE *comes in.*]

LUCIENNE: My husband! I'm lost!

OLYMPE: What's happening?

CHANDEBISE [*pulling* OLYMPE *round*]: Out of my way!

[CHANDEBISE *runs down the passage on the left.*]

OLYMPE: What?

LUCIENNE [*pushing* OLYMPE *below the stairs*]: Out of my way!

[LUCIENNE *runs to the bedroom and goes into the bathroom.*]

OLYMPE: But, madame ...

[RAYMONDE *comes from the left.*]

RAYMONDE: Oh, let's go! I won't breathe again till we're out of here. Out of my way! [*She pulls* OLYMPE *round in a circle.*]

OLYMPE: Ah ...

[TOURNEL *comes in from the left.*]

TOURNEL: Yes. Quick. This way. But for God's sake – out of our way! [*He pushes* OLYMPE.]

[RAYMONDE *and* TOURNEL *go up the central corridor.*]

OLYMPE: Are we on fire! What's going ... ?

HOMENIDES [*off stage*]: Let me find them! Let me find them! Then I can kill them! Then I can strangle them with my bare hands!

OLYMPE: Now what is it?

[RAYMONDE *comes running in from the central entrance.*]

RAYMONDE: Homenides de Histangua! Out of my way!

[RAYMONDE *pushes* OLYMPE.]

OLYMPE: Ah ...

[TOURNEL *enters and also pushes* OLYMPE.]

TOURNEL: Damned dago! You're always in the way!

[TOURNEL *goes out left.* OLYMPE *staggers.*]

OLYMPE: Oh, dear – oh, dear – what's – what's this?

[HOMENIDES *comes in from the hotel entrance.*]

HOMENIDES: So Tournel with a woman! It must be my wife – the mitherable strumpet!

OLYMPE [*stopping* HOMENIDES]: Excuse me. Where are you going, sir?

HOMENIDES: To kill the both of them. With my bare hands! Get out of my way! [*He pushes* OLYMPE *and goes out left.*]

OLYMPE [*staggering*]: Kill them! Oh, my God! Help! Help! Help! [*She sits down.*]

[FERAILLON *and* EUGÉNIE *come downstairs.*]

FERAILLON: What's all the noise about?

OLYMPE [*rising*]: An escaped lunatic! He says he's going to kill them!

FERAILLON: What?

OLYMPE: Ah – Ah – Aha!

EUGÉNIE [*running to support Olympe from behind*]: Help!

FERAILLON [*moving* C *and pointing up* L]: All right. Take her in there. Give her a whiff of smelling salts.

[*A commotion breaks out downstage left.*]

EUGÉNIE: Yes, sir!

[EUGÉNIE *and* OLYMPE *go out down the passage on the left.*]

FERAILLON [*hurrying to* SCHWARZ's *room*]: War's almost breaking out in there.

[SCHWARZ *enters, pulls* CHANDEBISE *out of his room and spins him so that* CHANDEBISE *bumps into* FERAILLON *on his way across, and lands on a stool.*]

SCHWARZ [*as he pulls* CHANDEBISE *out*]: Geh' doch von meiner Tür weg!

CHANDEBISE: No! No!

FERAILLON: What's going on here?

[SCHWARZ *goes back to his room.*]

FERAILLON [*moving to* CHANDEBISE]: Poche! You back again?

CHANDEBISE [*rising*]: What did you say?

FERAILLON: You useless nitwit! [*He kicks* CHANDEBISE *round in a circle.*]

CHANDEBISE: What are you doing?

FERAILLON: Dog's dinner!

CHANDEBISE: But ...

FERAILLON: A pig could teach you manners!

CHANDEBISE: Listen to me, my man!

FERAILLON: *What?*

CHANDEBISE [*putting on his hat and taking off his gloves*]: I am Monsieur Victor Emmanuel Chandebise, managing director for all France of the Boston Life Insurance Company.

FERAILLON: Tight as a drum! Soaked, sozzled, saturated ...

CHANDEBISE: Sir. [*He strikes him across the chest with his gloves.*] My seconds will call on you.

FERAILLON: Oh, yes? Well, take one of these for each of your seconds! [*He kicks* CHANDEBISE *round in a circle again.*]

CHANDEBISE: Oh – oh ...

FERAILLON: And that for Monsieur Chandebise!

CHANDEBISE: Oh!

FERAILLON: And that! And that!

CHANDEBISE: That'll be quite enough from you! [*He pulls his arm away.*]

FERAILLON [*pulling* CHANDEBISE's *jacket off his shoulder*]: What's the idea?

CHANDEBISE: If you don't mind!

FERAILLON [*turning* CHANDEBISE *round and taking his jacket off*]: This your idea of a joke? Parading in civies?

CHANDEBISE: You're going too far ...

FERAILLON [*taking off* CHANDEBISE's *hat*]: You can do without that as well. [*He moves to coat-rack, hangs up the hat and jacket, and takes down the uniform cap and coat.*]

CHANDEBISE [*facing front*]: My God! It's a raving maniac!

FERAILLON: Get your cap on now! [*He puts the cap on* CHANDEBISE'S *head.*]

CHANDEBISE: No! No!

FERAILLON: And your jacket! [*He gets one of* CHANDEBISE'S *arms in the sleeve.*]

CHANDEBISE: I won't wear it!

FERAILLON: Won't wear your uniform? I'll tell you when to wear your uniform. Get dressed – at the double.

CHANDEBISE: Yes! Yes, sir! [*He puts on the coat.*] Yes ...

FERAILLON: Now! Dis-miss. To your room! Like greased bloody lightning!

CHANDEBISE: Yes, sir. Yes. It's a raving – raving ...

FERAILLON: What did you say? You want another touch of my boot?

CHANDEBISE [*moving to the stairs*]: No! No!

FERAILLON: All right then!

CHANDEBISE [*facing front*]: Maniac! Complete maniac!

FERAILLON: Will you – dismiss!

[CHANDEBISE *runs upstairs.*]

You see! The terrible effect of vermouth! Still dead drunk! It's sad, when you find a decent servant, he has to turn out a hopeless sot ...

[EUGÉNIE *comes in from the passage on the left.*]

EUGÉNIE: Oh, there you are, sir.

FERAILLON: What is it now?

EUGÉNIE: Madame's got the screaming hab-dabs.

FERAILLON: Oh, my God, what's next on the menu I wonder? What do you want me to do about it? What do you take me for? An army nurse?

EUGÉNIE: For Heaven's sake, sir, what are we going to do about madame?

FERAILLON: In case of shock I always recommend a quick slap around the chops. She'll find that very reassuring. Try it.

EUGÉNIE: Thank you very much. I'd get a quick slap back.

FERAILLON: Yes, might do you a bit of good. All right. Run up to Number Ten and ask Doctor Finache to come and look at her. At a convenient moment!

EUGÉNIE: At the double, sir.

FERAILLON: What a bloody nuisance. [*Going out down the passage on the left.*] Now then, my precious. Feeling a little bit seedy, are we?

[*As soon as he is out of sight,* POCHE *comes in singing the 'Marseillaise', and moves to the coat-rack.*]

POCHE: Now – off to the post office. Well! What joker's pinched my uniform? Cheeky bastard! [*He takes* CHANDEBISE'S *hat and coat.*] He's left his hat and coat instead of mine. [*Putting them on.*] Not a bad fit, for going to the post office. I'll give them back when he hands over mine.

[*The buzzer sounds – Number 11.*]

Good! Someone wants me. They do love me here! Coming! Coming!

[POCHE *goes out left.* EUGÉNIE *and* FINACHE *come downstairs.*]

EUGÉNIE [*as she comes down*]: This way, Doctor.

FINACHE: You don't imagine I came here to practice medicine? What's the matter with your mistress?

EUGÉNIE: Nothing much. Just the screaming hab-dabs.

FINACHE: Whatever's that?

EUGÉNIE: A sort of blue fit. She had a fright and ...

FINACHE: A fright? Why not say so?

EUGÉNIE: It froze her blood! Now it's spread to her nerves, I should imagine.

FINACHE: And you interrupted me for that? Get a good big soda-water siphon and give her a squirt. That'll calm her down.

EUGÉNIE: You'd better see her. You've gone to all this trouble ...

FINACHE: Yes, I have!

EUGÉNIE: This way, Doctor ...

[EUGÉNIE *and* FINACHE *go out left.* CHANDEBISE *comes downstairs.*]

CHANDEBISE: The maniac's gone. What I've been through! If that's how he welcomes his guests, I can't see them coming back a second time! What a maniac! [*Moving to the coat rack*] Good heavens! Where's my jacket? And my hat! He hung them there! They've vanished. [*He looks under the table.*]

[RAYMONDE *and* TOURNEL *come in from the left.*]

RAYMONDE: We've given him the slip! Quick, call a cab!

TOURNEL [*seeing* CHANDEBISE]: Yes. Here's the porter.

RAYMONDE: The hall porter ...

CHANDEBISE: What a thing to happen ...

RAYMONDE: Quick, Poche. A cab!

CHANDEBISE: What?

TOURNEL: A cab!

CHANDEBISE: My wife!

RAYMONDE: My husband! It is him. It is ...

[RAYMONDE *runs out up the central corridor.*]

CHANDEBISE: And with Tournel!

TOURNEL: It really is! [*He backs and sits on the stool.*]

CHANDEBISE [*following* TOURNEL *and pushing him down each time he rises*]: What are you doing here? You! What are you doing with *my wife*?

TOURNEL [*rising*]: You know quite well!

CHANDEBISE [*pushing him down*]: What? What do I know?

TOURNEL [*rising*]: We just explained it all to you.

CHANDEBISE: [*pushing him down*]: Oh, yes! You explained it all! What did you explain? Answer me! Will you answer . . . ?

TOURNEL [*rising*]: Now, just a moment . . .

[FERAILLON *comes in from the left.*]

FERAILLON: Haven't we had enough of this bloody row! Poche!

CHANDEBISE: The maniac!

FERAILLON: Poche!

[TOURNEL *goes out left.* FERAILLON *kicks* CHANDEBISE *round in a circle.*]

FERAILLON: You animal!

CHANDEBISE: Eh! Oh! Help!

FERAILLON: Beast!

CHANDEBISE: Oh!

FERAILLON: Pig!

CHANDEBISE [*running to the stairs*]: Now then, my man. Look here.

FERAILLON [*following him*]: Haven't you had enough?

CHANDEBISE: Yes! Yes! Quite enough. Help! Help me! Help! There's a maniac. A raving maniac . . .

[CHANDEBISE *runs up the stairs.*]

FERAILLON [*following*]: I'll give you maniac, you vermouth besotted sponge! Back to your cell till tomorrow morning. Go and sleep it off. Double! Double! And twice as quick as that, you dozy bastard!

[CHANDEBISE *and* FERAILLON *run upstairs.* SCHWARZ *enters from his room, putting on his jacket.*]

SCHWARZ: Verflucht nochmal! Ich muss selbst sehen, ob diese Sache ewig dauern wird!

[SCHWARZ *goes out centre stage.* CAMILLE *enters from the back bedroom.* LUCIENNE *comes in from the bathroom and moves to the bedroom door.*]

CAMILLE: Nobody about. Oh, I do wish I could find my silver roof!

LUCIENNE: It's gone quiet again! [*She moves out of the small bedroom.*]

CAMILLE [*seeing* LUCIENNE]: Madame Histangua!

LUCIENNE [*closing the bedroom door behind her*]: My husband must have gone.

[LUCIENNE *and* CAMILLE *scream on seeing each other.* LUCIENNE *grabs* CAMILLE *by the arm.*]

Oh, Camille – please! Don't leave me. My husband's breathing down my neck. With a revolver! He wants to kill everyone!

CAMILLE: Good God!

LUCIENNE: I beg you. Don't leave me!

CAMILLE: No! No! I won't . . .

HOMENIDES [*off upstairs*]: Where are the wretcheth? Where are you hiding?

[LUCIENNE *and* CAMILLE *scream.*]

LUCIENNE: My husband!

CAMILLE: That's him!

LUCIENNE ⎱
CAMILLE ⎰ [*together*]: Let's run!

[CAMILLE *rushes into the small bedroom and puts his back against the door.* LUCIENNE *runs into* SCHWARZ'*s bedroom.* SCHWARZ *comes in stage centre.*]

SCHWARZ: Ach Mensch! Was für ein hübsches Mädchen!

[SCHWARZ *goes into his room, taking off his jacket,* HOMENIDES *rushes downstairs.*]

HOMENIDES: Where are they? I want to kill them! To slay them both! Just tell me! Where is the room of Chandebise? Is everybody dead?

[HOMENIDES *runs out stage centre.* POCHE *returns.*]

CAMILLE: Who's making all this noise?

[LUCIENNE *comes backing out of* SCHWARZ'*s room.* SCHWARZ *follows her.*]

SCHWARZ: Sei' lieb, mein Schatz. Komm zurück.

LUCIENNE: Kindly stop that suggestive behaviour! [*She slaps* SCHWARZ'*s face.*]

SCHWARZ: Nochmal! Ach, wie ist das scheusslich!

[SCHWARZ *spins round and goes out left of* LUCIENNE.]

POCHE: Good shot!

LUCIENNE [*falling into his arms*]: Monsieur Chandebise!

POCHE: What?

LUCIENNE: God's sent you – to save my life!

POCHE: What's the matter, madame?

LUCIENNE: My husband's after me. He wants to kill me!

POCHE: What's that again?

LUCIENNE: Save me! Save me!

POCHE: Come on, then. This way out.

[LUCIENNE *and* POCHE *go up the central corridor.*]

HOMENIDES [*off stage*]: Ah! Caramba! Caught you!

[LUCIENNE *returns, runs and tries to open the small bedroom door, which* CAMILLE *is barring.*]

LUCIENNE: It's him! Open, please!

CAMILLE: No one's coming in here!

[POCHE *returns.* LUCIENNE *runs stage left.*]

POCHE: Hurry up! Not in there, Herr Shutyourhole.

LUCIENNE: Where then?

POCHE [*moving to the back bedroom*]: In there! Baptistin's room!

> [LUCIENNE *goes into the back bedroom.* POCHE *follows and shuts the door behind them.* HOMENIDES *comes in down the central corridor.*]

HOMENIDES: Don't bother to hide yourselves. I've theen you. Death!

> [EUGÉNIE *comes in and moves to* HOMENIDES.]

EUGÉNIE: Did you want something, sir?

HOMENIDES: I want Chandebise! And the woman with him!

EUGÉNIE [*pointing to the downstage bedroom*]: In there, sir. He's mad!

> [EUGÉNIE *goes.*]

HOMENIDES [*knocking on the bedroom door*]: Open up! So I can kill you!

CAMILLE: Nobody at home.

HOMENIDES: Will you open up! [*As he counts, he shoulders the door three times.*] Uno! Dos! Tres!

> [*On the third count,* CAMILLE *dives to the chair.* HOMENIDES *rushes into the bedroom and through it into the bathroom. There is a crash of glass. Then* HOMENIDES *re-enters and stands over* CAMILLE.]

My wife. Just you give me my wife! So I can kill her. Tho' I can slay her! I'm a dead shot. See that target? [*Indicating the bed button.*] Toro! [*He produces his revolver and fires at the button.*] Bull's-eye!

> [*The bed revolves, bringing on* POCHE *and* LUCIENNE. HOMENIDES, *returning to* CAMILLE, *does not see this.*]

Caramba! When I find her, she dies! Hasta la meurte!

CAMILLE: I promise. I haven't got her. Search me!

LUCIENNE: My husband!

> [LUCIENNE *rushes out of the bedroom and up the central corridor, followed by* POCHE.]

HOMENIDES: My wife! [*He fires at the bedroom door, then rushes from the room.*]

> [FERAILLON *comes running downstairs, meeting* HOMENIDES.]

FERAILLON: Do I hear shots? War's broken out! In my hotel? Now then, what's going on here exactly? Oh, my God, apprehend him! A madman! A stark raving ... Poche! Eugénie! Apprehend him!

> [FERAILLON *and* HOMENIDES *struggle. More shots are fired.* SCHWARZ *returns.*]

Stop the carnage! Ah – got you, my beauty! You're not getting away with this. Police! Send for the police!

> [*During the ensuing chaos,* OLYMPE, EUGÉNIE *and two* MEN *and two* WOMEN *guests rush on from the corridors and down the stairs to join in the turmoil. In the bedroom,* CAMILLE *jumps on the bed and under the coverlet. The bed revolves continuously, bringing on* BAPTISTIN *and* CAMILLE *in turn, both shrieking. All the following speeches are spoken simultaneously.*]

EUGÉNIE:	Barbaric behaviour! Ou uncouth savage, you! Police! Police! Thank God – the maid. Got my orders, have you? Jump to it . . .
	All right, all right – what's the matter now? Good heavens, who's he got hold of there? Look, sir – look. It's the chief – he's got himself in the soup, all right. Oh, no, it's a bit too much. I'm not staying in this monkey house a moment longer, Madame! Madame! Look, sir, Madame! Madame!
1ST MAN.	[to 1st Woman]: Don't be afraid, my little darling. Your Paul's here to look after you. What's going on down there? Will you kindly stop this ridiculous horseplay! What'ee you waiting for? Stop it! Stop it! Mannerless apes. And this is meant to be a quiet little hotel. It'll be a long time before I set foot in here again. Fernande, where are you? Please! Answer me, Fernande . . . Fernande!
OLYMPE:	I thought I heard a noise! Aaaah! Help! Help! Feraillon! He's going to kill me! Help! I can feel it coming on again! I'm about to faint dead away . . . Eugénie! Help me! Eugénie!
1ST WOMAN:	Can't you see? Help! They're going to kill us. To slaughter us – in our beds! I told you I didn't want to come here! Don't shoot – not at me! Not at me. Help! Paul, don't just stand there, save me!
2ND MAN:	Don't make such a noise! Please – try to be quiet. What's happening, exactly? Stop it – come on, this way, we're getting out – come along. Police! Police!
2ND WOMAN:	My husband! I know it's my husband! Oh, please! Edouard, don't shoot! I beg you, don't shoot! Aaaah – it's not him! Help, help! This is the absolute limit! Help!

Eventually, HOMENIDES *is overpowered and forced out up the central corridor.* OLYMPE *faints,* EUGÉNIE *bends over her, the bed stops revolving with* BAPTISTIN *in view screaming, as the lights Black-Out and –*

THE CURTAIN FALLS

ACT III

SCENE – *The Chandebises' drawing-room. Half an hour later.*
   As the CURTAIN rises, ANTOINETTE *enters and moves down stage, doing up her blouse buttons.*

ANTOINETTE: Help! Etienne's back! I'll never have time – I'm all fingers and thumbs! Right! Now we'll see!

ETIENNE [*off stage*]: Antoinette! Antoinette!

ANTOINETTE: Oh! [*She runs to the central doors and bolts them.*]

ETIENNE [*off*]: Antoinette!

ANTOINETTE [*grabbing her apron from the sofa and putting it on*]: Help!

ETIENNE [*off*]: Antoinette! Will you open! The little slut's locked herself in! Just wait!

ANTOINETTE: Quick! [*She unbolts the doors.*]
   [ANTOINETTE *goes and* ETIENNE *enters.*]

ETIENNE: Antoinette! Where's she got to? Antoinette!
   [ANTOINETTE *comes in from the left.*]

ANTOINETTE [*moving to the table*]: Was it you making that extraordinary noise?

ETIENNE: Of course it was. What's the idea? Locking yourself in?

ANTOINETTE: What?

ETIENNE: I want to know why you were locked in.

ANTOINETTE: Me? Of course I wasn't locked in.

ETIENNE [*moving to the centre and opening the door*]: Now look! That's peculiar ...

ANTOINETTE [*picking up the magazines from the table*]: The wonders of science! Etienne learns how to open a door! [*She puts the magazines on the small table.*]

ETIENNE: Never mind. The door's unimportant. Just you tell me – what were you doing at the Hotel Coq d'Or.

ANTOINETTE: What did you say?

ETIENNE: The Hotel Coq d'Or.

ANTOINETTE: What on earth is 'The Hotel Coq d'Or'?

ETIENNE: What on earth? Oh, very good! But I've got you now. It wasn't half an hour ago – that I caught you there . . .

ANTOINETTE: You caught me? *Me?*

ETIENNE: Yes, you!

ANTOINETTE [*sitting on the sofa*]: I haven't moved out of here!

ETIENNE: A likely story!

ANTOINETTE: It's perfectly true.

ETIENNE: I thought you'd do better than that. I mean something like 'It was my long lost twin sister' or 'I just popped in to collect the fish'. But not 'I wasn't there'. Not a barefaced denial.

ANTOINETTE: I can't say what didn't happen.

ETIENNE: You miserable sinner! I saw you with my own eyes . . .

ANTOINETTE [*rising*]: What does that prove?

ETIENNE: Oh!

ANTOINETTE: It doesn't matter to me if you saw me or not. I still wasn't there.

ETIENNE: The nerve! The pure ice cold! So! So, I didn't catch you there? Half naked – all wrapped around by an Alsatian wolf-hound.

ANTOINETTE: Me?

ETIENNE: Yes, you! You! And he didn't get violent with me either, I don't suppose!

ANTOINETTE: Me, with an Alsatian gentleman? It's ridiculous. I don't even speak the language.

ETIENNE: Oh, yes! Very convincing. Certain things are beyond the barriers of language. Certain things – can be explained by signs! So – you weren't being hugged by a Hun?

ANTOINETTE: Never moved out of the house.

ETIENNE: God Almighty! Subtle little bitch! She lies like a respectable woman! So you never moved out of the house? All right. We'll find out.

ANTOINETTE: What are we going to do?

ETIENNE: Ask the concierge.

ANTOINETTE [*moving up to* ETIENNE]: The concierge!

ETIENNE: He'll tell me, if you went out!

ANTOINETTE		
	[*together*]:	You're out of your mind! You can't involve Monsieur Plommard in a ridiculous family squabble. Do you want the whole street to laugh at you?
ETIENNE		That's got you, hasn't it? You didn't think of that. Now you're hooked, clever puss!

ANTOINETTE [*beating on* ETIENNE's *chest*]: Listen, Etienne!

ETIENNE: I'm not listening ... [*He pushes her down stage.*]

ANTOINETTE [*moving below the table*]: Oh, do what you like! [*She leans on the table.*]

> [ETIENNE *moves into the hall, picks up the telephone and leans on the door jamb.*]

ETIENNE: Hullo ... Oh hullo, Monsieur Plommard. Good! ... Slightly odd request, old man, but I need the information. Did you happen to notice what time my wife went out this afternoon? ... What? She didn't go out? It's not possible! ... Perhaps she slipped past you ... What? She had a bite to eat with you. Onion soup! Oh, yes. I see. No one's in for dinner up here so she just popped down. Oh, yes, indeed ... Really? You don't say so ... ?

ANTOINETTE: Five francs – that call cost me!

ETIENNE: I can't understand it! It's incredible ... All right. Thanks, old man. Sorry to bother you. [*He replaces the receiver.*]

ANTOINETTE: And, so ... ?

ETIENNE: Let me alone! What am I? Soft in the head? Short-sighted?

ANTOINETTE: What fools jealousy can make of us!

ETIENNE: Yes ... all right. Go on! Back to the kitchen! We'll talk about this later.

> [*The doorbell rings.*]

ANTOINETTE: Oh, whenever you like.

> [ANTOINETTE *goes. The doorbell rings again.*]

ETIENNE: All right! Just coming. This woman'll stick at nothing. I must keep her under close observation.

> [*The doorbell rings again.*]

I'm coming.

> [ETIENNE *goes through the central door and returns with* RAYMONDE *and* TOURNEL.]

RAYMONDE: Didn't you hear us ringing?

ETIENNE: Yes, madame. I was coming ...

RAYMONDE [*taking off her hat and gloves*]: Monsieur Chandebise not back yet?

ETIENNE: What? Oh, no. No, madame.

RAYMONDE: All right. You can go.

ETIENNE: Yes, madame. [*To the front*] You little – bitch!

TOURNEL: What did you say?

ETIENNE: I wasn't talking to you.

> [ETIENNE *goes up centre, closing the doors.*]

TOURNEL: I should hope not. Well, my dear. Now I've seen you home – I think I'll be off.

RAYMONDE: You're not going to abandon me?

TOURNEL: Well ...

RAYMONDE: Thank you very much! How do we know what Victor Emmanuel's next mood is going to be? You know when we met him in the hotel the second time? You may not have noticed, but he was trying to strangle you! Perhaps he's got a taste for it ...

TOURNEL: You think I ought to stay?

RAYMONDE: I can't face him alone.

TOURNEL: Oh, all right. [*He sits on the sofa.*]

RAYMONDE: You don't sound very keen on the idea.

TOURNEL: Are you surprised?

RAYMONDE: Men are all the same! Ready for anything except responsibility!

TOURNEL: Responsibility for what? Nothing happened ...

RAYMONDE: It wasn't your fault nothing happened. And Victor Emmanuel doesn't know nothing happened. Finding us there he's quite entitled to think – whatever he thinks. And unless he thinks whatever he thinks why do you think he's so angry?

TOURNEL: What I can't understand is – why did he take so long to make up his mind – about what he thinks?

RAYMONDE: Well, yes.

TOURNEL: I mean, when he rolled in the first time, sitting on his bed, swigging vermouth ...

RAYMONDE: Yes ...

TOURNEL: He didn't seem so very shocked! He was really quite glad to see us.

RAYMONDE: He even gave us a kiss!

TOURNEL: Exactly! And then – we see him again in that ridiculous cap and he leaps at my throat. I mean, in these little adventures one usually jumps to a conclusion right away. It's not something that needs mulling over ... for hours and hours ...

RAYMONDE: That's what I was thinking! It's most peculiar ...
    [*The doorbell rings.* TOURNEL *rises.*]
    My God – someone's at the door. Perhaps it's him.

TOURNEL: Already?

LUCIENNE [*off*]: Is your mistress back?

ETIENNE [*off*]: Yes, madame.

RAYMONDE: No. It's Lucienne. [*Opening the door*] Come in!
    [LUCIENNE *enters*]

LUCIENNE: Raymonde, darling. What dramas!

RAYMONDE: Don't I know it!

LUCIENNE [*holding out her hand*]: Look. I'm trembling like a leaf.

[RAYMONDE *takes* LUCIENNE's *hand.*]

RAYMONDE
TOURNEL } [*together*]: Oh!

LUCIENNE: And I can't go home. Never! Never! Oh, hullo, Monsieur Tournel. I'm sorry ...

TOURNEL: Don't mention it. Formalities later ...

LUCIENNE: I'll sleep out under bridges – and railway embankments! Just as long as I never see that wild beast again! No! I should be too frightened to ...

RAYMONDE: Oh, him! That's not a husband you've got, it's a tornado. When he saw us at the Hotel Coq d'Or, Monsieur Tournel and I – I really don't know what got into him; but he chased us with a revolver! Just as if he wanted to kill us.

TOURNEL: Yes, us! Would it be awfully inquisitive to ask why?

LUCIENNE: You mean he was hunting you as well? It's too much ...

TOURNEL: What a firebrand!

RAYMONDE: What a volcano!

LUCIENNE: I'm not out of the wood yet. Luckily your husband helped me to escape. Without him, God knows what'd have happened!

RAYMONDE: My husband?

LUCIENNE: *He* frightened me a bit, too.

RAYMONDE: Why?

LUCIENNE: I don't know if all the worry affected his mind ...

RAYMONDE: You noticed it, too?

LUCIENNE: Most certainly I did! I mean he talked quite sensibly and begged me to go. Then oof! War broke out! We tumbled down the stairs, got to the bottom, and there he was looking most peculiar and saying, 'Who is this Red Skin. Anyone you know?' 'Do I know him? He's my husband,' I said, 'you know as well as I do!' And then he said, 'Who are You? I don't know you.' 'Dear Heaven!' I said. 'There he goes, poor old Victor Emmanuel, unhinged.' Then he started talking gibberish, and I couldn't understand a syllable!

RAYMONDE: He did that to us!

TOURNEL: Exactly the same!

RAYMONDE: Insane!

TOURNEL: Afraid so ...

LUCIENNE: And suddenly – I don't know what crossed his mind! He asked me to wet my whistle! Me! *Me!*

RAYMONDE
TOURNEL } [*together*]: Oh!

LUCIENNE: 'Now steady on,' I said, 'Chandebise.' And he went, 'Poche. Poche.'

RAYMONDE ⎱ [*together*]: Yes. That's what he does. 'Poche. Poche.'
TOURNEL ⎰

TOURNEL: It's his motto.

LUCIENNE: Well! Then, I'm afraid I got cold feet. I left your husband and
 I bolted. Oh, dear – I'm bolting still! [*She sits at the table.*]

RAYMONDE: Oh – what a day!

 [*The doorbell rings.*]

LUCIENNE: Someone – someone rang?

RAYMONDE ⎱ [*together*]: Yes.
TOURNEL ⎰

TOURNEL: Perhaps it's – Chandebise!

RAYMONDE: That'd be odd! He's got a key.

TOURNEL: Sometimes he forgets it.

RAYMONDE: That's true.

TOURNEL: I well remember one time when old Chandebise forgot his key!
 It was winter, and the snow was coming down ...

RAYMONDE: This is hardly the moment for reminiscences.

TOURNEL: Oh, all right.

RAYMONDE: Oh, help!

LUCIENNE: Isn't anyone going?

RAYMONDE: I don't know. But if someone rang ...

TOURNEL: It probably means someone's at the door.

RAYMONDE: Obviously.

TOURNEL: All right.

 [ETIENNE *comes in by the central doors, closing them after him.*]

ETIENNE: Madame! Madame!

RAYMONDE: Well? What is it?

ETIENNE: Oh dear, madame.

RAYMONDE: What?

ETIENNE: The master!

TOURNEL ⎱ [*together*]: The ...
LUCIENNE ⎰

RAYMONDE: Well?

ETIENNE: Well. I don't know what's the matter with the master. I opened
 the door to him, and he came in like *this*, and said, 'Is this where
 Monsieur Chandebise lives?'

ALL: What?

ETIENNE: Yes, madame. Of course I thought, 'Oh, dear me, that's the
 master's little joke.' I thought I'll join him in a bit of harmless fun, and
 I said, 'Ha ha ha,' I said, 'certainly this is where Monsieur Chandebise
 lives.' But he didn't bat an eyelid. He just said, 'Will you tell him that
 I've come about the matter of my uniform.'

ALL: No!

RAYMONDE: We're not going to start *that* all over again? Where is he?

ETIENNE: In the hall. He's waiting ...

TOURNEL
LUCIENNE } [*together*]: What?

RAYMONDE: He's *waiting*?

TOURNEL
LUCIENNE } [*together*]: In the hall?

[ETIENNE *opens the central doors.*]

RAYMONDE: Oh, for heaven's sake!

[POCHE *is seen sitting in the bench in the hall.*]

ALL: Oh!

RAYMONDE: What on earth are you doing there?

POCHE: What did you say?

RAYMONDE: Waiting like a tradesman?

POCHE [*rising and moving down to the doorway*]: Madame?

EVERYONE: 'Madame?'

RAYMONDE: 'Madame.' Oh, do come in ...

POCHE: I'm waiting for Monsieur Chandebise.

TOURNEL
LUCIENNE } [*together*]: What?

RAYMONDE: What did you say?

ETIENNE: You see, madame. What did I tell you?

POCHE [*taking off his hat*]: I remember you! I saw you, at the Hotel Coq d'Or. [*He slaps* ETIENNE'*s chest with his hat.*]

ETIENNE: Yes, sir. That's right.

POCHE: You're the chap whose wife ...

ETIENNE: Oh, please, Monsieur ...

RAYMONDE: What did he say?

POCHE: And you. You as well, madame! You're the lady from the hotel. You're the one that give us the cuddles, aren't you? All right, are you, madame? [*He lurches to* RAYMONDE.]

RAYMONDE: Oh, my God! Tournel! What's wrong with him?

TOURNEL: Steady on, old fellow.

POCHE: And the fancy man! How are you, darling? Give us a kiss!

TOURNEL [*pushing* POCHE *away*]: Now. That's quite enough of that, Victor Emmanuel! Victor Emmanuel!

POCHE: No. Poche! I tell you Poche!

LUCIENNE: You see. Poche. Poche. That's what he does.

POCHE: And you, madame! We were chased by redskins! Can you believe it! We were scared to death ... [*He bangs the table with his hat.*]

LUCIENNE [*running across* RAYMONDE *and holding her hand*]: Yes – weren't we? Quite so . . .

POCHE: And all you birds – live together? In the same nest! Highly comical!

ALL: Oh . . .

POCHE: Did I say something wrong?

ALL: No. Not at all. Nothing . . .

POCHE: Nice family – but a bit simple! [*He paces up and down.*]

RAYMONDE: But what's the matter with him?

LUCIENNE: Poor man. Let the doctor have a look at him.

ETIENNE: Shall I telephone Doctor Finache?

RAYMONDE: Oh, do what you like.

ETIENNE: Yes, madame.

POCHE: You off?

ETIENNE: Yes, sir. Yes . . .

POCHE: All right. But don't forget to tell Monsieur Chandebise.

LUCIENNE: Hear that?

ETIENNE: Yes, of course, sir. Yes, I will . . .

[ETIENNE *goes through the central doors.*]

TOURNEL: Is he playing charades?

RAYMONDE: He's working up to something!

POCHE: You see my uniform was on the peg and . . .

LUCIENNE ⎫
TOURNEL ⎭ [*together*]: Oh, yes? Really?

RAYMONDE: We've had quite enough of this!

POCHE: Ah . . .

RAYMONDE: If you're ill for heaven's sake say so, and we'll get you taken care of. If it's a sort of game then it's very silly.

POCHE: Ah!

RAYMONDE: We've explained everything. We've proved it's mathematically impossible for anything to have gone on between me and Monsieur Tournel. Lucienne will bear us out.

LUCIENNE: Certainly!

RAYMONDE: That ought to be enough! So, if you persist in thinking – whatever you think – well, do as you like. After all Monsieur Tournel's here to answer for himself . . .

TOURNEL: Me?

POCHE: Oh!

RAYMONDE: Absolutely! So whether you believe us or not, at least rise to the occasion! Stop making an exhibition of yourself!

POCHE: Me?

RAYMONDE: Yes, you! When you're confronted with the evidence you take us in your arms and kiss us. Ten minutes later you're trying to strangle Monsieur Tournel!

POCHE: Did I try to strangle you?

TOURNEL: Yes.

RAYMONDE: Do you believe us or not?

POCHE: Of course I believe you.

RAYMONDE: Good! So let's have one big kiss and never mention it again! [*She opens her arms.*]

POCHE [*wiping his mouth*]: Why stop at one? [*He moves to* RAYMONDE.]

ALL: At last!

RAYMONDE [*pushing* POCHE *away*]: Oh!
    [POCHE *treads on* TOURNEL'*s foot.*]

TOURNEL: Ow!

ALL: What's the matter?

RAYMONDE: You've been drinking!

POCHE: What?

RAYMONDE: You smell of drink!

POCHE: Me?

RAYMONDE [*pushing* POCHE *to* TOURNEL]: Try a whiff of that!

TOURNEL: Overpowering!

RAYMONDE: So, you've taken to drink now, have you?

ALL: Oh ... !

POCHE: What me? Drink? Just a couple of swallows to restore the bloodstream and so on. You know how it is. [*He slaps* RAYMONDE'*s stomach with his hat.*]

RAYMONDE: Tight! Completely tight!

ALL: Oh ... !

POCHE: Me? How could you say that? Not a word of truth! And you know it, my girl ... [*He slaps her behind with his hat.*]

RAYMONDE [*pushing* POCHE *away*]: Go away. Go and sleep it off somewhere else.

POCHE: What?

TOURNEL: Oh, Victor Emmanuel! That you should sink so low ...

POCHE [*right into* TOURNEL'*s face*]: No, no, Poche – I tell you, Poche!

TOURNEL: All right, if that's how you want it. [*He pushes* POCHE *away down.*]

LUCIENNE: Oh ... [*She moves up stage to* RAYMONDE.]

POCHE: Yes! That's how I want it! Of course I do! If you all go on like this I'll get really angry.

RAYMONDE: It's disgusting!
    [ETIENNE *enters through the central doors.*]

ETIENNE: Here's the doctor, madame.

[FINACHE *comes in after* ETIENNE.]

ALL: *Ah ... !*

FINACHE: What's the matter? Etienne says he was just telephoning me. Hullo, Chandebise. [*He moves down to* POCHE.]

POCHE: Where is this Chandebise?

FINACHE: Very witty! Ha ha. Yes. What's the matter?

RAYMONDE: Just that the gentleman's dead drunk.

FINACHE: What? *Him!*

ETIENNE: What? Monsieur Chandebise!

TOURNEL
LUCIENNE } [*together*]: Yes.

POCHE: What? *Me?*

RAYMONDE: Just take a sniff. Go on.

FINACHE: It's not true, is it, old man?

POCHE: *Me?* Pffh!

FINACHE: Oh ... !

POCHE: They're joking!

FINACHE [*recoiling slightly*]: Yes, indeed. Strong stuff!

ETIENNE: Oh, sir. *You ...*

FINACHE: My poor, dear friend. What did you drink to get into a state like this?

POCHE: What? You as well! Look here, my good man ...

FINACHE: My good man?

POCHE: You finished your little joke, have you? I'm no more tight than you are!

FINACHE: All right. Now, then, old fellow ...

POCHE: I tell you! [*In* TOURNEL'*s face*] You're driving me out of my mind!
    [TOURNEL *recoils.*]
Ever since I came in at that door my head's been spinning round – [*in* LUCIENNE'*s face*] – like a top!
    [LUCIENNE *recoils.*]
I don't know you! [*In* RAYMONDE'*s face*] What are you trying to do, anyway?
    [RAYMONDE *recoils.*]
I'm here to see Monsieur Chandebise, and – [*in* FINACHE'*s face*] – Monsieur Chandebise I'll see. I've nothing more to say. [*He paces up and down.*]

FINACHE: Oh dear, dear.

RAYMONDE: You see?

LUCIENNE: Just a few lucid flashes and then – pfft!

TOURNEL: He's been like that since this afternoon.

FINACHE: It's a serious attack.

RAYMONDE: Can you believe it?

[POCHE *turns a chair to face the window.*]

TOURNEL: What's he doing now?

[POCHE *makes a rude noise at the others, then sits.*]

LUCIENNE
TOURNEL } [*together*]: Oh!

FINACHE: Any previous disturbances?

RAYMONDE: Never. Isn't that right, Etienne?

ETIENNE: Never.

FINACHE: There are obviously strong hallucinatory symptoms. I would say – an amnesia of a very pronounced degree and a complete loss of contact with his true personality. One finds that with inveterate alcoholics.

ALL: No!

FINACHE: After this, we'll be getting delirium tremens.

ALL: Oh ... !

[POCHE *rises, bangs the table with his hat, and sits again. They all gasp.*]

RAYMONDE: It doesn't make sense! He only has one small glass of cognac after dinner.

TOURNEL: He often leaves half of it.

ETIENNE: And I have to finish it off, to prevent the waste ...

LUCIENNE: One small glass wouldn't make him like that.

FINACHE: In some cases half a small glass of cognac is more than enough! Alcoholism isn't a question of amount, it depends on the idiosyncratic tendencies of the personality factor.

ALL [*except* TOURNEL]: On the *what?*

FINACHE: The personality tends, in a greater or less degree ...

TOURNEL: Yes! To make an idiot of itself!

FINACHE: What? No – certainly not!

TOURNEL: Oh? Sorry, I thought it did.

[As FINACHE *speaks, the others huddle round him.*]

FINACHE: The personality factor regulates an individual's personal re-actions. Some people can absorb a bottle a day – and it doesn't do them the slightest harm; others only need one little glass and poof ... alcoholism!

POCHE: I bet they're saying something nasty about me.

FINACHE: And there, of course, lies the great danger. A glass of cognac after dinner? What's wrong with that? Nothing, apparently! Until the day of reckoning. And then – well, look at the pitiful result.

[*They all form a line again and look at* POCHE.]

ALL: Oh ... !

POCHE: All right, you lousy string of onions! Enjoying yourselves?

ALL: What?

POCHE: You know what I mean! This has got to stop, or it'll all end in tears!

FINACHE: What is it, my poor friend? What's the matter?

POCHE: I'm not a fool, you know!

FINACHE: There! There! Irritable with it, you see? One of the well-known symptoms.

POCHE: What?

FINACHE: Nothing, my dear fellow. Nothing at all. Now then, stretch out your hand.

POCHE: My hand?

FINACHE: Like this. [*Holding out his hand*] Can you manage that?

POCHE: What for? [*He holds out a very shaky hand.*]

ALL: Oh. Look he's got the shakes!

FINACHE: You see that, the alcoholic tremor? Typical of the condition.

POCHE [*stamping his foot*]: Ahaha! Ahaha! Ahaha!

ALL [*recoiling up stage*]: Ahaha?

POCHE [*stamping*]: Stop it! Stop it! *Stop it!*

ALL: Oh, my God!

FINACHE: What's the trouble, old fellow?

POCHE [*continuing to stamp about*]: You want to drive me loony, don't you? That's what you want to do!

ALL: No. Certainly not!

RAYMONDE: Please. [*Taking a pace down to* POCHE *as he passes.*] Keep calm, dear.

POCHE: Piss off! [*He moves away and paces up and down.*]

RAYMONDE: *What* did he say?

FINACHE: Take no notice. They don't know what they're doing during these attacks. This way. We'll try not to excite him. [*He indicates the door.*]

RAYMONDE: He's going too far! It's all jolly fine and large for him to be an alcoholic, but to tell me to pi ... Is that what he told me to do?

FINACHE: What do you expect? He's over-excited. Leave me alone with Etienne. We'll try and get him to bed.

RAYMONDE: Yes. Put him to bed! Because really ...

FINACHE: Yes. Yes. [*Showing* LUCIENNE *the door*] Pardon me, madame.

LUCIENNE: Of course. What a terrible thing – at his age!

[LUCIENNE *goes out stage right.*]

FINACHE: Go along, Tournel.

TOURNEL: Yes. You know, I once saw a very small alcoholic. He was about twelve years old! It was one summer ...

RAYMONDE: For heaven's sake! Tell us another time!

[RAYMONDE *and* TOURNEL *go out right.* FINACHE *and* ETIENNE *look at* POCHE, *then at each other. They move down level with* POCHE.]

FINACHE: Well now, my old friend ...

POCHE: Good thing you got rid of them. It could've led to violence.

FINACHE [*moving to* POCHE]: That's what I felt so strongly.

POCHE: What the hell's wrong with them all? Soft in the turnip?

FINACHE: Exactly. Soft. Yes, quite so. In the turnip.

POCHE [*gesticulating*]: What did I tell you?

[FINACHE *tries to hold* POCHE's *gesticulating hand.*]

ETIENNE: Soft, sir. In the turnip as you say.

POCHE: You should've tipped me the wink. You know, just whispered, 'They're all cracked.' Are you trying to hold my hand?

FINACHE: Pure friendship, old fellow.

POCHE: Oh, well – it's no good getting angry with them. You've got to humour the poor devils.

FINACHE: Damned odd. Hardly ticking over.

POCHE: What?

FINACHE: I've been listening to your pulse. Nothing doing. He's hardly ticking over.

POCHE: Of course not! [*Slapping* FINACHE *on the stomach with his hat*] No ticks on me at all!

FINACHE [*following* POCHE]: Oh, riotously funny! Oh, yes, irresistible. [*He signs to* ETIENNE *to laugh.*] Ha! Ha! Ha!

ETIENNE: Ha! Ha! Ha! Ha! Ha! [*He follows* FINACHE.]

POCHE: At least we made the flunkey laugh!

FINACHE: Oh, yes. Very quick. Delightful pun! And now we've had a good laugh we must try and be sensible – again.

POCHE: What?

FINACHE: I'm your old friend. You know me.

POCHE: No!

FINACHE: All right. I'm the doctor! The nice, kind doctor! Who looks after you all! Little aches and pains? Touch of the collywobbles ... That's when the Medicine Man comes to call.

POCHE: So, you're a doctor.

FINACHE: You've got it! [*He nods to* ETIENNE.]

POCHE [*facing front*]: Why is he acting so childish?

FINACHE: Now looking at you – I can tell – I can tell ... You must be quite exhausted ...

POCHE: Me?

FINACHE: Yes. You're exhausted. [*To* ETIENNE] He's exhausted!

POCHE: Exhausted! What do you expect? Up at five. Sweep out. Polish the floors. Lug up the logs ...

FINACHE: Naturally. Naturally.

ETIENNE: Naturally.

POCHE: Naturally!

FINACHE: So why not get your clothes off and pop straight into bed?

POCHE: Bed? Certainly not!

FINACHE: All right. At least slip out of that jacket and let Etienne bring you a nice comfortable dressing-gown!

POCHE: All right. But my uniform ...

FINACHE: Just while you're waiting for it to arrive. Etienne!

ETIENNE: Yes, Doctor.

[ETIENNE *goes out stage left.* FINACHE *takes* POCHE *by the shoulders and sways him to and fro.*]

FINACHE: Now. There we are! There's a lovely bed in there ...

POCHE: Why can't he keep still?

FINACHE: Wouldn't you like to stretch out in there?

POCHE: He's making me seasick.

FINACHE: And have a delicious forty winks.

POCHE [*breaking free*]: Me? Don't be stupid. What about Monsieur Chandebise?

FINACHE: Monsieur Chandebise? Oh! Good Heavens! If he says anything to you about it, come and tell me.

POCHE: Oh, all right ...

[ETIENNE *returns with a dressing-gown.*]

ETIENNE: Here's the dressing-gown.

FINACHE [*turning* POCHE *round and removing his jacket*]: Now. Off with that nasty old jacket.

POCHE: This doesn't mean you've got permission to do just what you like with me!

[ETIENNE *helps* POCHE *to put on the dressing-gown.*]

FINACHE: There's a good chap! Don't say that doesn't feel better.

POCHE: Do I look like the Pope at all?

FINACHE [*handing the jacket to* ETIENNE]: There. You see ...

[ETIENNE *puts the jacket on the chair above the table.*]

POCHE: Better quality stuff than my uniform.

FINACHE: Certainly is! And now a little bird keeps telling me that you're getting thirsty.

POCHE: Oh. What a sly little bird!

FINACHE: Isn't she? So, I'm going to give you a little drink. It may taste just a tiny bit disgusting, but I want you to gulp it all down.

POCHE: Strong stuff?

FINACHE: What? Oh, yes – strong stuff ...

POCHE: Come on then. I can manage it!

FINACHE: Good man. You got some ammonia?

ETIENNE: I think so, sir.

POCHE: What a godsend!

FINACHE: Right. We'll give him ten drops in a glass of water.

ETIENNE: Yes, sir.

FINACHE: And when he comes to, you make him take – I'll give you a prescription ...

ETIENNE: Yes, sir.

FINACHE: Where's something to write with?

ETIENNE: Over there.

FINACHE: Good. But first put him to bed. [*He sits at the desk.*]

ETIENNE: Yes, Doctor. Now, sir. [*Moving to* POCHE] If you'd like to step this way. Take my arm, sir.

> [POCHE *rises and takes* ETIENNE's *arm.*]

POCHE: You're not a bad lad, are you?

> [FINACHE *prepares to write.*]

ETIENNE: You're very kind to say so, sir.

POCHE: Quite a decent individual in fact.

ETIENNE [*opening the door*]: Thank you, sir, thank you very much.

POCHE: Pity you married a tart.

> [POCHE *goes out stage left.* ETIENNE *follows.*]

FINACHE: My God! What a stench! Talk about perfumed writing paper! Strong smell of maids' bedrooms! Must be Camille.

> [CAMILLE *comes in through the central doors. He has not yet recovered the palate.*]

CAMILLE: You – oh, Doctor! I'll never forget your hotel! What hasn't happened!

FINACHE: Don't talk so fast.

CAMILLE: If you knew ...

FINACHE: Put your palate in! After all the trouble I went to!

CAMILLE: I've lost my palate.

FINACHE: What?

CAMILLE: A horrible Hun person knocked it out when he punched me! In the chops!

FINACHE [*scarcely understanding*]: A Hun punched you in the chops?

CAMILLE: If that'd been all. Oh, it's been a nightmare! And who did I happen to bump into? Tournel! And Raymonde! And Chandebise with a load of logs! Why a load of logs in the name of God? And Madame Homenides, and her husband after her with a pistol. Bang! Bang! I saw them all! What tragedies! My God! What disasters! [*He sits at the table.* ANTOINETTE *enters stage right.*]

ANTOINETTE: The mistress wants to know if the master's any better.

FINACHE [*rising*]: Oh. Tell her he's a little better. No. I'll tell her my-self ...

CAMILLE: Now what's happened?

FINACHE: Nothing much. Chandebise's a little under the weather.

CAMILLE: There you are!

[ETIENNE *comes in stage left.*]

ETIENNE: He's in bed.

FINACHE: Good!

ETIENNE: Good evening, Monsieur Camille.

CAMILLE: Hullo, Etienne.

FINACHE: Right, Etienne. Get the ammonia ready while I go and see your mistress.

[FINACHE *goes out right, followed by* ANTOINETTE.]

ETIENNE: Yes, Doctor.

[ETIENNE *goes.* CAMILLE *rises.*]

CAMILLE: Helpless! That's what I am! A useless pawn! A little bit of fluff, caught up in a whirlwind.

[*There is a knock on the door stage left.*]

Oh, come in! I'm about to lose my reason!

[POCHE *comes in from the left.*]

POCHE: Excuse me ...

CAMILLE: Victor Emmanuel!

POCHE: Here's a young man I caught sight of at the Hotel Coq d'Or.

CAMILLE: Now for it ...

POCHE: Another one, in fact.

CAMILLE: He recognized me. I'll explain. [*Moving to* POCHE] If I was there it was for a reason. As a matter of fact it was for a very good reason. I'd heard that a certain lady there ...

POCHE: Got something stuck in his gullet.

CAMILLE: What?

POCHE [*slapping* CAMILLE *on the back*]: Cough it up, old man. Spit it out, whatever it is ...

CAMILLE: I haven't got anything stuck in my gullet. I was telling you there was a lady there interested in life insurance.

POCHE: I'm not interested in all that. I'm dying of thirst. They said they'd bring me a drink but it's my view they've totally forgotten me.

CAMILLE: Who has?

POCHE: Hoo har?

CAMILLE: Hoo har!

POCHE: Oh, who has? Hoo har! The doctor.

CAMILLE: Oh. I'll see to it at once. [*He moves up stage.*]

POCHE: You're a good lad!

[POCHE *winks and exits left.*]

CAMILLE: Good lad! Extraordinary. I thought I'd be covered with abuse. He almost congratulated me. I was wrong about Uncle Victor Emmanuel. I thought the old boy had a narrow mind. It's as broad as can be. [*He sees* CHANDEBISE *approaching.*]

[CHANDEBISE *enters through the central doors.*]

CHANDEBISE: What is it?

CAMILLE: Oh, my God! There! There!

CHANDEBISE: What on earth?

[CAMILLE *bangs the table.*]

CAMILLE: I'm losing my reason!

CHANDEBISE: Camille – for heaven's sake!

CAMILLE: I've gone mad! Mad ...

[CAMILLE *goes out stage centre.*]

CHANDEBISE: Delirious! It's infectious today. That hotel – what a nightmare! [*Seeing his jacket on the chair above the table*] My jacket! [*He takes off his uniform and hat and starts to put on his jacket, moving up to the table.*] I wonder who brought it back? At last I can get out of this ridiculous uniform. Having to come back in that get-up! The porter showed me to the servants' entrance!

[CAMILLE *and* ETIENNE *enter stage centre.*]

CAMILLE: Etienne! I've gone mad ...

[CAMILLE *goes out right.*]

CHANDEBISE: Why does he keep doing that?

ETIENNE: What's the matter with Monsieur Camille?

CHANDEBISE: Etienne! I can't imagine.

ETIENNE: Sir! You recognize me!

CHANDEBISE: Don't be silly! Why shouldn't I recognize you?

ETIENNE: No reason. Of course, sir. No reason at all.

[ETIENNE *makes a dignified exit.* CAMILLE *comes back.*]

CAMILLE: There's two! I tell you. Two of them. Look. There! There!

[RAYMONDE, TOURNEL, FINACHE *and* LUCIENNE *return from the right.*]

ALL [*as they enter*]: What? Where?

CAMILLE: I'm mad! That's what it is. Mad!

[CAMILLE *goes again.*]

ALL: What's the matter with him?

RAYMONDE: It's us, my dear. We've come to see you ...

CHANDEBISE: You! Here, madame? And your paramour?

RAYMONDE
TOURNEL } [*together*]: What?

[*During the following speeches,* CHANDEBISE *grabs* TOURNEL *by the lapels and pushes him round the table.* FINACHE *and* RAYMONDE *follow them, ending up in their former positions.* LUCIENNE *also follows.*]

CHANDEBISE: So, what are you doing, eh? What were you doing when I caught you – in that disorderly house?

ALL: Oh!

RAYMONDE: Not again!

TOURNEL: But my dear chap, we've explained it a hundred times.

CHANDEBISE: Explained – what? Get out! You think you can go on pulling the wool over my eyes for ever! Out of my house!

RAYMONDE: Now, dear . . .

CHANDEBISE: Out of my house!

LUCIENNE: Look here, Monsieur Chandebise . . .

CHANDEBISE: Not you, dear lady. [*To* TOURNEL] But *you*. I never want to set eyes on you again! [*He moves and stands in front of the window.*]

FINACHE: Come along, everyone. Don't excite him! He's clearly in the middle of a fit! You can come back when it's over.

RAYMONDE: His fits! I've really had enough of his fits . . .
    [RAYMONDE *goes out right.*]

FINACHE: Come along. Come along. Tournel. Please.
    [LUCIENNE *goes out right.*]

TOURNEL: He's berserk. Changes his mind every five minutes . . .
    [TOURNEL *goes out right.*]

FINACHE: Now then, my dear fellow. What's the matter now?

CHANDEBISE: I'm sorry, Finache. I lost my temper!

FINACHE: It was an outlet for your inner frustrations. A catharsis! Probably did you good.

CHANDEBISE: It should've done me good.

FINACHE: Of course. You're already a bit more rational. You can recognize people. You have an idea of your own identity.

CHANDEBISE: What?

FINACHE: You're coming on! Coming on!

CHANDEBISE: Recognize people – idea of my own identity . . . No. Not you, too!

FINACHE: What?

CHANDEBISE: Aren't I in the habit of recognizing people?

FINACHE: Oh, I wouldn't say you weren't but . . .

CHANDEBISE: I may lose my temper, but I'm not out of my head you know!

FINACHE: Of course not. Of course not . . .

CHANDEBISE: Ah.

FINACHE: No, no, no, no no! All the same . . . not that it really matters,

I don't think we should have got out of bed quite so soon, should we?

CHANDEBISE: *What?*

FINACHE: And why did we have to put on our jacket again?

CHANDEBISE: Because I'm tired of running around looking like a com-missionaire.

FINACHE: Like a com – commissionaire. Oh, I see ...

CHANDEBISE: Perhaps you'd find it amusing to go about in fancy dress?

FINACHE: Oi, oi, oi! Oi, oi, oi!

CHANDEBISE: But not me! I hate uniforms ...

FINACHE: An obsession.

CHANDEBISE: I certainly saw life at your Hotel Coq d'Or.

FINACHE: You went there then?

CHANDEBISE: I went there!

FINACHE: You shouldn't have gone!

CHANDEBISE: Well, I went! What a joy-ride! Punched by one of them – kicked by another! The owner a raving maniac! He shoved me into uniform! Locked me into a room – so I had to escape across the roof! Nearly broke my neck! And to top the lot, Homenides. Ho-me-ni-des! There can't be any disaster left! I've lived through them all!

FINACHE: Oh, my God. How sick he is!

[ETIENNE *returns with a glass of water and ammonia.*]

CHANDEBISE: I'll never forget it ...

ETIENNE: Here we are!

CHANDEBISE: What have you got there, Etienne?

ETIENNE: Oh! Just something for the doctor.

FINACHE: Yes. For me.

CHANDEBISE: Oh, good.

FINACHE: Thanks. [*He puts some drops in the glass.*]

[CHANDEBISE *paces up and down.*]

ETIENNE: Is it all right, Doctor?

FINACHE: Two – three – What?

ETIENNE: The master's better?

FINACHE: Afraid not.

ETIENNE: Not better?

FINACHE: Oh, dear, no. Six – seven ...

ETIENNE: Oh ...

FINACHE: Delirious. Quite delirious. Ten.

CHANDEBISE: You in some sort of pain, Doctor?

FINACHE: No. No. [*Moving to* CHANDEBISE *with the glass*] Now. Drink this up!

CHANDEBISE: Me?

FINACHE: It'll set you up. After all you've gone through.

CHANDEBISE: All right. [*Taking the glass*] Losing my temper quite exhausted me.

FINACHE: Of course it did. All in one gulp now! You may find it a little strong ...

CHANDEBISE: Oh, yes ... [*He drinks as* FINACHE *instructs him.*]

FINACHE: Big swallow now! Swallow! Don't say I didn't warn you! Down it goes ... !

CHANDEBISE: Ah ... [*He gasps, gives* FINACHE *the glass, runs to the window, opens it, and spits the liquid out.*]

ETIENNE: Oh!

FINACHE [*running after Chandebise*]: Oh!

CHANDEBISE: Doctor! I call that a joke, in quite appalling taste ...

FINACHE: Look now, Chandebise.

CHANDEBISE [*pushing* FINACHE *aside*]: Oh, let me alone – you great oaf!

FINACHE: Where are you going?

CHANDEBISE: To wash my mouth out! Do you think I want to savour the bouquet?

[CHANDEBISE *goes out left. The doorbell rings.*]

ETIENNE: Someone's ringing!

[ETIENNE *goes out of the central doors.*]

FINACHE: All that work for nothing. He spat it out! [*He puts the glass on the table.*]

FERAILLON [*off*]: Is Monsieur Chandebise at home?

ETIENNE [*off*]: This way, sir.

FINACHE: Good heavens – Feraillon ...

[FERAILLON *appears at the central door.*]

FERAILLON: Doctor!

[ETIENNE *appears behind* FERAILLON.]

FINACHE: Come in then.

FERAILLON: May I?

[ETIENNE *closes the doors.*]

FINACHE: Did you call about your insurance?

FERAILLON: Not that, Doctor. Any time'll do for that. [*Producing the palate*] No. I found this – object – in my hotel, which I take to be the property of Monsieur Camille Chandebise.

ETIENNE: *I* found that – I ...

FERAILLON: Sir?

ETIENNE: I'm Etienne. Monsieur Chandebise's butler.

FERAILLON: Charmed, naturally.

FINACHE: Show me. It's his palate! He lost it when he went out! How did you deduce it was his?

FERAILLON: It's got his name and address on it.

FINACHE: No! Oh, yes. Camille Chandebise, Ninety-five Boulevard Malesherbes. Clever idea that!

FERAILLON: Must be useful. If you've run out of visiting cards you just – leave the roof of your mouth . . .

FINACHE: I'll give it to him. He'll be relieved.

[ANTOINETTE *comes in at the central doors and moves between* FERAILLON *and* FINACHE.]

ANTOINETTE: Doctor! Doctor! Something's come over Monsieur Camille. I found him in the bathroom stark naked, in a cold shower. Singing the *Marseillaise*.

[ANTOINETTE *and* ETIENNE *move upstage talking together.*]

FINACHE: Well, whatever next!

FERAILLON: The *Marseillaise!*

FINACHE: You're right. It's madness! You see how he carries on, your precious Monsieur Camille? Singing the *Marseillaise* in the shower! No one has any sense. Where is he?

ANTOINETTE: This way, Doctor.

[ANTOINETTE *goes out by the central doors.*]

FINACHE: There's a plague in this house. Take me to the bathroom.

[FINACHE *goes.*]

FERAILLON: The *Marseillaise* under a cold shower? Curious behaviour! [*Picking up the cap and showing it to* ETIENNE] Poche's uniform, if I'm not very much mistaken! Beautiful cap this – but what's it doing here? Has my porter been around here?

[CHANDEBISE *comes in from the left.*]

ETIENNE: Your porter? No, why?

FERAILLON: My God – there he is!

CHANDEBISE: Revolting taste!

FERAILLON: Here, Poche. Just you come here!

CHANDEBISE: The maniac! In my house! [*He runs,* FERAILLON *chases him around the table.*]

FERAILLON: Oh, you great animal! What're you doing here?

CHANDEBISE: Oh, help! Help – help!

FERAILLON: So – proud of your uniform, are you?

CHANDEBISE: Help! Help!

ETIENNE: Sir! What are you doing?

FERAILLON: Dismiss!

CHANDEBISE: No! Help! Help! Help! Hold him tight!

[CHANDEBISE *escapes up centre, closing the doors.* ETIENNE *holds* FERAILLON.]

FERAILLON: Just let me go. [*He breaks from* ETIENNE *and moves up stage, picking up the hat and coat from the table. Off stage we hear a door slam.*]

ETIENNE: That's Monsieur Chandebise, my master!

FERAILLON: That's your master? It's my servant! I know him of old.

[FERAILLON *goes through the central doors.*]

ETIENNE: No, it's not! It's not!

[ETIENNE *goes out centre stage. There is another door-slam off.* CHANDEBISE *comes in from the right.*]

CHANDEBISE: Is the coast clear? I had the happy idea of banging the front door. He thinks I've gone out and he's busy chasing me down the street. [*He sits on the sofa.*] Thank God, he's gone.

ETIENNE [*off*]: I will announce you, sir, as is my custom.

HOMENIDES [*off*]: I will go in! I tell you, I will pass!

CHANDEBISE [*rising*]: What's happening?

[HOMENIDES *comes in through the central doors and points at* CHANDEBISE.]

HOMENIDES: Him!

CHANDEBISE: Homenides! [*He starts to move away.*]

HOMENIDES: Don't move!

CHANDEBISE [*turning to face him*]: How are you, dear friend?

HOMENIDES: Not dear friend any more! [*He takes off his hat and puts it with his stick and gloves on the sofa.*] You have escaped so far. But now we face each other. If it hadn't been for the idiots who took me to the police station – you might have already made the acquaintance of a revolver! But the police inspector took it away. He made me swear – never to use a revolver again! I gave him – my word of honour!

CHANDEBISE: You did? Very sensible. A sound fellow, that police inspector.

HOMENIDES: My word of honour – no revolvers! So now I have brought pistols instead. [*He pulls out two pistols.*]

CHANDEBISE: What?

HOMENIDES: Don't worry! I'm not going to slay you now. The moment for that was when I found you having – what do you French call it? – a *flagrante delighto*.

CHANDEBISE: I know what you mean.

HOMENIDES: Now it would be murder! That would be dangerous.

CHANDEBISE: I quite agree.

HOMENIDES: I have here – two pistols. One loaded – one not.

CHANDEBISE [*stepping to Homenides*]: Good! I'll take the first one ...

HOMENIDES: Oi – gar!

[CHANDEBISE *steps back.*]

[*Taking a piece of chalk from his pocket and moving to* CHANDEBISE] I take the chalk – and just draw a circle round your heart.

CHANDEBISE: Please – my best suit!

HOMENIDES [*backing away*]: I do just the same! [*He makes a circle on his own heart.*]

CHANDEBISE: He must be a tailor.

HOMENIDES: We each take a pistol and fire at the bull's-eye! [*Levelling the first pistol*] Bang! [*He levels the second pistol.*] Whoever gets the bullet – *muerte*! Dead!

CHANDEBISE [*moving to* HOMENIDES]: What about the other one? [*He steps back.*]

HOMENIDES: And so – we duel in my country.

CHANDEBISE: Most interesting, but . . .

HOMENIDES [*moving to* CHANDEBISE]: Take one.

CHANDEBISE: What?

HOMENIDES: Take one, I tell you! Take one!

CHANDEBISE [*backing away*]: I never take anything between meals!

HOMENIDES [*moving to* CHANDEBISE]: Take one! Or I'll kill you!

CHANDEBISE: He's not joking! Oh, my God – help! Help!

    [CHANDEBISE *runs out of the central doors, closing them after him.*]

HOMENIDES [*following*]: Chandebise. Will you come back! *Will you!*

    [HOMENIDES *goes after* CHANDEBISE, *leaving the doors open.*]

CHANDEBISE [*off*]: Help! Help!

HOMENIDES [*off*]: Come back! Wait . . .

    [CHANDEBISE *comes in stage right.*]

CHANDEBISE: Help! Help! Aaah! I'm asleep in my bed! We're haunted, the house is full of spirits . . .

HOMENIDES [*as he enters*]: Where is the miserable coward – wait a minute, wait a . . .

CHANDEBISE: Help! Help!

    [CHANDEBISE *goes out centre, shutting the doors.*]

HOMENIDES [*moving to the doors, finding them locked, and banging on them*]: Open, miserable coward! Will you open – hey, Chandebise! You think you're safe because you lock the door, but you don't know me. When I set out to do something I see it through to the end, and if I have to break down every door in the house I shall do it. You hear me, Chandebise? I'm going to break down the . . .

    [POCHE *comes in from the left.*]

POCHE: Who's making all this noise? How do you expect me to sleep?

    [HOMENIDES *locks the door on the left, and moves below the table.*]

HOMENIDES: You won't escape me now.

CAMILLE: My God, the redskin!

HOMENIDES [*holding out the pistols*]: Take one, so I can kill you!

POCHE: What? Help! Help! [*He tries the central doors and then the door on the right. They are locked. During the following dialogue,* POCHE *moves to*

the sofa. HOMENIDES *chases him round it.* POCHE *goes through the french*
window and dives off the balcony.]

HOMENIDES: Stand your ground!

POCHE: Help! Help!

HOMENIDES: Take your medicine!

POCHE: Medicine! Help! Help!

HOMENIDES: Advance two paces and fire!

POCHE: Help! Help! Help! Aaaaaahh!

[HOMENIDES *follows* POCHE *to the window and looks out.*]

HOMENIDES: Oh, poor man – he's going to kill himself! No! He's all right.
So – I'll kill him! Si! Slay him! I need a drink. [*He moves to the table, picks*
up the glass, and drinks.] Ah! Porrah! [*He runs to the window and spits*
it out.] Another filthy French drink! [*He moves to the desk and leans on*
the chair in front of it.] A filthy French perfume! The perfume of the
letter. The perfume of my wife. [*He picks up a piece of notepaper.*] The
paper's the same. And her writing. [*Reading*] 'Dear Sir, having noticed
you the other evening at the Palais Royal . . .' The twin brother of the
letter to the husband. Why is it here? In Señora Chandebise's writing-
case? [*Unlocking the right hand door and knocking*] I want to know!

[TOURNEL *comes in from the right.*]

HOMENIDES [*grabbing* TOURNEL *by the lapels and swinging him round*]: I
want to know!

TOURNEL: Stop it! No more cowboys and Indians.

HOMENIDES: The letter!

TOURNEL: Oh, let me go!

[RAYMONDE *comes in from the right.*]

RAYMONDE: Now what is it?

HOMENIDES [*pushing* TOURNEL *away and turning to face* RAYMONDE]: No
– you! I found the letter in your papers.

RAYMONDE: You've been rifling my letters!

HOMENIDES: And found my wife's handwriting! That's the point.
Why?

RAYMONDE: Well, now . . .

HOMENIDES: This is where she makes up love letters!

RAYMONDE: Yes. This is where she does it! And then you go and get
hold of the wrong end of the stick. Now you can see – it's all quite
innocent.

HOMENIDES: So – ow?

RAYMONDE: What do you mean: 'so – ow?' Do you think if she was
carrying on a secret romance with my husband I'd let her write to him
on my mauve writing-paper?

TOURNEL: Out of her writing-case?

[LUCIENNE *comes in from the right.*]

HOMENIDES: Egthplain!

RAYMONDE: Egthplain. Egthplain. Here's your wife! Ask her yourself!

HOMENIDES [*moving up to* LUCIENNE]: Tell me, madame ...

LUCIENNE: My husband!

HOMENIDES: Please. Wait a moment. With one word – you can bring peace to my heart. The letter – that letter!

LUCIENNE: What?

HOMENIDES: I found it *there.* [*He points to the desk.*] Why?

LUCIENNE: It's not my secret.

RAYMONDE: Oh, tell him the answer to the riddle! He's like a bear with a sore head.

LUCIENNE: You want me to?

RAYMONDE: Go on.

LUCIENNE: All right. You're as bad as Othello and that stupid handker-chief! Couldn't you understand? What a clown the man is! Raimunda creía tener motivo de dudar de la fidelidad de su marido. [RAYMONDE *thought her husband was unfaithful.*]

HOMENIDES: Como? [*Why?*]

LUCIENNE: Entonces para probarlo decidio darle una cita galante – a la cual ella también asistiría. [*For proof she arranged a meeting to which she would go as well.*]

HOMENIDES: Pero, la carta! La carta! [*But the letter, the letter.*]

LUCIENNE: Ah! La carta! La carta! Espera, hombre! Si ella hubiese escrito la carta a su marido, éste hubiera reconocido su escritura. [*Ah! The letter! The letter! Wait, man! Had she written the letter to her husband, he would have recognized the writing.*]

HOMENIDES: Después! Después! [*After! After!*]

LUCIENNE: Entonces ella me ha encargado de escribir en su lugar. [*She asked me to write for her.*] Ask Raymonde.

HOMENIDES [*moving to* RAYMONDE]: Es verdad? Es verdad? [*That is true? That is true?*]

RAYMONDE: Yes. What did you say exactly?

HOMENIDES: Es verdad lo que ella dice? [*Is it true what she says?*]

RAYMONDE: It's all as verdad as can be. What have I got to lose?

HOMENIDES [*kissing* RAYMONDE's *hand*]: Ah, Señora, Señora! Cuando pienso que me he metido tantas ideas en la cabeza! [*When I think I put so many ideas in my head.*]

RAYMONDE: Please. Don't mention it!

HOMENIDES [*moving to* LUCIENNE]: Que estupido! [*He moves to* TOURNEL.] Ah! Soy un bruto! Un bruto! Un bruto! [*How stupid! I am a brute! A brute! A brute!*]

192

TOURNEL [*facing front*]: A man could do himself a fatal injury, talking to himself like that.

> [LUCIENNE *hands* HOMENIDES's *hat and stick to* RAYMONDE, *and stands below the sofa.* HOMENIDES *moves and takes* LUCIENNE's *hand.* RAYMONDE *puts the hat and stick on the chair.*]

HOMENIDES: Ah! Querido! Perdóname mis estupideces. [*Ah, darling! Forgive my stupidity.*]

LUCIENNE: Te perdono [*I forgive you*], but don't do it again!

> [HOMENIDES *and* LUCIENNE *sit on the sofa.*]

HOMENIDES: Ah! Querida mía! Ah. Yo te quiero. [*Ah! My darling! I love you.*] [*He kisses* LUCIENNE's *hand.*]

RAYMONDE: How quickly people understand each other, in Spanish!

> [FINACHE, CAMILLE, CHANDEBISE *and* ETIENNE *come in through the central doors.* CAMILLE *is now wearing the palate.*]

FINACHE: Be sensible, you know you've taken leave of your senses.

CAMILLE: I tell you I saw them at the same time. [*Pointing*] There and there!

CHANDEBISE: And I came face to face with myself! I was in my room. I saw me in my bed!

FINACHE: Oh, yes?

HOMENIDES: What's that? What?

CHANDEBISE: You – still here?

HOMENIDES: Don't worry. At the moment I am calm. I know my wife wasn't the stranger at the Palais. She didn't write you a love letter. It was yours!

CHANDEBISE [*to* RAYMONDE]: What – you?

RAYMONDE: That's the fourteenth time you've been told.

CHANDEBISE: What?

TOURNEL: And each time we kiss each other – to absolutely no effect. [*He bangs the chair on the floor and moves to* RAYMONDE.]

CHANDEBISE: What's he say?

HOMENIDES: And for that – I made you go and jump out of the window ...

ALL: Out of the window?

HOMENIDES: Ah – then I felt a moment of pity for you!

CHANDEBISE [*moving up stage to* HOMENIDES]: *You* made *me* jump out of the window?

HOMENIDES: Of course I made you! You ran out of there. And hoop la! Through the window.

CHANDEBISE: Yes! Yes! You as well. We're all the victims of the same extraordinary hallucination! What you saw jumping out of the window was what I saw on my bed – me!

CAMILLE: And what I saw – there and there!

CHANDEBISE: And it's proved by the fact that I never – absolutely never in any circumstances – jumped out of the window!

HOMENIDES: What are you trying to tell us?

FINACHE: It's beginning to tell on me. I knew it would.

TOURNEL: We're bewitched!

[FERAILLON *comes in through the central doors with* CHANDEBISE'S *dressing-gown.*]

FERAILLON: Excuse me, ladies and gentlemen . . .

CHANDEBISE [*dropping on all fours and crawling under the table*]: The maniac!

FINACHE		Feraillon!
CAMILLE	[*together*]:	Feraillon!
RAYMONDE		The proprietor!
TOURNEL		From the hotel!

FERAILLON: I was just walking down the street when my hall porter happened to drop on my head. I can offer no explanation . . .

ALL: What?

TOURNEL		
CAMILLE	[*together*]:	It was the porter!
HOMENIDES		

FERAILLON: It would appear he jumped through a window, wearing this article of clothing . . . [*He holds out the dressing-gown.*]

RAYMONDE: That's my husband's! It's yours, dear. Where's he got to? Victor Emmanuel! Victor Emmanuel!

[FINACHE *and* CAMILLE *open the left hand door up and call.* ETIENNE *opens the central door and calls.* TOURNEL *goes to the french window and calls.* CHANDEBISE *crawls half out and tries to hush* RAYMONDE.]

ALL: Victor Emmanuel!

FERAILLON [*seeing* CHANDEBISE]: Ah! [*He puts the dressing-gown on the table, and hauls* CHANDEBISE *out by the collar.*]

ALL [*slamming their various doors and turning on stage*]: What?

FERAILLON: Poche! Poche again!

ALL: What do you mean, Poche?

CHANDEBISE: Ah – help! Help!

FERAILLON [*kicking* CHANDEBISE *round in a circle*]: You scoundrel – you beastly individual! You low form of humanity! You – pig's abortion . . . [FERAILLON *finishes kicking* CHANDEBISE.]

ALL: Ah!

[RAYMONDE *moves between* FERAILLON *and* CHANDEBISE.]

RAYMONDE: Excuse me, sir! You're referring to my husband!

FERAILLON: What?

CHANDEBISE: He's got an obsession. Every time we meet he kicks me round in a circle!

FERAILLON: Him! Your husband?

RAYMONDE: Exactly. Monsieur Chandebise!

FERAILLON: He's the spitting image of my hall porter! Monsieur Poche!

ALL: Poche!

RAYMONDE: And the one we saw in the hotel swigging vermouth ...

TOURNEL: Who kissed us ...

ALL: That was Poche!

LUCIENNE: And the one who wanted me to wet my whistle ...

CAMILLE: Who carried the load of logs ...

ALL: That was Poche!

CHANDEBISE: Poche! Poche! Nothing but Poche! I'm sorry he left in such a hurry. I'd like to have seen him close to. My second self!

FERAILLON: We can arrange that – call in any day. At the Hotel Coq d'Or.

CHANDEBISE: No, thank you very much! I've seen quite enough of the Hotel Coq d'Or!

RAYMONDE [teasing CHANDEBISE]: Not even to meet a lovely stranger from the Palais Royal?

CHANDEBISE: You may mock! But who started this whole ridiculous ball rolling?

RAYMONDE: I'm sorry! Really I'm sorry! But what could I do? I thought you were unfaithful to me ...

CHANDEBISE: Good heavens! Why? Whatever gave you that idea?

RAYMONDE: Well, because you – because ...

CHANDEBISE: No! Not for such a little ...

RAYMONDE: But *because* there was such a little ...

CHANDEBISE: Oh – well!

RAYMONDE: I know. I was very silly. The fact is – I had a flea in my ear!

CHANDEBISE [putting his arm round her]: All right! I'll squash that flea, tonight!

RAYMONDE: You?

CHANDEBISE: Yes. That is – [he lets her go] – well, at least I'll try!

TOURNEL: Listen to this. You'll never believe it – not in a million years – but I must tell you ...

ALL: Oh, no – save it up! Till tomorrow! Till tomorrow!

The lights Black-Out and –

THE CURTAIN FALLS

THE
LADY
FROM
MAXIM'S

CAST OF FIRST LONDON PRODUCTION

The Lady from Maxim's was first presented in this version by the National Theatre Company at the Lyttleton Theatre, London, in October 1977

PETYPON	Stephen Moore
GÉNÉRAL	Michael Bryant
MONGICOURT	Edward Hardwicke
LE DUC DE VALMONTÉ	Timothy Davies
CORIGNON	Christopher Good
ÉTIENNE	John Normington
THE DUSTMAN	Michael Beint
THE ABBÉ	Martin Friend
CHAMEROT	Michael Stroud
GUÉRISSAC	Robert Ralph
VARLIN	Peter Tilbury
ÉMILE	Harry Lomax
VIDAUBAN	Brian Kent
TOURNAY	Louis Haslar
SAUVAREL	Antony Higginson
THE SHRIMP	Morag Hood
MADAME PETYPON	Sara Kestelman
THE DUCHESS	Rosamund Greenwood
MADAME VIDAUBAN	Ruth Kettlewell
MADAME PONANT	Barbara Ogilvie
MADAME SAUVAREL	Anne Leon
MADAME CLAUX	Yvonne d'Alpra
MADAME HAUTIGNOL	Diana Payan
MADAME VIRETTE	Rose Power
MADAME TOURNAY	Elizabeth Benson
CLÉMENTINE	Jeananne Crowley

The play was directed by
CHRISTOPHER MORAHAN
Designed by
MICHAEL ANNALS
Stage Manager
DIANA BODDINGTON

CHARACTERS

DR MONGICOURT	Dr Petypon's friend and colleague
ÉTIENNE	Dr Petypon's butler
DR PETYPON	A Parisian doctor
MADAME PETYPON	His wife
THE SHRIMP	A Dancer from the Moulin Rouge
GÉNÉRAL PETYPON DU GRÊLÉ	Dr Petypon's uncle
THE DUSTMAN	
THE ABBÉ	The General's neighbour in Touraine
MADAME VIDAUBAN	A country lady
MADAME PONANT	A giggling country lady
MADAME CLAUX	A provincial 'femme fatale'
MADAME VIRETTE	A provincial housewife
MADAME SAUVAREL	The wife of the prefect of Touraine
MADAME HAUTIGNOL	A provincial blue stocking
LA DUCHESS DE VALMONTÉ	A deaf duchess
LIEUTENANT GUÉRISSAC LIEUTENANT CHAMEROT LIEUTENANT VARLIN	Army officers and friends to Lieutenant Corignon
CLÉMENTINE	The General's niece
ÉMILE	The General's butler
MONSIEUR VIDAUBAN	A country gentleman
LE DUC DE VALMONTÉ	The Duchess's son
MONSIEUR SAUVAREL	The prefect of Touraine
A FOOTMAN	At the General's house
MONSIEUR TOURNAY MADAME TOURNAY	The General's neighbours
LIEUTENANT CORIGNON	Clémentine's fiancée, an old flame of the Shrimp's

ACT I

DR PETYPON's *consulting room. A large room, comfortably but austerely furnished. Downstage right a window with lace half-curtains and full curtains. Upstage right a door facing the audience, which leads into the hall: a table near it. Upstage left a door leading to* MADAME PETYPON's *room. Upstage centre a large recess closed off by a double tapestry curtain on a curtain rod, which is worked by cords. This recess opens onto Petypon's bedroom and when the curtains are drawn, the bed and a chair beside it are visible to the audience. On the other side of the bed is a bedside table with a shaded electric lamp. Stage left is a big leather couch with a straight back and only one arm. Right a desk, facing it an armchair. Left of the desk a pouffe covered temporarily with a table cloth. Another table and chair. At the back against the wall between the recess and the door to the hall is a chair. Above this chair is a bell-pull. On the desk there are a blotter, an ink well, and large medical books. An electric wire coming out from the wings and passing the window goes up the far right hand leg of the desk-table. At the end of it an electric socket.*

When the curtain rises the stage is dark. Window curtains across the recess are closed. It's a scene of great disorder and the sofa is overturned. The wing chair is also overturned and on one of its feet hangs what was once a top hat. On the desk is an open umbrella and the pouffe has rolled along the floor. The table cloth lies further on.

The stage is empty and we hear midday strike. From the hall the sound of voices gradually coming nearer.

MONGICOURT [*offstage*]: Good morning, Étienne. How is the good doctor?

ÉTIENNE [*offstage*]: Good morning, Monsieur. Doctor Petypon is still asleep.

MONGICOURT [*offstage*]: You're pulling my leg, Étienne. He's not still asleep?

ÉTIENNE [*offstage*]: Ssh ... M'sieur le docteur.

    [DR MONGICOURT *and* PETYPON's *butler,* ÉTIENNE, *enter.*]

MONGICOURT [*whispers*]: He's not still asleep?

ÉTIENNE: I can't understand it! My Doctor Petypon's always up by eight. Now he's lounging in bed at midday. Like a rake!

MONGICOURT: Your master's a bit of a cardboard rake. If you want my opinion.

ÉTIENNE [*outraged*]: But my Doctor Petypon's no sort of rake at all!

MONGICOURT: I did say 'cardboard'. 'Cardboard' makes all the difference.

ÉTIENNE: My master's a most respectable gentleman. I'd trust him with my wife.

MONGICOURT: I didn't know you were a married man, Étienne.

ÉTIENNE: Married? Of course I'm not married! Why should I be married? It's a figure of speech.

MONGICOURT: Let's have a bit of light on the subject. It's as dark as hell [*sniffs*] and smells of Parma violets.

ÉTIENNE [*whispers*]: Not so loud, M'sieur.

MONGICOURT [*sniffs and whispers*]: Smells of Parma violets.

[ÉTIENNE *draws the window curtains, daylight floods into the room.*]

MONGICOURT: Good heavens! It's a Roman orgy!

ÉTIENNE: What did you say?

MONGICOURT: Just talking to myself.

ÉTIENNE: I thought perhaps you said 'orgy'. That's hardly the word for my Doctor Petypon ... who drinks nothing but Perrier Water, and only puts a slice of lemon in it at Christmas.

MONGICOURT: But I said 'Roman'. 'Roman' makes all the difference.

ÉTIENNE [*a gesture embracing the wrecked room*]: I see ... What M'sieur has in mind is the destruction of Pompeii.

MONGICOURT [*pointing to the uncovered, overturned pouffe*]: Exactly! Even the pouffe seems to have lost all sense of decency!

[ÉTIENNE *putting the pouffe the right way up and covering it with a table cloth which is lying near to it.*]

ÉTIENNE: Oh, that's a temporary measure. Madame is at work on a tapestry to cover its nakedness. It will soon be decently clad with a martyrdom of the Blessed Saint Violetta done in needlepoint. [*He looks round the room again.*] The destruction of Pompeii!

MONGICOURT [*picking up the battered opera hat from the foot of the chair*]: The destruction of his Opera hat ...

[ÉTIENNE *takes it from him.*]

ÉTIENNE: I don't like it! When a man starts to misuse his Opera hat he ends up by kicking his butler.

MONGICOURT: Look here! I want to see your Master urgently. On a medical matter. Would it be asking too much to wake him up?

ÉTIENNE: You'd have to take full responsibility.

MONGICOURT: As a fellow doctor, I prescribe your Master ... a good waking up.

ÉTIENNE: We'll have to do it gradually ... Perhaps to music. Quietly at first, then mounting to a crescendo.

MONGICOURT: Music? Anything special?

ÉTIENNE: What about Tra la la la [*He sings a tune from 'Faust'.*]

MONGICOURT: You – an expert on Gounod's 'Faust'?

ÉTIENNE: I've no choice. Madame Petypon plays it all day on the piano.

MONGICOURT: Well, why not? It's rather suitable. Quietly at first, eh?

ÉTIENNE [*singing*]:

> Careless, idle maiden
> Wherefore dreaming still?
> Day with roses laden
> Cometh o'er the hill
>
> The blithe birds are singing
> List to what they say!
> Through the meadows ringing,
> The harvest is so gay

MONGICOURT [*singing at the same time*]:

> Tra la la
> Tra la la
> Don't know the words
> So I'll just have to vamp the tune
> Tra la la

[*Sound of a groan*]

MONGICOURT: Sssh!

ÉTIENNE: What?

MONGICOURT: Sssh! Down in the forest something stirred.

ÉTIENNE: Where?

MONGICOURT: It was a sound, like an animal in pain ...

ÉTIENNE: My Master, Doctor Petypon. Waking up!

MONGICOURT: Ahh ...!

[*We hear* PETYPON'*s groans.*]

PETYPON: Oooh ...!

MONGICOURT: Are you there, Petypon?

PETYPON: Noo ...

MONGICOURT: Aren't you getting up?

PETYPON: I've only just gone to bed.

ÉTIENNE: On the disembodied side, that voice, wouldn't you say, M'sieur?

MONGICOURT: Strange ... It seems to come from just behind us ... Petypon! Where the devil are you?

PETYPON: In my bed, of course.

[*They rush to the sofa and lift it up from behind so that we see* PETYPON *in his shirt sleeves, evening dress, tie undone, sleeping, stretched out.*]

MONGICOURT: Boring evening, was it, Petypon? So you slipped under the sofa for forty winks?

[PETYPON *opens his eyes, turns his head, looks at them, stunned.* MONGICOURT *and* ÉTIENNE *burst into laughter.*]

PETYPON [*turning over*]: Leave me alone.

MONGICOURT: Eh, Petypon. [*Taps his feet*] Circulation still ambling through you, is it?

PETYPON: Well. What? [*He sits up and leans his head against the sofa*] Was there an earthquake? [*Stretches on his back*]

[MONGICOURT *and* ÉTIENNE *are laughing.*]

MONGICOURT: An earthquake! The destruction of Pomp ...

[MONGICOURT *almost completely lifts up the sofa by drawing the back of it towards him in order to uncover* PETYPON.]

PETYPON: It's extremely rude ... To stand about on people's beds.

MONGICOURT: Do you call this your bed? You're under the sofa!

PETYPON [*on his back*]: Of course I'm under the sofa. What sofa?

[MONGICOURT *lets down the back of the sofa so as to cover* PETYPON *up again completely.*]

MONGICOURT: This one!

PETYPON [*in a rage, struggling under the sofa*]: What idiot put the sofa on top of me?

MONGICOURT [*half lifting the sofa again*]: Better ask yourself who put you under it.

PETYPON: Let me out!

[*They completely lift up the sofa, against which* PETYPON, *who is sitting up again, leans exhausted.*]

PETYPON: Terrible headaches you get, sleeping under sofas.

[MONGICOURT *who has gone round the couch, comes back down on the extreme left and goes and sits on the couch.*]

MONGICOURT: I don't imagine you did it for your health.

PETYPON [*rubbing his eyes, pathetic voice*]: Is it morning?

MONGICOURT [*joking*]: There's still a bit of it left.

PETYPON [*headache*]: Oooh! [*To* MONGICOURT] Ahh ... My friend!

MONGICOURT: Your best friend ... And fellow Doctor.

ÉTIENNE [*coming down on the right of the couch*]: Would M'sieur like me to help him up?

PETYPON [*cross*]: Étienne! What are you doing here?

ÉTIENNE: Or would M'sieur like breakfast down there ... ?

PETYPON: It was a hot night ... a hot summer night. I envied the explorers lying out under the stars! We don't get enough of that in Paris. I decided to sleep rough. Under the sofa. Why shouldn't I sleep where I want to ...?

ÉTIENNE: No reason at all. [*Aside*] Try the kitchen stove tonight ...

[ÉTIENNE *picks up* PETYPON's *tailcoat from the floor.*]

PETYPON [*gets up painfully, helped by* MONGICOURT]: Do I have to ask your permission?

ÉTIENNE [*shaking the tailcoat*]: Oh, no, M'sieur. [*Aside*] He must have got out the wrong side of the sofa!

[ÉTIENNE *puts the tailcoat on the arm of the sofa.*]

PETYPON [*grumbling to* MONGICOURT]: Humiliating to be under the furniture when the servants arrive. Aah! [*He seizes his head.*]

ÉTIENNE [*considerate*]: M'sieur would like luncheon ...? We have liver pâté and a nice fat roast goose.

PETYPON [*jumps*]: Uggh! [*Disgust*] Eating! Disgusting habit!

ÉTIENNE [*going right*]: Very well, M'sieur.

PETYPON: Where's Madame Petypon?

ÉTIENNE [*who's taken the umbrella and hat off the table*]: Madame has just gone to visit M'sieur Le Curé at Saint Sulpice ... for coffee and ...

MONGICOURT: Gossip.

PETYPON: Gossip about the martyrdom of the Blessed Saint Violetta. Raped and beheaded by the Roman soldiers ... I know exactly how Saint Violetta felt. [*To* ÉTIENNE] Are you still hanging about, Étienne?

ÉTIENNE: Yes, M'sieur. [*Aside as he goes up*] Oh, he's very low today.

[*He goes upstage right with the hat and umbrella.* MONGICOURT, *looking at* PETYPON, *who is holding his head, his right hand on his forehead, his left on top of his head, groaning horribly.*]

MONGICOURT: Touch of the collywobbles?

PETYPON [*his eyes to heaven, pitiful voice*]: What a brilliant diagnosis!

[*He gets to the chair in the middle and sits.*]

MONGICOURT [*standing gaily*]: Serves you right. For leading me astray.

PETYPON: *I* led *you*?

MONGICOURT: Certainly.

PETYPON [*collapsed on his chair*]: We'd just spent two hours together operating on the Mayor of Clignancourt.

MONGICOURT: You kept on finding new complaints! Like Aladdin's Cave.

PETYPON: And when we'd put it all back and got it sewn up ...

MONGICOURT: You said 'After a stomach like that, one's entitled to a large Perrier'. [*He strides upstage.*]

PETYPON: So I did! [*He has made an effort to get up and is trying to reach the couch.*]

MONGICOURT: And I told you I knew a little place round the corner.

PETYPON: Your little place round the corner happened to be *Maxim's*! On a Gala Night! I thought the Perrier was a funny colour ...

MONGICOURT: Of course, we bachelors can spend hours in Maxim's, every evening. But you wretched married fellows! Five minutes of bubbling wine and flashing stockings and you all go down with Maximitis!

PETYPON [*he sits on the couch, exhausted*]: I've got Maximitis?

MONGICOURT: Never seen a worse case!

PETYPON: It's extremely painful. How did you escape it?

MONGICOURT: I told you. I've been immunized ... after a long, painful course of champagne and dancers. You came to Maxim's straight from married life. Of course you were hit by the change of climate. That's why you collapsed, under the sofa!

PETYPON: I couldn't be feeling worse if I were the Mayor of Clignancourt himself. By the way, is his condition satisfactory?

MONGICOURT: Perfectly. He's dead.

PETYPON: That's all right. He was dying anyway.

MONGICOURT: Then the operation was unnecessary!

PETYPON: An operation, my dear friend, is never unnecessary. [*We hear* MADAME PETYPON's *sing-song voice offstage.*] My wife!

MME PETYPON: Ah ... M'sieur le Docteur's up at last. Careful with the brown paper parcel, Étienne. It's a statuette of Our Lady of Lourdes ...

PETYPON [*grabbing his tailcoat from the sofa*]: Can you tell I've been sleeping rough?

MONGICOURT [*serious*]: Not at all ...

PETYPON [*reassured*]: Ah.

MONGICOURT [*helps him put on his tailcoat*]: You do rather look as if you'd dossed down on a slab in the mortuary. Apart from that ...

PETYPON: If I could greet her with a smile ... [*He gets up and puts a hand through his hair, trying to force a smile*] Is that better?

MONGICOURT: Worse!

[MADAME PETYPON *enters in her hat, rushing in from the right, her arms outstretched.*]

MME PETYPON: Good morning, Lazybones. Had a good lie-in!

[*She draws* PETYPON *energetically to her to kiss him.*]

PETYPON [*his head jarred by the clasp of his wife*]: Good morning ... Gab ... oooh ... rielle ...

MME PETYPON: Good morning, Doctor Mongicourt.

MONGICOURT [*very polite*]: Madame. Your servant!

MME PETYPON: Petypon. You don't look quite up to snuff!

PETYPON: Never felt better in my life.

MME PETYPON [*worried*]: But you're green! [*To* MONGICOURT] Why is my husband green, Doctor?

MONGICOURT: After a thorough examination I have diagnosed, 'Maximitis'.

MME PETYPON [alarmed, without understanding]: Oh dear! Not that!

MONGICOURT [grave]: Yes, Madame.

MME PETYPON [frightened]: It's serious!

MONGICOURT [important, reassuring]: With constant care and attention, I have every hope for his eventual recovery.

MME PETYPON [profoundly thankful]: Oh, thank Heaven! [Affectionate and commiserating to PETYPON] My poor friend. Well, it's God's will. You have 'Maximitis'. We must all be very brave.

PETYPON [embarrassed]: Well, I don't know. It's Mongicourt who ...

MME PETYPON [lively]: Oh, but you must be looked after. [To MONGICOURT] What should I get for him? A little drop of brandy? He never takes it but ...

  [She sets out to find some.]

PETYPON: For God's sake! [Nauseated] No! No alcohol!

MME PETYPON [coming back downstage]: Such a sainted man, my husband. No alcohol! Even as a medicine.

MONGICOURT [important]: For 'Maximitis' most doctors prescribe – a half bottle of castor oil!

MME PETYPON [going back upstage, satisfied]: Castor oil. Certainly.

PETYPON: Certainly not.

MONGICOURT [taking pity on PETYPON]: But as we are dealing with the less serious tertiary stage ...

MME PETYPON: Less serious?

MONGICOURT: I would personally recommend strong black coffee.

MME PETYPON [hurrying out]: Coffee! Of course. I'll get Étienne to strengthen some at once ...

MONGICOURT: And lemon juice ...

MME PETYPON [as she passes PETYPON]: Lemon juice. Of course. I never guessed you were ill. You were sleeping like a baby.

  [PETYPON, stupefied, looks at MONGICOURT, astonished.]

MME PETYPON: You didn't even move when I kissed you, my darling.

PETYPON [astonished]: You what?

MME PETYPON: Kissed you.

PETYPON: Where was I, at the time?

MME PETYPON: In your bed, of course.

PETYPON: In ... In my bed? Oh yes, of course.

MME PETYPON: Where else could you be? I kissed that dear little quiff of hair that was just peeping out over the sheet. You didn't feel it?

PETYPON [stupefied]: My hair's very insensitive ...

MME PETYPON [*going to the door upstage*]: Strong black coffee! And the juice of one lemon?

MONGICOURT [*goes to the door with her*]: That's right!

[*As soon as* MME PETYPON *has gone* MONGICOURT *runs downstage.*]

PETYPON [*who has stayed dumbfounded on the spot, his eyes fixed on the sofa*]: She kissed me in my bed! And I was asleep under *there* ... Wasn't I ...?

MONGICOURT: Undoubtedly.

[*With fierce concentration* MONGICOURT *gets hold of the chair near the couch with his right hand and places it in front of him.*]

PETYPON [*shaking his head*]: Is there some simple scientific explanation?

MONGICOURT [*bestrides the chair and sits in meditation*]: Somnambulism! You were in bed, as your wife kissed you, dreaming that you were a Persian rug.

PETYPON [*falling onto the sofa*]: Was I?

MONGICOURT: So naturally you went and lay under the sofa.

PETYPON: 'Naturally'! I am not in the habit, Mongicourt, of dreaming that I'm a Persian rug.

[*They remain for a moment in these meditating poses, their backs turned on each other,* PETYPON *facing downstage left,* MONGICOURT *facing downstage right. Suddenly a loud and long yawn is heard coming from the recess.*]

THE VOICE: Aaaah!

PETYPON [*turning his head towards* MONGICOURT]: What did you say?

MONGICOURT [*turning his head towards* PETYPON]: Me? I didn't say anything!

PETYPON: You said, 'Aaah!'

MONGICOURT: It wasn't me!

PETYPON: Pull yourself together, Mongicourt. It certainly wasn't me ...

THE VOICE [*another yawn*]: Aaah! Aaah!

PETYPON [*getting up and turning towards the direction of the noise*]: Jesus Christ!

MONGICOURT [*getting up at the same time*]: Don't jump to conclusions.

THE VOICE: Aaah! Ah! Ouaah!

[PETYPON *moves towards the tapestry curtain at the back, followed by* MONGICOURT.]

PETYPON: It sounds as if it were in my bedroom ... What can it be?

MONGICOURT: I rather imagine. Whatever got kissed!

[*Simultaneously they pull back the two tapestry curtains,* PETYPON *pulling the left hand one,* MONGICOURT *the one on the right. Each of them leaps back on seeing, lying in the bed, a young woman, awake, with a pretty face and her blonde hair cut short. Her dress and petticoat are on the chair by the bed.*]

PETYPON *and* MONGICOURT: Ah!

SHRIMP [*sitting up*]: Good morning, everybody. [*Laughing at him*] Cheer up, darling. How's your father?

PETYPON [*astonished*]: What is it?

   [*The* SHRIMP *starts to put on a bodice and drawers from the chair by the bed.*]

MONGICOURT [*sitting down, convulsed with laughter, on the chair on the right against the casing of the recess*]: It's a girl! Have you forgotten what they look like?

PETYPON [*his hair standing on end, totally bewildered, at the foot of the bed*]: Eh! Certainly not! [*To the* SHRIMP] Mademoiselle. You are a girl. That's what you are. Obviously. No doubt about it. But what I want to know is – why are you in my bed?

SHRIMP [*in an amused voice*]: 'Cos you invited me in special Cocky. Don't you remember?

PETYPON [*indignant*]: How could I have? I don't know you! I wouldn't even have invited you for coffee.

SHRIMP: Don't be soft, you big baby. Of course you know me.

MONGICOURT [*killing himself*]: A cup of coffee!

PETYPON: This is an extremely serious situation! [*Furious, to* MONGICOURT] It's not funny! [*To* SHRIMP] Who are you?

SHRIMP: Name and address! Honestly, you'd think I was being hauled up before the Beak. I'm the Shrimp, aren't I. *You* know that Cocky darling.

PETYPON: I don't know anything of the sort.

MONGICOURT: A bachelor does have a rather wider knowledge of the world, Petypon. This is the charming little dancer from the Moulin Rouge. Known to those of us who are still at liberty – as 'The Shrimp'.

SHRIMP [*tapping* MONGICOURT *on the cheek with the flat of her hand*]: That's right, sweetheart! So called because of my hard shell and lovely pink, soft centre ...

MONGICOURT [*getting up and roaring with laughter on the left, near the table*]: Don't you remember her? Cocky darling?

PETYPON: Don't start that, please! Mademoiselle. My name is Doctor Lucien Petypon and last night ...

SHRIMP: Last night we was tight as ticks, Doctor Patapouffe and his little Shrimp. So he invites me home for a good lay down ... [*Looking round appreciatively*] Lovely place you got here, Patapouffe. Very tastefully done!

PETYPON [*astonished*]: I asked you here ... to lie down?

SHRIMP [*without changing her expression, looking to the left and right*]: Well, it's *your* home, isn't it? I couldn't 've been asked to lie down in here by the President of the Republic.

PETYPON [*abruptly*]: My God!

[*The* SHRIMP *has jumped out of bed niftily, on the far side.*]

MONGICOURT: What?

PETYPON: A horrible thought occurs to me! [*Going to* MONGICOURT] My dear wife ... who is sewing hassocks when she is not knitting mittens for the little sisters of Saint Theresa ... must have actually kissed this appalling Shrimp!

MONGICOURT: It's all part of life's rich pattern.

[*They stay stiff, unmoving, shoulder to shoulder, their legs giving way, their astonished eyes fixed on the* SHRIMP. *Meanwhile, she picks up her dress, comes downstage, and looks at the two men.*]

SHRIMP: You two still hanging about – like a bunch of bananas?

[*She puts her dress on a chair downstage and with the movement of a dancer she twirls and her leg goes over the back of the chair, in the middle of the stage.*]

Cheer up, darling. How's your father?

[*She flops down on the sofa and stretches herself out, her head to the left.*]

Christ on a bicycle! I do love you, Patapouffe!

[PETYPON, *bounding, beside himself, to the* SHRIMP, *whilst* MONGI-COURT *picks up the chair in the middle and puts it against the wall of the recess.*]

PETYPON: *Petypon*, Mademoiselle. Docteur Lucien *Petypon*!

SHRIMP: Petypon! [*Looking at him, teasingly*] Silly name. It makes no difference! I still love you!

PETYPON [*pulling her legs to the ground*]: Will you please get *dressed*!

SHRIMP: Patapouffe, darling! You're such a caveman!

MME PETYPON [*offstage*]: A lemon, Étienne. Run to the greengrocer. His life may be at stake!

PETYPON [*jumping at the sound of his wife's voice and speaking over hers*]: Oh, my God! Gabrielle!

MONGICOURT: Your wife!

PETYPON [*leading the* SHRIMP *to the back*]: In there! Vanish!

MONGICOURT [*leading her back too*]: Yes, vanish. That's the best thing for you to do.

SHRIMP [*astonished*]: Vanish? Whatever for?

MONGICOURT [*pushing her into the bedroom*]: Some people ... are allergic to shellfish.

[MONGICOURT *and* PETYPON *energetically close the tapestry curtains. At the moment when* MME PETYPON *appears they only have time to turn and stay where they are,* MONGICOURT *to one side of the curtain,*]

PETYPON *the other, desperately trying to look at ease.* MME PETYPON *comes bustling in from the right. She's carrying a tray on which there's the coffee-pot, sugar bowl and a cup and saucer, glass and a lemon squeezer. Without looking at the two men she goes down to the table and puts down the tray.*]

MME PETYPON: There we are! The coffee! I've sent Étienne out for the lemon.

[PETYPON, *beside himself, with his eyes fixed on his wife, taking the opportunity while she's not looking, he says very loudly through the join in the curtains to warn the* SHRIMP.]

PETYPON: It's my dear wife! Madame Gabrielle Petypon. My lawful wedded *wife*!

MONGICOURT [*same game*]: Your *wife*. Good heavens, yes! So it is! Your dear *wife* with whom you've been living happily for twenty years! Of course I haven't got a wife. I've never had anything approaching a wife. But *you* have, Petypon. And here she is...!

PETYPON: Yes, here she is. My wife! And I'd like you to meet her!

MME PETYPON [*astonished, turns towards her husband, crosses the stage towards him*]: Petypon! Why are you introducing me to our oldest friend?

MONGICOURT [*without thinking*]: Enchanted to meet you, Madame! I've heard so much about you!

[*Whilst speaking he comes down to behind the sofa.*]

PETYPON [*to* MME PETYPON *who is sitting on the sofa*]: No, no ... You didn't let me finish ... I was saying, 'Madame Petypon, my lawful wedded *wife* ... don't you think it's frightfully stuffy in here?'

MME PETYPON: In here? Not particularly.

PETYPON: I'm suffocating! [*Abruptly he seizes her wrist*] Air! For pity's sake! Fresh air!

MME PETYPON [*resisting being led away by* PETYPON]: No! No!

PETYPON [*leading her towards the right*]: Oh, yes! Yes!

[*He pulls his wife so hard that she is projected violently towards the chair on which are the* SHRIMP's *clothes.*]

MME PETYPON [*on the right of the chair, seeing the clothes*]: Who left that about?

PETYPON [*on the left of the chair*]: What?

MME PETYPON [*taking up clothes and coming downstage*]: It looks like a dress!

PETYPON [*beside himself, aside*]: God in heaven! The Shrimp's dress!

MONGICOURT [*whistling between his teeth, flopping onto the sofa*]: Phew!

MME PETYPON: What on earth do you want with a dress ... in your consulting room?

PETYPON [*coming energetically down to stand between* MME PETYPON *and* MONGICOURT]: Oh we use a lot of those. In the consulting room. For diagnosing ... Dress-o-mania ... [*To* MONGICOURT, *irritated by his silence and amusement*] Can't *you* think of anything?

MONGICOURT [*without conviction*]: What? Oh ... Yes! Yes!

PETYPON [*to his wife*]: I know. It came to the wrong address! I'll send it back! Stupid mistake!

[*So saying he grabs the dress and passes in front of* MME PETYPON *as he makes for the door.* MME PETYPON *who hasn't let go of the other end of the dress, pulls it towards her, making her husband turn and be pulled towards her.*]

MME PETYPON: There's no mistake.

PETYPON: What?

MME PETYPON: Well, I wrote my dressmaker a sharp little letter!

PETYPON: Your ... ?

MME PETYPON: She should have delivered this dress to me yesterday.

PETYPON [*whose only idea is to get back the dress*]: But no! It's impossible! I know your taste. This is no good to you! You couldn't go near a Mass in this! Give it to me!

[*He has seized the dress and is about to make off with it.*]

MME PETYPON [*defending her rights*]: You know very well I never choose the material. I just say to my dear little dressmaker round the corner 'Make me a dress'! I leave it to her. It *is* a little on the pinkish side.

PETYPON: Disgustingly pink! [*Seizing the dress and trying to tear it away from his wife*] I'll have it dyed!

[MME PETYPON *pulls her side of the dress and with a sharp snatch makes* PETYPON *let go of it.*]

MME PETYPON: Oh, come on! Can't I indulge myself in a little bit of pink for once. This would be perfectly all right for a summer confessional ...

[*She goes out upstage left, taking the dress with her.*]

PETYPON [*who's rooted to the spot between the sofa and the recess*]: Help me!

MONGICOURT [*laughing*]: You've lost the dress, Petypon.

PETYPON: She'll look ridiculous! Pink in the confessional!

[*Saying this, he's gone up to near the junction of the curtains.*]

SHRIMP [*looking out of the curtains*]: Panic over?

PETYPON [*jumps back startled on seeing a head by his nose*]: Women everywhere!

SHRIMP [*following* PETYPON *downstage*]: Naughty Patapouffe! [*Pinches his nose*] You didn't tell me you were married ...

PETYPON [*disengaging his nose by turning his head, says crossly*]: Please go away! My wife's a very religious woman!

SHRIMP: She must be a bucket of fun for you, Patapouffe!
[*She goes to the right.*]

PETYPON [*drily*]: Come on! Hurry up! Get dressed, mademoiselle.

SHRIMP [*coming back to him, graciously*]: You can call me 'Shrimp' if you want to.

PETYPON [*drily*]: Thank you. Hurry up ...

SHRIMP: But call me Shrimp. I call you Patapouffe. Let's not stand on ceremony ... Patapouffe and his little Shrimpy!
[*She goes right.*]

PETYPON: All right, hurry up ... Mademoiselle 'Shrimp'. God in heaven!

SHRIMP [*sitting on the pouffe, her legs crossed in front of her, her back to the table*]: Don't rush me. I don't move all that quick in the mornings.

PETYPON [*leaping to her*]: Well move quick now. I mean ... move quickly now. Please. I beg of you. [*Points to the door*] Get out!

SHRIMP: 'Get out!' Charming! I'm used to gentlemen that respect a girl's finer feelings.

PETYPON: Ah! [*Gets out his purse*] How much?

SHRIMP [*frowns*]: What?

PETYPON [*mid-stage*]: How much ... respect exactly ...?

SHRIMP [*left knee up, says teasingly*]: What sort of girls are you used to, Patapouffe? The way you carry on! Oh, if only I had a sou's worth of pride ...

PETYPON [*coming down*]: But as you haven't ...

SHRIMP: I don't really do it for the money. Cut me throat if I tell a lie!

PETYPON [*puts back his purse*]: Don't you? That's good. [*He takes her hand*] Thank you very much. [*Tries to lead her in the direction of the door*] I don't suppose we shall meet again ...

SHRIMP: I've hurt your feelings!

PETYPON: No, really.

SHRIMP: I was a brute to turn down your offer, made in all sincerity. Look, Patapouffe, I'll be generous. As it's you, I'll take a small cash present.

PETYPON: Thank you very much!
[*Gets two twenty-franc coins out of his purse, holds them out.*]
There you are. Forty francs!

SHRIMP: Forty francs! Oh! [*She pushes away his hand.*] That's for the maid!

PETYPON: But it's all *I* get for a visit!

SHRIMP: My visits come a bit more welcome, darling. So naturally they come more expensive. [*She looks at* PETYPON *clutching his purse.*] You hold your money so tight you're strangling the President of the Republic!
[MONGICOURT *laughs.*]

SHRIMP: And you can wipe that smile off your face. You know, when I was young I earned my living as a singer ...

MONGICOURT: In the Opera House?

SHRIMP: No. In gentlemen's bedrooms. They paid me to keep quiet and not draw attention to myself.
[*She sings loudly.*]

PETYPON [*desperate*]: Quiet! State your price and let's have done with it.

SHRIMP: But who's asking for money, my little Patapouffe? [*Pinches his nose*]

PETYPON [*disengaging his nose*]: You are!

SHRIMP: I don't want your filthy money! If you say you've grown tired of me ...

PETYPON: I've grown tired of you.

SHRIMP: Then we're all washed up!

PETYPON: Wrecked!

SHRIMP: There's nothing left ... Except the 'goodbye' present.

PETYPON: What 'goodbye' present?

SHRIMP: I bought a new dress yesterday. Patapouffe ... I'll do you a favour. You can pay for it.

PETYPON: Thank you very much!

SHRIMP: That's all right! I want you to have a little memento of the Shrimp ... Cheer you up during your wife's prayer meetings in the long winter evenings.

PETYPON: How much exactly?

SHRIMP: What?

PETYPON: Your ... dress. Would forty francs ... ?

SHRIMP [*as if it were nothing*]: Twenty-five louis.

PETYPON [*swallows*]: Five hundred francs!

SHRIMP [*comic admiration*]: Marvellous arithmetic! Clever little Patapouffe! [*Pinches his nose*]

PETYPON [*in a rage, disengages his nose*]: Doctor Lucien Petypon!
[*He starts to give her hundred franc notes.*]

PETYPON: One hundred ... Two ... Three ... Four hundred ... [*He has only a fifty-franc note left.*] Four hundred and fifty. That's all I've got. It'll have to do.

SHRIMP: Oh no, it won't!

MONGICOURT [*taking a fifty-franc note out of his wallet*]: Here you are, Petypon. Have the last fifty francs worth on me.

SHRIMP [*snatching the note*]: You're a gentleman!

MONGICOURT [*to PETYPON*]: We bachelors are used to paying for our pleasures. It comes far cheaper in the long run. How long could you keep Gabrielle on five hundred francs?

PETYPON: Gabrielle! If my wife should ever hear of this! [*To* SHRIMP] Good! You've had your twenty-five louis. Now! Out!

SHRIMP [*goes to the chair where her dress was*]: Christ on a bicycle! Who pinched my dress?

PETYPON: What do you mean – pinched it?

    [SHRIMP, *not finding the dress where she thought it was, goes to another chair.*]

SHRIMP: It's done the vanishing trick!

PETYPON: That's right. Vanished! No use waiting about for it. You look very nice like that. Come on! Out with you!

SHRIMP: Are you mad, Patapouffe?

PETYPON: Petypon!

SHRIMP: All right, Petypon. Do you think I'm going to parade down the street in my unmentionables?

PETYPON: In your what?

SHRIMP: Drawers, darling. If you must talk vulgar.

PETYPON: All right, if you insist. Put this on!

    [*He snatches the tablecloth, puts it round her shoulders. She takes off the tablecloth, throws it at* MONGICOURT.]

SHRIMP: I've got a reputation to keep up! I'm not walking down the Boulevard Malesherbes in a tablecloth! Give me my dress!

PETYPON [*desperate*]: I haven't got it.

SHRIMP [*marches to him*]: Well, who has, Pet*y*pon? Just tell me that, darling.

MONGICOURT [*laughing*]: Yes. Tell her that, darling!

PETYPON [*almost crying*]: If you must know ... My wife took it!

    [*With his heel,* PETYPON *pushes the pouffe half under the table and sits sulking on the corner of it.*]

SHRIMP: Oh, Petypon. You fine cheeky chappy! You skunk! Do you think I had a twenty-five louis dress made, as a present for your wife!

PETYPON [*leaning on the table*]: What can I do about it?

SHRIMP: I hope you're going to pay me for it, darling. That's the least you can do.

PETYPON: Pay for it? I just *have* paid for it.

SHRIMP: You paid for it ... [*Pause*] So I could keep it. [*Pause*] Not so I could give it away as a present ... To Christian gentlewomen in reduced circumstances!

PETYPON: But that makes two dresses!

SHRIMP: Naturally. [*Pause*] The one you give me ... [*Pause*] And the one you give her!

MONGICOURT: That seems reasonable.

PETYPON: It seems exorbitant!

MME PETYPON [*offstage*]: That little dressmaker's gone out of her mind …
I don't know what measurements she used for this?

[MME PETYPON *goes on chattering offstage during the following scene.*]

MME PETYPON [*offstage*]: She must have thought I'd shrunk in the wash,
or gone on a starvation diet. It's ridiculous … And she's cut it so
low. I couldn't pass a church in it, let alone go inside for confession,
even in the summer! Petypon! And I absolutely forbid you to pay for
it!

PETYPON: I'll show you. [*Jumping at hearing his wife, seizes the* SHRIMP *by
the hand*] Heavens! My wife! Vanish! Vanish!

SHRIMP: You not feeling well, darling?

MONGICOURT [*also panic*]: Quick! Quick!

SHRIMP: Your wife's been lurking about all this time … ?

PETYPON [*throws himself with his back against the door and says to* MONGI-
COURT]: For God's sake, hide her!

MONGICOURT [*panic*]: Of course.

SHRIMP: Where?

MME PETYPON: Lucien, the door's stuck.

MONGICOURT [*pushing her to the ground to hide under the table*]: Down there!

SHRIMP [*on all fours*]: The pouffe's in the way!

PETYPON: For God's sake hurry up!

MME PETYPON: Lucien, Lucien! Lucien, why's the door stuck?

MONGICOURT: Wait, don't move!

[*He covers the* SHRIMP *with the tablecloth and sits on her back as if he
were on the pouffe.*]

MME PETYPON [*offstage*]: Why's the door stuck?

[MME PETYPON *now gives the door such a violent push that it flies open
and she hurtles in.* PETYPON *leans back against his wife's stomach and,
making little inarticulate cries like someone out of his head, in this way
pushes his wife, by little jerks, across the middle of the stage, almost in
front of the sofa.*]

PETYPON: Aha! Aha! Aha!

MME PETYPON [*distraught as she holds her husband as he leans back on her
stomach*]: What's the matter with him? Doctor, quick! Is it the 'Maximitis' back? In a terrifying form?

MONGICOURT [*not moving from the* SHRIMP*'s back*]: No doubt of it. Hold
him up! Don't let go of him!

MME PETYPON: No!

[*To* PETYPON, *who is still moaning and who has moved so that his wife
is forced to turn her back on* MONGICOURT.]

MME PETYPON: Lucien! My husband! Oh, but he's too heavy! Doctor
Mongicourt! Come and help me!

[*She moves to turn towards* MONGICOURT. PETYPON, *with a twist of his back, brings her back into her former position with her back to* MONGICOURT.]

PETYPON: No! Don't ask him!

MME PETYPON [*her arms still under* PETYPON'*s armpits*]: It's just that you're a little ... on the heavy side!

PETYPON [*facing the audience so that his wife is behind him, in a voice as though he's dying*]: That doesn't matter! For God's sake! Turn me to the north! Turn me to the north!

MME PETYPON [*flabbergasted, turns her husband to face* MONGICOURT]: To the north? Where is the north?

PETYPON [*briskly, at the same time with a jerk of his back turning her to face downstage left again*]: No! That's the south. It's essential to keep the patient facing north in a crisis like this! For pity's sake! Turn me to the north!

MME PETYPON [*exasperated*]: I haven't got a compass! Where's north?

PETYPON: Opposite south!

MME PETYPON: Oh, let's sit down! I can't keep this up! [*Without turning round, talking over her shoulder*] Doctor Mongicourt. Bring me the pouffe!

PETYPON: No! Not that! Not the pouffe!

MME PETYPON: Just so we can sit down!

PETYPON [*shouting*]: Aha! Mongicourt! Do you hear me? Take the pouffe away! I'm allergic to the pouffe!

MONGICOURT: You want me to take the pouffe away?

MME PETYPON [*shouting like* PETYPON]: Take the pouffe away! Better humour him.

PETYPON: Yes! Yes! [*He pretends to faint and closes his eyes*]

MONGICOURT: Keep calm, Petypon. Calm. Let's take the pouffe away then! Let's take it away!

[MONGICOURT *puts his hands under the* SHRIMP'*s knees and carries her in a kneeling position still covered with the tablecloth, into the bedroom.*]

PETYPON [*his eyes still closed*]: Has it gone?

[MONGICOURT *comes back downstage again, having deposited the* SHRIMP *and throwing the tablecloth on the chair backstage right.*]

MONGICOURT: Yes, yes. All clear now.

PETYPON [*immediately coming back to life again*]: Thank God! That feels better!

MME PETYPON [*letting go of her husband*]: Oh, Petypon. You gave me such a nasty turn ... [*She goes to the right of the table and pours a cup of coffee.*]

PETYPON [*very alert*]: There! It's passed! It's passed! The pouffe allergy's very violent! And then, all of a sudden – over! [*To* MONGICOURT] Isn't that so? [*Low*] Well, say something, you idiot!

MONGICOURT [*lively, moving away to the right a little*]: Yes! Yes! All of a sudden. Over! And then ... And then ...

PETYPON: And then it's finished! That's right?

MONGICOURT: And then it's finished! That's right!

MME PETYPON [*from behind the table, coming downstage with the cup of coffee in her hand*]: Provided it doesn't come over you again! Oh, dear! [*Holding out the cup of coffee to* PETYPON] Here you are!

PETYPON: Thank you.

MME PETYPON: You know, this terrible illness ... I really think it might be the good God punishing your lack of faith ...

PETYPON [*turning his astonished face to his wife*]: What?

MME PETYPON: When you were making fun of me yesterday, about the miracle at Clermont Ferrand. I said to you, 'You're wrong not to have faith! It'll bring you bad luck!'

PETYPON: Bad luck? It's certainly brought me that.

MONGICOURT [*coming up to* MME PETYPON *and pretending to be very interested*]: The Clermont Ferrand miracle? What's all that about?

MME PETYPON: Don't you read the papers? The blessed Saint Violetta appeared at Clermont Ferrand to the Station Master!

MONGICOURT: And asked for a return ticket to Dieppe? [*Kills himself laughing.*]

MME PETYPON: Oh, you may mock! Monsieur le Curé says that now the blessed Martyr has returned ... She will certainly call on me!

MONGICOURT: Shouldn't you meet her at the Gare de Lyon?

MME PETYPON: I have prayed to her regularly ... She has me in her special care ...

PETYPON: You?

MME PETYPON: Monsieur le Curé expects her to come to me and say, 'My daughter! Heaven has singled you out for great things! There is a great mission for you to accomplish ...!' [*With a dramatic gesture, her arms outstretched, palms upwards*] 'Go!'

PETYPON: That's splendid, darling! [*He puts his cup into his wife's outstretched hand*] If you could just put that in the kitchen on your way out ...

MONGICOURT [*to* MME PETYPON *as she moves to a table to put the cup down*]: Has the blessed Saint Violetta dropped in yet?

MME PETYPON [*simply*]: I'm waiting for her!

PETYPON: Well, of course ... You might as well wait ... You've really got nothing much else to do.

SHRIMP [*offstage. Her voice is impatient, coming from the back of the room*]: Well, *I* have!

PETYPON [*jumping, startled*]: God in Heaven! The Shrimp! [*He goes quickly upstage near to the recess.*]

SHRIMP [*offstage*]: I can tell you, darling. I've got plenty else things to do.

PETYPON [*very loudly to cover the* SHRIMP*'s voice*]: Ah! Ha ha! Well you believe in visions, do you? Mongicourt, my wife believes in visions. Aha! Oh! [*Low and brisk*] For God's sake say something!

MONGICOURT [*loudly*]: Ah! Ha ha! Your wife believes in visions. Well, then. My wife can't believe in visions. Because I haven't got a wife. But if I had one, she might. And as for *your* wife . . .

PETYPON *and* MONGICOURT [*together*]: Aha! She believes in visions. Aha!

MME PETYPON [*imperative voice*]: Be quiet! Someone spoke to me!

PETYPON [*desperate to make a lot of noise*]: Where? I didn't hear anything! Did you hear anything Mongicourt?

MONGICOURT [*loudly*]: Not at all! I didn't hear anything! Quiet as the tomb!

MME PETYPON: But I'm sure I did! From your bedroom!

PETYPON *and* MONGICOURT: No! No! Impossible!

SHRIMP [*offstage. In a heavenly, far-off voice*]: Gabrielle!

GABRIELLE: Someone's calling me.

PETYPON [*jumping backwards*]: She's gone mad! She's calling my wife!

SHRIMP: Gabrielle!

GABRIELLE: Someone's calling me! I must see about this! [*She moves upstage*]

PETYPON [*interposing himself between his wife and the recess*]: No! No!

MME PETYPON [*pushing him away*]: But yes! [*She pulls the curtains of the recess and immediately leaps backwards.*] Hallelujah!

MONGICOURT [*trying to stop laughing*]: Hallelujah!

[*We can make out, on the foot of the bed, in the half-light, a white figure, transparent and luminous. It's the* SHRIMP *who has made herself look like a vision. She has a sheet that covers everything except her face. The spray of a shower is on her head like a halo. Under the sheet she is holding an electric lamp which throws up light onto her face. All the rest of the room is in darkness, which makes the* SHRIMP *all the more luminous.*]

MME PETYPON: I must go to her! [*She is about to go upstage towards the bedroom.*]

SHRIMP [*using her celestial voice until the end of the scene*]: Turn away!

[*This order stops* MME PETYPON *short. Her arms go stiff and she wheels about, which leaves her facing the audience on the left of the table.*]

SHRIMP: I've come for you, Gabrielle!

MME PETYPON [*her arms stiff, her head bent*]: What!

SHRIMP: Those unbelievers cannot see me! I am visible only to you!

MME PETYPON: Is it possible ...?

SHRIMP: My daughter, prostrate yourself! I am the martyred Saint you have been waiting for!

MME PETYPON [*in a radiant voice*]: The Blessed Saint Violetta! [*Kneeling, says to* PETYPON *and* MONGICOURT] Kneel! Kneel, you two!

PETYPON and MONGICOURT [*hardly able to conceal their laughter and joining in the* SHRIMP's *game*]: Why? Why?

MME PETYPON [*as if having a vision*]: She's here! You can't see her! But I can hear her! I can see her! She is speaking to me alone!

SHRIMP [*aside*]: Don't flatter yourself, darling!

MME PETYPON: Kneel! Kneel!

[*The two men obey, trying not to laugh,* MONGICOURT *kneeling in front of the sofa,* PETYPON *between the sofa and the foot of the bed.* MME PETYPON *on the left of the table.*]

ÉTIENNE [*coming in suddenly from the door on the right and coming down to the right of the table with the lemon on a saucer*]: Here's the lemon!

MME PETYPON [*with a start*]: Quietly!

PETYPON [*aside*]: Oh my God, Étienne! Never knows when he's not wanted!

ÉTIENNE [*frightened when he perceives the apparition on the bed*]: Mother of God!

MME PETYPON [*still on her knees, imperious*]: No. Saint Violetta ...! Down on your knees!

ÉTIENNE [*staring at the* SHRIMP]: How did she get on the bed?

MME PETYPON [*getting to the corner of the table on her knees, says in a voice of pious admiration*]: You have faith, Étienne. You can see the blessed lady.

ÉTIENNE [*going down to almost in front of the table, his eyes never leaving the apparition*]: Blessed lady? She looks a bit tousled to me.

MME PETYPON [*scandalized*]: You'd look tousled, Étienne, if you'd been raped by a Roman centurion – and then beheaded. Seven hundred years ago!

ÉTIENNE [*bewildered*]: I suppose I would.

MME PETYPON: On your knees! And listen to the words from on high!

ÉTIENNE [*resigned*]: If Madame says so.

[ÉTIENNE *kneels on the right of the table, whilst* MME PETYPON, *going to the side one step on her knees, takes up her first attitude of bowing very low in devout meditation.* ÉTIENNE *speaks abruptly.*]

ÉTIENNE: I'll put the lemon here! [*He puts it on the table.*]

MME PETYPON [*cross*]: This is no time to chatter about lemons! [*In a reverent voice to the* SHRIMP] I am listening to you, oh my Blessed saint.

SHRIMP [*in a heavenly voice*]: Gabrielle! I have come down to earth particular to tell you of the high mission which I got in store for you!

MONGICOURT [*aside*]: You've got to hand it to her! Wonderful sense of Theatre!

SHRIMP: Woman! Are you listening?

MME PETYPON: I am all ears, Blessed Lady!

SHRIMP: You will get up, and look sharp about it! You will proceed at once to the Place de la Concorde and you will walk round it five times.

PETYPON [*low*]: I see what she's up to.

MONGICOURT [*low*]: She's not stupid!

SHRIMP: You will then hang around by the side of the Obelisk until a man speaks to you! Listen to his pious words, Gabrielle, for they will make your loins fruitful and a son will be born to you!

MME PETYPON: To me?

PETYPON [*aside*]: Very potent phrases ...

[PETYPON *and* MONGICOURT *try to suppress their laughter whilst the* SHRIMP *makes faces at them.*]

SHRIMP [*carrying on her charade*]: Your son will save France! He will reign over us and give birth to a new line of sainted Kings. You can call him Louis ...

MME PETYPON [*in a swooning voice*]: Louis ... Oh, I shall!

MONGICOURT [*aside*]: Louis Petypon!

SHRIMP: Lose no time! Go, my daughter! For your son! [*Pause*] For your saintly King! [*Pause*] For France!

MME PETYPON [*rising and without turning round, brandishing an imaginary standard*]: For my son! [*Pause*] For my saintly King! [*Pause*] For France!

SHRIMP: Go! [*Pause*] And take that servant with you!

MME PETYPON [*whilst* MONGICOURT *and* PETYPON *nod encouragingly*]: To the Place de la Concorde?

SHRIMP: Anywhere, so long as it's out of here! And may no man for the rest of this blessed day cross the threshold of this sanctified room! As for me, I shall vanish from mortal eyes to return to those celestial regions where I feel sure my heavenly dinner is on the table ... Obey me, Gabrielle!

[*She falls flat on her stomach, still covered over with her sheet. At the same time her lamp goes out.* MME PETYPON *remains in the same pose for a second, then, not hearing anything more, turns round again towards the bed.*]

MME PETYPON: She's left me. Farewell! The poor martyr. The wonderful, Blessed Lady! Did you hear her?

PETYPON and MONGICOURT [*getting up at the same time and acting stupid*]: But no! No. Hear who? [*They come downstage a little.*]

ÉTIENNE [*also getting up but staying in the same position*]: I never thought there was anything particularly holy about the Place de la Concorde . . .

MME PETYPON [*exulted to* PETYPON]: Oh! Your unbelieving ears heard nothing?

MONGICOURT [*aside*]: She's well and truly hooked!

MME PETYPON [*briskly but excited*]: Listen, Lucien! Seconds are precious! Saint Violetta came; she spoke to me; she expects me to do my duty!

PETYPON [*melodramatic*]: My dear wife . . . You look transfigured!

MME PETYPON [*leading him across the stage*]: I must go to the Place de la Concorde! By the Obelisk! A man will speak to me!

PETYPON [*indignant*]: I shouldn't be at all surprised!

MME PETYPON: From his words will be born a son!

MONGICOURT: That's a risk you take, standing by the Obelisk!

MME PETYPON [*lively*]: My son will be King of France! His crown and his halo await him! His destiny awaits him! It is the will of heaven!

PETYPON [*with tremors in his voice*]: Another man. How can I bear it?

MME PETYPON [*bombarding him with sentences, as though to convince him more quickly*]: Think, it's only words! Celestial syllables! You can't be jealous!

MONGICOURT: Not of a son conceived by a past participle . . . After a hectic affair with a subordinate clause . . .

PETYPON [*same voice*]: It's asking too much!

MME PETYPON [*same voice*]: I don't suppose the Petypons have had a Saint in the family before, let alone a King!

ÉTIENNE [*very prosaic*]: If I were in M'sieur's place, I'd say 'yes' like a shot.

MME PETYPON [*to* MONGICOURT]: For heaven's sake, Doctor Mongicourt! He won't get this opportunity again! Persuade him!

MONGICOURT [*in a comically persuasive voice*]: France expects it of you, Petypon!

MME PETYPON [*throwing herself at* PETYPON*'s knees*]: Lucien! Lucien! Let us obey the words of the saint!

PETYPON [*one hand on his wife's head and in a suffering voice*]: Oh God! Is it truly thy will . . . ? [*as if illuminated*] Voices! Do I hear voices . . . ? And those shadowy angels . . . holding out their entreating arms towards me?

MME PETYPON [*radiant*]: Oh! You can see . . . you can see! You have been touched by the finger of the Blessed Saint Violetta!

MONGICOURT [*aside*]: I shouldn't be at all surprised ...

PETYPON: The angelic voices are imploring me! 'For your son, for your King, for France!'

MME PETYPON [*standing up again*]: For France!

SHRIMP'S VOICE [*under her sheet, sounds far-off*]: For France!

MME PETYPON [*to* PETYPON]: Did you hear that?

PETYPON [*as if touched by grace, moves in front of his wife*]: Yes! Yes! I hear! I hear the angel voices! I believe! My duty is clear. I have seen the light! [*Taking his wife's hand and sending her off*] Go! Go! I consent! For my son! For my King! For our Fatherland!

MME PETYPON: For our Fatherland! [*A theatrical gesture*] Let us go! [*She goes back up to the exit door.*]

ÉTIENNE [*with lyricism*]: For the Fatherland! [*Taking the plate and the lemon*] I don't know what they wanted the lemon for!

 [*He goes out after* MME PETYPON.]

PETYPON: Did I go too far?

MONGICOURT: Much!

SHRIMP [*emerging from the sheets and sitting astride a chair by the sofa*]: There's a future for you, Petypon ... In the Comédie Française!

PETYPON: God forbid! And as for you ... the ice cold cheek ... !

SHRIMP: Fair's fair. Where would you be without me, your little Shrimp!

PETYPON: At peace! That's where I'd be ... half way through the day's work with a good lunch inside me. What on earth are you using for a halo?

SHRIMP: It's the spray. From your shower bath.

PETYPON [*outraged*]: My shower bath! That's one of the finest shower baths in Paris. I gave over a thousand francs for that shower bath! You've ruined it!

SHRIMP: It was a shower bath. Now it's a halo. It's gone up in the world.

PETYPON: All right! Not another word about the shower bath. Just go!

SHRIMP: You want me out!

PETYPON: How did you guess?

SHRIMP: All right, darling. Get me dressed. [*She looks at* PETYPON *who's staring at her with his mouth open.*]

MONGICOURT: Wake up, old fellow! Looks so bad to the neighbours, having girls popping out of your front door in their under-drawers around lunchtime. You've only got to put a few clothes on her.

PETYPON: What clothes? My wife always locks her wardrobe ...

SHRIMP: Whatever for? She can't have much to lose.

PETYPON [*going to* MONGICOURT]: My old friend!

MONGICOURT: Yes, old friend?

PETYPON: Would you be very kind and slip down to the shop on the corner and get something? A dress ... A dust sheet if necessary.

MONGICOURT [takes his hat off the table and goes]: I'm gone. Like a flash of light!

PETYPON [returning to the SHRIMP]: I'll see if I can find a dressing gown ... while you're waiting.

SHRIMP: There's a good little Patapouffe.

PETYPON: If anyone comes in ...

SHRIMP: Anyone?

PETYPON: Anyone like my wife ... Hide in the bedroom! [He goes.]

SHRIMP: Not very hospitable. He may not mean it but he's starting to make me feel just a tiny bit in the way.

GÉNÉRAL [offstage]: Left, right! Left, right! Left, right!

SHRIMP: Sounds like the army's arrived, to inspect me drawers. [She rushes into the alcove and is about to draw the curtains, but they have stuck.]

GÉNÉRAL [offstage]: Of course I'm going into his consulting room, you idle little man!

SHRIMP: They won't shut! Jesus Christ on a ... [She flops onto her stomach on the bed, pulls the sheet over her head and keeps perfectly still. Softly.] Bicycle ...

[The General marches briskly into the room followed by ÉTIENNE, who waits nervously on the threshold.]

GÉNÉRAL: You can tell him his uncle's here. Général Petypon du Grêlé!

ÉTIENNE: Yes, M'sieur le Général.

GÉNÉRAL: What the devil are you doing, lurking about in the doorway? Come in, man!

ÉTIENNE: Please, M'sieur le Général. I can't cross the threshold.

GÉNÉRAL: Can't cross the threshold? Why on earth can't you cross the threshold?

ÉTIENNE: The Archangel wouldn't like it!

GÉNÉRAL: The Archangel! What sort of an animal's that?

ÉTIENNE [self-important]: No doubt Generals don't have much to do – with Heavenly bodies!

GÉNÉRAL: Insolence! And not so dumb either.

ÉTIENNE: Excuse me. M'sieur le Général. If you want to find M'sieur le Docteur Petypon in this room you'll have to get down on your hands and knees.

GÉNÉRAL: That is not a position I'm accustomed to!

ÉTIENNE: You see, Doctor Petypon's often to be found under the sofa.

GÉNÉRAL: It's a madman! 'Often found under the sofa!' Madman. Dis ... miss!

ÉTIENNE: Yes, M'sieur le Général! [*He goes and shuts the door after him.*]

GÉNÉRAL: Well, I'm not grubbing about for my nephew under the furniture! He's not in here. Let's try in here. [*He goes into the recess and looks at the end of the bed*] No one here ... [*He goes into another part of the bedroom, out of sight of the audience*]

[SHRIMP *slowly pokes her nose out from the sheet.*]

SHRIMP: It's gone all quiet!

[*She pushes herself up, still covered by the sheet, kneeling in a position with her bottom higher than her head. The* GÉNÉRAL *re-appears at the foot of the bed and, thinking it's* PETYPON *as he can't see the* SHRIMP*'s head, raises his hand playfully.*

GÉNÉRAL: Now ... I'll liven you up, my little nephew!

[*He administers a resounding smack. She jumps in the air and finishes sitting on the bed.*]

SHRIMP: Christ on a bicycle! You clumsy great camel!

GÉNÉRAL [*sweeping off his hat and looking at the* SHRIMP *who's looking at him sulkily and rubbing her bottom*]: Devil take it! I've slapped my niece ... on the sit upon! What an introduction!

SHRIMP: What an extraordinary fellow!

GÉNÉRAL: Not a fellow, my dear. An uncle ... [*holds out his hand*] Delighted to meet you at long, long last.

SHRIMP [*weakly*]: Same to you, M'sieur.

GÉNÉRAL: I'm Général Petypon du Grêlé. Back in circulation after nine hot, smelly years in Senegal. My nephew's told you about me ...?

SHRIMP: Your nephew?

GÉNÉRAL: Petypon! Your husband ...

SHRIMP [*aside*]: My God, he thinks I'm Madame Patapouffe!

GÉNÉRAL: I don't know what idiot told me he'd married an old boiler. You're the sort of spring chicken we could have done with in the Mess ... on Saturday nights.

SHRIMP [*bowing low*]: Ah ... Général ... What a beautiful thing to say ...

GÉNÉRAL [*bowing low back*]: I speak as I feel.

SHRIMP [*aside*]: Very polite – military gentlemen!

GÉNÉRAL: Why are you still in bed? Feeling seedy?

SHRIMP: I'm hanging about for a dress.

GÉNÉRAL [*sitting on a chair at the head of the bed*]: You got my letter?

SHRIMP: Not yet.

GÉNÉRAL: Disgraceful! I'll have the postman shot! Don't bother to read it! I'll tell you what's in it.

SHRIMP: Oh, do!

GÉNÉRAL: You know Clémentine. My niece ...

SHRIMP [*sitting on the bed*]: Never heard of her.

GÉNÉRAL: Adopted her on the death of her parents. Clémentine Borré. Your husband must have told you ...

SHRIMP: Oh God, yes! The little Borré!

GÉNÉRAL: Well it can't be me. I function splendidly as a General ... but as a young mother ... Well, I just don't have the equipment! Anyway, Clémentine needs a man ...

SHRIMP [*sighs*]: Don't we all!

GÉNÉRAL: She must get married.

SHRIMP: Oh. She needs one for *that*!

GÉNÉRAL: She will become the beautiful young bride of Lieutenant Corignon!

SHRIMP: Not Lieutenant Corignon! Of the Twelfth Dragoons!

GÉNÉRAL: You've met him?

SHRIMP: Never in my life!

GÉNÉRAL: Never ...?

SHRIMP: Well, of course I knew him. I mean, my husband knew him. Till the Lieutenant gave me the boot.

GÉNÉRAL: Gave you the *what*?

SHRIMP: My marching orders!

GÉNÉRAL: Oh yes, he could give orders to march, that boy. I had him under me in Senegal.

SHRIMP [*squatting on her heels*]: Lucky you!

GÉNÉRAL: Smart soldier! Outdid the men on parade! When it came to about-turn. 'Form fours!' 'Quick dress!' Atten ... shun!

SHRIMP: I remember.

GÉNÉRAL: Attention! Why he'd stand rigid for hours through the heat of the day ...

SHRIMP [*her eyes half close sensually, her teeth clenched, hugging herself on her knees*]: I know just what you mean ...

GÉNÉRAL: Delighted we see eye to eye. [*He moves downstage.*]

SHRIMP [*aside*]: He's made me fancy that cheeky devil Corignon all over again!

GÉNÉRAL [*returning to her*]: So you agree ... to do the honours? This afternoon we leave for my château in Touraine!

SHRIMP [*aside*]: The Shrimp doing the honours at the wedding of Lieutenant Corignon! I can't wait to see his face ... [*To the* GÉNÉRAL] All right, Général. You can count on me!

GÉNÉRAL [*moving back towards the* SHRIMP]: Come to my arms. My darling little niece!

SHRIMP [*still kneeling on the bed and over the* GÉNÉRAL's *shoulder as he embraces her*]: There's nothing like family life!

[PETYPON *enters from the left, behind the sofa.*]

PETYPON: That idiot Étienne's hidden my dressing-gown. Who's that?

GÉNÉRAL [*turns and recognizes* PETYPON]: There you are!

PETYPON [*staggered and supporting himself against the headpiece of the sofa*]: This is ghastly! It's my uncle!

SHRIMP [*aside*]: Now the balloon's going up!

PETYPON: How wonderful! It's my uncle! My uncle du Grêlé! My own uncle! In the flesh ...! Well then. It's uncle ...

SHRIMP: This is getting boring.

GÉNÉRAL: What the devil's the matter with you, man? Embrace your uncle!

PETYPON [*aside*]: My uncle ... and that cursed Shrimp still in her under-drawers. [*Aloud to the* GÉNÉRAL] Well. For Heaven's sake! It's *you*, Uncle!

GÉNÉRAL: Surprised?

PETYPON [*taking the* GÉNÉRAL*'s hand*]: Amazed!

GÉNÉRAL: You haven't changed a scrap in nine years, except you look a great deal older. Now listen to me! I'm taking you down to the country ... for young Clémentine's wedding. You can spare us a day or two? Remember, you're the only nephew who gets a mention in my Will ...

PETYPON: Anything to oblige my dear uncle the General!

GÉNÉRAL: All right. Just 'yes' or 'no' 'll do. Cut out the fine phrases ... And your wife's coming with you!

PETYPON: She'll be delighted.

GÉNÉRAL: I know she will. I've just asked her.

PETYPON: You asked ... Who?

GÉNÉRAL: Your wife.

SHRIMP [*from the bed*]: Remember me?

PETYPON [*outraged*]: That! That's not my wife! You didn't for a moment imagine ... Ha! ha! [*He moves downstage left*] The idea's ridiculous!

GÉNÉRAL: If she's not your wife, what on earth's she up to! In the matrimonial bed? At lunch-time?

PETYPON: My wife is never in the matrimonial bed at lunch-time.

GÉNÉRAL: We'll see about that!

[*He moves rapidly to the bell-pull.*]

PETYPON [*rushes to the* GÉNÉRAL *to stop him ringing the bell*]: What are you doing?

GÉNÉRAL: The servants must have some idea whether it's your wife or not.

PETYPON: Please ... Don't ask them!

GÉNÉRAL: The game's up, Petypon! It *is* your wife!

PETYPON [*moves off laughing desperately*]: You're brilliant, uncle. There's no hiding anything from you! Well ... All right, then. It is my wife!

GÉNÉRAL: I knew it all along. Your wife's charming, delightful ...

SHRIMP [*bowing to him from the bed*]: Thank you ... Général ...

GÉNÉRAL [*turning and bowing to the SHRIMP*]: Enchanted, I'm sure. [*To* PETYPON] Who ever said you were married to an old boiler?

PETYPON: I can't imagine. [*Aside*] Poor Gabrielle. She'll *love* that ...

[*There's a knock at the door.*]

GÉNÉRAL: Come in!

PETYPON: Stay out!

[*The door opens.* ÉTIENNE *is standing firmly on the threshold with a large cardboard box which he holds out.*]

ÉTIENNE: This has arrived from Madame's little-dressmaker-round-the-corner.

GÉNÉRAL: Your wife said she was waiting for her clothes.

PETYPON [*aside*]: My God ... He's giving her my wife's clothes!

[*The* GÉNÉRAL *grabs the box and throws it at the* SHRIMP, *who catches it.*]

GÉNÉRAL: Now you can parade in full regimentals, Madame!

SHRIMP [*taking one of Madame Petypon's dresses out of the box*]: What am I going to look like in that? The Undertaker's widow! I suppose it's better than nothing ... Unky!

PETYPON: 'Unky'! The ice-cold cheek!

GÉNÉRAL: Yes, my little niece?

SHRIMP: Better pull the curtains ... Unless you want an exhibition of galloping drawers.

GÉNÉRAL [*drawing the curtain*]: 'Galloping drawers'! What a little firework! She'll make the country cousins sit up and take notice!

PETYPON: That's just what I'm afraid of!

[MONGICOURT *comes in from the right with a parcel, which he puts on the chair near the table.*]

MONGICOURT: This is the best dress I could find.

GÉNÉRAL: This must be the dressmaker!

MONGICOURT [*seeing the* GÉNÉRAL]: Excuse me ...

PETYPON [*aside*]: Mongicourt! He's bound to put his foot in it! [*Aloud*] Uncle. May I present my old friend and colleague, Doctor Mongicourt. Général Petypon du Grêlé.

GÉNÉRAL: Doctor! My apologies ... Took you for the dressmaker ...

MONGICOURT [*affable*]: Not at all. Perfectly natural! Are you staying long in Paris, Général?

GÉNÉRAL: Unfortunately I have to go down to Touraine ... My niece

Clémentine is marrying ... an old friend of yours, Petypon. Lieutenant Corignon.

PETYPON: An old friend? I never heard of him!

GÉNÉRAL: But your wife told me ... he's an old friend. Taught her marching apparently ...

PETYPON: Well. He's an old friend then ... [*Aside*] Just as you like!

MONGICOURT: Your wife's back then?

GÉNÉRAL: Of course she's back! She's in there. [*He points to the curtains.*] Giving an exhibition of galloping drawers.

PETYPON: Doctor Mongicourt. A word with you in private ... [*To the* GÉNÉRAL] Professional secrets!

GÉNÉRAL [*sitting on the sofa*]: Go ahead!

PETYPON [*leading* MONGICOURT *aside, in front of the table*]: The old idiot's found the Shrimp, and naturally he thinks ... Well, he thinks I'm married to her.

MONGICOURT: Poor old Petypon!

PETYPON: Just so long as Gabrielle doesn't come back. [*He hears* MME PETYPON*'s voice in the hall.*] There she is!

[MME PETYPON *comes in, radiant, and moves to the sofa.*]

MME PETYPON: Saint Violetta be praised! My mission is accomplished ...! [*She sees the* GÉNÉRAL] Oh, pardon me.

PETYPON: Ah, my dear *friend*! This is my Uncle, Général Petypon du Grêlê.

MME PETYPON [*going to the* GÉNÉRAL]: What a delightful surprise! [*She kisses him*] I've heard such a lot about you!

GÉNÉRAL [*during the embrace*]: Delighted. Of course. [*Aside*] What a remarkable friendly old boiler!

MME PETYPON: I'm sorry, Général. I'm a little out of breath.

GÉNÉRAL: Breathe then. For God's sake!

MME PETYPON [*to* PETYPON]: Oh, my dear one. I went to the Place de la Concorde ... And he spoke to me!

GÉNÉRAL: Who spoke to you?

MME PETYPON: The one whose words must bring fruit to my loins!

GÉNÉRAL [*looks at her, astonished*]: What the devil's she talking about?

MME PETYPON: I waited half an hour by the Obelisk, when suddenly coming from the Champs Élysées, surrounded by galloping soldiers I saw – The President of the Republic in his carriage! 'There you are,' I said, 'The man whom God had chosen to impregnate me with words – so that I may give birth to the Saviour of France!'

GÉNÉRAL [*aside*]: A completely cracked old boiler!

MME PETYPON: I threw myself at his carriage – but I was stopped by a huge arm ... The President rushed by like the wind – without even looking at me! And from the humblest of mouths I heard the divine words, 'Move along there, Madame'. God had chosen as his vessel – a simple gendarme!

MONGICOURT *and* PETYPON [*together*]: Fancy that.

GÉNÉRAL: They're all cracked!

MME PETYPON: What a day it's been! I feel totally exhausted!

MONGICOURT [*rushing to her*]: Yes, of course. Exhausted! As your Doctor ... I order you to lie down. [*He begins to move her towards her room.*]

MME PETYPON: I must try and rest, for His sake. Will you excuse me, Général?

GÉNÉRAL: Oh, don't mind me.

MME PETYPON [*breaks away from* PETYPON *and* MONGICOURT. *Seeing the parcel* MONGICOURT *put on the chair.*]: I knew she must have made a mistake. This must be from the dressmaker.

MONGICOURT: Oh no, it isn't!

GÉNÉRAL: Oh yes, it is. You said so yourself!

PETYPON: Oh yes, it is. But you don't want it.

MME PETYPON: I certainly do want it!

MONGICOURT: No, you don't ...

[*In spite of* PETYPON*'s and* MONGICOURT*'s efforts,* MME PETYPON *gets hold of the parcel. Clutching it firmly to her she goes down graciously to the* GÉNÉRAL.]

MME PETYPON: While you're in Paris I hope we shall see you often ...

GÉNÉRAL: Oh no! That's impossible! I'm going to my château in Touraine this afternoon.

MME PETYPON: Oh, really?

GÉNÉRAL: It's been closed for nine years. [*To* PETYPON] The country people say it's haunted.

MME PETYPON [*shivering a little*]: Doesn't that frighten you?

GÉNÉRAL: It would take more than a ghost to frighten Général Petypon du Grêlé!

MME PETYPON: It doesn't matter whether it is or not. I wouldn't dream of going there! Good day, Général. I'll leave you with my husband!

[*She goes out left clutching the parcel leaving* PETYPON *and* MONGICOURT *appalled, one each side of the sofa.*]

GÉNÉRAL: Her husband?

PETYPON [*sighs*]: Just when it was all going so well.

GÉNÉRAL [*advances on* MONGICOURT]: M'sieur, I owe you a thousand apologies! I had no idea the lady was your wife.

MONGICOURT: My w ...

GÉNÉRAL: But it's my nephew's fault; he never mentioned her name when he introduced us.

MONGICOURT: What? Not at all.

PETYPON: On the contrary, my uncle's quite right, it's completely my fault, I just wasn't thinking; of course I should have said Mme Mongicourt. Anyway it's all straightened out now. [*To* MONGICOURT] It's all straightened out now.

MONGICOURT: My God!

GÉNÉRAL [*to* MONGICOURT, *shaking his hands*]: My compliments! She seems a very friendly lady.

MONGICOURT [*rather pinched*]: Thank you very much. That's taking friendship too far!

GÉNÉRAL [*aside to* PETYPON]: Bit of an old boiler your friend married, didn't he?

SHRIMP [*coming out of the recess in* MME PETYPON's *dress*]: I'm ready! You all still hanging about like a bunch of bananas? [*She walks past the* GÉNÉRAL] Cheer up, darling. How's your father?

GÉNÉRAL [*laughing loudly*]: She's a wit your wife. 'Cheer up darling. How's your father?' Isn't she hilarious?

PETYPON: Simply killing!

GÉNÉRAL: Now you two love-birds. Parade at the station barrier ... at sixteen thirty hours.

SHRIMP: Why not!

GÉNÉRAL [*embracing the* SHRIMP]: Permission to kiss her, Petypon?

PETYPON: Feel absolutely free.

GÉNÉRAL [*kisses the* SHRIMP *on the cheek*]: Good day, Mongicourt. My respects to the old boi ... to your wife. 'Cheer up darling. How's your father?'

[*He goes out roaring with laughter.*]

SHRIMP: See you at the station, cocky-bird!

PETYPON [*looks at her, appalled*]: You're not going ...

SHRIMP [*jumps up and sits on the table*]: Free grub and as much champagne as you can pour down your throat. Of course I'm going!

PETYPON: What've I done to deserve you ...?

SHRIMP: Count yourself lucky, darling. I got you out of a nasty scrape again!

PETYPON: Only yesterday ... I was blissfully unaware of your existence. And now I'm married to you!

MONGICOURT [*very gloomy*]: And I to Madame Petypon!

PETYPON: All right. What choice have I got? Half past four. No later. At the barrier of the Gare de Lyon. [*He uncrosses her legs and lifts her down from the table.*] Quick. My wife could come in at any moment.

SHRIMP [*waving to* MONGICOURT]: Goodbye, sweetheart. Mind how you go now.

MONGICOURT: Goodbye.

SHRIMP [*she grabs* PETYPON*'s nose*]: Don't you go mucking around with other girls. You old devil! We're married now, remember?

[ÉTIENNE *appears at the door and stands obediently on the threshold.*]

PETYPON: Why can't you give my nose a rest?

SHRIMP [*as she passes,* ÉTIENNE *gives him a little tap on the cheek*]: Goodbye, Flunkey! [*She goes.*]

ÉTIENNE [*rooted on the threshold*]: The men are here with your medical chair, M'sieur.

PETYPON [*excited*]: Ah, good! Excellent! Bring it in. Bring it in.

MONGICOURT: What on earth ...?

PETYPON: This'll interest you, Mongicourt. The famous electrically operated Chair of Oblivion, perfected by the great Doctor Tunekunc of Vienna!

MONGICOURT: The Chair of Oblivion ...?

PETYPON: Chloroform is dangerous! Ether expensive ... But this gently vibrating chair rocks the patient into a state of smiling ecstasy and total oblivion – during which you can perform the most dangerous operation ...

MONGICOURT: Like presenting your bill?

[ÉTIENNE *stands in the doorway as two* PORTERS *bring in the Chair of Oblivion which looks like a primitive dentist's chair with a trailing wire, many switches and dials and a control box.*]

PETYPON: You see ... Here it is. Down there now ... Put the switch box on the desk. Oh yes, it plugs in here ...

[*As the* PORTERS *move the chair he plugs it into the wire on the desk. A* PORTER *holds out a pair of rubber gloves.* PETYPON *takes them from him and puts them in a drawer of the desk.*]

Thank you very much. Hold on a minute. Here's five sous. Share it among yourselves! Now for the moment of truth! Press this and contact is established!

[*The* PORTERS *go.* PETYPON *presses a switch on the control box. Lights flash and dials move on the chair, which vibrates gently. He presses another switch.*]

MONGICOURT: What are the rubber gloves for?

PETYPON: Insulation. Otherwise you'd go to sleep yourself when you touched your patient. There's another button on the arm so you can switch it on and off from here as well. [*He presses a button on the arm of the chair*] Now you position the patient. Good Lord ... I need a patient ... [*He looks round and then his eyes light on* MONGICOURT *who's listening, fascinated*] You'll do! Just take a seat.

MONGICOURT: No! Thank you very much. You sit in it.

ACT I

PETYPON: But I'm the operator. I can't sit there and … operate as well! Please. Just for a minute …

MONGICOURT: You won't send me to sleep?

PETYPON: I promise …

MONGICOURT: All right. You promise! [*He sits gingerly in the chair*] Not bad. In fact it's quite comfy. [*He looks at a switch on the control box*] What do the other switches do?

[PETYPON *turns with his back to* MONGICOURT *and works the control box.*]

PETYPON [*pressing a switch*]: Puts the back down. [*The back of the chair goes down. Presses another switch*] That one puts it up again … [*The back comes up, he presses another switch*] That one twiddles you round and round. [*The chair revolves.*] And that one sends the patient off to the land of nod.

MONGICOURT: But you promised …!

[PETYPON *presses the switch.* MONGICOURT *is frozen, grinning inanely in his last attitude.* PETYPON *is standing with his back to him.*]

PETYPON: My dear colleague. The patient under the influence of the current … falls into the most delightful slumber. You can open him up, operate, sew him together … all in the comfort of your own home. Isn't science wonderful? It almost takes your mind off married life. Well, say something! Don't just sit there, Mongicourt! What's the matter? [*He turns to see* MONGICOURT] Oh, bother! I've put him to sleep. [*He runs to the door of* MME PETYPON'*s room*] It works. Gabrielle! Quick. Come and look! Mongicourt's gone to sleep!

[*She comes in wearing the very unsuitable dress* MONGICOURT *bought for* SHRIMP.]

MME PETYPON [*looks at* MONGICOURT]: Gone to sleep …! In our house? How rude!

PETYPON [*aside*]: Oh, my God. He bought that for the Shrimp. It doesn't suit her! [*To* MME PETYPON] It's my new Chair of Oblivion. Excellent for operations.

MME PETYPON: Poor Mongicourt. He does look funny.

PETYPON: Don't touch him!

MME PETYPON: Why ever not?

PETYPON: The current will pass straight into you if you touch him, and knock you out as cold as he is. He looks happy. Ridiculously happy. [*He shouts*] Life's not as good as that, Mongicourt!

[*He presses a button in the arm of the Chair.* MONGICOURT *wakes, smiling as he feels for* MME PETYPON.]

MONGICOURT: I love you, my darling. And you look enchanting in that little dress.

PETYPON: Stop it, Mongicourt! It's my wife!

MONGICOURT [*disappointed*]: Your wife? Oh dear, I was dreaming of someone else entirely. Can I go to sleep again? It was delicious.

PETYPON: Don't be greedy!

[MONGICOURT *gets reluctantly out of the chair.*]

PETYPON: Isn't it wonderful? Think of the operations you'll be able to perform! In the privacy of your own home. That reminds me ... speaking of operations. Gabrielle. I leave in fifteen minutes.

MME PETYPON: Fifteen minutes ...? Do you like this little dress? I think it rather suits me.

PETYPON: Enchanting! But duty calls! An urgent appendicitis ... in the country.

MME PETYPON [*understanding*]: A doctor's life. Always on call ...

PETYPON: I keep a valise ready packed, for such emergencies ...

[*He goes to his bedroom,* MONGICOURT *follows him.*]

MONGICOURT: You're leaving her behind?

PETYPON: Really, Mongicourt. I can't turn up with two women. I'm not a Turk!

MONGICOURT: Then I'll leave you ...

PETYPON: Goodbye. I say, Mongicourt ...

MONGICOURT: Yes, Petypon?

PETYPON: It's not a day we'll ever forget!

[PETYPON *goes into his bedroom.* ÉTIENNE *appears on the threshold with a letter on a salver.*]

ÉTIENNE: This just arrived for Madame.

[MME PETYPON *takes the letter and opens it.*]

MME PETYPON [*reading the letter*]: Pardon me ... Doctor Mongicourt ... The General wants us to go to a wedding ... in Touraine! His niece! Why didn't he say anything about it ...? And Lucien's away operating. He wants me to do the honours ...

MONGICOURT: Good day, Madame. [*He goes with* ÉTIENNE]

MME PETYPON: Oh, good day, Doctor Mongicourt. I'll have to go! And do the honours. It's so sad Lucien can't come ...

[PETYPON *reappears with a hat and an umbrella, carrying a valise.*]

PETYPON: Look, I'm ready!

MME PETYPON: Lucien. You can't guess what this letter's about ...

PETYPON: Tell me when I come back ...

MME PETYPON: But you *must* know ...

PETYPON: My dear. I can't wait. It's a matter of life and death. Seconds may be precious!

GÉNÉRAL [*offstage*]: Isn't my nephew ready yet? Show a leg there, Petypon!

PETYPON: Oh my God! My uncle! [*Pulling* MME PETYPON *towards the bedroom*] Come in here. Quick! You can read it to me in your bedroom.

MME PETYPON [*pulling away from him*]: Whatever for? I can read it perfectly well in here ...

PETYPON [*pulling her*]: No, come in here!

MME PETYPON: Leave me alone! [*She pulls violently away from him and falls into the Chair of Oblivion.*] I'm exhausted. And so hot! [*She starts to fan herself with the letter.*]

GÉNÉRAL: Left, right! Left, right! Left, right!

PETYPON: It's the only way!

[*He rushes to the switch box and presses a button. The chair vibrates. Immediately* MME PETYPON *freezes as she fans herself and is totally immobile.*]

GÉNÉRAL [*offstage*]: In *there*, did you say?

PETYPON: I've got to hide her.

[*He picks up the tablecloth and throws it over his wife as the* GÉNÉRAL *bursts in.*]

GÉNÉRAL: Petypon ... I've come to pick you up ... Can't rely on you getting to the Gare de Lyon under your own steam ...

PETYPON: I'm coming!

GÉNÉRAL [*looks at the shrouded figure*]: What the devil's that?

PETYPON: That? Oh, that's nothing. An anatomical model ... Don't touch it!

GÉNÉRAL: Why?

PETYPON: Wet paint. You go on downstairs. I'll be with you in a second.

GÉNÉRAL: No more than a second! I'm not having you parading late! [*He goes.*]

PETYPON [*looks guiltily at the chair*]: I can't go away for the weekend and leave my wife frozen stiff!

[*There's a noise at the door and* ÉTIENNE *appears on the threshold with a large and vociferous* DUSTMAN *who comes in with a cigarette stuck to his lower lip and shouting.*]

ÉTIENNE: Just a moment, my friend. I'll tell M'sieur le Docteur ...

DUSTMAN: But I'm expected ... I'm an honoured guest. I am ... [*Seeing* PETYPON] Hullo again. Doctor Petypon!

PETYPON: Who's that?

ÉTIENNE: No one is allowed to cross the threshold.

PETYPON: Let him in.

DUSTMAN [*triumphantly to* ÉTIENNE]: You see! A bloody honoured guest!

[ÉTIENNE *goes. The* DUSTMAN *advances on* PETYPON, *smiling, still smoking.*]

DUSTMAN: Remember me, don't you, Doctor Petypon? I'm the dustman from the Rue Royale.

PETYPON: What on earth do *you* want?

DUSTMAN: What do I want? I've come to dinner.

PETYPON: You've *what?*

DUSTMAN: You asked me to dinner. This morning.

PETYPON: This morning?

DUSTMAN: There I was, emptying the dustbins around dawn, in the Rue Royale, and there you was, going home with your arm about your little bit of fancy goods and you said, 'I like your face' and you asked me to dinner!

PETYPON: What?

DUSTMAN [*takes a card out of his belt, cleans it on his shirt and presents it, holding his cap out like a salver*]: Your card what you gave me. 'Doctor Lucien Petypon. Operations at all times.'

PETYPON: Look ... Here's forty sous ... You can have dinner in the kitchen ... My salvation!

DUSTMAN: My benefactor!

PETYPON: Listen! When I've gone I want you to go and eat in the kitchen. Then just press this button here, understood?

DUSTMAN: Understood! God bless you, M'sieur. You'll never forget it. Forty sous!

PETYPON: Goodbye, Gabrielle! [*He goes.*]

DUSTMAN: As a matter of fact, my name's Georges ... Now ... *That* button, he said ...

[*He presses the button.* MME PETYPON *starts to stir under the table-cloth.*]

MME PETYPON: Mmm! It's a man! My God! I've gone blind!

[*She hits out, striking the* DUSTMAN *on the cheek.*]

DUSTMAN: Steady on!

MME PETYPON [*rushes up right, towards the table by the door*]: Who are you?

DUSTMAN [*barring her way*]: I'm the dustman what you asked to dinner.

MME PETYPON [*changing course and running towards the other door*]: Étienne! Étienne!

DUSTMAN: But I'm the dustman what you asked to dinner.

MME PETYPON: Étienne! Étienne!

[MME PETYPON *goes.*]

DUSTMAN: But I'm the dustman what you asked to dinner. Some people are so common! I mean, they're very free with their invitations, but when it comes to carving the joint, they all go absent. That Dr Petypon! I would say definitely not a gentleman. [*He goes and sits on the chair. He starts to light a fresh cigarette from the stub of his previous one.*] But I'm sitting here! Until I gets my dinner. Even if it means sitting here all night. I'm definitely not moving. [*He stubs his cigarette butt out hard – on the button on the arm of the chair. With his other hand halfway to his mouth with the newly lighted cigarette, he freezes stiff.*]

THE CURTAIN FALLS

ACT II

The Château du Grêlé in Touraine.

A large salon, upstage three arched French windows open onto a terrace which overlooks the Park. Console tables against the wall. Right two large doors, between them a chimney-piece with an ancestral portrait over it. A door left with a piano near it. Five chairs near the piano and a chair and a piano stool in front of it. On the right there's an easy chair facing the piano, and other chairs. Near the French windows on the right a buffet is set out on a table. There are lamps and hanging electric lustres worked by a switch on the left. Bouquets of flowers, moonlight on the terrace, and the GÉNÉRAL's *uniform cap on the piano.*

As the Curtain rises the room is full of guests. THE DUCHESSE DE VALMONTÉ, *who is deaf and carries an ear trumpet, and her son* THE DUC DE VALMONTÉ, *and the following other guests:*

SAUVAREL	The Prefect.
MME SAUVAREL	Prefect's wife, middle aged, middle class, desperately anxious to be a worthy wife for an aspiring Politician.
VIDAUBAN	Tries to be very elegant.
MME VIDAUBAN	Very 'county', huntin' and shootin'.
MME PONANT	Giggly and silly.
MME CLAUX	Provincial femme fatale, tries to be very fashionable.
MME HAUTIGNOL	Spectacles. Provincial 'blue stocking'.
MME VIRETTE	Plump, stolid housewife.
OFFICERS: CHAMEROT, GUÉRISSAC, VARLIN	

The butler ÉMILE *is behind the buffet. On the terrace there are three* SERVANTS *in livery. In the centre of the room the* GÉNÉRAL *is presenting a handsome clock to the* ABBÉ. *A* FOOTMAN *is holding it. He lifts the large clock case to show it off: it's elaborate in bronze and gilt. The* OFFICERS, *thumbs in mouths, blow a mock bugle call. The* GUESTS, *enraptured, say* It's a clock!

GÉNÉRAL: To celebrate my return to my ancestral home after nine years in smelly Senegal and also the forthcoming marriage of my niece Clémentine. I wish to present this handsome timepiece to our local church. [*Applause*] This clock was looted from the Cathedral in Venice by Napoleon's old Guard, so it ought to be good. It's yours, M'sieur l'Abbé.

[*Another mock bugle call by the* OFFICERS. *The* GUESTS *all clap.*]

ABBÉ: M'sieur le Général is too generous! I must embrace you, General. [*He rushes to embrace the* GÉNÉRAL.]

GÉNÉRAL [*fending him off*]: Just a kiss on the cheek. After all, you're not beautiful and you're not a girl!

[*As they embrace the* GUESTS *clap politely again.*]

GÉNÉRAL [*to the* FOOTMAN]: Put the cover back and leave the clock on the table. M'sieur l'Abbé can take it after the party. [*To the* FOOTMAN] All right. Scoot!

[*The* FOOTMAN *puts the clock on a console table and goes. The* SHRIMP *comes in from the terrace, dressed as if she were going to a lover, with* CLÉMENTINE, *the* GÉNÉRAL'*s niece and* PETYPON *who is guarding the* SHRIMP, *terrified of her giving him away.*]

SHRIMP: Atten-shun! Having a nice time? Alright, Duchess?

GÉNÉRAL: There's my adorable Mme Petypon. Isn't she charming?

MME VIDAUBAN: Devilish handsome! [*Whispers to the other ladies*] Looks a little go-er.

MME PONANT [*whispers, giggling wildly*]: Did you ever see so much of anyone's undies?

MME CLAUX: It's the latest thing in Paris! [*Whispers*] I think it's so terribly romantic, showing your undies.

MME VIRETTE: Brussels lace! [*Whispers*] I wonder how much that cost a metre!

MME SAUVAREL [*whispers*]: My Sauvarel's promised me lace undies when he's made a Minister.

MME HAUTIGNOL [*whispers*]: She looks a tremendously *intelligent* lady. No doubt reads a tremendous lot of Alfred de Musset. Well, they all do in Paris.

DUCHESS [*loudly*]: A touch of class! So unusual at the General's! [*To* SHRIMP] You're a Queen of Elegance, my dear!

SHRIMP: Jesus Christ on a bicycle, Duchess! You're pulling my leg.

MME HAUTIGNOL: Such wit! Such brilliance!

MME PONANT: She's killing! [*Giggles*]

MME VIDAUBAN: Sparkish! I told you she was a go-er.

MME CLAUX: 'Jesus Christ on a bicycle' – that's terribly Parisian!

GÉNÉRAL [*to the three* OFFICERS]: Isn't she a wild success here ... My little niece, Petypon.

GUÉRISSAC: It's the Parisian glitter, shining in the Provinces!

CHAMEROT: Doesn't she remind you of someone, though? I'll be damned if I haven't met her somewhere.

VARLIN: So will I! Was it the Ball ... at the Brazilian Embassy?

CHAMEROT: My God, you're right! Or was it the Ball *somewhere* else?

GÉNÉRAL [*to* CLÉMENTINE *and the* SHRIMP]: You have everything you want, my dear nieces?

SHRIMP *and* CLÉMENTINE: Oh yes, Uncle.

PETYPON: Oh yes, Uncle.

GÉNÉRAL: You're not a niece! You're long in the tooth for a nephew. You'd be ridiculous as a niece! [*To the* SHRIMP] You should give Clémentine a few tips ... on the Parisian glitter!

SHRIMP: Oh, I'm going to Uncle. I promise you I'll let her into all my secrets ...

PETYPON: God forbid!

GÉNÉRAL: Come up to the picture gallery, Petypon. I want you to meet M'sieur Sauvarel, our Préfet ... He's up there admiring the water colours.

PETYPON [*aside to the* GÉNÉRAL]: I can't leave my wife.

GÉNÉRAL: Of course you can leave your wife. They won't eat her. [*He seizes* PETYPON*'s arm and propels him out of the door. As they go the* GÉNÉRAL *speaks to the audience*] My God – he's a jealous bugger!

> [*There's a moment of general conversation as the guests split into two groups. The* DUCHESS, VIDAUBAN *and* MADAME VIDAUBAN *are in one group. The* DUCHESS*'s voice rings out.*]

DUCHESS: My dear, it's false and malicious gossip to say that the Baroness has fallen in love with her Coachman. I have it on excellent authority it's the Cook! [*She turns and calls*] Guy!

SHRIMP [*who is at the buffet with the* GUESTS, *comes quickly down to the* DUCHESS]: You want something, Duchess?

DUCHESS: I called my son to bring me a glass of water.

SHRIMP [*yodelling for* ÉMILE]: Yoodle ... eye ... ee ... o! Émile!

> [ÉMILE, *astonished, comes downstage from the buffet.*]

ALL: Ah!

ÉMILE: Madame?

SHRIMP [*grandly*]: A glass of water for the Duchess!
    [ÉMILE *bows and goes.*]
SHRIMP: Quick as a tortoise, that flunkey. [*The* DUCHESS *laughs*] What's
    so funny?
DUCHESS: You calling him 'flunkey'.
SHRIMP [*laughing back*]: Don't you know the word 'flunkey'?
DUCHESS: Naturally I know it!
SHRIMP [*starts a little dance, slapping her bottom and doing a little kick as she
    chants*]:

> The Duchess don't say 'Flunkey'
> She thinks it's not polite
> She calls her man her monkey
> And keeps him up all night!

    [*To* MADAME VIDAUBAN, *who's looking at her, amazed*] Hear that,
    darling? The Duchess don't say 'flunkey' ...
MME VIDAUBAN [*slapping herself on the bottom, imitating the* SHRIMP]: The
    Duchess don't say 'flunkey'! Marvellous!
SHRIMP [*slaps her bottom*]: The Duchess don't say 'flunkey'.
MME VIDAUBAN: Marvellous!
EVERYONE: Marvellous!
MME VIDAUBAN: My husband goes to Paris once a month. He keeps up
    with the fashions, don't you, Roy?
VIDAUBAN [*elegantly slapping his bottom*]: The Duchess don't say 'flunkey'.
    She thinks it's not polite ...
    [ÉMILE *brings the* DUCHESS *her glass of water on a tray.*]
DUCHESS: Thank you, flunkey. [*She takes the glass of water.*] Hilarious!
ÉMILE [*going, annoyed, with his tray*]: Flunkey! Charming!
DUCHESS [*smiling at the* SHRIMP]: I'm so out of touch with your Parisienne
    wit. Now I want you to meet my eldest son. Guy!
    [*A large, sturdy young man, chattering with other guests and with his
    back to the audience, detaches himself from the group. He is smoking.*]
THE DUKE [*coming downstage quickly*]: – Yes, Mama?
SHRIMP: I don't believe it! Is this great big bouncing boy, *yours*, Duchess?
DUKE: Absolutely, Madam.
DUCHESS: Believe it or not.
SHRIMP: Christ on a bicycle!
DUCHESS: He grows so fast ... And I'm worried about sending him to
    Paris ...
    [*The* DUKE *winks at the audience and moves to the* SHRIMP.]
    But then he's got to work. And he's got no talent of any sort.
    [*The* DUKE *looks sulky.*]
SHRIMP [*looking at the* DUKE, *under her breath*]: Thick as two planks!

DUCHESS: So he's going to be an author.

SHRIMP: That's obvious!

DUCHESS: I mean, any fool can write: but it has to be done in Paris. You see, the terrible worry about my great baby is – he's enormously rich!

[*The* SHRIMP *twirls round to face the* DUKE *who lowers his eyes modestly.*]

LADIES: Ah!

SHRIMP: Ah!

[*The* DUCHESS *moves and whispers to the ladies so her son won't hear her.*]

DUCHESS: Now ... he's growing up to be quite a little man.

SHRIMP: I can see that!

DUCHESS: And we all know ... Men are the victims of certain carnal lusts ...

SHRIMP [*looks up piously*]: I've read that somewhere ...

DUCHESS: If he happened to meet ... one of *those* terrible women ...

SHRIMP: She'd eat him alive? Oh, Duchess, darling. Do let me take your glass!

[*The* DUKE *was about to take it, but the* SHRIMP *is too quick for him, and his hand is left suspended in the air.*]

DUCHESS: Don't you bother! The flunkey's there!

SHRIMP: No trouble!

[*She grabs the glass and passes very near the* DUKE*, so she gazes into his eyes and then, seizing his hand, pulls him quickly to her and then passes on, leaving the* DUKE *staggering to the left. The* SHRIMP *puts the glass on the buffet.*]

DUCHESS [*to* MME VIDAUBAN]: What a charming girl!

MME VIDAUBAN: Charming!

[*The* SHRIMP *returns and, in passing, pinches the* DUKE*'s lower lip and wobbles it up and down.*]

MME CLAUX: Parisian compliments, such style!

MME HAUTIGNOL: So elegant! So romantic!

SHRIMP: Hullo, my big green rabbit!

DUCHESS [*to* MME VIDAUBAN]: She could charm the birds out of the trees.

MME VIDAUBAN: A little go-er! Doesn't funk her fences.

MME PONANT: She's a scream!

MME HAUTIGNOL: We're so starved here – for really *witty* conversation.

SHRIMP [*moving innocently to the* DUCHESS]: I done the job. I do fancy your son. [*She looks at the* DUKE] Something amazing.

[*The* DUKE*, totally confused and embarrassed, twists round and strides towards the terrace.*]

SHRIMP [*under her breath as he goes*]: Fat head!

DUCHESS: You fancy him something amazing? You're too kind!

[PETYPON *comes in from the door on the left with* SAUVAREL.]

SAUVAREL: You're not interested in politics, M'sieur?

PETYPON: I hardly have the time.

SAUVAREL: A Prefect's life is not a happy one. I've just had another stupid order from the Minister in Paris. We are to count all the telegraph poles ...

PETYPON [*aside*]: My God! The Shrimp with the Duchess! [*He rushes to her and slaps her hard on the bottom.*]

SHRIMP: Clumsy camel!

DUCHESS: Excuse me?

SHRIMP: I was just chattering to my idiot of a husband. You don't mind?

DUCHESS: Please ...

SHRIMP [*to* PETYPON]: What's up with you, Patapouffe?

PETYPON: You're mad! Flinging yourself at the Duchess!

SHRIMP: Thank you very much. I'll talk to who I like. [*She moves away and kicks her leg over the chair between her and* PETYPON, *saying loudly*] Cheer up darling. How's your father?

PETYPON [*appalled*]: No!

EVERYONE [*amazed*]: Ah!

[*They all stand,* MESDAMES VIRETTE, *the* BARONESS, PONANT *and* HAUTIGNOL *move to the piano. The* DUCHESS *and* MONSIEUR *and* MADAME VIDAUBAN *move to join* MADAME CLAUX *at the buffet.*]

SHRIMP [*suddenly realizing the impression she's made*]: Have I said the wrong thing?

PETYPON: Oh no!

GÉNÉRAL [*moving to the front of the piano*]: Charming, her little jokes! Cheer up darling. How's your father? [*Moves to the* DUCHESS *at the buffet*]

PETYPON: Oh, yes. It's the latest thing in Paris! All the chic ladies of the Faubourg Saint Germain say that.

SHRIMP: The chicest of the chic!

EVERYONE: Really! You don't say! Chicest of the chic! Indeed! [*etc, etc.*]

PETYPON: It was started by the Princess of Waterloo and what she says ... Everyone just has to say it. Isn't that right, Madame Vidauban? You know about these Parisienne crazes.

MME VIDAUBAN: Of course. [*To* MONSIEUR VIDAUBAN] You know I'm always saying it, Roy! [*She kicks her leg over a chair, imitating the* SHRIMP.] Cheer up, darling. How's your father?

EVERYONE [*amazed*]: Ah!

SHRIMP [*clapping like a child*]: Encore! Encore!

SAUVAREL [*to his wife*]: You'd better start learning to behave like a Parisienne my dear or I'll never get on in the world. Study it!

MADAME SAUVAREL [*carries a chair to the extreme left and tries clumsily to kick her leg over it, muttering*]: Cheer up darling. How's your father?
   [*There's a fanfare outside the door.*]

GÉNÉRAL: It's the firemen, parading to pay their respects! Come on everyone … Let's inspect the firemen! [*Taking* PETYPON*'s arm*] Come along you!

PETYPON: But Uncle …

GÉNÉRAL: You can leave your wife for five minutes. Jealous bugger!
   [*He takes* PETYPON *off. As they go they pass* MADAME SAUVAREL *who is in agony trying to get her leg over the chair.*]

GÉNÉRAL [*encouraging*]: Bravo, Madame Sauvarel!
   [*Nearly everyone has gone. The* DUKE *is last. Seeing him the* SHRIMP *tiptoes towards him and traps him by the buffet. As he moves away she twists him round to face her.*]

SHRIMP: Kiss me!

DUKE: What?

SHRIMP: Kiss me, fat head!
   [*The* DUKE *looks embarrassed at the audience. Then he tries to kiss the* SHRIMP *on the cheek, but she turns her head so that he gets her lips instead. He looks at the audience astonished, smacking his lips reflectively.*]

SHRIMP: Did it taste nasty?

DUKE: Actually it was … absolutely delicious, Madame …

SHRIMP: I fancy you!

DUKE: I can't believe it.

SHRIMP: Cut my throat if I tell a lie? You'll come and see me in Paris?

DUKE: But … what about your husband?

SHRIMP [*takes his hand, leads him towards a chair and sits down*]: Don't give him a thought. You'll come, won't you? It's very chic, where I live …

DUKE: I'm sure it must be …

SHRIMP: Cheer up, darling. How's your father? [*With a brisk movement she pulls the* DUKE *down so that he's sitting on her lap.*] Oh … The Little Dukey and his Shrimp! [*She puts her arms round him and nurses him like a baby.*] Are you comfy, darling?

DUKE [*delighted, kicking happily*]: Yes! Absolutely!

SHRIMP: All right then. Kiss me, my big green rabbit. Does it like to have its nose rubbed by its Shrimpy, then?
   [PETYPON *comes in from the left and sees the couple intertwined.*]

PETYPON: Excuse me!

DUKE [*twisting round on the* SHRIMP*'s lap*]: Confound it! It's your husband! Put me down!

SHRIMP: Take no notice of him, darling!

DUKE: Put me down! [*He leaps off her lap and moves to the extreme right.*]

PETYPON [*moving to the* SHRIMP, *who gets up calmly*]: Are you out of your mind? If anyone saw you …

DUKE [*astonished*]: *What* did he say?

SHRIMP [*bored*]: Don't you start again, Patapouffe.

PETYPON: What on earth did you think you were doing – with a Duke on your knee?

SHRIMP: Where did you want me to put him?

PETYPON: Do what you like in Paris. While you're here for Heaven's sake behave yourself! [*He moves to the* DUKE] Of course, it's perfectly natural, M'sieur le Duc. She's very pretty, you're young … and strong. You'll have plenty of opportunities in Paris. Can't you just wait a little?

DUKE [*to the* SHRIMP]: That seems absolutely reasonable doesn't it. Madame?

SHRIMP: Don't take any notice of Patapouffe. He's a stuffed shirt!

PETYPON: Me! A stuffed shirt!

DUKE: You can't really blame him …

PETYPON [*moving to the door*]: If M'sieur le Duc could be a little discreet …

DUKE: Discreet? Absolutely! By the way, what's your address in Paris?

PETYPON: 66, Boulevard Malesherbes. Why do you want to know?

DUKE [*writing it on his cuff*]: So … [*He looks at the* SHRIMP.] So I can call on you when you're out.

PETYPON: Then I'll be delighted to receive you. [*He looks through the door*] God in heaven, it's Gabrielle! What's she doing here? [*He seizes the* SHRIMP *by the thumb and drags her to the door on the left.*]

SHRIMP: What's the matter?

PETYPON: This isn't the time to ask questions!

SHRIMP [*blowing kisses to the* DUKE]: Goodbye little Dukey! See you soon, darling. [*She is pulled out left.*]

DUKE [*who has followed her to the doorway*]: I've conquered a woman of the world! How absolutely wonderful! I'm starting to have affairs! If only I could tell Mama! She always said I'd take up with one of those terrible women.

> [ÉMILE *comes in carrying* GABRIELLE*'s valise, followed by* GABRIELLE *in a travelling costume.*]

ÉMILE: No one else was expected tonight, Madame.

MME PETYPON: What are you saying? You mean there's no room reserved for Madame Petypon?

ÉMILE: Madame Petypon? Yes, of course she has a room.

MME PETYPON: Good! Put my luggage in it.

ÉMILE: Really? If you say so ... [*He goes out carrying the case.*]

DUKE [*to himself*]: I've conquered a woman of the world! [*To* MADAME PETYPON] Oh, excuse me, Madame.

MME PETYPON: No! Excuse *me*! I'm still dressed for the train. [*She puts her handbag on the piano.*]

DUKE: That's perfectly all right.

MME PETYPON: The Général's not here?

DUKE: I think he's in the garden. Reviewing the firemen.

MME PETYPON: I came as quickly as I could. I expect the dear Général has been lost without a lady to help him out.

DUKE: Absolutely. [*Aside*] What an old boiler! I'd rather have Madame Petypon.

MME PETYPON: I'll go and see if they've unpacked my suitcase.

GÉNÉRAL [*offstage*]: Welcome to you, gallant firemen. There's beer and wine for you in the kitchen, men. Try not to get tight!

FIREMEN [*offstage*]: Long live the Général.

GÉNÉRAL: Try not to get sozzled!

[*The* GÉNÉRAL *comes in with the other* GUESTS. MADAME PETYPON *moves towards him, smiling. The* GÉNÉRAL *is surrounded by the* LADY GUESTS, *to whom he makes his comments.*]

MME PETYPON: Ah, my dear Général! There you are!

GÉNÉRAL [*aside to the other* LADIES]: Who the devil invited *her*? [*To* MADAME PETYPON] My dear lady! Delighted to see you! Of course ...

MME PETYPON: I'm sorry to be dressed like this. I didn't know it was a party.

GÉNÉRAL: The devil you didn't!

MME PETYPON: I'll go up and change. I've already sent my luggage upstairs.

GÉNÉRAL [*aside to the other* LADIES]: She's making herself at home! [*The other* LADIES *giggle*]

MME PETYPON: I came by express train. I wish I could have brought my husband – but he was busy unfortunately ... Please excuse him ...

GÉNÉRAL: Don't mention it! Couldn't you have brought the rest of your family? [*The other* LADIES *laugh*]

MME PETYPON: Alas, I have no other family ... yet.

GÉNÉRAL [*aside to the other* LADIES]: Thank God for that!

[*The* DUCHESS *comes in on the arm of the* PRÉFET.]

MME PETYPON: You see, I've done my duty and turned up. In spite of the ghosts!

GÉNÉRAL: Ghosts! No such thing as ghosts!

MME PETYPON: Well I've come. That's the great thing! Now, aren't you going to introduce me to these ladies?

GÉNÉRAL: Of course! Pleasure! [*To the other* LADIES] Devil take it, I've entirely forgotten this old boiler's name. She's some sort of a friend of Madame Petypon's.

MME PONANT: A Parisienne?

GÉNÉRAL: Old vintage.

THE LADIES: Enchanted to meet you!

[*They stretch out in a line in the following order –* MESDAMES VIRETTE, CLAUX, HAUTIGNOL, SAUVAREL, VIDAUBAN, *and by the piano* MADAME PONANT *is chatting with the* OFFICERS, *and after her* THE ABBÉ.]

GÉNÉRAL: Mesdames. May I introduce … Madame … What's her name! Madame Vidauban …

MME VIDAUBAN [*kicking her leg over a chair*]: Cheer up darling. How's your father?

GÉNÉRAL: Madame Sauvarel.

MME SAUVAREL [*kicking her leg over a chair*]: Cheer up, darling. How's your father?

GÉNÉRAL: Madame Hautignol.

MME HAUTIGNOL [*kicking her leg over a chair*]: Cheer up, darling. How's your father?

MME PETYPON [*aside*]: Extraordinary! It must be an old custom in Touraine!

GÉNÉRAL: Mesdames Claux and Virette.

[*The two* LADIES *do a kick at the same time and succeed in kicking each other.*]

MME VIRETTE: I'm sorry! I hurt you!

MME CLAUX: Not a bit. Are you all right?

MME VIRETTE: Stupidly clumsy of me.

MME PETYPON [*aside*]: You have to come down to the country to see this sort of thing!

GÉNÉRAL: And my dear old friend, the Abbé Chantreau.

ABBÉ: Cheer up, darling. How's your father? [*He kicks his leg over a chair – his* CHAPLAIN *applauds.*]

MME PETYPON [*aside*]: Even the clergy at it!

GÉNÉRAL: My dear Duchess. May I present Madame Thingamyjig … The Dowager Duchess of Valmonté.

MME PETYPON [*kicks her leg over a chair*]: Cheer up darling. How's your father? [*Aside*] Since they're all doing it!

DUCHESS: Forgive me. I can't get my leg up. I'm deaf.

MME PETYPON: Ladies and gentlemen. More champagne. [*Calls to* ÉMILE] Fill the glasses, my man.

[*A* FOOTMAN *enters and announces*]

FOOTMAN: M'sieur and Madame Tournay!

[*The* TOURNAYS *enter. The* GÉNÉRAL *comes up to the* TOURNAYS, *but* MME PETYPON *gets to them before him and pushes him aside.*]

MME PETYPON: Ah M'sieur and Madame Tournay – how good of you to come! [*She kicks her leg vaguely over a chair*] Cheer up darlings. How's your father? [*Rattling on*] I must say you're dreadfully late. Whatever happened to you both?

M. TOURNAY: It's my wife. It takes her simply *hours* to dress!

MME TOURNAY: Oh yes. It's me. It takes me simply hours to dress.

MME PETYPON: Well I haven't had time to dress at all! I'm just as I am when I stepped off the express train. I was in such a mad rush to get to the dear Général's party.

M. TOURNAY: Think nothing of it. We quite understand ...

MME TOURNAY: We quite understand. Think nothing of it.

GÉNÉRAL: Madame! I'm very grateful to you for receiving my guests, but ...

MME PETYPON: Think nothing of it. It's a pleasure ... [*To the* TOURNAYS] Have you two latecomers met the dear Général. Général, M'sieur and Madame Tournay. She takes simply hours to dress.

GÉNÉRAL: Dammit! She's taking over my Château. [*To* MME TOURNAY] Dear Madame ...

MME PETYPON: Come. Let's find you a drink. [*Surges in front of the* GÉNÉRAL *and leads the* TOURNAYS *to the buffet.*] Your husband can come too of course.

GÉNÉRAL: Madame. Will you kindly allow me ...

MME PETYPON: Just relax, Général. Remember, I'm in charge. [*To the* TOURNAYS] Just take whatever you fancy.

GÉNÉRAL: This old boiler's beginning to drive me off my rocker!

MME PETYPON [*leaving the* TOURNAYS *at the bar*]: There! You see ... Mission accomplished!

GÉNÉRAL: Congratulations! But from now on, Madame ...

MME PETYPON: Please. Don't call me Madame ...

GÉNÉRAL: What the devil should I call you?

MME PETYPON: Call me niece – and I'll call you 'Uncle'.

[*She kisses him and the* SERVANTS *giggle behind their hands.*]

GÉNÉRAL [*aside*]: She's completely cracked! [*He sees the* SHRIMP *and*

CLÉMENTINE *coming in arm in arm from the terrace.*] Ah! The cousins ... [*To* CLÉMENTINE] Has she been teaching you how to behave in Paris, Clémentine? What! She's put a bit of spit and polish on you ready for the bridal parade!

SHRIMP [*jumps to left*]: Old mother Petypon! I know why the Doctor jumps like a rabbit whenever he sees her! [*She moves near the* GÉNÉRAL]

GÉNÉRAL: My niece Clémentine. Who'll be a bride tomorrow.

MME PETYPON: But she's ravishing. Congratulations my dear!

GÉNÉRAL: And may I introduce Madame Petypon!

[MADAME PETYPON *is about to speak when the* SHRIMP *interrupts her desperately.*]

SHRIMP: Introduce us! Christ on a bicycle! That's a joke, that is! He wants to introduce us! Lovely to see you, darling. How *are* you...?

MME PETYPON [*astonished*]: Me? I'm perfectly well ... Thank you. And you?

SHRIMP: Still kicking, thanks. Oh, I'm so glad to see you. You look blooming.

GÉNÉRAL: She looks blooming!

SHRIMP: You know I was hardly able to get away. Émile's terribly ill.

MME PETYPON [*bewildered*]: Émile?

SHRIMP: Touch of the old trouble. And you know Jeanne's going to marry Charles...?

MME PETYPON: Charles?

SHRIMP: Isn't it amazing! Well, she had to – but with that terrible nose! Of course he's got pots of money ... Oh dear ... You heard about Gustave?

MME PETYPON: Gustave...?

SHRIMP: Shot himself? Well, the flics were on to him. What you going to drink, darling? Orangeade? Iced coffee?

MME PETYPON: Beer!

SHRIMP: Lovely to see you, darling! I'll get it.

MME PETYPON: Who on earth's that woman?

GÉNÉRAL: What woman?

MME PETYPON: The woman who thought she knew me?

GÉNÉRAL [*laughing heartily*]: *Thought* she knew you! Bless my soul. You Parisiennes ... Quite cracked!

[*The other* GUESTS *join in the loud laughter and then join the* SHRIMP *at the buffet.* MADAME PETYPON *goes to them, asking desperately*]

MME PETYPON: But who *is* she? Who?

MME VIDAUBAN: Parisienne wit! It's hilarious!

MME PETYPON [*to the* ABBÉ]: Can't you tell me? Who *is* she...?

ABBÉ: Funny! Very, very funny! Who is she? Best joke I ever heard!

MME PETYPON [*aside*]: It seems very easy to make them laugh! [*She stops* ÉMILE, *who is passing with his tray*] Tell me, my friend. Who's that woman talking to the Général?

ÉMILE: That? Oh, that's Madame Petypon, to be sure! [*He goes off, collecting empty glasses.*]

MME PETYPON: What? Madame Petypon? My dear! And I never knew the Général was married! [*She rushes to the* SHRIMP *with her arms outstretched*] The footman just told me you were Madame Petypon!

SHRIMP [*alarmed*]: Oh ...

MME PETYPON: Aunty...! [*She kisses the* SHRIMP *warmly.*]

GÉNÉRAL: Why the devil are you calling her Aunty?

MME PETYPON [*leaving the* SHRIMP *and going to* MADAME VIDAUBAN]: She's my aunt! And I never realized ...

GÉNÉRAL: Completely cracked! She called me Uncle!

MME PETYPON [*to the* ABBÉ]: She's my aunt, father!

GÉNÉRAL: He's her *father* now!

MME PETYPON [*crossing the room*]: I'll just slip up and change. I won't be a minute ... [*She goes*]

GÉNÉRAL [*to* GUÉRISSAC]: I suppose you're her nephew!

GUÉRISSAC [*laughing*]: God forbid!

GÉNÉRAL: Well then. You're not her nephew! But you probably will be. By the time she gets down again. Who let her in, that's what I want to know? Who the devil let the old boiler in?

[CLÉMENTINE *comes in and goes to the* GÉNÉRAL, *worried.*]

CLÉMENTINE: Uncle, I'm so miserable. My fiancé's still not here. What can I do?

GÉNÉRAL: I don't know. Ask your cousin about it. She'll have the latest idea on keeping your Lieutenant Corignon up to scratch.

[CLÉMENTINE *is moving up to the* SHRIMP *when* PETYPON *rushes in from the door on the right and up to the* SHRIMP.]

SHRIMP: Psst!

PETYPON: There you are!

SHRIMP: Your wife's here ...

PETYPON: I know!

SHRIMP: What're you going to do about it?

PETYPON: I saw her go into our bedroom ... The key was on the outside ... So ... I gave it a couple of turns ... And we're safe for the moment!

SHRIMP: What good's that going to do?

PETYPON: I'm buying time. It's the best I can hope for now ...

[*He moves back a pace as the* DUCHESS, *who has been talking to the* GÉNÉRAL, *comes up anxiously to the* SHRIMP.]

DUCHESS: The fiancé doesn't seem to be turning up after all. I really think ... dear Madame Petypon, that he's not coming. [*She starts to laugh*] We've all been brought here on false pretences!

SHRIMP [*laughing*]: On false pretences! Yes ...

DUCHESS [*laughing*]: We've all been tricked!

SHRIMP [*laughs*]: Tricked! Of course ... [*Stops laughing*] He's not coming. Oh *shit*!

    [*A moment of general horror.* PETYPON *is rooted to the spot. There's an icy silence, then the whispering starts. What did she say etc., etc.*]

PETYPON: It's all the rage in Paris. Started by the Baroness Birkheim who first said it ... [*He looks round, aware that he's making no impression*] ... at the Rothschild Ball ... Shouldn't we dance?

GÉNÉRAL [*from behind the piano*]: Of course we should!

SHRIMP [*pirouetting on her way to the piano*]: Lovely! Come on, twinkletoes, let's have a quadrille!

PETYPON [*catching the* SHRIMP *as she pirouettes*]: No! I'm not having you dancing here!

SHRIMP: Not me darling! I'm going to tinkle the ivories!

PETYPON [*letting her go*]: That's better ...

    [*The* DUCHESS *sits down at the piano.*]

DUCHESS: I think I can remember the quadrille.

    [*The* SHRIMP *pirouettes up and sits down beside her at the piano.*]

SHRIMP: We'll make it a duet!

    [CHAMEROT *is at the buffet with* GUÉRISSAC *as the music starts and the dancers get into place.* CHAMEROT *suddenly strikes his forehead.*]

CHAMEROT: I've got it!

GUÉRISSAC: What?

CHAMEROT: Who she reminds me of.

VARLIN: Who?

CHAMEROT: The Shrimp from the Moulin Rouge! [*Looking at the* SHRIMP] It's uncanny!

GUÉRISSAC: Nonsense! Doctor Petypon would never have married the Shrimp from the Moulin Rouge.

VARLIN: All the same – there is a sort of resemblance.

CHAMEROT: Shrimp or not – she's a fine filly!

DUKE [*passes them on his way from the buffet*]: What's that?

CHAMEROT: Madame Petypon. A fine filly, what!

DUKE [*off-hand*]: If you like that type of thing ...

SHRIMP [*as they play*]: Everyone ready?

EVERYONE: Ready!

    [*The quadrille starts.* CLÉMENTINE *is dancing with the* PRÉFET. *Everyone dances – as they do so* ÉMILE *comes in to speak to* CLÉMENTINE *and does so by keeping in step with her at a respectful distance and speaking in a very loud voice.*]

ÉMILE: The dressmaker's brought your bridal gown, Mademoiselle. Has Mademoiselle any message for her?

MME PONANT [*dancing*]: Your wedding dress! We must see it!

CLÉMENTINE: That's easy!

LADIES: Yes! We must see the dress!

ÉMILE: Has Mademoiselle any message for her?

CLÉMENTINE [*still dancing*]: After the dance you can bring the dress in here, Émile.

ÉMILE: Very well, Mademoiselle. [*He dances with the rest to the door on the left and escapes*]

SHRIMP [*shouting from the piano*]: All change!

EVERYONE: All change! Carry on, Duchess!

[*They move into the next figure. The* SHRIMP *shouts encouragement from the piano.*]

SHRIMP: Tralala ... lalala ... lalala ... Come on, darlings! Hot it up a little!

PETYPON: Please!

SHRIMP [*to* PETYPON]: Shut up! [*To the* DANCERS] You dance like a wet weekend! Where's your brollies?

PETYPON [*whispering desperately to the* SHRIMP]: For God's sake! No running commentary...!

SHRIMP: Why ever not? Where are we? Sunday School? Oh, no! What a bunch of clodhoppers. Have you ever seen anything like it? [*She throws herself into the quadrille*]

PETYPON [*grabbing her skirt*]: For pity's sake!

SHRIMP [*pulling her skirt away from him*]: Take your hands off me! Come on everyone! Look! This is how the living shake a leg!

[*She dances a hectic solo as if she were on the stage of the Moulin Rouge. The others are motionless, watching fascinated.*]

EVERYONE: Oh!

[PETYPON *is holding out the tails of his coat like a screen, he's trying to dance in front of the* SHRIMP *to hide her from the public gaze.*]

PETYPON: My dear wife! Please! That's enough of that! Quite enough!

[*At which moment, on the final chord, the* SHRIMP *turns her back to the audience, bends over, flips her skirts over her head and displays her knickers to the general consternation of all the ladies concerned and the pleasure of some of the men.*]

PETYPON [*collapsing on the chair near the piano*]: It's the end! Catastrophe!

[*He leaps up with an energy born of despair.*] It's all the rage in Paris! It was started by the Princesse de Hohenbrau-Gallitaine at the Élysée Ball ...

EVERYONE: Oh. Not again ...

PETYPON: Not? All right. Perhaps not. [*He has an inspiration*] The Daisy Chain!

SHRIMP [*who's now upright and by the piano*]: Yes! The Daisy Chain!

EVERYONE: The Daisy Chain!

[*They start to form into a long line holding hands, to dance like a daisy chain. As they do so* CHAMEROT *and* GUÉRISSAC *pass the* SHRIMP.]

CHAMEROT: Hullo, Shrimp!

SHRIMP [*turns her head automatically*]: Hullo.

CHAMEROT [*triumphant*]: You see! Got you – in my net!

SHRIMP [*whispers*]: It's the lobster! No jokes here, please. Keep your jokes for Paris. [*Winks.*] Get me?

CHAMEROT: I'll call on you in Paris ... We'll have a little laugh together.

SHRIMP [*whispers*]: All right, darling [*Aloud.*] Daisy chain everyone! Come on, General!

GÉNÉRAL: I'm too old. You stand in for me, Petypon!

PETYPON: No! Oh no!

EVERYONE: Oh yes!

[PETYPON *is forced into the line and everyone dances out, singing, onto the terrace and away.*]

GÉNÉRAL [*looking after them*]: Young people! How they enjoy life! [*He turns as* LIEUTENANT CORIGNON *enters by the door on the right.*] Ah! The fiancé at last!

CORIGNON [*saluting*]: My General!

GÉNÉRAL: You're late, M'sieur. Your little bride has just gone off in a daisy chain.

CORIGNON: Oh, really? [*Unconcerned*]

[*He salutes the* DUCHESS, *who returns his salute, still playing.*]

GÉNÉRAL: Don't trouble yourself with all that finger slogging, Duchess. They've all gone!

[*The* DUCHESS *stops playing and stands.*]

[*To* CORIGNON] I'll go and find your Clémentine. She may have a little surprise for you! [*To the* DUCHESS] On parade, Duchess! Quick march!

[*The* GÉNÉRAL *and The* DUCHESS *go.*]

CORIGNON [*takes off his sabre and cap and puts them on a chair*]: A little surprise! What's that, I wonder? A hand-knitted egg cosy? Marriage! ... The idea makes the old days with the Shrimp seem like heaven. [*He sees* CLÉMENTINE *coming in from the terrace.*] Here comes little Mademoiselle Sunday School ... [*He goes to her*] My darling! I've been dying for this moment ... [*He brings her downstage, kissing her hand gallantly.*]

CLÉMENTINE [*shyly, then gaining confidence*]: How are you, my big green rabbit?

CORIGNON [*dropping her hand in alarm*]: Pardon me?

CLÉMENTINE: Why're you so late, cocky bird. Some little ballet girl you couldn't get out of.

CLÉMENTINE [*can't believe his ears*]: It's incredible!

CLÉMENTINE: Come here. [*She takes his hand.*] Let's have a look at you! [*She pulls him onto her knees*] Here we are ... Little Corignon and his Clemmy ...

CORIGNON [*trying to escape*]: Put me down!

CLÉMENTINE: You sit still, my big baby. Does it like to have its nose rubbed by its little Clemmy then? [*She rubs his nose with hers, he frees himself and rushes to the right, she stands.*]

CORIGNON: It's like a voice from the past!

CLÉMENTINE [*a high kick over the chair*]: Cheer up darling. How's your father?

CORIGNON: Clémentine! You're only just out of the convent!

CLÉMENTINE [*pirouettes round him*]: I learnt a thing or two since then, fat head! [*She sees the* SHRIMP, *who has come in from the terrace and is watching them*] Darling, you just *have* to meet ... my cousin Petypon.

CORIGNON: Shrimp!

CLÉMENTINE: My fiancé Lieutenant Corignon.

CORIGNON [*astonished*]: Shrimp?

SHRIMP: Learns quick don't she, Lieutenant Corignon...?

CORIGNON: You...! *Here?*

CLÉMENTINE: You two know each other?

CORIGNON: Yes! That is, no! [*Pause*] That is to say ...

SHRIMP: We met at the photographer's ...

CORIGNON: My darling, sweet fiancée ... Could you leave us for a moment? I've got something to say ... to your cousin.

CLÉMENTINE: She taught me everything! She said you'd love the new me! [*She does a little circular kick.*] Cheer up darling. How's your father? [*She goes out onto the terrace.*]

CORIGNON: What the hell are you doing here?

SHRIMP: Same to you!

CORIGNON: It's my party. But what are you up to, in a respectable household?

SHRIMP: Charming! I thought your marriage might be amusing. Anyway, I'm here with my lover.

CORIGNON [*winces*]: Will you please not say things like that!

SHRIMP: You're never jealous!

CORIGNON: Jealous! Don't be ridiculous! Not in the least jealous ... All the same. I *was* madly in love with you. It might have been more tactful ...

SHRIMP: Look. When I was with you I never talked about lovers. But seeing as you've gone off me ...

CORIGNON: Why do you say that? I don't know that I've gone off you, exactly!

SHRIMP: Well, you better had. Seeing as you're getting married!

CORIGNON: Why do you keep going on about my marriage?

SHRIMP: Are you going off *that*, too?

CORIGNON: I don't know if I'm not going off it. Look here ... Shrimp!

SHRIMP: What?

CORIGNON: Do you think you could still love me?

SHRIMP [*smiles*]: I might force myself.

CORIGNON [*his arms round her*]: Right. Don't say a word. Let's go!

SHRIMP: You'd ditch your little fiancée?

CORIGNON: Oh, she doesn't love me! She's only marrying me because her uncle told her to.

SHRIMP: You're quite right.

CORIGNON: How do you know?

SHRIMP: She told me.

CORIGNON [*moves away from her*]: The little bitch!

SHRIMP: Ssh ... I'll go and get my cape ... A veil over my head ... and we'll slip away when no one's looking. [*She moves back into* CORIGNON's *arms and kisses him eagerly as he holds her in the air.*] Oh, my little Lieutenant and his Shrimp!

CORIGNON [*letting her down*]: Will we be happy? ...

SHRIMP: As a couple of ticks! I wasn't cut out for a doctor's wife. I won't be a minute ... [*She goes out of the door on the left, before she goes she turns to look at him.*] Cheer up darling. How's your father?

CORIGNON [*moving down to the piano*]: It's God's will! He shouldn't have sent me a temptation I can't resist. He should have known me better than that.

> [*As he speaks he tries on the* GÉNÉRAL's *cap, which falls down over his ears, he puts it back on the table but the other way round, steps back and salutes it smartly. As he's on his way out* MME PETYPON *rushes in and grabs him desperately.*]

Excuse me, Madame!

MME PETYPON: Oh, M'sieur! If you knew what I'd been through!

CORIGNON: A hedge backwards? [*He tries to escape but* MME PETYPON *continues to bar his way.*]

MME PETYPON: I went into my room – and simply closed the door!

CORIGNON: Fascinating! [*He's side-stepping,* MADAME PETYPON *is side-stepping opposite him.*]

MME PETYPON: And when I tried to get out ... The lock had been turned! *Twice!* The key had simply moved of its own accord. I yelled for half an hour ... Luckily someone ... came at last. And they told me ... About the ghosts.

[*She lets go of his arm,* CORIGNON *salutes smartly.*]

CORIGNON: Good evening, Madame. [*He clicks his heels and goes smartly.* MADAME PETYPON *is left with her mouth hanging open.*]

MME PETYPON [*to the audience*]: He didn't seem very interested! I will tell the Général. I'll tell him, 'There are more things in heaven and earth, Général' ... Now. Where did I put my handbag...? It's got the keys of my suitcase ... [*She goes to the piano*] Perhaps it slipped inside ...

[*She delves into the piano, nothing can be seen of her but her bottom sticking in the air.*]

PETYPON: Oh, my God! What an evening! [*He's brought face to face with his wife's bottom.*] I recognize that woman! She's escaped!

[*He rushes to the switch and turns off all the lights.* MADAME PETYPON *moves away from the piano.*]

PETYPON: I'm getting out of here.

MME PETYPON: What's happening? Oh, dear God. What are these shadows that throng about me?

PETYPON: Damned moonlight! She won't see me if I duck behind the piano. [*He starts to creep behind the piano.*]

MME PETYPON: Courage, Gabrielle Petypon! It's nothing. Probably just a fuse.

[PETYPON *falls against the piano and hits some wild chords.*]

PETYPON: Damned piano! [*He crouches behind the piano so only his head is visible.*]

MME PETYPON: Who's there? Who's there by the piano? No answer ... Come on, Gabrielle Petypon, Courage. [*Unconvinced*] It's not a ghost – is it? [*She moves towards the piano,* PETYPON *brings out a hand and plays a chord,* MADAME PETYPON *leaps back.*] Ah! [*Encouraged,* PETYPON *starts to play 'Chopsticks' on the piano.*] Help! The piano's haunted! It's playing itself!

[*She rushes to the door and is halfway out of the room when she stops and returns, walking backwards, away from the terrible vision in white which is moving relentlessly towards her. As she does so we see that it is* ÉMILE, *carrying the wedding dress on a wicker tailor's dummy, so that it looks like a headless ghost. As he crosses, we hear the line of* DANCERS *coming back from the garden shouting and singing.* ÉMILE *goes out left*] *and the* DANCERS *stream in and dance round* MADAME PETYPON, *who is crying ...*]

MME PETYPON: Mercy! Mercy, dear ghosts! Please...!

[*The* DANCERS *dance off in line.* PETYPON *comes creeping from behind the piano and takes the case of the clock and pops it over his wife's head.*]

PETYPON [*disguised voice*]: Gabrielle! Gabrielle! I am your good angel ... Listen carefully ...

MME PETYPON: The Archangel Gabriel!

PETYPON: Keep this cover on your head and the ghosts can't touch you. Go quickly from this haunted château. Take your suitcase and don't come back.

MME PETYPON: Oh. Thank you! Good Angel!

PETYPON: Go! And give thanks to God for your salvation!

GÉNÉRAL [*offstage*]: What? Where? I'm trying to find Petypon!

PETYPON: No! It's the Général! [*He crouches down again behind the piano*]

GÉNÉRAL: Some idiot switched off the lights! [*He switches them on again, sees* MADAME PETYPON *with her head in the clock case.*] What the devil! [*He recognizes* MADAME PETYPON's *clothes.*] Oh, it's you again. What're you doing in there? [*He tries to lift off the clock case by the nob on the top.*]

MME PETYPON [*clutching the clock case*]: Don't take it away!

GÉNÉRAL [*pulling the nob*]: I certainly will!

MME PETYPON: Leave it alone...!

GÉNÉRAL: You can't have my clock case!

MME PETYPON [*escaping from him*]: But the Archangel Gabriel put it on my head. Don't you understand? The Archangel Gabriel!

GÉNÉRAL: Come here! It's a complete lunatic!

[*She rushes out onto the terrace, with the* GÉNÉRAL *hot foot after her.* PETYPON *comes out from behind the piano. At the same time* MONGICOURT *appears on the terrace, dirty, sweating and out of breath.*]

PETYPON: Right, she's gone! Now to get rid of the other one.

[MONGICOURT *sees* PETYPON *and comes in to him.*]

MONGICOURT: Ah, there you are.

PETYPON: What are you doing here?

MONGICOURT: Your wife's here!

PETYPON: Where?

MONGICOURT: She came down to visit the Général. I caught the train by the skin of my teeth and rushed 250 kilometres to warn you. The wretched train stopped at every station, but thank God I'm in time.

PETYPON: In time? She's been here an hour. I had a terrible time getting rid of her ...

MONGICOURT: Getting rid of her? Then it's all passed off well ...

PETYPON: What do you mean, it's all passed off well? I've still got that cursed Shrimp to contend with. Every time she opens her mouth she puts her foot in it! Look. My best friend. My old colleague. Find the Général! Tell him I have to leave for an urgent operation. A matter of life and death.

MONGICOURT: A matter of life and death? I'll do it. Where's the Général?

PETYPON: In the garden.

MONGICOURT: I'll run. [*As he goes*] It's the last time I take you to Maxim's!
    [CORIGNON *comes in with a letter.*]

CORIGNON: If I can find a footman to give this to the Général ... [*Looks at* PETYPON] Would you do me a favour, M'sieur?

PETYPON: What is it?

CORIGNON: A letter for the Général ...

PETYPON: Certainly. [*He takes the letter*]

CORIGNON: Thank you.
    [*The* SHRIMP *comes in veiled and cloaked, sees* PETYPON.]

SHRIMP [*aside*]: Patapouffe! [*She bends double and speaks in an old lady's quavering voice.*] Goodnight, M'sieur ... God be wi' you!

PETYPON [*bowing*]: Goodnight Madame. [*As the* SHRIMP *and* CORIGNON *go out onto the terrace*] His grandmother, no doubt. [*He looks at the letter.*] Rather odd to write to the Général when you're in his house.

GÉNÉRAL [*offstage*]: Corignon!

PETYPON: Ah! There he is ...

GÉNÉRAL: Have you seen Corignon? I can't put my finger on him ...

PETYPON: He gave me this for you.

GÉNÉRAL: A letter? Extraordinary idea! [*He glances at it*] Hell and damnation! What? He gave me his word of honour he'd given his mistress the boot! Émile!
    [*He shouts at* ÉMILE, *who's passing on the terrace.* ÉMILE *comes into the room.*]

ÉMILE: Général?

GÉNÉRAL: Have you seen Lieutenant Corignon?

ÉMILE: Why yes, Général. He has just driven off with Madame Petypon.

GÉNÉRAL: What? What's that? Gone! With Madame Petypon! Corignon! [*He spins* ÉMILE *round and pushes him away.*] Get out of here! [*He marches to* PETYPON *as* ÉMILE *goes out of the door on the right.*] Well, M'sieur! What do you make of that? Corignon's gone off with your wife ...

PETYPON [*shrugs his shoulders*]: Oh, really?

GÉNÉRAL: 'Oh really.' Is that all you can say? 'Oh really'! You bear the honourable name of Petypon, M'sieur. And we don't have damned complacent cuckolds in this family! [*He strides to the door and shouts*] Émile!

ÉMILE [*coming into the room*]: My Général!

GÉNÉRAL: Pack for me and Doctor Petypon! [*He spins* ÉMILE *round and pushes him away.*]

ÉMILE [*as he goes*]: Very well, my Général.

PETYPON: But why?

GÉNÉRAL: 'But why?' You think we're going to let them get away! Where're your guts, man! We're going to catch these love birds and drag them back by the scruffs of the necks!

[*He's moved upstage when* MADAME PETYPON *who's been in the garden looking for the way out, staggers back onto the terrace.*]

MME PETYPON [*still trembling*]: Général! I'm lost! Totally lost! I've been at least three times round the garden ...

GÉNÉRAL: The Mad Woman! Leave me in peace, madam.

[*The* GÉNÉRAL *goes out onto the terrace by the left doorway.*]

PETYPON: Oh, hell! She's back again!

MME PETYPON [*seeing* PETYPON]: Lucien! You're here! Thank God! What happened to the operation? Was it successful...?

PETYPON: The operation? An absolute fiasco! What operation are you talking about?

MME PETYPON: You told me you were called away, to perform an appendicitis.

PETYPON: Oh, yes! An appendicitis. Complications set in. And then the complications developed complications. I'll explain later.

[*He moves away. She follows.*]

MME PETYPON: Lucien, don't leave me! I beg you! The château's haunted ... Oh dear, why am I so sensitive to the occult? I've been frightened out of my wits.

PETYPON: Frightened out of your wits! That's first rate! We'll leave immediately. This way [*He pushes her towards the central arch leading to the terrace.*] Don't hang about ... Or the ghosts'll be after you. [*He sees the* GÉNÉRAL *coming back from the terrace by the right archway.*] Oh, hell! It's the Général! [*He gives his wife a final push which causes her to land up near the buffet. He comes down to behind the piano.*]

GÉNÉRAL: It's absolutely true! They've bolted. [*To* PETYPON] Let me tell you, Lucien. That Madame Petypon is nothing but a little tart.

MME PETYPON: A little ... A little *what*? What did he say? [*Furious*] What did you say? You *beast*! [*She rushes to the* GÉNÉRAL, *seizes him by the arm to turn him towards her and stepping back, gives him a resounding slap.*] There!

PETYPON: Ouch!

GÉNÉRAL: Mutiny!

PETYPON [*as if he'd been hit*]: Ouch!

MME PETYPON: So! Madame Petypon is a little tart, is she? [*She goes out of the door on the right, furious.*]

GÉNÉRAL [*striding to the right*]: Devil take it! That's the first time a woman's struck me ... in anger.

MONGICOURT [*comes panting in from the terrace*]: There you are Général! I've been looking for you!

GÉNÉRAL: Well met, M'sieur. I can't stand a fellow that can't control his wife! Take that! [*He gives* MONGICOURT *an enormous smack which knocks him to the ground.*]

PETYPON: Ouch!

GÉNÉRAL [*to* MONGICOURT]: I'm at your disposal, M'sieur. Swords or pistols? [*To* PETYPON, *who is hurrying towards the terrace*] Hurry! You'll still catch them!

PETYPON [*as he passes* MONGICOURT]: It's all gone wrong! I really can't understand why ...

THE CURTAIN FALLS

ACT III

Same as at the end of ACT ONE, *except that the Chair of Oblivion has been covered with a tablecloth and we cannot see what's under it, it has also been turned with its back to the audience.* MME PETYPON *comes in in her travelling costume, followed by* ÉTIENNE *carrying her suitcase.*

MME PETYPON: Has M'sieur le Docteur returned yet?

ÉTIENNE: No, Madame, but there's a young man I put in the waiting room ...

MME PETYPON: A patient...?

ÉTIENNE: He said he had an urgent appointment with you. [*He goes out right with the suitcase, leaving the door open.*]

MME PETYPON: Really, I can't understand my husband. He heard me insulted down there and then he totally abandoned me and left by train – with the Général!

[MME PETYPON *goes out left. The* DUKE *bursts in at the door right, very impatient, carrying a bouquet of flowers.* ÉTIENNE *is following him.*]

ÉTIENNE: But I told you to wait, M'sieur. Madame Petypon's just arrived and she's tired after her long journey and ...

DUKE: Tell her. It's the Duc de Valmonté ... Here ... [*he takes a small coin out of his pocket and gives it to* ÉTIENNE] Tell her it's absolutely urgent ...

ÉTIENNE [*looking at the coin in his hand*]: These aristocrats! They can lend dignity to the most trivial gestures!

[MME PETYPON *comes in from the left.*]

ÉTIENNE: Apparently it's absolutely urgent, Madame!

DUKE [*bowing coolly*]: Madame.

MME PETYPON: M'sieur le Duc de Valmonté?

DUKE: Absolutely.

MME PETYPON: We met at the Général's château in Touraine.

DUKE: Absolutely. [*He's looking at the door behind her.*] Is Madame Petypon well?

MME PETYPON: As well as can be expected. A little tired after her long journey – and in the middle of unpacking her suitcases!

DUKE: What a pity! [*He's staring right,* MME PETYPON *is staring right also.*]

MME PETYPON: What on earth's he looking at?

DUKE: She's not ill?

MME PETYPON: Who?

DUKE: Madame Petypon.

MME PETYPON [*aside*]: Why does he talk about me in the third person – like a butler? [*To the* DUKE] No. Thank you for asking!

DUKE: That's a relief!

MME PETYPON: Excuse me, M'sieur. I'm rather busy and …

DUKE: Please. Don't mind me … You get on with … whatever it is you want to get on with. [*He turns his back on her.*]

MME PETYPON: No I didn't mean that … But I can't wait all day …

DUKE [*turns to her*]: Madame. Allow me …

> [MME PETYPON *thinks he's offering her the bouquet and tries to take it from him.*]

MME PETYPON: Oh, thank you!

DUKE: No! [*He snatches back the bouquet.*] Allow me to ask you a question …

MME PETYPON: Well … All right.

DUKE: Will it take long … unpacking the suitcases?

MME PETYPON [*with rising irritation*]: Not if there aren't any more silly interruptions! I don't suppose you came here to ask how long it takes to unpack suitcases! I heard it was urgent!

DUKE: Absolutely urgent!

MME PETYPON: Well then, tell me! What's it all about?

DUKE: Certainly not! It's an absolutely private matter!

MME PETYPON: What? [*Aside*] A genuine eccentric! [*To the* DUKE] But why did you come here?

DUKE: That's my affair. Absolutely! I shall leave now. I can see that Madame Petypon's busy. I'll come back when Madame Petypon's rested a little. [*He goes out right with his bouquet.*]

MME PETYPON: He came to ask me how long it takes to unpack suitcases…! A genuine eccentric! Ha!

> [PETYPON *comes in to the room with a case, just arrived back home.*]

PETYPON [*offstage*]: Gabrielle! Gabrielle! I must say you let me down very badly at the château! [*He puts his case down by the door and moves towards the desk.*]

MME PETYPON: I did?

PETYPON: Raising your hand to my Uncle! The first time he's ever been struck by a woman in anger.

MME PETYPON: But that wasn't my fault!

PETYPON: It certainly was! You behaved disgracefully, Gabrielle. Absolutely dis ... gracefully.

> [*To emphasize his point, he brings his fist hard down on the desk, and hits one of the buttons that control the chair. The chair swings round towards the audience disclosing a figure shrouded by the tablecloth.* MME PETYPON *screams.*]

MME PETYPON: Not more ghosts!

> [PETYPON *pulls the cloth from the figure, and we discover the* DUSTMAN *in the same position he was in at the end of Act* I.]

MME PETYPON: Who on earth's that?

> [PETYPON *touches the button on the arm of the chair and the* DUSTMAN *awakes with a belch.*]

DUSTMAN: I'm the dustman what you asked to dinner.

PETYPON: Just a patient! They're lying about everywhere. Nobody's tidied this place since we've been away. [*Goes to the door and calls*] Étienne!

DUSTMAN: Marvellous dinner, too. [*Another belch*] Fish soup. Gigot of lamb. Lyonnaise potatoes. And a huge great Camembert cheese. All washed down with a lovely Château Beauregard ...

ÉTIENNE [*appearing at the doorway*]: M'sieur?

PETYPON: Show this patient out, will you?

ÉTIENNE: This way, M'sieur?

DUSTMAN [*passing* ÉTIENNE *as they both leave*]: Thank you, M'sieur. [*Final belch*] Lovely dinner.

> [ÉTIENNE *and* DUSTMAN *go.*]

MME PETYPON [*looking after them*]: I've seen that man before!

PETYPON: Impossible!

MME PETYPON [*shrugs*]: Perhaps in a previous existence?

PETYPON: A previous existence! Of course. That's it. You've had so many lately.

MME PETYPON: Who did he say he was...?

PETYPON: A dustman. A patient ... Thinks we invited him to dinner. A common delusion of dustmen. Brought about medically ... by the dust. But we were discussing my Uncle.

MME PETYPON: Yes. He insulted me!

PETYPON: He didn't mean to.

MME PETYPON: You mean he was paying me a compliment? Calling me a little tart!

PETYPON: Well perhaps he meant someone else. I mean there may be more than one lady called ... Madame Petypon!

MME PETYPON: But who else ...

PETYPON: Who indeed? I can't imagine!

MME PETYPON: I can!

PETYPON: Who?

MME PETYPON: Your aunt, of course!

PETYPON: Of course! [*His eyes up to heaven*] Sorry, aunty. If you can hear us up there!

MME PETYPON: Whoever would believe that your aunt was a little tart ... of course, I did find her ... somewhat eccentric.

PETYPON: You found her! You never met my aunt!

MME PETYPON: Oh yes I did. Yesterday.

PETYPON: Yesterday?

MME PETYPON: The General introduced us ...

PETYPON [*aside, astonished*]: Let's get this perfectly clear. My aunt's been dead for eight years and the General introduced them yesterday! [*To his wife*] Now, I want you to be very calm about this ...

[ÉTIENNE *comes in with the* DUKE'*s bouquet and a letter.*]

ÉTIENNE: These are for Madame.

MME PETYPON: For me?

PETYPON: Is it your birthday? [*He takes the bouquet and gives the letter to his wife.*]

MME PETYPON: Not as far as I know!

ÉTIENNE: M'sieur le Duc de Valmonté insisted that Madame got the letter personally.

PETYPON: Good heavens! [*He throws the bouquet at* ÉTIENNE.]

ÉTIENNE [*catching the bouquet*]: Oh!

PETYPON: That will be all!

ÉTIENNE [*going out with the bouquet*]: I'll put them in water. Poor things! They'll need it after that!

PETYPON: Give it to me. I'll deal with it.

MME PETYPON: No, I can read it perfectly well myself. He's out of his mind! This young Duc de Valmonté. [*Reading*] 'Madame, when your enchanting voice spoke words of love, my heart was full to overflowing ...' Words of love? The fat head!

PETYPON [*grabbing the letter and reading it*]: 'I have burnt my boats. I am all yours. I shall come back in ten minutes and kiss your lovely mouth. Absolutely!' Oh, Gabrielle! At your age!

MME PETYPON: What?

PETYPON: You've hooked M'sieur le Duc de Valmonté.

MME PETYPON: Nonsense! I only said a couple of sentences to him. 'The Général's not here.' and 'I'll go upstairs and see if they've unpacked my suitcase.'

PETYPON: It's not the words. It's the tone of voice. Perhaps you said ... [*soft sensual voice and rolling lascivious eyes*] 'I'll go upstairs and see if they've unpacked my suitcase.' You can say so much in a sentence like that!

MME PETYPON: I assure you ...

PETYPON: Oh, Gabrielle! There's no smoke without a fire!

MME PETYPON: I never lit a fire!

PETYPON: You don't know your own strength! Gabrielle! I absolutely forbid you to see M'sieur le Duc de Valmonté again. Do you swear...?

MME PETYPON [*raising her hand*]: I swear! On your head!

PETYPON: My head's got nothing to do with it. [*Aside, moving down right*] That's settled that!

[MONGICOURT *comes in, furious.*]

MONGICOURT: Petypon! I've got a bone to pick with you!

PETYPON: A bone? Ah, yes. Of course ... Would you leave us a moment, Gabrielle? [*He takes her by the shoulders and pushes her gently out of the room.*] Professional secrets ...

MME PETYPON: See you later, Doctor Mongicourt ...

MONGICOURT: Madame! [*She goes out left.*]

PETYPON: Now Mongicourt, what's your little trouble?

MONGICOURT: Little trouble! I was perfectly happy. I was gay ... carefree ... A young bachelor.

PETYPON: Well, a bachelor anyway.

MONGICOURT: And then out of pure spite, you land me with a wife!

PETYPON: It wasn't spite. It was pure necessity!

MONGICOURT: And what's more – your wife. A religious maniac who's accustomed to treat her husband like a hassock.

PETYPON: Don't speak like that ... of Gabrielle.

MONGICOURT: Oh, you can keep your Gabrielle! Ever since you married us off she's been a liability. She even got me into trouble with your Uncle! He landed me a couple of thumps.

PETYPON: Only one Mongicourt! You can't count.

MONGICOURT [*collapses on the sofa*]: One ... or two. What's it matter?

PETYPON: You're right! It's the thought that counts ...

MONGICOURT: And it's not going to end there ...

PETYPON [*sits nonchalantly on the arm of the sofa*]: Really?

MONGICOURT [*raises his arms in despair*]: It'll come to a duel.

PETYPON: What a nuisance! [*He gets up.*] My dear friend, I'd like to act as your second – but unfortunately I'm leaving the country.

MONGICOURT: What do you mean 'second'?

PETYPON: You can't fight without a second. It's just not done.

MONGICOURT: Fight? Why should *I* fight?

PETYPON: It's difficult to duel without fighting.

MONGICOURT: It's up to *you* to do the fighting!

PETYPON: But the Général thumped *you* ...

MONGICOURT: He thumped me on account of *your* wife.

PETYPON: Because he thought she was *your* wife.

MONGICOURT: Exactly. I've had quite enough of that. I shall find the Général – and tell him the truth! [*He starts for the door.*]

PETYPON: No! No ... My dear colleague. My dear friend. My oldest friend and colleague. I beg you. Don't complicate matters! Look, I've solved everything ...

MONGICOURT: Promise?

PETYPON: Oh, yes. I wrote to the Général this morning. Special delivery! I told him I'd forgiven my wife and we were leaving immediately for Italy. An urgent operation on the Pope!

MONGICOURT [*impressed*]: Macchiavelli!

PETYPON: That'll solve everything!

MONGICOURT: And I just pocket a couple of thumps ...

PETYPON: And forget it!

MONGICOURT: I rushed 250 kilometres! Just to get thumped!

PETYPON: That's going a bit far ...

MONGICOURT: Exactly!

PETYPON: But you are extraordinary!

MONGICOURT: Why?

PETYPON: France is a big country. But when there's a thump going in some obscure château in Touraine – you have to rush 250 kilometres just to collect it! Anyway, you can't betray professional secrets!

MONGICOURT: What?

PETYPON: You wouldn't discuss my pancreas with the Général. My married life's exactly the same ...

MONGICOURT: We'll see about that!

[*Sound of shouting outside*]

GÉNÉRAL: Left, right! Left, right! Left, right!

MONGICOURT: What's that?

GÉNÉRAL [*offstage*]: Where's that nephew of mine?

MONGICOURT: I must tell him ...

PETYPON: No! No! I'll explain it all. Come on, quickly. [*He gets* MONGI-

COURT's *hat from the sofa and hurries him out.*] I'll see it's all settled. In a friendly fashion.

MONGICOURT: Promise?

[*They go out as* ÉTIENNE *shows in the* SHRIMP *and the* GÉNÉRAL, *who is carrying two sabres in their scabbards.*]

GÉNÉRAL: Now! Tell M'sieur le Docteur that Général Petypon du Grêlé wants him at once!

ÉTIENNE: The Général. And Madame?

GÉNÉRAL: Don't bother about her. Just tell *him* I'm here!

ÉTIENNE [*goes, looking at the scabbards*]: Very odd umbrellas!

GÉNÉRAL: Good! Now we'll settle the whole business. [*He puts his hat on the table.*]

SHRIMP: You really think he'll be pleased to see me?

GÉNÉRAL: Of course he will! I'd better have a word with him first. You pop into the waiting room, my dear. I'll call you when the time is ripe!

SHRIMP [*going out right*]: Oh yes, Uncle! Call me when it's ripe!

[*There's a knock at the door left.*]

GÉNÉRAL: Come in!

MME PETYPON [*putting her head round the door*]: Your conference over?

GÉNÉRAL: My God! The looney!

MME PETYPON [*aside*]: It's Uncle. [*Smiling to the* GÉNÉRAL] Oh, Uncle. I'm delighted to see you ...

GÉNÉRAL [*thumps the table*]: Really, Madame! After all that's happened!

MME PETYPON: Are you still going on about that?

GÉNÉRAL: Madame. You have struck a General of France. My God, it was not only mutiny. It was practically Treason!

MME PETYPON: But Uncle ...

GÉNÉRAL: Kindly don't call me Uncle. Show a little respect! Call me 'Général'! [*He sits in the armchair by the corner of the table.*]

MME PETYPON: Don't you *want* me to be your niece, Général?

GÉNÉRAL: Before you assaulted me I was prepared to humour you. But now ...

MME PETYPON: You don't understand ... I'd just been spoken to by an Archangel.

GÉNÉRAL [*again thumps the table and rises, shouting at her*]: Let me give you a bit of advice, Madame. Next time you see an Archangel, take careful aim and give him a good sound kick up the rump!

MME PETYPON: Wouldn't that be blasphemy?

GÉNÉRAL: Exactly! You see the effect Archangels have on you? They make you do things you regret.

MME PETYPON [*effusive, going to him*]: Oh, Général! And I do regret it! With all my heart. Will you accept my apologies?

GÉNÉRAL: Only ... if your husband grovels a little.

MME PETYPON: Of course he will!

GÉNÉRAL: You don't understand, Madame. I thumped your husband!

MME PETYPON: He never told me.

GÉNÉRAL: Naturally. It's not something you boast about.

[PETYPON *comes in rapidly and stops suddenly.*]

PETYPON: Ah, my dear Uncle! [*Aside*] Blast! It's my wife!

MME PETYPON: Lucien. The Général will forgive me. But he wants you to grovel ...

PETYPON: Grovel? Why ever not?

MME PETYPON [*whispers to* PETYPON]: You didn't tell me he struck you!

PETYPON: I was a very irritating little boy ...

MME PETYPON: Yesterday!

PETYPON: Yesterday? Yes, of course. But very gently ... Just a little friendly thump from an uncle ... Please, Gabrielle. Leave us while I grovel ... [*He pushes her out and shuts the door. The* GÉNÉRAL, *much amused, has been watching all this from the sofa.*]

GÉNÉRAL: My God, Petypon! You must fancy that old boiler!

PETYPON: Fancy her? Me? Good heavens! Why do you say that?

GÉNÉRAL: Every time I come here – there she is! I can never remember her name ... Madame ...

PETYPON: Mongicourt ...

GÉNÉRAL: Exactly. I can't ever remember it. It doesn't matter. [*Gets up and moves to* PETYPON] My dear boy. I've managed a reconciliation!

PETYPON: What?

GÉNÉRAL: Lieutenant Corignon and your wife never actually ... Well. They never went into action!

PETYPON: Never?

GÉNÉRAL: Preliminary manoeuvres perhaps ... But the charge was called off. So the order of the day is, 'Forgive and forget'! What do you say?

PETYPON: Oh yes, Uncle. I shall forgive her ... and tonight we go to Italy ...

GÉNÉRAL: Well done! You'll never regret it! [*He thumps* PETYPON *on the shoulder.*] Now I've got a surprise for you!

[*The* GÉNÉRAL *moves briskly to the door right.* PETYPON *nurses his shoulder.*]

PETYPON: What a cannon ball the man is! Thank God I'm not fragile!

[*The* GÉNÉRAL *bursts back into the room with the* SHRIMP *and pushes her to* PETYPON.]

GÉNÉRAL: He forgives you! Throw yourself into your husband's loving arms.

SHRIMP [*playing the part, she goes to* PETYPON *with her arms outstretched*]: Lucien!

PETYPON: No! No! Take her away! Don't start that all over again!

GÉNÉRAL: What's this, my boy. Reluctant now, are you? [*Aside*] Unforgiving bugger!

PETYPON [*retreating extreme left*]: For God's sake! Take her away!

GÉNÉRAL: Don't bear a grudge my boy.

SHRIMP [*a small sob*]: If he doesn't want me, I'm off. I tried for your sake, Général ... But that's enough. He can stay with his old boiler!

GÉNÉRAL: Eh? What?

PETYPON: What did she say?

SHRIMP: Goodbye! [*She goes to the door*]

GÉNÉRAL: Oh, my dear. Don't be rash! I'll have a word with him. Just slip into the waiting room.

SHRIMP: I've seen quite enough of that waiting room!

GÉNÉRAL: Please, my little one. I'll call you ...

SHRIMP [*going*]: How long do you expect me to hang about? For *him*?

[*The* SHRIMP *goes. The* GÉNÉRAL *sees her out and then returns to* PETYPON.]

GÉNÉRAL: Are you mad? You told me you were forgiving her – and taking her to Italy. And when I throw her into your arms ... You throw her out again!

PETYPON: I'm sorry, Uncle. But after what's happened!

GÉNÉRAL: I told you. Nothing's happened! Not a shot fired ... Only blanks! Think again!

PETYPON [*emotional, after a short pause*]: You're right, Uncle. Call her back.

GÉNÉRAL [*slapping his shoulder*]: That's my boy!

[PETYPON, *much moved, holds out his right hand. The* GÉNÉRAL *takes it with his right hand, then tries to go to the door, but* PETYPON, *still holding him, pulls him back to him.*]

What the devil!

[PETYPON, *still holding the* GÉNÉRAL'*s right hand, puts out his left hand under his right. The* GÉNÉRAL *lets go of* PETYPON'*s right hand and takes* PETYPON'*s left hand with his left hand.*]

Yes, yes!

[*He starts to go again but* PETYPON, *pulling his left hand, twirls the* GÉNÉRAL *round and pulls him back. He then holds out his right hand under his left. The* GÉNÉRAL *looks down at this apparent third hand, amazed.*]

Got any more of them?

PETYPON: No!

GÉNÉRAL: Just as well.

PETYPON [*aside*]: I'll wait till he's gone. Then I'll kick her out.

ÉTIENNE: There are two gentlemen here on behalf of a Lieutenant Corignon.

GÉNÉRAL: Good! [*To* PETYPON] It's your duel.

PETYPON: What?

GÉNÉRAL: You're fighting Corignon. I told him to send round his seconds ...

PETYPON [*moving to the sofa*]: Duel. Not at all. What a ridiculous idea. Me! Fight Corignon? No!

GÉNÉRAL: Certainly you'll fight Corignon. [*To* ÉTIENNE] I'll talk to them in the waiting room. No. Your wife's there. In the dining room! [*To* ÉTIENNE, *who is going*] Send Madame Petypon in to her husband.

ÉTIENNE: Very well, Général. [*He goes*]

PETYPON: No! Oh, no!

GÉNÉRAL: Yes! Oh, yes!

[*The* GÉNÉRAL *draws a sabre from its scabbard.* PETYPON *nearly runs into it.*]

GÉNÉRAL: Careful! Don't get yourself wounded. That's Corignon's job!

PETYPON: You're not serious!

GÉNÉRAL [*making passes at him with the sabre, almost slicing off his nose to make his points*]: Of course I'm serious! The cad needs teaching a lesson. As his General I can't do it. But you're the betrayed husband! It's up to you, Petypon! [*A final swipe at the air and he puts the sabre on the table.*]

PETYPON [*moves to the extreme left*]: Why do they all want to get me fighting duels?

MONGICOURT [*putting his head through the bedroom curtains*]: Hey there, Petypon!

PETYPON [*whispers*]: What? Oh, it's you! I'm arranging it all. Keep quiet. I'll call you.

[MONGICOURT *disappears, the* GÉNÉRAL *turns round.*]

GÉNÉRAL: Who the devil's that?

PETYPON: No one. An impatient patient. He can wait. He's got a long illness ...

[MADAME PETYPON *comes in.*]

MME PETYPON: You want to see me, my Général?

GÉNÉRAL [*shrugs his shoulders and moves right*]: You, Madame? Certainly not!

PETYPON: It's all a mistake. Go to your room, my darling. Come on now.

GÉNÉRAL [*standing by the chair of oblivion, aside*]: 'My darling'?

MME PETYPON: Étienne told me the Général wanted me in your consulting room.

GÉNÉRAL [*laughing loudly as he collapses into the chair of oblivion*]: What an idiot the man is! He's sent me Madame Mongie ... Mungie ... What's her name? By mistake?

PETYPON [*looking at the* GÉNÉRAL *in the chair*]: What?

MME PETYPON: What did he say?

GÉNÉRAL: When I distinctly told him I wanted Madame Pet ...
[*Before he can finish* PETYPON *has pressed the button. The* GÉNÉRAL *is frozen rigid.*]

PETYPON [*sits on the arm of the sofa*]: Close thing!

MME PETYPON: Poor Général! Are you all right...? [*She goes to the chair.*] Please, wake up! [*She touches the* GÉNÉRAL'*s shoulder – and freezes stiff.*]

PETYPON: Gabrielle! [*He moves to her.*] What've you done? [*He touches her and freezes, his arm outstretched, touching his wife.*]
[*PAUSE. Then* ÉTIENNE *appears at the doorway.*]

ÉTIENNE: Monsieur Chamerot.
[*He looks round, can't see anyone and then moves in, looks astonished at the frozen tableau and coughs politely.*]
Madame Petypon. A Monsieur Lieutenant Chamerot is asking for you, Madame.
[*He touches* PETYPON *and freezes. PAUSE. Then* CHAMEROT *comes in gaily.*]

CHAMEROT: You told me to call on you in Paris, little Shrimp – but it's like waiting at the dentist's! [*He sees the group.*] Oh, hell! People. Oh, God! My Général! [*He stands talking to the* GÉNÉRAL, *his cap in his hand.*] Excuse me, Général. I was on the way to the dentist. I must have got out of the lift at the wrong floor and ... My God! They're all frozen stiff! What's the matter with them? It must be the change in the weather. [*He runs to the door left and opens it to call*] Help! They're frozen stiff!
[MONGICOURT *comes out of the bedroom curtains.*]

MONGICOURT: What on earth's the matter?

CHAMEROT [*running back to him*]: I don't know, M'sieur. Look at them! Look!
[*He grabs* MME PETYPON'*s arms – and is immediately frozen, one leg in the air, his cap just over* PETYPON'*s head.*]

MONGICOURT: It's incredible! Madame Tussaud's in the privacy of your own home! [*He hits the button on the chair.*] Come on, you Sleeping Beauties!
[*The* OTHERS *come to life.*]

PETYPON: Life's not so good as that! [*He moves downstage.*]

CHAMEROT: Shall I spit in the basin now?

GÉNÉRAL: Parade ... Atten ... shun!

MME PETYPON [*to* ÉTIENNE]: I love you ... My little monster ...

ÉTIENNE: Give us a kiss then. You big brute …

[ÉTIENNE *kisses* MME PETYPON. *She opens her eyes in horror.*]

MME PETYPON: Étienne! Take your mouth away! I don't know where it's been!

ÉTIENNE: My God! The mistress!

CHAMEROT: I'll creep off. Before my Général notices me …

[*He rushes to the door.* MME PETYPON *is in his way, he spins her round and goes.*]

MONGICOURT [*to the* GÉNÉRAL]: Général. I think I should tell you!

GÉNÉRAL: We have nothing to say to each other, M'sieur. Except through our seconds. [*To* PETYPON] I'll go and fetch your wife.

MME PETYPON: What did he say he'd fetch?

PETYPON: His pipe.

MONGICOURT: He said, 'Your wife'.

PETYPON: He said, 'Urwyf'. That's what they call pipes in Senegalese. Quick before he comes back …

MONGICOURT: But you were going to talk to him …

PETYPON: I'm going to talk to him. I'm going to talk to him alone! In here … [*he pushes them out of the door*]

GÉNÉRAL [*offstage*]: Are you there, my boy?

PETYPON: Back in a minute, Général!

[*He goes out with* MONGICOURT *and* MME PETYPON *as the* GÉNÉRAL *comes in.*]

GÉNÉRAL: What the devil! They vanish as soon as we appear! Come in, my child. I'm going to bring you to a husband as true and loving as ever.

[*The* SHRIMP *comes in, cautiously.*]

SHRIMP: All right, Général. But I'm only doing it for you!

GÉNÉRAL [*his arm round her*]: Don't be afraid!

SHRIMP [*her head on his chest*]: You're so wonderful, Général. [*She strokes his moustache*] You understand me … You're the only one who's got any idea how to treat a lady!

GÉNÉRAL: Yes. I am quite wonderful. Come on now. Kiss your old Uncle.

[*She holds his face and turns it to her, gives him a long kiss.*]

What the devil! What … the … devil!

SHRIMP [*lyrical*]: That kiss did me a bit of good!

GÉNÉRAL: If you weren't my niece! My God, we'd make the sparks fly!

SHRIMP [*stroking his hair*]: I could fall for a man like you, Général. A man like you who can understand a girl like me.

GÉNÉRAL: Poor innocent creature! Marriages are destroyed by thoughtless husbands!

[*He aims a huge kiss at her and scores a hit.*]

SHRIMP: Good shot, Uncle!

> [*The* GÉNÉRAL *moves away from her and strides up and down, very distressed.*]

GÉNÉRAL: Why the devil did she have to be my niece? This little angel! Her husband forced her into the arms of a cad! I mustn't kiss her again. [*He goes to the* SHRIMP, *kisses her.*] Not once more! [*He kisses her again.*] Listen, my child. [*He leads her to the Chair of Oblivion.*] Sit there! [*She sits down, he moves left.*] I shall speak to your husband. And we shall see what we shall see! [*He moves to the desk.*] Why are you my niece? Why are you married to that brute? Devil take it! [*He sits at the desk, puts his fist under his chin, and his elbow on the chair switch – and the* SHRIMP *is fast asleep, he goes to the door.*] Don't move! [*He gets up and goes. A beat, and* ÉTIENNE *shows in the* DUKE.]

ÉTIENNE: M'sieur le Duc de Valmonté.

> [*He goes. The* DUKE *comes in with a new bouquet.*]

DUKE: Madame! I despaired of ever seeing you. Absolutely! Oh, it's so wonderful. I've thought of you night and day. I told Mama I was coming to see you and she sent her love ... [*Aside*] What's she staring at? [*He feels his fly buttons nervously.*] Madame ... [*Aside*] She's playing tricks! [*To the* SHRIMP] Madame. If you play tricks with me I shall pay you back. By kissing you! Oh, you may smile. But you don't know what a passionate brute I can be ... Absolutely!

> [*He kneels, kisses her, and is immediately transfixed, with his bouquet in his hand, as the* GÉNÉRAL *comes in with* PETYPON.]

GÉNÉRAL: Come along, Petypon. Cast your eyes on a picture of perfect innocence! [*Seeing the couple in the chair*] What the devil!

PETYPON: Don't worry. I only have to press a button ... [*He goes to the chair.*]

GÉNÉRAL: What are you playing at, Petypon?

PETYPON [*pressing the button*]: It's meant to be in the interests of science. But it has other uses ...

> [*The* DUKE *and the* SHRIMP *begin to stir.*]

DUKE: Mama. Where are you, Mama...? I'm the lover of a woman of the world. Absolutely!

SHRIMP: Oh, little Dukey and his Shrimp. Oh, my green rabbit!

> [*They embrace.*]

GÉNÉRAL: What the hell are they talking about?

> [*The* DUKE *and the* SHRIMP *part and come downstage, looking lost.*]

DUKE: Where am I?

SHRIMP: God knows, darling.

DUKE [*seeing* PETYPON]: The husband!

> [*He rushes to the door, knocking the* GÉNÉRAL *out of his way and goes.*]

GÉNÉRAL [*to* PETYPON *and the* SHRIMP]: Now, my children, you're together. Kiss and make up!

PETYPON [*aside*]: There's nothing for it! [*To the* SHRIMP] Come to my arms – my darling wife!

GÉNÉRAL [*pushing her at* PETYPON]: In you go!

SHRIMP [*throwing herself into* PETYPON*'s arms*]: Lucien!

[MME PETYPON *comes in from the left and sees the picture.*]

MME PETYPON: Good gracious!

PETYPON [*releasing himself from the* SHRIMP]: My wife!

GÉNÉRAL [*aside, moving right*]: Looney's back again!

MME PETYPON [*seeing the* SHRIMP, *goes to her with outstretched arms*]: Oh, it's you, Aunty!

SHRIMP: Ooooh!

MME PETYPON: How are you? Dearest Aunt.

PETYPON: Aunty?

MME PETYPON: I can't tell you the terrible things that happened to me at the château.

SHRIMP: Can't you?

PETYPON: It's not worth telling! We know all about it!

MME PETYPON: But your Aunt doesn't.

PETYPON: This is hardly the time and place ...

MME PETYPON: Then we'll go and talk in my room. Come along, Aunty!

[*The* TWO WOMEN *move to the door.* PETYPON *tries to stop them.*]

PETYPON: She doesn't want to know!

MME PETYPON: Of course she does. Stop! Petypon.

SHRIMP: Really, Lucien. Why don't you leave my little niece alone?

[*The* TWO WOMEN *go out left.* PETYPON *moves reluctantly to the* GÉNÉRAL.]

GÉNÉRAL: How could you ever have neglected a little darling like that? She's adorable. You idiot! [*Thumps* PETYPON *on the shoulder.*] She's exquisite! You beast! [*Thumps him again.*] If only she wasn't your wife ...

PETYPON: What would you do?

GÉNÉRAL: By thunder! What wouldn't I do?

PETYPON: Then do it!

GÉNÉRAL: What?

PETYPON: She isn't my wife!

[*The* GÉNÉRAL *looks at him, then bursts out laughing.*]

I promise you. She's not my wife.

GÉNÉRAL: I dearly love a joke! Not your wife! Very witty! Oh yes ... You're a card, Petypon!

[ÉTIENNE *appears at the door.*]

You. What's your name? Who's Madame Petypon married to?

ÉTIENNE: Why, to Monsieur Petypon!

GÉNÉRAL: There you are! Got you!

ÉTIENNE [*aside*]: Military intelligence! [*To* PETYPON] M'sieur le Docteur. Two gentlemen are still waiting for you from Lieutenant Corignon.

GÉNÉRAL: His seconds! I'll be your second, but we need a second second. Or we can't have a proper duel …

[*The* DUKE *pops his head through the curtains, sees* PETYPON.]

DUKE: He's still here!

GÉNÉRAL: Bit of luck! [*He goes to the curtain and pulls it, reveals the* DUKE *still holding his bouquet.*] What on earth are *you* doing there?

DUKE [*at a loss*]: Well, as a matter of fact …

GÉNÉRAL: It doesn't matter. You can be a second second at a duel.

DUKE [*enthusiastic*]: Absolutely! As a matter of fact that's exactly why I came here. To be a second second at a duel!

PETYPON: *He* won't do!

GÉNÉRAL: Nonsense! He'll do perfectly …

ÉTIENNE [*comes in again to announce*]: Messieurs Guérissac and Varlin!

[GUÉRISSAC *and* VARLIN *come in briskly, click their heels at the* GÉNÉRAL *and salute. The* DUKE *sits on the sofa, looking at the door, waiting for his loved one to come in.*]

GUÉRISSAC: We are here on behalf of our principal, Lieutenant Corignon.

GÉNÉRAL: I am here on behalf of my principal, M'sieur le Docteur Petypon. I believe we have the choice of weapons …

VARLIN: Pistols?

GUÉRISSAC: Sabres?

VARLIN: Foils?

PETYPON: Hypodermics!

VARLIN: He's joking!

GUÉRISSAC: It's an insult!

GÉNÉRAL: Petypon! Have you gone out of your mind?

[MME PETYPON *comes out of her room left.*]

MME PETYPON: What's going on exactly?

PETYPON [*to the* GÉNÉRAL]: I've got to do the duelling … and I've had a lot of practice with hypodermics.

MME PETYPON [*throwing herself between* PETYPON *and the* GÉNÉRAL]: What do you mean, a duel? You're not to fight a duel! Think of your Gabrielle! I love you, Lucien!

GÉNÉRAL: The devil you do! Ah … Now I understand why you're always hanging about. [*To* VARLIN *and* GUÉRISSAC] Leave us, Messieurs!

[VARLIN *and* GUÉRISSAC *click their heels, salute and go. The* GÉNÉRAL *turns to the* DUKE.]

GÉNÉRAL: And you! Scoot! Scoot!

[*The* DUKE *goes after the* OTHERS. *The* GÉNÉRAL *turns on* PETYPON *and* MADAME PETYPON.]

GÉNÉRAL: I see it all now! She's your mistress!

PETYPON: What?

MME PETYPON: What did you say?

PETYPON: But Uncle ...

GÉNÉRAL: You cad! [*He moves to the door left and goes out.*]

MME PETYPON: *Me!* His mistress!

PETYPON: Don't put your oar in. [*He moves right.*]

MME PETYPON: What's he talking about?

[*The* GÉNÉRAL *reappears with the* SHRIMP.]

GÉNÉRAL: Come in here, my poor child, and learn the truth about that woman you call your friend! She's deceiving you with your cad of a husband.

SHRIMP [*aside*]: Christ on a bicycle!

MME PETYPON: But Général! I'm his wife!

GÉNÉRAL: You!

PETYPON: Let me explain ...

GÉNÉRAL: Look at her! Bluebeard! [*Points to the* SHRIMP.] Here stands your poor insulted wife!

MME PETYPON [*to* GÉNÉRAL]: But she's your *wife!*

PETYPON [*aside*]: She had to put her oar in!

GÉNÉRAL: My ... wife! ... Please ... My wife! ... Don't make me laugh...! [*He sinks laughing into the Chair of Oblivion.*]

PETYPON: The Chair!

[*He rushes for the button and presses at the moment the* GÉNÉRAL *stands up again, still laughing heartily.*]

MME PETYPON: *Not* your wife? Général, explain yourself!

PETYPON: No need, Général. It's perfectly obvious ...

[MONGICOURT *comes in left.*]

MONGICOURT: Ah, Général. I must talk to you.

PETYPON: That's torn it! [*He sinks, exhausted, into the Chair of Oblivion, gives a sudden 'Youpp!' and there he is, frozen with his desperate smile fixed on his face.*]

GÉNÉRAL: Talk to me! Certainly not!

MONGICOURT: But allow me ...

GÉNÉRAL: Useless, M'sieur. After all, she is your wife. I hold you responsible ...

MONGICOURT: My wife? Who's my wife?

GÉNÉRAL [*pointing to* MADAME PETYPON]: This ... this ... Lady. Though she may not be very bright. And is no better than she should be. And is forever leaping into bed with that scoundrel Petypon.

MONGICOURT: She's not my wife!

MME PETYPON: I, Monsieur, am the wife of Doctor Lucien Petypon!

SHRIMP [*who has been moving nearer the door*]: Seems a good time to hop it! [*She goes out of the door right.*]

GÉNÉRAL: Don't talk rubbish! I know Petypon's wife perfectly well. He brought her to my château in Touraine!

MME PETYPON: He brought *her*! I'll see about that!

GÉNÉRAL: And I know perfectly well you're the wife of M'sieur Thingamyjig here. Only it seems to be thought very funny in this house to pretend everyone's married to everyone else. But when you tell me I'm married to my nephew's wife! That takes the biscuit! Where the devil's my niece?

MME PETYPON [*her head in her hands*]: What's he talking about now?

GÉNÉRAL: I've had quite enough of your sense of humour, Madame. My niece ... Where the devil are you? My poor deceived little niece ... [*He goes out calling for her*] My niece!

MME PETYPON [*moves to* PETYPON]: Ah ... you! You'd try and pass your little mistress off as your lawful wedded wife ... would you? [*To* MONGICOURT] Look at him! He's actually smiling! You wait, Petypon! [*She raises her hand to slap his face.*]

    [MONGICOURT *grabs her hand.*]

MONGICOURT: Look out! You're not insulated. Use the rubber gloves.

MME PETYPON: Where are they?

    [MONGICOURT *opens the drawer and* MME PETYPON *puts on a rubber glove.*]

MONGICOURT: Right! Carry on!

MME PETYPON: You'd deceive your Gabrielle. Don Juan! [*She slaps him back and forth across the face.* PETYPON *stays smiling.*] Lecherous! Treacherous! Petypon!

MONGICOURT: That's enough! [*He pushes the button on the chair.*]

PETYPON [*rises, smiling happily*]: Life is full ... of wine and kisses ...

MME PETYPON: What?

PETYPON: Wine and kisses ...

MME PETYPON: I'll give you wine and kisses! [*She gives him a huge slap.*]

PETYPON: Ouch!

MME PETYPON: Good! You felt it! [*She takes off the glove and leaves it on the desk.*]

PETYPON: Gabrielle!

MME PETYPON: It's no use! The Général's told me everything! It's all over!

PETYPON: But Gabrielle ...

MME PETYPON: No 'But Gabrielle'. I'm leaving this house!

PETYPON [*playing resignation, his head bowed*]: Very well.

MME PETYPON: I'll get a divorce!

PETYPON: Very well.

MME PETYPON: I'll take back my marriage settlement!

PETYPON: Very well. [*He looks up*] Not all of it?

MME PETYPON: Every sou! Now ... [*Gesture*] Get out of my sight! Lecher!

PETYPON: Very well. [*He does a heavy, tragic, theatrical walk to the door and turns dramatically.*] I'll go back to Mama. [*He goes.*]

MONGICOURT: You were a bit hard on him!

MME PETYPON: I've got no pity for that type of man! If he wants to play the giddy goat at his age. I'll have to look around myself!

ÉTIENNE [*appearing at the door*]: M'sieur le Duc de Valmonté.

MME PETYPON: In the nick of time!

DUKE [*comes in as* ÉTIENNE *goes*]: This time I hope she's here ... [*He comes face to face with* MME PETYPON.] Not you again! [*He starts to go but* MME PETYPON *grabs him.*]

MME PETYPON: Come here, M'sieur. Strike while the iron's hot!

MONGICOURT *and* DUKE: What?

MME PETYPON: You wrote that you love me madly ...

DUKE: I did?

MME PETYPON: Don't be afraid. I'm not a cruel woman!

DUKE: What are you talking about?

MONGICOURT [*laughing on the sofa*]: Bad luck, M'sieur!

MME PETYPON: Come here, my young lover! [*She holds the* DUKE*'s hand and pulls a flower from his bouquet.*] I'll wear your flower in my bosom!

DUKE [*trying to defend his bouquet*]: No! No!

MME PETYPON: As a trophy of your love! [*She puts the flower in her corsage.*]

DUKE [*furious*]: You've absolutely ruined my bouquet!

MME PETYPON: And now! [*She takes a run and throws herself into his arms.*] I'm all yours! Take me!

DUKE: Take you? Where? [*He tries to escape.*]

MME PETYPON [*grabs his coat tails and embraces him again*]: I am a woman thirsting for revenge! And hungry for love!

DUKE [*drags* MADAME PETYPON, *who's clinging to him, to the door*]: Let me alone! Help! Mama! Mama! [*He wriggles out of her grasp and goes.*]

MME PETYPON [*at the door*]: What? Has he gone?

MONGICOURT [*laughing*]: Looks like it!

MME PETYPON: That's men for you! Fine words but when it comes to the point ...

[*She bites her thumb, thoughtful, and then hears* PETYPON*'s voice, far off, ethereal.*]

PETYPON [*offstage*]: Gabrielle … My daughter …

MME PETYPON: Who's that calling me?

PETYPON [*offstage*]: It is I. Your good angel.

MME PETYPON [*moves forward with her head bowed*]: The Archangel Gabriel! I'd know that voice anywhere!

    [MONGICOURT *goes to the bedroom curtains, and pulls them back, discovering* PETYPON *dressed in a sheet, standing on the bed in the same position as the* SHRIMP *in Act One.*]

MONGICOURT: Petypon!

PETYPON: Shut up! [*In a celestial voice to* MME PETYPON, *who's prostrated herself facing the audience.*] Gabrielle! Gabrielle!

MME PETYPON: Yes, my Angel.

PETYPON: You're making a terrible mistake. You've got the best of husbands. You … [*He sees the* GÉNÉRAL *coming in right*] My God! My Uncle! [*He hides his face, raising his left elbow.*]

GÉNÉRAL: What's going on in here? [*Seeing the apparition on the bed*] What the devil!

PETYPON: Avaunt!

    [*In the hope of intimidating the* GÉNÉRAL *he flaps his sheet.*]

GÉNÉRAL: What is it?

MME PETYPON [*rising*]: It's you, Général. [*To the apparition, but without turning to it*] Excuse me, Archangel. I must convince a heretic!

    [*She grabs the sabre from the table and brandishes it over her head.*]

PETYPON: What's she up to?

MME PETYPON: Look, Général. I'll prove it to you. It's a disembodied spirit! [*She moves to the bed with the sabre at the ready.* MONGICOURT *is laughing.* PETYPON *is terrified.*]

PETYPON: Gabrielle! Look out! That's sharp!

MME PETYPON: It's you! Don Juan! So … You'd make fun of me!

PETYPON [*jumps off the bed on the opposite side*]: No, please! Gabrielle!

MME PETYPON [*starts to climb on the bed*]: Come here a minute!

    [PETYPON *runs to the door with the sheet floating behind him.*]

PETYPON: Help! Help!

MME PETYPON [*in pursuit with the sabre*]: Come here a minute! Lecherous! Treacherous! Petypon!

    [PETYPON *runs to* MONGICOURT, *twists him round to face* MME PETYPON, *does the same with the* GÉNÉRAL *and then rushes out of the door left with* MADAME PETYPON *at his heels.*]

MONGICOURT [*laughing*]: Poor Petypon!

GÉNÉRAL [*laughing*]: She has no luck with spooks! [*To* MONGICOURT] M'sieur! I owe you an apology!

MONGICOURT: You what?

GÉNÉRAL: That dear sweet innocent girl has explained it all to me. Can you imagine! She's never even been to Senegal! It seems you're not married to Madame Mongicourt ...

MONGICOURT: No, Petypon is. I mean ...

GÉNÉRAL: So! He's responsible for her. He's the one I should have thumped. I gave it to *you*, M'sieur.

MONGICOURT: You certainly did!

GÉNÉRAL: I tell you what. You can pass it on ...

[PETYPON *appears at the door, leading in* MADAME PETYPON.]

GÉNÉRAL: You again!

MME PETYPON [*going to the* GÉNÉRAL]: Général! Forgive my husband ...

GÉNÉRAL: Why ever should I?

MME PETYPON: You see, it's all perfectly simple. He knew this appalling Shrimp had been the mistress of Lieutenant Corignon. So he heroically pretended she was his wife. It was to avoid a scandal – at your niece's wedding! The dear, good, Pious Petypon!

MONGICOURT: A man of endless invention.

[*The* SHRIMP *appears at the door and looks at the* GÉNÉRAL.]

SHRIMP: Are you coming, my little green rabbit?

GÉNÉRAL: Of course my child. Here I am!

[MONGICOURT *moves to* PETYPON.]

MONGICOURT: So. It all ends happily. I've settled my problem with the Général ...

PETYPON: Good, excellent!

MONGICOURT: His thump wasn't meant for me.

PETYPON: It wasn't...?

MONGICOURT: I was meant to pass it on!

[*He fetches* PETYPON *a resounding slap across the face.*]

PETYPON: Ouch!

[*He jumps backwards, into the* GÉNÉRAL, *who's collecting his hat and the sabres.*]

GÉNÉRAL: Touché!

PETYPON [*rubbing his cheek*]: My best friend! It's a bit hard ...

MME PETYPON [*rushing to her husband*]: My poor Petypon!

MONGICOURT: With the Général's compliments!

GÉNÉRAL [*to the* SHRIMP]: I'm at your disposal!

PETYPON [*worried*]: Mine?

GÉNÉRAL [*offering his left arm to the* SHRIMP *and pointing to her with his right hand*]: Certainly not. I was talking to Madame ...

SHRIMP: Cheer up, darling. [*She pats the* GÉNÉRAL*'s cheek.*] How's your
father?
   [*She goes out with the* GÉNÉRAL.]

CURTAIN

MORE ABOUT PENGUINS, PELICANS
AND PUFFINS

For further information about books available from Penguins please write to Dept EP, Penguin Books Ltd, Harmondsworth, Middlesex UB7 0DA.

In the U.S.A.: For a complete list of books available from Penguins in the United States write to Dept DG, Penguin Books, 299 Murray Hill Parkway, East Rutherford, New Jersey 07073.

In Canada: For a complete list of books available from Penguins in Canada write to Penguin Books Canada Ltd, 2801 John Street, Markham, Ontario L3R 1B4.

In Australia: For a complete list of books available from Penguins in Australia write to the Marketing Department, Penguin Books Australia Ltd, P.O. Box 257, Ringwood, Victoria 3134.

In New Zealand: For a complete list of books available from Penguins in New Zealand write to the Marketing Department, Penguin Books (N.Z.) Ltd, Private Bag, Takapuna, Auckland 9.

In India: For a complete list of books available from Penguins in India write to Penguin Overseas Ltd, 706 Eros Apartments, 56 Nehru Place, New Delhi 110019.

PLAYS IN PENGUINS

☐ **Edward Albee** *Who's Afraid of Virginia Woolf?* £1.60
☐ **Alan Ayckbourn** *The Norman Conquests* £2.95
☐ **Bertolt Brecht** *Parables for the Theatre (The Good
   Woman of Setzuan/The Caucasian Chalk Circle)* £1.95
☐ **Anton Chekhov** *Plays (The Cherry Orchard/The Three
   Sisters/Ivanov/The Seagull/Uncle Vania)* £2.25
☐ **Henrik Ibsen** *Hedda Gabler/Pillars of Society/The
   Wild Duck* £2.50
☐ **Eugène Ionesco** *Absurd Drama (The Rhinoceros/The
   Chair/The Lesson)* £2.95
☐ **Ben Jonson** *Three Comedies (Volpone/The Alchemist/
   Bartholomew Fair)* £2.50
☐ **D. H. Lawrence** *Three Plays (The Collier's Friday
   Night/The Daughter-in-Law/The Widowing of
   Mrs Holroyd)* £1.75
☐ **Arthur Miller** *Death of a Salesman* £1.50
☐ **John Mortimer** *A Voyage Round My Father/What Shall
   We Tell Caroline?/The Dock Brief* £2.95
☐ **J. B. Priestley** *Time and the Conways/I Have Been
   Here Before/The Inspector Calls/The Linden Tree* £2.50
☐ **Peter Shaffer** *Amadeus* £1.95
☐ **Bernard Shaw** *Plays Pleasant (Arms and the Man/
   Candida/The Man of Destiny/You Never Can Tell)* £1.95
☐ **Sophocles** *Three Theban Plays (Oedipus the King/
   Antigone/Oedipus at Colonus)* £1.95
☐ **Arnold Wesker** *The Wesker Trilogy (Chicken Soup with
   Barley/Roots/I'm Talking about Jerusalem)* £2.50
☐ **Oscar Wilde** *Plays (Lady Windermere's Fan/A Woman
   of No Importance/An Ideal Husband/The Importance
   of Being Earnest/Salomé)* £1.95
☐ **Thornton Wilder** *Our Town/The Skin of Our Teeth/
   The Matchmaker* £1.95
☐ **Tennessee Williams** *Sweet Bird of Youth/A Streetcar
   Named Desire/The Glass Menagerie* £1.95

CLASSICS IN TRANSLATION IN PENGUINS

☐ **The Treasure of the City of Ladies**
Christine de Pisan   £2.95

This practical survival handbook for women (whether royal courtiers or prostitutes) paints a vivid picture of their lives and preoccupations in France, *c.* 1405. First English translation.

☐ **Berlin Alexanderplatz** **Alfred Döblin**   £4.95

The picaresque tale of an ex-murderer's progress through underworld Berlin. 'One of the great experimental fictions . . . the German equivalent of *Ulysses* and Dos Passos' *U.S.A.' – Time Out*

☐ **Metamorphoses** **Ovid**   £2.50

The whole of Western literature has found inspiration in Ovid's poem, a golden treasury of myths and legends that are linked by the theme of transformation.

☐ **Darkness at Noon** **Arthur Koestler**   £1.95

'Koestler approaches the problem of ends and means, of love and truth and social organization, through the thoughts of an Old Bolshevik, Rubashov, as he awaits death in a G.P.U. prison' – *New Statesman*

☐ **War and Peace** **Leo Tolstoy**   £4.95

'A complete picture of human life;' wrote one critic, 'a complete picture of the Russia of that day; a complete picture of everything in which people place their happiness and greatness, their grief and humiliation.'

☐ **The Divine Comedy: 1 Hell** **Dante**   £2.25

A new translation by Mark Musa, in which the poet is conducted by the spirit of Virgil down through the twenty-four closely described circles of hell.

CLASSICS IN TRANSLATION
IN PENGUINS

☐ *The Magic Mountain* **Thomas Mann**   £3.95

Set in a sanatorium high in the Swiss Alps, this is modern German
literature's most spectacular exploration of love and death, and the
relationships between them.

☐ *The Good Soldier Švejk* **Jaroslav Hašek**   £4.95

The first complete English translation, with illustrations by Josef
Lada. 'Hašek was a humorist of the highest calibre . . . A later age will
perhaps put him on a level with Cervantes and Rabelais' – Max Brod

These books should be available at all good bookshops or news-
agents, but if you live in the UK or the Republic of Ireland and have
difficulty in getting to a bookshop, they can be ordered by post.
Please indicate the titles required and fill in the form below.

NAME _____ BLOCK CAPITALS

ADDRESS _____

_____

_____

Enclose a cheque or postal order payable to The Penguin Bookshop
to cover the total price of books ordered, plus 50p for postage.
Readers in the Republic of Ireland should send £IR equivalent to the
sterling prices, plus 67p for postage. Send to: The Penguin Bookshop, 54/56 Bridlesmith Gate, Nottingham, NG1 2GP.

You can also order by phoning (0602) 599295, and quoting your
Barclaycard or Access number.

Every effort is made to ensure the accuracy of the price and availability of
books at the time of going to press, but it is sometimes necessary to increase
prices and in these circumstances retail prices may be shown on the covers of
books which may differ from the prices shown in this list or elsewhere. This list
is not an offer to supply any book.

**This order service is only available to residents in the UK and the Republic of
Ireland.**